Jack & Scarlett

Tyler Roberts

Copyright © 2024

All Rights Reserved

Jack and Scarlett. All rights reserved. No part of this publication maybe reproduced, distributed, or transmitted in any form or by any means, including photocopying, recording, or other electronic or mechanical methods, without prior written permission of the publisher. Jack and Scarlett is a work of fiction. Any references to historical events, real people, or real places are used fictitiously. Names, characters, and places are products of the author's imagination.

ISBN: 979-8-35095-824-9 (print)
ISBN: 979-8-35095-825-6 (eBook)

DEDICATION

TO MY WIFE OF 44 YEARS FOR HER SUPPORT AND INSPIRATION. Her insight and wisdom make this a better book. Most of all, I am thankful for her patient endurance. Only an author's spouse knows how much time we spend locked away in our writing room attempting to put order to the English language in the form of a story. All those reading this benefit from her skills and she has my tremendous thanks.

And a special thank you to Ann, my friend in New York and number one Beta reader. She fell in love with the characters as much as I have and mentioned several times how the story took her straight back to the center of the seventies. Her editing and contributions have made this a much better read. Thank you, Ann. You are greatly appreciated!

CONTENTS

PART ONE: JACK'S STORY

Chapter One 3
Chapter Two 10
Chapter Three 22
Chapter Four 31
Chapter Five 42
Chapter Six 53
Chapter Seven 68
Chapter Eight 72
Chapter Nine 78
Chapter Ten 87
Chapter Eleven 104
Chapter Twelve 111
Chapter Thirteen 117
Chapter Fourteen 125
Chapter Fifteen 132
Chapter Sixteen 140
Chapter Seventeen 151

PART TWO: SCARLETT'S STORY

Chapter Eighteen 161
Chapter Nineteen 165
Chapter Twenty 171
Chapter Twenty One 182
Chapter Twenty Two 188

Chapter Twenty Three 192
Chapter Twenty Four 196
Chapter Twenty Five 200
Chapter Twenty Six 209
Chapter Twenty Seven 214
Chapter Twenty Eight 228
Chapter Twenty Nine 234
Chapter Thirty 243
Chapter Thirty One 252
Chapter Thirty Two 260

PART THREE: JACK AND SCARLETT

Chapter Thirty Three 277
Chapter Thirty Four 293
Chapter Thirty Five 304
Chapter Thirty Six 316
Chapter Thirty Seven 323
Chapter Thirty Eight 331
Chapter Thirty Nine 336
Chapter Forty 354
Chapter Forty One 359
Chapter Forty Two 368
Chapter Forty Three 378

PART ONE:
JACK'S STORY

CHAPTER ONE

THE SILENCE OF THE DEAD PHONE LINE CONTRAST WITH THE ringing in Jack's ear. Her shrill, ear-splitting voice and the jolt of the phone slamming into its cradle left him at the mercy of a razor-edged blade, carving at his heart. Weak and barely able to stand, Jack clutched at his belly and tried to breathe. Then, dropping the handset atop the black Western Electric rotary dial telephone, Jack swallowed a sob. His mind spun with the sound of her furious voice as he stumbled down the stairs to his room in the basement.

Over the next few hours, Jack's head cleared just enough to leave him with nothing but pure, unadulterated heartache. And paired with it came the familiar desire to hit the road and leave everything behind. Fortunately, he already had plans to leave the following morning. Wanting nothing more than to erase the entire history of the two-year relationship, Jack's desire to flee to the refuge of the road in the next few minutes nearly overcame him. But it was too late in the day, and he didn't feel like spending a night camped in the mountain pass when it got dark.

Lying in bed that evening, reviewing the events leading to the precipice his heart had just been thrown from, he wondered what was the point of love if it did nothing but slice up a person's heart and stab them in the back.

The next morning, he packed a single bag and said goodbye to his concerned grandparents whose house he'd just finished painting in

Ritzville, Washington. He knew they felt his heartache, but what could they do? Heartache is a road taken alone.

Easing his lanky frame into the driver's seat before storming onto the freeway, he raced west through endless wheat fields bordering Highway 90. A clear blue sky promising more hot weather greeted him and assured a perfect day for a road trip. Cranking up Foghat on the cassette deck, he searched for the relief that usually came when taking refuge in loud music and high-speed driving. Looking to distance himself from the wreckage of his life, he accelerated to ninety miles an hour, something he viewed as the perfect cruising speed.

The 289 V-8 tucked under the hood of his two-door Ford Falcon Sprint agreed. Jack swore it ran the smoothest at that speed. It was the same engine as the one found in the Ford Mustang, but few recognized it as such, often leading to some fun and exciting race challenges.

Experience taught him that there would be no cops on the freeway until approaching Seattle, and he settled in for a high-speed trip. The warm wind blowing through the window caressed and tossed his dark, semi-curly shoulder-length hair just like the fingers of the girl he was doing everything to forget. Jack put his foot down and accelerated to one hundred.

But nothing he did, no matter how fast he drove or how loud the music pounded in his ears, could leave his heartache behind. It wasn't long before the first empty beer bottle flew out the window. A left-handed hook over the top of the car from the driver's side window nearly hit its mark – a seventy-mile-an-hour speed sign – and smashed into the rocky hillside behind.

Not bad for a first try.

Jack knew he'd have been in the tank if he were a whiskey drinker. And though he'd heard a lot of country western music speak of drowning memories in whiskey, whiskey never appealed to him.

Come on, man, it's not like you haven't been down this road before! You split with the girl, things suck for a while, and then another one comes along. It always works out. Rinse. Repeat.

So what was different this time? Why did he feel like he was dying inside? He'd given numerous girls their freedom before, and it never felt like this. *Uh, ya, Jack. Catch a clue. It's the other way around this time. Taste of your own medicine?*

Teeth clenched, his square jaw line taut, Jack swore. Nothing like love gone wrong to make a man feel so lost and free all at the same time. Had this been real love? Was that the difference? Jack didn't know. *Time to party.*

"Don't be stupid now." He mumbled out loud.

Where did that come from? It startled him as if someone sitting beside him had said it. *You're messed up, man. Have another beer, and forget it.*

The voices were always there, but today they were unrelenting. Swearing he'd never give his heart away again, he pried the cap from another bottle, flipped it out the window, and tilted the cold brew back for a deep pull. His dry lips delighted in the liquid treat.

I trusted her, and she betrayed me.

Wasn't really love Jack.

She said it was and that she'd be there forever.

Another voice. This one not nearly as nice.

Fool!

What's with the voices? Must be something funny in that Ritzville weed I picked up.

Oh, give me a break, Jack. What's new? It's what women do, and it's not like you haven't done it yourself more than a few times!

Jack rubbed his head. *Geez! Do I have to listen to this?*

Never again. Swear it! It was the stern voice again. *You learned this lesson the hard way years ago when abandoned on the farm—Aint no one watching out for you but number one. So get it straight, Jack, because you obviously haven't figured this out yet. You screwed up believing this time was somehow different. It's the price you pay for a hard lesson. Now, get over it and move on.*

But Jack's heart told him this was more in the order of a mortal injury, one that wounded his mind as well as his heart. It was a hurt so deep Jack wondered if he could ever recover from it, and he winced at the thought.

Why this time, Jack? She was no different than all those other women.

"Just shut up and get out of my head!" He screamed above the music.

Then, as if to leave the voice behind, he floored the accelerator while swearing out loud that no woman would ever get inside his heart again. "That's a promise. You happy now? Love ain't nothing but trouble. Love 'em, leave 'em, move on."

As much as he wanted to disappear into the music and rid his mind of the broken relationship and heartache, the voices were insistent and pursued him for many more miles. Then, another thought pierced his mind, and he swore again.

How'd you miss it, Jack? You should have figured it out long before now.

Back in June, while visiting his girl in Seattle, her parents had thrown him out of the house because he refused to cut his more than shoulder-length hair. Their stinging words still echoed in his head.

"We told you last time you wouldn't be welcome back if you didn't cut your hair. And that crazy headband, those beaded jeans..." The old man shook a stubby finger inches from his nose before throwing his hands up. "What would the neighbors think?"

Probably think you're an asshole.

He'd been foolish to believe their love was strong enough to weather that storm. It was her parents, for crying out loud! Now, it was some smooth talker bedding his girl simply because the guy presented a slick, uptown, big-wheel image. Her parents swallowed it all: hook, line, and sinker. The worst part was that Jack knew the guy from the shady circles he occasionally frequented around campus. If only her parents knew. He was one of the worst womanizers and corrupt drug dealers on campus!

And she fell for it, Jack!

Don't remind me. Makes me feel like such a fool.

Rounding a sweeping curve, Jack swiped the hair out of his face, popped out the expiring cassette tape, and reached into the passenger seat for new tape - right where she used to sit.

An image of his hand resting on a firm, silky smooth thigh flashed across the parched landscape of his mind. It was followed by the picture of bare feet on the dash of his car and long bare legs barely clad in short, cut-off jeans. Outside the open window, her hand glided up and down in the wind. The tube-top-clad girl with the long chestnut hair blowing in the wind smiled back at him, taunting and haunting. It was a memory from the previous summer. He shook his head to rid himself of the image. What a difference a year made.

She'd promised forever in her kisses and spoke of everlasting love. Their shared dream was a cabin in the woods, but it was all a lie! What a fool he'd been, and damned if he would be fooled again.

The Who song "Won't Get Fooled Again" came to mind, and Jack changed cassettes. Again, he was forced to acknowledge it was one of those wounds a person didn't soon walk away from. Like so many other wounds life so profoundly inflicts that will never be forgotten, the thought somehow, made him feel better.

The hard knocks began in the 60s when he was eight. Told he would only be there for the weekend while his parents slipped away for a short vacation together, Jack was left off at a farmhouse far out in the country. When they failed to return for him, the damage the rejection brought was deep and everlasting.

Another boy on the farm was about the same age. His name was Larry, and he'd also been abandoned. The two soon became close friends, watching out for and sticking up for each other. Whenever they got into fights at school, which, to the angst of their adoptive parents, happened far too often, it was always the both of them involved.

Then, one day, Jack returned home after a trip to the dentist to discover that Larry was gone. No one said a word and the answers to his inquiries were vague and unclear. Again, he found himself unexpectedly alone.

Without his one and only friend, things took a turn for the worse. Middle school was a nightmare, and when he entered high school, he was tall, rail thin, and often picked on. After one particularly tough day, Jack decided to run away. But with no place to go, it lasted less than a week before the police hauled him in. By this time, he was numb to the repercussions. They had little impact on him. People didn't understand.

As a sophomore, he began to earn some respect on the football field. Jack was no superstar, but the sport became the perfect outlet for his anger. By the time he was a Junior, Jack had earned a place on the varsity team. His hard-knuckled, iron-willed approach made him perfect for defense, and soon, opposing teams found it was a lot easier to take their running game away from him toward the other end of the line. By the time he was a Senior, he led the team in sacks of opposing quarterbacks.

But regardless of how well he played, his high school football games were never once attended by his adoptive parents. It's not like any college would recruit him, but on a local level, he did all right. To Jack, none of that mattered. He just wanted someone to care enough to be there for him. A couple of the other kid's fathers, aware of his situation, occasionally congratulated him after a particularly good game. Though he appreciated their support, it wasn't the same, and off of the playing field, Jack suffered from a profound lack of confidence, especially when it came to girls. Too often, they laughed and giggled at his thin, ungainly form. The impact of those years in high school never left him.

By the time he was seventeen, the facts of life were obvious, and Jack grew up understanding two things: it was him against the world, and you couldn't trust anyone. Life had always been that way, and there was no reason to expect it to change.

Lesson learned, idiot! Get what you want, and don't worry about the rest.

Yeah, this time, I won't forget.

For the moment, it didn't matter if there was a brilliant bluebird sky overhead, filled with dazzling sunshine, inviting him to enjoy the perfect day. Jack ran with a hot mix of anguish, hurt, and anger for being so stupid and not protecting himself. His go-to when the world got too crazy was to get away from it all and leave everything behind. Shed the mess like an old snake skin and leave the train wreck behind for someone else to figure out. There was always something new down the road to fill the void; right now, the Zeppelin concert seemed the perfect place.

It was the summer of '73, and Jack swore things would be different from this point forward. He wouldn't allow himself to be hurt like this again. His broken childhood taught him his own survival was the only priority. Success was the only real reward in life, and working harder and harder was the key to both. He didn't recognize it then, but these events combined to make Jack quite selfish and self-centered.

CHAPTER TWO

THE THICK, ACRID SMOKE REMINDED JACK OF A TYPICAL Friday night at college, watching Monty Python with his friends. A room full of smoke, bongs, and marijuana cigarettes passed freely about ensured an excellent time for everyone. But this was a public, in full view of the cops setting, yet everyone was so casual about it. It blew him away. Even though there were drugs everywhere and none of them were legal, the cops stood back and ignored all but the most unruly individuals, and there were few of them.

When the gates to the coliseum opened, the line moved surprisingly well for a bunch of stoners, and soon, Jack was situated near the stage. It was relatively dark inside compared to the bright, sunny afternoon outside. Sound checks reverberated off the walls, and lights flashed on stage as sound check managers made final preparations.

Jack's stash was hidden in an empty red and white Marlboro cigarette pack tucked in the pocket of his tie-dye T-shirt.

Maybe see what's happening before lighting up and check out what gets passed around. Not a lot of cops in here, but still, better keep an eye out. Oh, what the hell. Smoke em if ya got em. They can't arrest all of us.

The mental wrestling match settled, Jack freely joined in.

It was July 1973, and marijuana was not legal in the state of Washington. The last thing he needed was a drug rap. Gas was nearing 50 cents a gallon, up from the 19 cents he'd known as a kid filling up his adoptive dad's gas can at a local gas station. He was often dropped off about a half mile from the gas station while his adoptive father ran other errands. Jack was to get a gallon of gas for the lawn mower and meet him back at the drop-off point. Each time, he was given a quarter to buy the fuel, and Jack could then buy a penny candy and a nickel Heath or Look candy bar with the six cents left after purchasing the gas.

Allen elbowed Jack, flicked a Bic, put the flame to his joint, and the two lit up. The crowd grew louder, chanting for the band and pushing toward the stage, but remained peaceful despite being filled with anticipation.

Jack enjoyed Allen's company and was glad he'd stopped to pick him up from the side of the road just west of Vantage. (Vantage – that tiny little berg on the Columbia River where curiously good stories –and other mysteriously good things often occurred.)

"Where you headed?" Jack asked after pulling over to pick him up. Allen stared back with a dumbfounded look, saying, "Dude, come on, you serious?"

Jack told him to get in.

He soon learned Allen was hitching from Wazzu to the Zeppelin concert in Seattle. Six feet tall, clad in blue jeans and a tie-dyed t-shirt, his long black ponytailed hair held in place with a blue handkerchief rolled into a headband, he portrayed the look of the times. Allen's confident grin lit up dark, smiling eyes, which Jack had little doubt had charmed the pants off many a girl.

Jack immediately grew comfortable with his new stranger friend. It was just the kind of distraction he needed. Reaching over to shove a "Buffalo Springfield" cassette into the player, Jack got a quiet "I can dig it" acknowledgment from Allen when "For What It's Worth" began to play.

Allen reached for his shirt pocket and shot Jack a sideways look with raised eyebrows.

"Sure, man, go for it." Jack grinned.

"Cool." Allen's easy smile lit up his face as he extracted Zig-Zag papers from his shirt pocket. Then, easing back in his seat, Jack kept them headed down the road, square between the white lines, and quietly observed the stranger's skills. Rolling a good doobie on your pant leg while riding in a car took some talent and even more practice to avoid spilling the weed and wasting it. It soon became apparent this wasn't Allen's first rodeo, and the two men were soon sharing the first of what would be many a "J."

Cruising down the four-lane concrete ribbon of liberty at nearly a hundred miles per hour, it was freedom personified. The V-8 power plant thrumming away under the hood of the dark blue Falcon Sprint hummed, offering up even more speed and excitement. Bucket seats embraced the two and four on the floor provided sporty fun. They didn't know it then, but the car, the music rocking the interior, and the warm wind blowing through their lengthy hair embodied the best of the 70s.

The previous owner raced the car, and everything under the hood, right down to the power steering pump, was a gleaming chrome. But the recently rebuilt engine, coupled with the lightweight Falcon body, could really make that bird fly! Jack hadn't hesitated for a moment when he got the chance to purchase the car for eight hundred dollars.

Allen glanced at the speedometer and suggested Jack back off from one hundred miles per hour.

"There's no hurry, man." Jack thought he sounded like the guy from Cheech and Chong. "Kick back and relax." Then, giving Jack a sideways look, "Something eating at you, man?"

"Sorry." Jack eased off the pedal, dropping his speed back to eighty.

"Come on, dude. I can tell something's not right. What's going on?"

Jack stalled and reached into the console for another cassette tape while deciding how much he wanted to share. "Just broke up with my girl." His grip tightened on the wheel, and he stared straight ahead. "Never felt like this before."

"Let me guess. First love, right?"

Glancing at Allen, then back to the road, he opened up. "Well, no, not quite. But maybe my first real love, ya, maybe. I don't know. How's a guy supposed to know about that stuff?"

"If it feels like your heart has been cut out of your chest, stomped on with hate, and that shrill, high-pitched voice stealing your peace of mind never stops, well then…" Allen drifted off.

"Yeah. Guess you're right." Jack mumbled.

"Been there, done that, man. Happens to everyone. We all wear the cloak of misery at some point. Get involved with women, and you're gonna get burned. It's a fact." Allen nodded as if it was a commonly known truth.

Jack tilted his head in agreement. "Afraid you're right."

"Let me guess. Hurt and angry about sums it up. Right?"

Jack swallowed hard and, in a tight, barely audible voice, replied, "Yep."

"It happens, man. Go light on yourself and promise you'll never let it happen again."

Jack reached for the joint. "Gotcha, man." He loved the smell of a marijuana cigarette and held it under his nose for a moment before taking a hit.

The two swapped the joint and rode silently until Jack decided it was time to change the music. He grabbed the Lee Micheal cassette, dropped it into the player, and dialed up "Do You Know What I Mean." The stirring organ and drum beat pushed the speakers to their limit.

Allen began rocking to the tune and drumming on the dash. Soon, a goofy smile spread over his face, and he looked across at Jack, "Come on, man! Loosen up. Take a breath already!"

"Little too close to home. Pretty torn up inside."

"Gotta give that stuff up, man. It'll eat you alive. Here."

Taking back the joint and drawing deeply, Jack inclined his head and looked at Allen through slanted eyes. "I just feel like cutting loose. I don't give a shit about much of anything right now. Ever been there?"

He took another hit and passed the joint back while reminding himself to go easy on the weed since he was driving.

"Sure, man. Been there done that more than once. But for now, be cool and keep this thing on the road. Alright? We'll party in a while."

Jack grinned broadly. "Alright. We're cool."

Allen raised the joint in a toast. "Better living through chemistry, man."

It took a few more miles before Jack could apply Allen's sage advice and begin to relax. The freedom of the road enthralled, the thrumming engine reminded him of the power of good rock and roll, and the warm wind blowing through the car began to cut Jack free of the ties binding him to his cares. It all combined to make a soothing balm for the pain in his heart and was the perfect elixir to wildly indulge himself in whatever might come his way next. More than anything else, he just wanted to escape from the bonds of reality, find something to soothe the pain and wasn't worried about what form it came in. Other than being burned by his first serious relationship, hell, he didn't have a care in the world - most of the time.

A few miles later, the cassette tape began Buffalo Springfield's song "Sit Down I Think I Love You." Jack fast-forwarded the tape to the next song. Allen passed the "J" and squinted through the smoke.

"Come on, man, it happens. You're not the first. Lotta chicks out there. And real love? Who can find that? Just go with the flow, man."

Jack loved the attitude, but it did little to assuage the pain, though he had to admit the marijuana was helping with that, and he passed the joint back. "You're right, man. It's cool."

The two sped down the freeway, passing the joint back and forth and sharing little pieces of themselves. Allen was more part-time college student and full-time free-wheeler. He worked ski resorts in the winter and fought fires in the summer but was taking this summer off from firefighting to catch up on a few college classes.

Jack told him about being dropped off on a farm at the age of eight. "Grew me up."

"Eight?" Allen questioned through a cloud of smoke.

"Grew up hard." He nodded absent-mindedly as if lost in the moment. "I got my butt kicked that first summer there by another kid a couple of years older. So, the farmer's teenage son decided to teach me how to fight. Long story short, when the same kid began picking on me again the following summer, I kicked his butt."

Jack exhaled a cloud of smoke with his chuckle. "Wasn't much of a fight, a nine-year-old and an 11-year-old."

Allen choked on his next hit. "Probably went all 15 rounds, huh." He laughed.

"Hardly. That farm boy I told you about had taught me to always aim for the nose. When the kid missed with his first punch, I nailed him on his beak. When he grabbed his nose, I kicked him in the nuts and ran away as fast as I could."

Allen howled. "Awesome, man." He mused for a moment while gazing skyward. "I'm a little more from the school of Lennon myself." Allen's half-mast eyes smiled.

"Gotcha man. It's cool."

"So..." Allen motioned with his hand for Jack to continue.

"Well, after beginning college, I started a painting business and signed up as many gigs as possible. Being on my own for most of my life, I'd become pretty independent. Probably too independent for my own good."

Allen smirked and rolled his eyes. "A person can be too independent?"

Jack ignored him. "It was just me and Wolfman Jack alone in that bunkhouse most summers. Full of myself from working alongside the adults and keeping up with every one of them, I began to feel like no one could touch me. So, when the painting business took off, I soon felt pretty bulletproof. I could make my own way, and the world couldn't hurt me anymore." He trailed off and reached for the clip holding the joint Allen was extending his way.

"Wolfman. He's the best." Allen's deep-set eyes peered out from under heavy lids to look out the window.

Jack toked, and Allen continued. "S'all good man. You may not feel like it right now, but soon, you'll put that girl in the rearview mirror where she belongs. Trust me. She's just another chick on a long list. And soon, you'll be right back to feeling like no one can touch you."

"Sure. We'll see." Jack rolled his head back and forth. "In my world, I'm trusted and known for my integrity and hard work. She just blew all that out of the water."

A skeptical Jack returned what remained of the joint. Allen drew what he could from the last of it before tossing the roach out the window and slipping the clip back into his shirt pocket.

Jack continued, more to himself than Allen. "People know they can count on me no matter what. My word is golden because I always back it up, and growing up as an orphan, it's the one thing of value I possess. Doesn't seem to mean much to the lady folk, though."

"So you paint houses? Sounds like a lot of work."

"It is, but it pays pretty well. I was painting my grandparent's house in Ritzville when I got the 'Dear John' letter." He held up both hands to make the quotations. "I tore up her Zeppelin ticket on the spot."

Allen coughed smoke from the Winston cigarette he'd just lit and cracked up. "That's too funny, man. You actually tore up a ticket to Zeppelin?"

"Sure did."

"Wow, that's awesome. Gotta hand it to ya!"

Allen reached for the small pack resting on the floor between his feet and broke out a package of Oreos. He passed a handful to Jack. It would be another 70 or 80 hot, free-wheelin' miles before their concert adventure began, and in the meantime, the munchies were making their demands. The taste of fresh Oreos made Jack's mouth water.

He reflected on how living in the moment, behind the wheel of a hot car, kicking down the miles, the wind in his hair, and sharing life with a newfound friend was simply the best. No expectations. No demands. There was nothing more freeing! And when he could block the girl from his mind, Jack found the peace he yearned for. And it was getting easier to do with each passing mile—most of the time.

The mid-July sun and endless blue skies were raining down a scorching 101 degrees as they climbed Snoqualmie Pass, but the Falcon ran cool. Near the forested summit, they spotted a tan, sun-faded van pulled off to the side of the road. It sported a somewhat commonly seen bumper sticker with the message, "Ass, grass or gas, no one rides for free" on the left side and a "Peace" sticker on the right.

Five people, two guys, and three gals, dressed in cut-offs, T-shirts, and halter tops, appeared to just be hanging out. Some sat on the wooded roadside bank, and a couple of others danced near the side of the van.

As they passed, Jack slowed and saw the steam blowing out from under the raised hood. He told Allen he was going back to help. Allen surfaced from the haze he'd sunken into just long enough to shrug, okay.

After pulling to the side of the road, Jack carefully backed up into the gravel along the shoulder, more by feel than fuzzy sight, until nearing the front of the van and stopped.

Two girls in revealing halter tops and exceedingly short shorts approached the car's passenger side and leaned in the window to introduce themselves to Allen. Jack noted how quickly Allen popped out from under the miasma and swiftly turned on the charm. Having never possessed that ability, but knowing it when he saw it, Jack had to admire how guys did it.

The mystery was why the girls never seemed to catch on. It wasn't real. Or maybe they just didn't care. Who knew?

While Allen was busy with the girls, Jack got out and walked back to see what the problem was with the van. His nose told him the vehicle was hot, and the steam confirmed it. A short, thickly built man in a Grateful Dead T-shirt turned from the front of the van and stuck out a meaty ebony hand to introduce himself.

"Names Josiah. We overheated, coming up the grade. Just waiting for my rig to cool down."

"Do you have any water for the radiator after it cools off?" Jack asked.

"Water? No, dude."

"Well, I've got some in the back of my rig. After things cool down, we'll get you filled up."

"Awesome man. I appreciate you stopping to help. So hey, help yourself to anything we have."Then, chuckling and running a hand through his thick black afro, "Just not Debbie. She's mine." And he laughed some more.

The two enjoyed a comfortable moment of instant friendship. Strangers helping strangers was a commonly shared experience in the 70's. Jack soon learned they were all headed to the Zeppelin concert. Things were looking up. The guy was cool and easy to be around. All of it added to the righteous trip that looked to be in the offing.

Jack never had much of a relationship with his real father, but his adoptive father passed along a few tips about car maintenance, and carrying a gallon of water in the car for times like this was one of them.

When Jack returned to his car to dig the jug of water out from the trunk, one of the two girls chatting with Allen walked over and tried to strike up a conversation. Blonde hair and a nice figure, she was cute enough, but Jack had had his fill of girls and wasn't in the mood. He brushed her off. Besides, he figured, she was losing the connection with Allen and viewed Jack as second best.

Not happnin', babe. Jack thought. *Her thighs are likely high mileage anyway.*

Then, pulling the water jug from the trunk, he quickly returned to the van after giving the woman the cold shoulder.

Back at the van, he was invited to join them for a beer, and someone fired up "Disraeli Gears" on the van's stereo before stepping out the side door, smoking a fatty, and passing it around. One of the girls bent over the cooler to get Jack a beer – sheesh –there were mountains everywhere you looked.

Everybody took a cold one and kicked back, absorbed in the music and the universal friendship of a joint and common bond. Jack was sitting in the gravel on the shady side of the van. He was leaning against the rear tire with one leg pulled up to rest his arm that held his beer. Having finally found that peaceful place he'd longed for, Jack relaxed. The mountain air refreshed, and he was free from all the crap attempting to bind him. Feeling like this was everything he needed, Jack allowed the solace of friends, freedom, and an excellent smoke to wash over him.

A little while later, the girl who'd first approached him at his car returned and sat beside him. The blonde was running her fingers through his long dark curls; he had to admit it felt pretty good, but there was no way he was allowing himself to be drawn in. What the hell was it about long hair anyway? After he grew it out, the shy, awkward guy he'd always been never had a problem with girls. How weird.

Though he tried to look away, it was hard not to notice what was nearly falling out of the front of her halter top. Did someone say her name was Ginger? Or was he thinking of Ginger Baker, the drummer for Cream, now playing on the van's cassette? She was no brick house but was pretty close. The brick house was the chick Debbie, the gal with the van driver.

Jack's attention returned to the girl playing with his hair. He'd been hit on before and wasn't having any of it. There was a time and place for the loose and loaded girls available in the 70s, but this wasn't one of them. Free of his shackles and on his own, life was uncomplicated when he only had himself to worry about, and he remained distant. She asked him what was wrong. Always a loaded question, he reminded himself.

"Just want to be alone." He smiled peacefully.

It wasn't what she wanted to hear. She quickly stood and left in a huff. Jack fell back into the quiet, peaceful space he'd possessed before the interruption.

Suddenly, the music stopped, and after a short pause, Robert Johnson's "Cross Roads," popularized by Eric Clapton, blasted from the stereo. The van vibrated with the music, and soon Josiah stepped out from the vehicle, playing air guitar like a pro. Jack considered himself pretty skilled on the air guitar but wasn't about to challenge this dude. Turned out the guy could play for real, and this was one of his favorite tunes.

When he finished, everyone applauded. The group hung out for a few more songs before deciding it was time to get back on the road. Allen and Jack would follow the van to Seattle, ensuring it didn't get stranded again, and meet up with friends of the van's occupants before heading to the concert.

After pouring every lick of water Jack had into the radiator, the driver slammed down the hood and turned to thank him. The two shook hands, and Jack told him, "Be sure to slow down before reaching Issaquah. We need to watch out for the man down there. You can always count on seeing the heat just this side of town."

Upon reaching his car and opening the door, what do you suppose Jack saw? Allen and the dark-haired girl were in the back seat, sharing kisses and a beer. He shook his head and popped the cassette out so he could slide in the new "Eagles" cassette. "Train Leaves Here This Morning," fired up and spoke to Jack.

Behind them, the wounded van spewed a cloud of blue smoke, and Jack heard the engine roar to life. Moments later, the driver eased the vehicle out onto the freeway. Jack watched from his driver-side window as it passed, only to see "what's her name" watching from the van's side door window. A tender smile peaked out from behind her gently waving hand.

Distraction, he thought and turned away. More than ever, he felt the need to be left alone. Cranking up the stereo, Jack sped out onto the freeway.

The hearty stroke of the V-8 engine rose through his legs. Jack was getting centered again when "Peaceful Easy Feeling" began to play. It eased the pain, stabbing at his mind and heart. Mercifully, he soon slipped back into that peaceful space he'd found while kicking back at the side of the van. He was good to go.

CHAPTER THREE

THE TRIP TO SEATTLE WAS UNEVENTFUL, AND FORTUNATELY for Jack, Allen and his girl showed some restraint in the backseat, coming up for air occasionally and engaging him in conversation.

Though they encountered cops about five miles east of town, it was no problem slipping through Issaquah unmolested, even though Jack could see the smoke and smell the weed coming from the van.

The traffic in Seattle was light, and a short while later, they pulled in behind the van and parked in the driveway with their new friends. Stepping from his car, Jack could hear Aerosmith blasting from inside a brown brick house surrounded by trimmed vegetation. He hoped to disappear in the crowd, kick back with a beer, and relax. It wasn't asking much, and his hazy mind hungered for the peace he knew he'd find by checking out.

Inside, someone shoved a beer into his hand, and after introductions, he collapsed into a bean bag chair in the living room. That's when he saw Ginger whats-her-name. She was all cozied up under some guy's arm, apparently trying to play the jealousy game by catching Jack's eye and smiling. He couldn't have cared less.

High mileage, dude. Ride at your own risk.

Skipping the masquerade, he fell back and attempted to get lost in the music. Ginger caught his eye several times, ensuring he saw her when passing by Jack's seat on the floor. But it wasn't going down the way she wanted, and Jack took a small measure of satisfaction in knowing what she was up to wasn't working.

The music was good, the music was loud, and Jack lay back in his chair, lost in his thoughts and a room full of bong smoke. His mind continued its review of recent events, and finding no answers, he gave up trying to figure out what had gone wrong. They'd shared secrets, the same dreams, the same view of the future, and had so much in common. How could it have ended like this? He didn't know, and in so many ways, he didn't want to care. But he did, and there was the rub. Closing his eyes, he drifted off in a smoky cloud and the sounds of a local Seattle boy – Jimi Hendrix.

A tender hand on his shoulder pulled him up from the depths a short while later. A petite little thing with blonde hair, piercing blue eyes, and an interest in joining him was offering another beer. *Well, why the hell not? It's sure to make Ginger, or whatever her name is, a little jealous.* If she could play the game, so could Jack.

"Blondie" sat down and nestled beside him in the bean bag chair. The shallow, small talk between strangers of the opposite sex ensued, and then suddenly, right out of the blue, she kissed him!

Geez, is the whole world just a game, or what? Something had to be up. Am I just always to be played the fool by the opposite sex? Yep.

About that time, Ginger whatshername walked by, frowned, and shook her head as if he didn't know what was going on. Jack chose to enjoy the moment. The feel of the girl at his hip and her honey-flavored lips enchanted him.

A short while later, the girl's boyfriend came by and tried to create a scene. Jack told him to be cool and that nothing was going on, but the fool insisted on playing the tough guy, and things began to heat up.

Jack stood and towered over the guy when he did. That took a little air out of the guy's balloon, but it was quickly becoming a pride thing. About then, the blonde stepped in between them. They'd had a fight, and she was making him jealous by cozying up to Jack.

I guess that's my purpose in life – to be used by girls who don't care.

"Leave my girl alone, asshole. Got me?"

Jack told him, "I don't want your girl."

The guy took the comment to mean she wasn't good enough and lunged at Jack. He stepped aside and half slugged, half pushed him into the wall. At that point, a bunch of guys stepped in and ushered the kid outside. Jack raised his hands in innocence. *Sheet! I've been trying to keep to myself since I walked in the door and look at what happens.*

In the background, Jack saw Ginger whatshername looking at him. Her blue eyes expressed longing and an offer of love, pleasure, and a lot of trouble. Turning away, Jack ignored her, picked up his beer, and went outside.

The sunny Seattle skies with cotton ball clouds helped Jack clear his head and improved his mood. The massive honeysuckle bush growing beside the front door filled his nostrils with sweetness. When two orange and yellow butterflies drifted past, he decided a short walk in the summertime air was just what he needed.

Upon returning a half hour later, he found the group preparing to leave, and Jack was quickly back in a party mood. Allen and his girl joined him, and once again, the three of them fell in behind the beige van, this time for the drive to the Seattle Coliseum. After parking the rigs, the group gathered before walking through the parking lot to stand in line.

Man, what a freak show.

Jack had never been to a concert in Seattle but knew from experience the freaks were always the gentlest and kindest of folk. Still, he was shocked by the number of people openly smoking weed. He'd been to numerous concerts and shared in a lot of the weed smoked there, but he'd never seen it smoked out in the open like this.

While waiting in line, he thought of how the Stones developed the sound systems necessary for monster concerts, though Alice Cooper made them into theatrical shows. But this was no theatrical show! Instead, these were rock and roll gods, soon to be on the stage right in front of him and surrounded by a nearly three-story wall of speakers and lights. It wasn't hard to understand how the girls could swoon for guys like the Zeppelin frontmen.

Once inside, they found their way to places near the front and waited for Zeppelin to come on stage. Soon, the air was thick with what John Hiatt would later refer to in a song as "smoking something that smelled exactly like cat pee." No matter how you described it, there was little doubt you could get a buzz just from breathing the air, not to mention all the stuff being passed around. *Gotta be careful you don't get some nasty shit.* Jack reminded himself.

Jack was hungry to cut loose, get a little crazy, and what he called a 'sound treatment.' It was what he'd come for, and Zeppelin was known for its loud, extravagant shows. No longer caring about what those in the group were doing, he drifted closer to the stage to an area with no chairs, where the crowd was standing about, waiting for the concert to begin. He wanted nothing more than to get high, get lost in the music, and feel it pounding in his chest as much as it registered in his ears.

Jack reached for the Marlboro pack in his shirt pocket and pulled out a joint. After returning the empty package of cigarettes containing his weed to his shirt pocket, he lit up and took a few hits before passing it off to the guy beside him. There was plenty more circulating about. For the moment, everything was forgotten, and he soon slipped into that sweet and mellow zone he craved.

The crowd was getting anxious. What had been a loosely packed throng began packing tighter together in anticipation and began chanting for the band. Jack had been to numerous concerts and noted how this crowd near the stage was relatively peaceful and unruffled when compared to other concerts he'd been to.

Easy-going bunch. Good crowd.

Jack was about ten to twelve people deep, where it wasn't packed as tight. Perfect. He was partaking of the newest joint passed his way when the band walked on stage and exploded into their opening number, "Rock and Roll."

Jack had never experienced anything like it, and the concert's impact would always be with him. Robert Plant's colossal stage presence drew everyone in, and his remarkably unique voice thrilled. No one could control a scream the way this guy did. But Jimmy Page was without equal, and Jack soon felt himself swept up in the vibe. It left him without words. Or was that the weed? As long as the music played, he was at peace. It was his shelter, his refuge, and once harbored safely inside, it was a secure place to escape the world.

There were moments when he felt he was the only person in the place and that the band was playing just for him. The rest of the group he'd come with was a short distance away and a bit to his left. It had been easy enough to distance himself from them and disappear into the depths of the music.

Somewhere amidst it all, when Zeppelin launched into "Since I've Been Loving You," Jack felt a slender arm gently slide around his waist, snapping him back into the here-and-now world. Turning to his right, he looked straight into the deep pools of two brown eyes and the welcoming smile of a striking brunette. The two were sharing a joint but had yet to say a single word to one another.

She returned their shared joint and looked up to him with an inviting smile. Jack liked how she bit her lower lip and found the comfort of her smile, well… comforting. He slipped his arm around her waist and drew deeply from the joint. Then, offering it back, she snuggled close and looked up into his sleepy blue eyes. After toking deeply, she paused momentarily before blowing the smoke in Jack's face and giggling.

Suddenly, the world seemed right, and Jack considered how good it felt to be free of all bounds and still be wanted by someone.

The two began tenderly swaying together. Wrapped up in the music, Jack drifted off into the musical haze, the comforting feel of a new friend against his side and the weed's smoky buzz.

There was nothing more between them than two people enjoying the music, the moment, and the warmth and comfort of another peaceful soul. Jack relished the thought they asked nothing of each other—no demands, perfectly free at the moment. He'd yet to find that one person who satisfied his soul, but this would certainly do for the time at hand. Someday, he'd find the right girl and settle down, but this moment restored him. *Living in the moment is always the best.*

Jack was in this hazy, mellow state of mind when whatshername Ginger approached and interrupted—momentarily breaking the spell.

Walking up during a break between songs, she interrupted Jack's moment of perfect harmony. Saying something like, "Why didn't you take me with you when you went for your walk?" In direct contrast to her grating voice, her bedroom eyes invited.

Jack struggled to focus. *Do I know this girl?* Then it dawned on him who she was. She'd put on a summer dress for the concert and was quite attractive despite her rude and pushy attitude. Jack told her he'd catch up with her later and turned away. It was his trip, and no one would be hijacking his ship.

Especially not this woman!

After sending Ginger away, the girl standing at his side rested her head on his shoulder. The connection with the stranger in his right arm grew more potent. Eyes closed, Jack slipped back under the spell of the music, smoke, and soft comforts of the brunette snuggling at his side. He soon floated away, enveloped in the melody and peaceful haze of Stairway to Heaven. The music lifted him, carrying him deeper into the quiet oblivion he craved.

Near the peak of the swelling music to "Stairway to Heaven," his newfound friend pulled him close, and Jack felt her cherry lips envelop his own. The flying carpet ride he was on kept improving, and he didn't want the party to end.

At the end of three hours of music, the band was into the last song for the night and saying their goodbyes long before he was ready for it to end. When the music stopped, Ginger was immediately at his side. Thinking he might like to get to know the girl he had his arm around a little better, he told Ginger to beat it in no uncertain terms. He owed her nothing.

When Allen approached, the new gal and Jack were discussing what they might like to do and where they'd like to go.

"Dude, come on, we're going."

"I might have other plans, Allen."

"Come on, man. We're all headed back to the house together, and besides, you've got a place to crash there," Allen was insistent. "On top of that, you hurt Ginger's feelings."

"What?" Jack felt a surge of resentment assault the rich fabric of peace he'd wrapped himself in. "I hardly know her!"

"Come on, man. It's all good. Besides, you agreed to take me back to Pullman with you."

Ultimately, Allen and Jack agreed to part ways. Jack would call him later and make arrangements to give him a ride back to WSU.

Outside the Coliseum, the clear sky and fresh nighttime air drew Jack from his haze. Brilliant stars pierced the black velvet sky, a rarity for Seattle. Casually walking her back to his car, Jack enjoyed the shoulder-to-shoulder closeness and the tender feel of her hand.

What a contrast to recent experiences.

Following her suggestion, the two of them returned to her apartment. Three delightful days of hand-in-hand strolling through Seattle's waterfront, the markets of Pike Place with its incense-laden head shops, stealing passionate kisses on the shadowy deck of a nighttime ferry ride in Puget Sound, and eating fresh and tasty clam chowder at Ivar's on the waterfront followed.

It wasn't love, and Jack was sure it was a shared sentiment. An occasion for healing, he told himself. He didn't know what might have brought her to this place in time but assumed it was similar to his own and didn't inquire, just as she didn't ask about his circumstances. The two enjoyed an unspoken agreement not to ruin their time together. If temporary comfort was what they each required, what was the point in destroying a healing moment?

By the fourth day, Jack knew it was time to return to Pullman if he wanted to get all the houses he'd scheduled for painting done. Hating to tear himself away, she understood, though the timing seemed good for both of them. The peace and calm of the new relationship were healing and precisely what he needed. Yet, Jack reminded himself, he'd built his business on integrity and wouldn't allow another girl to mess it up. As much as he hated to leave, he knew the time was now.

"Thank you, Jack. You'll never know what this time has meant to me."

"It's been good for each of us. Take care."

He kissed her goodbye and walked down the steps toward his car. The scent of her perfume followed him and lingered. Somehow, he knew he'd never see her again. Still, it was a time he'd always cherish, and he wished her the best in life.

Back home, he found himself working fourteen-hour days right up until harvest began. Though it had been an amazing time with the new girl in Seattle and a perfect moment for some much-needed healing after the breakup, the two gradually drifted apart over the summer. Jack was good with that, intuitively knowing she was as well and that it was never meant to be something to last.

The rare, trouble-free moment gave them the freedom to enjoy and then walk away from the warmth of a soothing relationship without hurt.

As shallow as it was, Jack cherished it. Life would teach him how moments like that are rarer than diamonds.

Standing atop a three-story ladder, balancing his paint can in one hand and painting with the other, Jack wondered. How many times did people escape to drugs, music, and a new girl when things went sour? Innumerable, he figured. Though he knew it was nothing that would last, it was still a sweet instance of peace he would long treasure. He was sure she would sometimes think of it and smile to herself as well.

Other things he was thinking about needed to be worked out, but this was different. It gave Jack confidence he could move into the future with the hope that someday someone special would care and that a real, lasting relationship could be built with a special girl he could trust with his life.

CHAPTER FOUR

(January 1974 - Six Months Later)

AN ANGRY, BRITTLE WIND PUSHED AND HAMMERED AT THE cobalt-blue Ford Falcon Sprint, working its way up the Lewiston grade. Turn after turn, at each bend in the road, the howling wind was there waiting for him around each corner, ready to shove the car off the road and into the canyon below. The car's V-8 engine hummed confidently under the hood while the wind whistled outside Jack's window. An experienced winter driver, having learned how to navigate the steep, slick, wintry hills in Pullman, Washington, as a kid, Jack confidently worked his way up the winding grade.

Calmly working his car through each of the familiar sixty-four turns that would take him from the Clearwater River at the bottom of the valley to the top of the two thousand-foot climb, Jack enjoyed the trip. The car cornered with ease, and the power at his fingertips added to the pleasure of his drive. The heat on his feet felt good, and the wooden shift knob atop the four-on-the-floor gear shift fit his hand perfectly while the spliff he was smoking calmed him.

Rumor had it that the highway was the subject of the 1950s rock n' roll song, Hot Rod Lincoln. A connoisseur of 70's rock music, Jack wasn't so sure. However, he was familiar with the Commander Cody version of the song and decided to give it a spin to see if there was any mention of the old Lewiston grade.

Leaning toward the passenger seat to open the case carrying some forty different cassette tapes, Jack jumped when the cherry fell from the end of his smoke and landed in his lap, causing him to swerve off the road. Swearing softly, he quickly brushed it away and promptly corrected his veer toward the guardrail.

That was a little too close, Jack.

When the song kicked off, Jack kicked back, and the wind kicked even fiercer at the grill of his car. It seemed the darker it got, the stronger the wind blew, and now it was streaming brilliant rivers of white snow straight into his low-beam lights. After topping the grade, his view through the tunnel of his headlights switched to snow-covered wheat fields, and the weather changed dramatically.

The angry wind attacking him while climbing the Lewiston grade was nothing compared to the blizzard sweeping across the frozen fields. Looking over the rolling hills, at least what he could see of them, the countryside was more than knee-deep in snow and the road he was on changed from wet slush to a gleaming sheet of ice.

The closer he got to Pullman, the more violent the storm grew, and he slowed to a mere twenty-five miles per hour. Still, it felt like the fifty-mile-an-hour wind could push him off the road, and Jack slowed even more. The mesmerizing tunnel of snow filling his headlights hypnotized him, making it nearly impossible to see. He struggled to discern the side of the road from the ditch and stay on the highway. The wind pounding at the side of his car threatened to break loose what little traction his summer tires had on the icy road surface and slide him off the highway. Commander Cody hadn't sung about anything like this.

He shut off the music and focused on the road. About halfway to Pullman, a perfectly straight stretch of road he recognized as the old Johnson half mile appeared in the channel of his car's headlights. The wind's low rumble and the near-whiteout conditions forced Jack to consider pulling over and waiting out the storm, but that had its own risks, such as being run into by another snow-blind driver or being stuck in a snow drift.

Jack slowed even more, preparing for the sharp corner at the end of the straightaway. That's when he saw the flashing lights ahead and to his right.

What in the world? Jack shook his head. *Those can't be headlights; they're way off the road.*

Forcing his eyes, dried out from the hot air blasting from the windshield defroster, to squint through the blowing snow, he confirmed the flashing lights were not an illusion. There was a car off the road in the wheat field. Even gently breaking caused his vehicle to skid on the frozen surface, forcing Jack to all but coast to a stop. Backing up was dangerous. Through the blowing snow, there was no way to tell where the road ended, and the drop-off into the field began.

His car tilted as he got too near the edge, and he quickly cut back onto the highway, barely avoiding being stuck and filling him with a shot of adrenaline. Still more than fifty yards away but no longer comfortable backing up, Jack stopped the car and turned on his four-way flashers. Since topping the Lewiston grade, he had not seen a single vehicle on the road. No one would be out in these conditions, but he still felt the need to turn on the flashers. Then, turning up the collar of his jacket, Jack prepared to take on the storm and see if someone in the car needed help.

A gust of wind threw the driver's side door back in his face in his first attempt to exit the vehicle, and the blast rocked the entire car. His second attempt was successful, but he soon found himself skating along the icy road surface, barely able to stay on his feet. The wind did all it could to push him off the road while attempting to maintain his footing on the arctic surface. With the storm howling down the neck of his jacket despite the turned-up collar, Jack already felt like he was freezing and had to fight to overcome a sudden urge to return to the warm environment of his car.

In the distance, the wrecked car lights blinked, and drawing near, he could hear the horn blasting above the roar of the wind and snow. Stepping off the road and down the bank toward the car, Jack quickly found himself waist-deep in a snow drift. His dim flashlight revealed that the car had missed the corner, spun around, smashed against the snow bank, and flipped upside down as it dropped over the bank into the snowdrift. Only the bottom of the car and the front of the vehicle facing the road were visible. The rest of the automobile lay buried in the snow.

Seattleites. Happens every year, with the first hard snow.

Honk, honk!

Jack abandoned his thoughts and slogged through the nearly chest-deep snow bank. Approaching the car, he was nearly overcome by the sharp bite of gasoline in his nostrils. He could barely make out the bottom of the upside-down car door in the remains of each flash of the headlights. The snow was piling up, and he realized the car would be completely buried in another hour.

Jack pounded on the small portion of the door protruding above the snow and yelled to the occupants inside. But they couldn't hear him over the wind, their screams, and the blaring horn. Digging ferociously with his bare hands, he began excavating access to the door. After digging nearly two feet down, the door still wouldn't budge, and his gloveless hands were getting numb. He cursed himself for not heeding a friend's advice to always carry a blanket and some gloves in the car during the winter.

Jack blew into cupped hands to warm them before sliding them inside his jacket and under his armpits. Again, he yelled and beat on the side of the door with his foot. Almost as one, the yelling inside stopped. He yelled again and told them to stop blowing the horn and flashing the lights, fearing a single spark could engulf the entire vehicle in flames. If that happened, there would be little he could do, and those trapped inside would be carboiled. He chuckled at his own dark humor.

The lights went out, and all grew quiet except for the howling wind. Ignoring his frozen hands, Jack redoubled his efforts and dug with all his strength. The door wouldn't budge until he cleared an area nearly four feet deep and a few feet wide. By then, his ears had frozen, and his face, caked in snow and ice, burned beneath the icy coating.

Nearly twenty minutes after arriving, Jack was reminded that the wind and cold were sapping his strength when he yanked on the door to open it. Unbeknown to him, the extended exposure to sub-zero conditions was already dropping his core temperature. Thankful he'd finally gotten the door pried open and gained access to the car, Jack ignored his weakening condition and focused on the state of those inside.

Visions of gore and bloody survivors, a dead body, and someone bleeding out coursed through his mind. Then, digging quickly with a new burst of energy drawn from deep within and enlisting the help of those inside, Jack pulled the door open enough for the first person to emerge.

On the verge of going into shock, frightened and frozen, she clung so hard to Jack that he struggled to move her aside to help the next person. Fortunately, the next girl still had her wits about her, and when Jack pulled her from the car, she stepped aside, and the two friends quickly hugged one another.

Jack turned to them and yelled into the wind. "Let's go!" He pointed. "My car is that way."

"NO!" One girl shrieked and grabbed him by the arm to turn him around. "We can't leave Scarlett. She's still inside!"

"What?" He yelled, unsure he'd heard them right.

"Go back." Both girls pointed."Scarlett's still in there."

Jack turned back toward the car but saw no one attempting to slide through the narrow opening he'd created to escape the metal tomb. His frozen limbs would barely move, and weakness threatened to smother him like a blanket. He staggered forward in the snow, suddenly realizing he'd been exposed to the howling wind and glacial cold for nearly an hour and was suffering the effects of exposure.

Keep your wits about you, Jack. He reminded himself.

Jack drew on the last of his strength, knelt, and painfully crawled through the door on frozen stiff limbs. The smell of gasoline was overpowering, and he immediately recoiled. Images of bodies engulfed in flames shot through his mind. Back outside in the wind, he drew a deep breath before returning to the deadly cavern of the car.

In the far corner, sitting atop the car's inverted roof, was a red-haired girl curled up in a ball and shining a dim flashlight at him. He reached out his hand and spoke softly, encouraging her to come with him, but she refused to move and stared back through glassy, unseeing eyes.

Clearly in shock, Jack got a sudden image of the two of them frozen to death in the back of a car buried in snow as he spent the last of his energy in an attempt to get her out. Shaking it off, he took his first breath inside the car and choked on the gas fumes. He had to get her out of there.

Stiffly, Jack moved closer. He spoke gently while encouraging her and saw a light flicker inside her eyes. She moved her hand and pointed the flashlight straight into Jack's face, momentarily blinding him. Jack shook his head, drew closer, and reached for her icy palm. She didn't recoil this time, and Jack was allowed to grasp it. Her stiff fingers contained no warmth. He pulled, but frozen with fear, she refused to move. Tugging harder, he attempted to pull her near him, but she remained unmoving in the corner.

The blank stare she'd first greeted him with returned, flushing the fear from her eyes and replacing it with an empty, emotionless gaze into space. Jack slapped her, and her eyes sprang wide open. Even in the dim light of the car's tomb-like interior, they gripped Jack in a way no pair of eyes ever had.

Quickly shaking it off, he took her hand and pulled. This time, she moved a short distance toward him before locking up again and fading into oblivion. Jack slapped her a second time. Anger burst forth on her face this time, and a firestorm lit up her eyes. It was precisely what Jack wanted, and together, they fought to move their stiff bodies toward the door.

When Scarlett knelt to crawl out through the snowbound opening, she stopped in place once again. Dizzy and thick-headed from exposure to the fumes and weak from the cold, Jack had had enough. After ignoring his verbal commands to crawl out, Jack raised both hands, placed them squarely on Scarlett's butt, and shoved.

She shrieked and landed face down in the snow outside. Her yelp, followed by boisterous cussing upon gaining her feet, was quickly followed by Jack's exit. He gasped for air and allowed the freezing wind to flush the fumes from his lungs. It helped to clear his head, but the pain in his frozen hands and limbs was nearly more than he could bear.

Jack barely had time to wonder how the three women had survived inside a car filled with gas fumes and no air circulation before Scarlett grabbed him so hard he nearly fell into the snowbank. She was shrieking and shaking with fright, the fresh air having cleared her head enough to comprehend the full extent of the accident.

Jack hugged her back and spoke tenderly while caressing the back of her head, giving her time to settle down. But he was running out of time and needed to get to his car and out of the weather. "It's ok. You're safe now."

Now, getting her wits together, she stepped back and shot Jack a severe look. "Don't you dare slap me again! And don't you ever touch my butt…!" She caught herself and stopped.

"I'm so sorry. I just… I just…" she stammered.

Looking into her frosted eyes, Jack watched as she blinked at the tears now freezing her eyes shut.

"I'm sorry." She took his hand. "Please get me out of this place."

Alright. Jack thought. *Now, we're making some progress. Let's get them all out of here.*

"Follow me." He yelled with all his strength to be heard above the screaming wind. Before he could step away, Scarlett grabbed at him again, pulling him into a fierce hug. "I can't leave yet. Please go back inside and get my purse?" She held up the fading flashlight still clutched in her right hand.

He could see it all now. This would be his reward. He'd crawl into the backseat one last time, only to be emulated in flame. It's how the world worked.

Drawing on the last of his strength, Jack reluctantly took the flashlight and knelt to crawl back inside the gas bomb, waiting for just one single spark to detonate it.

Sliding across the surface of the car's inverted roof, Jack quickly located her purse in the corner where she'd been sitting. The gas fumes burned his lungs and fueled a building angst. He was getting dizzy again and, in his weakened state, had difficulty turning around to exit the vehicle.

Crawling outside into the storm, Jack wondered if he could navigate the short climb to the roadside. He had to get to the shelter of his car. Looking at the three women huddled together, now covered in the blizzards coat of ice and snow just like the road signs, he marveled at their toughness.

"Follow me." *I might need your help.* He thought.

Scarlett reached for his stiff, frozen hand. Jack barely felt it and took her dying flashlight to follow what remained of the trail he'd broken through the drift over an hour ago. Seeing his tracks nearly filled with snow, Jack realized the three women would likely have frozen to death if he had not stopped.

Back inside his car, where the heater ran full blast, Jack shook uncontrollably. Dozens of needles stabbed at each of his fingertips.

"Mmmynammmeis Jack. Give mmme a mminute. I'll be alright." The pain in his hands was nearly unbearable as they began to warm.

The girls introduced themselves. "And the one holding your hand is Scarlett."

"Ignore them." She protested, "They're just trying to embarrass me."

Scarlett sat in front and carefully massaged his hands with her own to warm them. She turned and looked at one of the girls in the back. "Jody, his hands are frozen. He can barely flex them."

"Can you feel anything?"

Jack shook his head. "Just, p-p- pressure."

"We need to get you to the E.R."

"Jody's in nursing school; you need to listen to her."

Jack was in no condition to argue. Knowing he needed to get into town, he cautiously pulled onto the highway. Scarlett continued rubbing one hand while he drove with the other. A while later, when the pain of thawing skin peaked, Jack moaned and attempted to distract himself.

"You're not still mad at me?"

"Mad at you?" Scarlett's puzzled look in the glow of the dashboard lights was sincere.

"You swore at me for slapping you and touching…"

"I did? I'm so sorry."

From the backseat. "Scarlett treats all the guys she likes that way."

"Shut up, Jody!"

Jack glanced at her and forced a smile on his still-frozen face. "Apology accepted."

Scarlett squeezed his hand. "Eyes on the road, please."

A few miles later, the warm car began thawing out his mind, and he asked the women how long they'd been stuck inside the car.

"I just looked at my watch. It's been at least four hours since the accident. We can't thank you enough." Scarlett squeezed his hand again, and Jack realized how much he was enjoying her touch.

On the slow, treacherous drive back to town, Jack learned all three girls were attending Washington State University in Pullman. When asked if he was going to school there, he hesitated. "Well, I'm taking a break from school. I've started up a new business that's demanding all my time."

"Besides going to Led Zeppelin concerts?" Scarlett waved the ticket stub he had left on the dash of his car. Somehow, Jack hadn't been able to bring himself to throw it away.

"Um, well…that was a reward for all my hard work."

Scarlett smiled at the strikingly handsome man beside her. Even in the dim light of the dashboard, the strong chin, deep-set eyes, and dark eyebrows were prominent.

"Something tells me there's more to that story."

Jack glanced her way before returning his focus to the road ahead. "How'd you know?" His thawing face stretched enough to grin.

"Women know these things."

He canted his head towards her. "Well then. You can probably tell me all about what led to you ending up in a snow bank." But Scarlett didn't take the bait.

"We'd have to know each other better to continue that discussion. We're just so thankful you stopped to help."

After arriving in town, Jack drove to the police station so the girls could report the accident and arrange a tow for the car. After speaking to the officer in charge, each girl hugged Jack and thanked him. Jody made him promise to go directly to the emergency room.

Scarlett grabbed his arm to walk him outside. "I'll make sure he goes."

On the sidewalk, standing under the golden glow of the police station lights with snow still blowing all around, Scarlett thanked him again.

The wind shrieked and tore at them, making the conversation brief. Jack leaned in as if to hear better. "Sorry, I didn't catch that. Say again."

Scarlett leaned forward to repeat her thanks.

"I said I can't thank you…"

Then, she stopped after realizing he was playing games when his eyes lit up, and a smile burst across his face. She smacked him in the shoulder. "We'd still be in that car near dead if you hadn't stopped."

She reached up to tuck strands of shoulder-length hair behind his ear. "Now promise me you'll let a doctor check you out and ensure you're alright."

The wind tugged at the wet curls of red hair atop her head. Even in the dim light filled with blowing snow, Jack could see what a beauty she was. Raising on her tiptoes, she kissed him on the cheek. "Maybe I'll see you around." With that, she turned away and disappeared inside to escape the storm.

Wow, talk about getting the kiss-off, Jack thought as he got back into his car. Oh well. He would probably never see her again anyway, just as well. All three are sorority sisters, and you know how they are.

CHAPTER FIVE

A COUPLE OF MONTHS LATER, JACK RAN INTO SCARLETT AT A local pizza joint. On a Tuesday evening, when the pizza place was holding its weekly all-you-can-eat pizza for just a few bucks, a pair of soft hands slid over his eyes from behind.

"Guess who?"

Jack's back was to the door, and he had no idea who it might be. After he'd finished chewing most of the bite of pizza stuffing his mouth, he mumbled, "Dave?"

"Dave's not here, silly. Try again."

The Cheech and Chong reference was funny, and Jack turned around to look directly into the deep green pools that had haunted his dreams since the night of the car accident. Jack stood and greeted her. The two of them moved to the side to visit while Scarlett's friends found a table.

Jack's friends, Mark and Bobby, watched them momentarily before Mark nudged Bobby. "That's gotta be Scarlett."

"Scarlett?"

"You know. The redhead he always talks about pulling from the wrecked car."

Bobby's eyebrows shot up. "Really! I always thought that was just some stoner's story. She's for real? Why didn't you say so?" He turned and leaned forward to have a better look. "Whoa. That chick's totally hot. Way outta Jack's league."

The two shared a laugh before diving back into the pizza.

During their conversation, Scarlett asked Jack if he wanted to get together for a burger or something sometime. "I'd kinda hoped you would call so we could talk. It might help me deal with some of the things still bothering me about that terrible night."

But Jack turned her down. "Sorry, Scarlett, maybe another time. I've got a lot on my plate right now with work, and honestly, I probably wouldn't be that much help anyway."

The truth was Jack was seeing another girl, and the timing wasn't good.

"Jack, are you sure?" She flashed ruby-red lips and her most enticing smile. I thought maybe…"

"Sorry," he interrupted. "It was all just a dumb luck kind of chance thing that we met. We come from two different worlds, Scarlett. Maybe some other time."

Scarlett sighed. "Alright, Jack. But the invitation to call is still open."

She turned away and headed for the table with her friends. Jack joined his buddies, hungry for some more pizza.

"That's Scarlett, isn't it?"

Jack peered over the rim of his glass. "Yep. How'd you figure?"

"You idiot, Jack. I've never seen red hair like that before. And you turned her down! Unbelievable!"

"Do I have lots of money, drive a hot car, and take European vacations?"

"You do have the hot car."

Jack shook his head. "She's a sorority chick, Mark. High brow meets low brow. No way that works, and I don't need the trouble."

"You're just gonna let that chick walk away? She was hitting on you, man!"

"Sit down, Mark." Jack's buddies all chuckled. "She's outta your league too."

Munching on another piece of pizza, Jack wondered. *Stranger things have happened.*

But that was the end of it, and Jack and Scarlett parted ways.

Humble Pie's "30 Days in the Hole" began to play over the sound system, and Bobby drummed his fingers on the table before singing, "A dirty room and a silver coke spoon; give me my release."

"Thought you gave that shit up." Jack jabbed.

Bobby grinned. "Just singing, man, just singin..."

"Let's get him outta here."

Jack glanced over at Scarlett's table before following them out but failed to catch her eye.

Work for Jack's painting business had slowed like it always did in the winter months, and on a typical Friday night out, Jack found himself at the Rathskellers Inn across the border in Moscow, Idaho. The "Rat" had great pizza and hosted top bands from as far away as Seattle and Spokane. Their happy hour dollar pitchers of beer were also a huge hit. Jack often joined his brother in dominating the foosball tables until the beer and weed combined to defeat them, and he had to step away.

Still hurting from the summer breakup, Jack's gloomy mood hovered over him in a nearly visible dark cloud. The shallow distractions of parties, girls, and drugs had done little to soothe him. Attempting to ease his self-absorbed heartbreak, he found a little blonde cutie, who, at the moment, was sitting in his lap, giggling at every little thing he said. *Just something to ease my pain*, he thought to himself.

Across the table from where he sat, his friends rolled their eyes at him - typical Jack: too much beer and smoke, find the easy bimbo babe, and go home. It was the same old Jack.

When the band went on break, Blondie took off for a bathroom break—or, more likely, a chance to light up and keep the buzz rolling. Jack was laughing with his buddies when he heard a woman's high-pitched voice yelling from across the dimly lit room. She was screaming at some guy, and Jack was tuning it out when he heard her cry for help.

Looking to his left, where the couple stood next to their table, he saw a man brutally shaking a woman and yelling at her to be quiet. When she attempted to scream again, the guy raised his hand and fiercely slapped her across the face. The sound of the slap struck Jack almost as if he'd been the one hit, and the resulting shriek sent a shock through his system, dulled as it was.

No one should treat a woman like that.

The woman fell back into her seat in tears with one hand massaging her cheek. That's when Jack recognized the girl was Scarlett. In no condition to fight, Jack rushed over anyway.

Marching across the dance floor to the other side of the room, he approached the guy from behind and spun him around. Jack fired the best right hand he could muster at the guy's nose, but the guy leaned back, and his glancing blow did little harm. In retaliation, the black jacketed form responded with a solid right to Jack's left eye. Jack barely felt it in his condition and squared up to fight as another right hand came his way. This time, he was ready and blocked the shot with his left arm, then sliding his hand toward the back of the guy's head, he yanked it down to meet his upraised knee with the help of his right hand.

Blood streamed from the smashed nose that resulted, and the stranger collapsed to the floor, limp and barely conscious. Jack turned to Scarlett, who was just now realizing who had come to her rescue.

"Jack, are you alright?" Scarlett threw her arms around him and buried her face in his chest.

Calmly, Jack rested his hands on her hips and pushed her back a step before asking her to sit down. "Let me have a look at that," he said.

Even in the bar's smoke-filtered light, the red imprint of the guy's hand showed clearly on the side of her alabaster cheek.

"Reminds me of me." Jack's charming smile was already making her feel better.

"Jack, you never hit me like that."

"I never should have slapped you."

"From what my friends have told me, I think it was probably necessary. I was pretty freaked out."

Two burly bouncers in T-shirts stretched tight across their broad chests appeared and told Jack he needed to leave. Jack protested, then raised his hands, not wanting any more trouble.

"Leaving right now, guys. I just need to say goodbye to my friends. Then, turning to Scarlett, "Let's get you out of here." He offered his hand, and Scarlett took it.

The two returned to Jack's table and joined his friends. Jack found no other marks on Scarlett, but the side of her face where she'd been struck was bright red. He asked who the guy was, and an embarrassed Scarlett admitted she had been dating him for the last couple of months.

"I should have called it off some time ago," she said. Now, here you are again. It seems that whenever I'm in trouble, you somehow magically appear. It must be some kind of God thing. I'm indebted to you, Jack."

His friends couldn't resist.

"Oh, Jack." Mark cried out in a high-pitched voice and pumped his hands over his heart to simulate it beating, "I'll do anything for you."

His friends fell into a fit of laughter. "Anything?" One hooted.

Jack raised one hand to silence them. "Alright, guys. That's quite enough."

Then, turning back to Scarlett. "You'll have to excuse these guys. They all come from good families, but somewhere along the way, they developed some ways about them that just aren't right."

Scarlett chuckled. "It's alright, Jack. They look like good friends to me."

"Most of the time, but where were they moments ago helping me deal with that nut job you were with?"

"You're a big guy, Jack," Mark said. "We just wanted to watch the show."

"That's right," Bobby added. "Was a good one, too. You whipped the guy and got the girl. Can't do any better than that." That led to another round of hoo-hahs as his friends raised their glasses in a toast.

Jack smiled softly and shook his head. "I should take you home, Scarlett. You ready to go?"

"She was reaching for his hand when the blonde girl he'd been with returned from the restroom. Jack noted how roasted she looked.

"What are you doing, Jack?" Hands on hips, she scowled.

"Helping out a friend."

"Humph. What about us? We had a good thing going."

"I'm sorry. I need to go."

Jack took Scarlett's arm and pushed past the blonde. Then, turning back, he pointed at Billy. "I'm sure Billy here will be glad to show you a good time."

After driving back to campus and walking her to the door of her sorority, the two stood together outside for a moment.

Scarlett looked into Jack's blue eyes. "I don't know what it is. It's so crazy, but you always show up at my worst moments. Please don't think I'm some stupid damsel in distress. That's not me at all."

Scarlett patted his chest with a flat palm and felt the muscles there. "And though you ignored me at the bar when I told you it's a God thing, it has to be."

"Well, I don't know." Jack shuffled his feet.

She placed her hands on each side of his head and gently kissed his now swollen-black eye. "You need to get some ice on that." The square jaw, dark eyes, and firm mouth invited. She gave him a hard hug and quickly kissed him on the lips. "Call me."

Over the next few days, Jack's mind rattled with the invitation to call her. Though he tried to ignore it, the thought kept coming back as if there was some strange force behind it. Eventually, he gave in and asked her out to dinner.

At the sorority, he was taken to a small room next to the front door and asked to wait. When Scarlett entered the waiting room where Jack sat, he was caught off guard and struggled to catch his breath. She was clad in a form-fitting black dress, contrasting with red shoes and crimson hair. The tall, slim redhead presented a striking form.

"Scarlett." He couldn't find the words. "You're…..beautiful!"

She smiled back at him, her green eyes sparkling before waving him off. "Thank you, Jack." Then, deflecting the attention, "You don't look so bad yourself. Now, where are we going?" She slipped her arm through his and led him towards the door.

Caught unprepared, Jack's mind spun into high gear. He was not about to take her to the place where he'd planned on going. She deserved better than that, and the only high-brow place he knew of was in Moscow. Pulling onto the highway to make the ten-mile drive across the state line, Jack wondered what he'd gotten himself into.

Sorority girl, Jack. You are such a dope. You should have figured.

But it was hard to resist the smiling red lips or the shapely legs riding in the seat beside him. Trying to shake the feeling he was in way over his head, Jack did his best to make conversation on the short drive over.

"Jack, what's wrong?"

"Nothing." He glanced over, caught the suspicious look, and saw her raised eyebrows.

She continued. "I haven't been around you much, but you seem nervous tonight."

Jack looked straight ahead, eyes focused on the road.

"Scarlett, if you know anything about me, you know I'm a straight shooter."

"Um, hmm." She nodded.

"So, believe me when I say I'm more than a little overwhelmed by you tonight. Having only seen you in a bar, a pizza joint, and a car wreck, I wasn't prepared."

"Prepared for what?"

This time, he looked to see if she was toying with him but saw only sincere concern. "Scarlett, you're stunning." There, he'd said it.

Scarlett giggled and put a hand over her mouth before replying. "I appreciate that, Jack; now get over it. I'm just an ordinary girl who is a little surprised she can rattle the likes of you."

"The likes of me?"

"I don't date men without knowing a little about them first. The girls in the sorority know a lot of guys on this campus. It's a great resource. All we had to do was put out some feelers, and finding out about you wasn't that difficult."

"Really." Uh-oh. The reports couldn't have been that great, he figured. "And yet, here you are. Must have been all good then, right?"

Scarlett laughed. "Look, I'm a pretty straight shooter myself, so if you're ready."

Jack nodded.

"I know you can be a handful; you're often associated with trouble and may not be the best thing for a girl."

It was Jack's turn to laugh now. "Wow. That's what you heard, huh? Nothing good?"

"Well, for the most part, you are a man of your word."

Jack burst out laughing. It helped to ease the tension he was feeling.

"Uh-huh. The last part, a man of his word that makes up for all those other things?"

"Well, there was one other thing."

"And."

"I should never tell you this 'cause it will go straight to your head, but since we are being honest with one another, most girls would jump at the chance to go out with you. Didn't you see the bunch of them peering into the waiting room after I walked in to meet you?"

"Honestly, I didn't."

"How could you have missed it?"

"My eyes were only on you, Scarlett."

Over dinner and conversation, Jack grew comfortable with the striking redhead that shared his table. The tall, slim Scarlett attracted looks wherever they went, and Jack still had difficulty believing she was interested in him. They shared stories of growing up and what it was like for them. Scarlett told Jack she thought she was going to die in the snow bank and prayed someone would come along to save her.

"That was you, Jack."

"Well, I don't know about that. Anyone…"

"Forget it, Jack. God sent you to rescue us. How can you doubt that?"

"Look, if that works for you, then fine. For me, I never heard a word from God. So let's just leave it at that."

After dinner, Scarlett snuggled close to his side as the two casually strolled to his car. The conversation and wine brought a growing closeness. That's when Scarlett suggested they head out to Rathskeller's.

"Are you serious? You're dressed too nice for a place like that."

"I feel like dancing." Her cherry lips grinned broadly, and Jack fell under their spell.

"What about those heels?"

"I'll just take them off, silly. Now, are you up for it or not?"

"Uh, well, sure I am if you are."

The band played great dance music all night and Scarlett doffed her shoes to dance barefoot. She soon learned Jack cut a pretty mean rug, but she was no slouch either.

The evening couldn't have gone better, and in the following days, the two began dating regularly. The handsome couple was quite the hit at the sorority, with more than a couple of girls doing their best to catch Jack's eye. He ignored them.

Though Jack was reluctant to get involved in another serious relationship, he was transfixed by Scarlett's emerald green eyes and long, blazing red hair. He soon he couldn't stand to be away from her, though he did stand her up once just to prove he could.

After calling off their date, he'd spent a night out with the boys, partying, smoking, and playing air guitar to their loud music. It had been a lot of fun and was good for the moment. Still, after falling into bed that night, the ringing in his ears and lingering embrace of the marijuana he'd smoked was little consolation and a stern reminder of how empty his life had become without Scarlett.

He finally had to admit that Scarlett was unlike all the others. There was something different about her spirit, her character, and something else

Jack couldn't put his finger on. But he knew how right it felt when she held his hand or put her arms around him. She was special and caused him to wonder if there wasn't something about this God thing she spoke of. And there was the rub. Scarlett was a Christian, and Jack had no time for religion. For now, it was something he would have to ignore.

CHAPTER SIX

WEEKS LATER, JACK WAS KAYAKING ON AN IDAHO RIVER WITH friends. The river was running at flood stage, but the rapids were always at their best then. In the past, Jack and his two buddies had chosen not to run this particular river cascading down a steep, tight drainage, believing the challenge was beyond their abilities. This year, they felt they were up to the test.

Scarlett told him not to go because she didn't have a good feeling about it. Jack blew her off, and it led to their first fight.

"You said the same thing when we ran the Selway and Clearwater rivers. Scarlett, I know you mean well, but you are unfamiliar with white-water and kayaking. That's the only reason you're fearful."

The discussion devolved into a nasty argument, and Scarlett was in tears when Jack left that evening.

The following morning on the Potlatch River, things quickly went from bad to worse, and it didn't take long for Jack to realize he never should have gotten into the water. The white-capped river ran swiftly, leaving no place to pull out. There were no pools, eddies, or stretches of slow water, just a steep rampage down the narrow river chasm.

His buddy went into the water first. Unable to roll back up, he had exited his kayak and was being swept downriver. Jack attempted to get to him to offer help but soon found himself in the same predicament.

Naturally, they all wore life jackets, but it made little difference in the river's violent, raging waters. The snowmelt-powered runoff had a temperature of just 36 degrees, and it didn't take long for Jack to realize he was in real trouble.

Fight as he might, the icy water would effortlessly drive him down to the bottom, bounce him over the rocks, and attempt to thrash the life out of him. Only by chance did he receive random opportunities for a breath of air. Numb from the cold and drained of strength, he would later recall feeling like it would be just as easy to stay down as trying to fight his way to the surface. He'd swallowed too much water, and his world was growing dim.

At that very moment, as if a giant hand rising from beneath lifted him and placed him atop a submerged boulder in the middle of the river. He was saved from drowning. Pinned by the force of the water with his kayak between him and the boulder, the sound of it breaking up told him he would soon be cast loose again. A hundred yards away, downriver roared a massive wall of whitewater, where it smashed against a vertical rock cliff. He would likely be dashed to bits in the churning caldron there and knew getting to the shore was his only chance.

Jack coughed up more water and struggled to fill his lungs with air. Weakened by the freezing water and all but lifeless, he knew there were only seconds left before having to swim for it. The shoreline beckoned. It wasn't far away, but it looked more like a mile than the few yards it was, and he had no idea where the strength would come from to get there.

Then, with a loud pop, the kayak shuddered beneath him and broke away. Jack was launched downriver. He gave it everything he had, yet felt so feeble. The drop off into the boiling pool of water approached, and the roar of it drowned out even his thoughts.

Nearing the riverbank he grabbed at a branch that immediately pulled free. Drifting further and drawing near to his demise, he scrambled for any purchase available and caught hold of an underwater rock. There, he was forced underwater to maintain his purchase and had to raise his head periodically for air. He was within three or four strong strokes of making the rock-strewn bank and knew he didn't have it in him. The roaring maw of death below opened wide and called his name, hungry to engulf him.

When a surging wave broke his grip on the underwater rock, Jack swam for all he was worth, accepting his likely fate. Somehow, he found strength he didn't think he possessed and managed to swim through the torrent of waters and drag himself onto the bank.

Fortunately, no one drowned that day. Driving along the river afterward, the men realized the surging river had hauled them more than three miles away from where they went in.

Upon sharing the adventure with Scarlett, she grew angry. Glaring at him with tears in the corners of her eyes, she shouted. "I told you not to go. That I had a bad feeling about it."

"I'm sorry, Scarlett. But this is who I am, and running rivers in the spring is something I do."

"Jack! Don't you realize it was God who saved you? That giant hand you described, lifting you from the bottom and placing you on that rock, and the incredible strength you discovered when you needed it to swim to shore. How can you deny that? You were in trouble, and you know as well as I do you were not saved by your own strength!"

Jack shook his head. "I don't know Scarlett. I find that pretty far-fetched. I've always taken care of myself, and I don't think this was any different."

Scarlett fumed. "Jack, what made you like this? A normal person is not so frivolous with their life." Furious, she crossed her arms and turned away.

"I'm sorry. Guess I never thought about it like that. I've been on my own since I was a kid, and when the music, the drugs, the parties, and all that comes with it came along, I just got on the bus to enjoy the ride and see where it led. I've fended for myself all my life and learned the hard lesson that no one else will be there for me. This fire behind my eyes?" Jack pointed. "Well, now you have a little insight into it."

"I feel sorry for you, Jack."

"Why? Life's just a big adventure; you'd better get what you can before it all ends."

When she turned back, Jack saw the tears running from the corners of her bright green eyes.

"Yes, I know that fire Jack. It probably saved me from freezing to death the night we crashed into that snow bank. Instead, you nearly froze. Sacrificing yourself to pull three strangers from that upside-down car showed me all I need to know about the fire that burns within you. But be smart about it. Don't throw it away!"

"Well, I thought I was, but..."

"Jack! How plain do I have to make it?" She stomped her foot. "I love you, and you're breaking my heart."

The words 'I Love You' had yet to be shared between them. He figured it was true, even to the point of taking it for granted, but now it was out in the open, and he felt guilty for not treating her better.

Jack took her in his arms and caressed her back. Holding him tight before leaning back to look into his soft blue eyes, she took in the carved features of his face and wondered about staying with him. He wondered if she was about to give up on him. His history of messing things up reared its ugly head, and he couldn't help thinking this woman, who was entirely out of his league, wouldn't hesitate to leave.

Scarlett took his face in her hands and gently kissed him. She had no way of knowing she'd just cracked the ice dam surrounding his heart. Gazing into the deep pools of green filled with tears, Jack realized what a fool he'd been. This beautiful woman, clutching him in her arms, wanted him and was giving him her heart. He'd locked his own up so tightly he missed the love she showed for him on her glowing face every day.

Before that evening, Scarlett hadn't told him she loved him. And when Jack heard her say the words and saw the tears, it hurt. He was surprised to find that the cold, dead heart he'd locked away to protect at all costs was still alive, beating, and full of passion. He'd nearly missed out on this remarkable woman by refusing to risk it and swore things would change.

Over the next few weeks, the relationship bloomed and grew serious. Both were healing from the consequences of bad relationships, so slow and easy seemed to work the best. Scarlett convinced Jack to return to school after the summer break and promised to help him manage his painting business if he finished his degree.

The summer of 1974 brought more work than Jack had ever seen, and he hired four new employees to help out. But as summer wore on, he grew determined to break away and visit Scarlett in Seattle before harvest. A road trip would be good as well. Jack felt a little too "nine to fiveish," even though his hours were much longer than that, and he longed to take to the road with his Harley.

Scarlett wasn't sure if it was a good time to meet her parents and suggested he stay with some friends.

"I would love to see you, Jack, but my parents probably aren't ready. They're pretty straight, you know."

"Well, I guess I could stay at an old girlfriend's place over there. She'd probably give me a bed."

Scarlett didn't appreciate the joke. "Not a chance, Jack. Don't say those things. That's exactly what I'm afraid of."

He was surprised by her reaction. "Just kidding. You know I'd never do that to you. I know a couple of guys I can stay with."

"Call me from their place when you get into town, and we can arrange to meet."

"We'll get some rides in on my bike. It'll be fun."

The two of them spent three days exploring downtown Seattle, the waterfront, and riding the freeways. Scarlett would meet Jack at a local grocery store after telling her parents she would be spending the day with friends, leave her car there at the store, and jump on the back of Jack's motorcycle. Jack fell in love with Pike Place and was especially fascinated by the fish market, where he watched them toss salmon and stack it like cordwood.

When Scarlett could keep Jack out of the head shops, the couple strolled through the open-air farmer's marketplace, where fresh produce and locally grown flowers were laid out for sale on long wooden tables.

The open freeway invited them on adventurous road trips. Arms wrapped around Jack's waist, trusting him entirely with her safety; she'd never felt so close to any man.

Jack knew he'd never been so deeply in love. It scared him, but there was no turning back now. Their time together went by too fast, and soon, Jack found himself back in Pullman painting houses again.

When harvest began a few weeks later, he left a three-person crew in charge of finishing his final paint job and moved to the farm. As the main hired hand, he would oversee the other hired help and run a combine for the duration of harvest.

It would mean nearly two months apart from Scarlett, as the hours required him to arise before 5 AM and work until almost dark. And there would be some night work as required. By the time he had dinner each evening and got to bed, it was nearing ten o'clock, if not later. The long days and the short nights wore a guy down, and there was little time for meeting Scarlett in town once she returned to school.

Scarlett surprised Jack early one morning when she arrived at the farm unannounced to spend the day with him. She looked stunning in a simple white T-shirt, long red braids, cut-offs, and cowboy boots. They'd been apart too long, and he'd forgotten how attractive she was. It reinvigorated him, and instead of another long day in the heat, he knew this day would be special.

After greeting her and introducing the family he was staying with, Jack picked up his lunch and prepared to go.

"Um, Jack." It was Hazel, the farmer's wife."

Stopping at the edge of the kitchen, he turned around on the dusty linoleum floor. The gritty sound grated on Scarlett's ears, though Jack didn't seem to notice. "What can I do for you, Hazel?"

Hazel pointed to Scarlett's legs and shot him a disapproving look. "She's gonna regret wearing those shorts."

His puzzled look quickly turned to understanding. "Have you got something she can wear, Hazel? Won't take even half a day, and she'll be itching like crazy."

"Ha! Not in her size!" Her good-natured laugh filled the room. "But we can make some adjustments."

"Thank you, Hazel. I should have thought of that."

Scarlett got changed, and after adjusting the waist to fit, they had something that would work. Jack drove them through the yellow, stubble-covered fields in an old Dodge pick-up used for running errands. He began his daily maintenance routine after pulling alongside his green John Deer 95 combine. Each combiner fueled and greased their harvester every morning and made minor repairs.

Scarlett watched closely while he greased the combine with its baffling number of zerks.

"What's a zerk?"

"Here, see this little nipple sticking out here." Jack pointed, then wiped the dust off it with his fingers. "The grease gun fits over the end of it; depending on where it's at and what it's lubricating, I give it a certain amount of grease to keep things running smoothly." Jack pumped the handle of his grease gun. "Ol Bessie needs a certain amount of lube each morning to get through the day's work."

"Gee, I don't know Jack. Come to find out, you're out here in the field all alone, playing with ol Bessie's nipples when I'm not around to keep an eye on you." She winked, and Jack felt his knees grow weak.

"Um, Jack, your face is turning red? Are you blushing?" She crowed.

He'd never seen this side of Scarlett and was unsure how to act.

"I think there must be a little bit of country girl in you somewhere."

"Oh, you'd be surprised." Her coy smile was all tease.

Scarlett spent the day with him, riding in his combine's cab and learning how things worked. During lunch, they sat in the dirt eating a sack lunch while leaning against the combine tire on the shady side of the machine. It was over one hundred degrees out.

The work crew teased Jack that she was much easier on the eyes than him and that his job might be jeopardized.

Shortly after lunch, the three combines were making their way around the steep hillsides of a large bowl above its valley. It was a typical Palouse wheat field with deep valleys and steep hillsides.

Jack's boss, Frank, had come to a stop on the opposite side of the valley, and Jack told Scarlett when they made it around to that side, they would stop and give him a hand.

Frank was a short little man Jack had never seen in anything but overalls. He had dark, thinning, short-cropped hair, a Hitler mustache, smoked non-stop, and possessed a hilarious sense of humor. When Jack pulled up behind Frank's combine, he shut down his machine and helped Scarlett descend the metal ladder at the side of the combine while she tended to keeping up her pants.

Frank was working on something underneath the walkway of his harvester. The hillside was so steep the combine was leveled against it as far as the hydraulic jacks would go, leaving little room for even short Frank to stand underneath the iron catwalk. Walking up behind him, Jack asked what was wrong.

"Brokeatoothoffenthisgearhere." Scarlett looked at Jack in amazement. "Justneedtopullitbutthecottakeysstuck."

Frank had a way of speaking so fast his words often required an interpreter for those not used to being around him. Naturally, this included any new employee.

Wide-eyed, Scarlett mouthed, "What?"

"He said the gear has a couple of broken teeth, and he needs to pull it to put on a new one."

Just then, Frank turned around and grunted. "Gottapullerinmytoolbox," before ducking underneath the catwalk and walking around to the other side.

"He's going to get a gear puller," Jack said to Scarlett.

Upon his return, Frank forgot to duck and walked straight into the corner of the catwalk. The sharp edge of the angle iron struck Frank in the forehead right between his eyes. The blow staggered him, and his eyes rolled up like whitewashed tombstones. Jack rushed to catch him. *He thought, just like in the cartoons where the tilt sign pops up in the character's eyes.*

But this was serious, and as a reeling Frank took one step back and began to fall, Jack was there to catch him. After easing him down on the ground, the lights came back on as soon as Frank was off his feet and sitting. He looked to Jack, then Scarlett, and then up at the corner of the catwalk and pointed. "Now that there's iron, Mr. Jackie," before breaking into a titter.

Scarlett looked at Jack in amazement and shook her head. The man was a real character.

Jack pulled an unused bandana from his shirt pocket and, after soaking it with water, wiped away the blood from Frank's face. Then he gave it to Frank to hold over the gash in his head. Soon, the crusty old boy was back on his feet, working the gear puller after telling Jack he could manage.

"No point in shutting us both down."

"I'll hang around a bit if it's alright with you. That's a nasty smack on the head you took."

When Frank finally got the gear off, he grinned and looked up at Jack through a stream of cigarette smoke and squinty eyes.

"AndthattheressuccessMr.Jackie."

By the end of the day, Scarlett's long red braids were full of dust and wheat chaff. Her pants were also covered, and she thanked Jack for the chance to change out of her shorts. "I would have been miserable."

"Better thank Hazel. She's the one who thought of it." Though secretly, Jack missed the long, lean legs those pants had covered.

She may have been dirty, sweaty, and even a bit smelly, but Jack thought she never looked better.

After walking her to her car that evening, he took Scarlett in his arms and searched her green eyes. "Thank you. It's probably not what you expected today, but you sure made my day. It was the best."

Scarlett smiled, leaned back, and patted his chest with one hand before whispering, "There you were again, Jack, reacting in time to help your boss, caring for him after he was down."

"Now you're getting carried away. Anyone would have done what I did. It's no big deal."

"But you were there. You're always right there when needed."

Jack shook his head, smiled, and kissed her. It was alright with him if that's what she wanted to believe.

"I'll see you in another week. We should be finished by then."

Jack looked skyward as her car disappeared down the long driveway, leaving a cloud of brown dust hanging in the air. The brilliant pinpricks of light against the ink-black sky had never looked so beautiful. He felt as if he would never forget it.

It would only be a few days before he saw Scarlett again. Three days later, the harvest crew moved to a new field and were just opening it up when Jack's combine slid down the hill and rolled.

Being the last combine in line, he was the furthest up the hillside, on the steepest part. The combine was leveled to the maximum and still didn't feel level. Jack took it easy, but the back end of the combine kept breaking loose and slipping. It was no big deal, he thought. It happened sometimes—nothing to get excited about.

Using his skill and experience, he carefully guided the machine back into place. Then it slipped again. Jack noted how heavy and dense the stubble was. Heavy stubble was not a combiner's friend. It could be exceedingly slick, to the point of keeping the wheat trucks out of certain parts of the field.

Jack was working the ungainly machine back into place on the hillside when, in the blink of an eye, it broke free and slid down the hill. The combine rolled at the bottom, where the hillside began to level, allowing the tires to grab. Jack was crushed inside the cab.

Frank radioed back to the farmhouse, and Hazel called the hospital for an ambulance. Paramedics responded as soon as possible. They took Jack to the hospital in critical condition. Crushed ribs, a broken left arm, a lacerated kidney, and a collapsed lung left Jack clinging to life.

It took a while for word to get to Scarlett. The doctors sedated Jack for pain management, and on the evening of the second day, while visiting Jack at the hospital, Frank and Hazel found Scarlett's phone number in Jack's wallet.

Frank called her from the farm that evening to share the tough news. "I'm sorry to be so late in letting you know, but it took a while to come up with your phone number. He's in room 307, but you'll need to wait until tomorrow, Scarlett. It's past visiting hours."

She noted how he spoke more slowly, especially when giving her the room number.

Scarlett thanked him and hurried to the hospital, not caring it was after visiting hours. She barely noticed the medicinal smell and quiet atmosphere when rushing straight past the nurses' station and up to Jack's room. Sound asleep, he was unaware of her presence. After taking his hand and kneeling at his bedside, she prayed.

"Lord, he's a good man. Rough, course even, but his heart is right and good. Do not take him from me. I love this man and know we are to spend our lives together. Please, please, please." She pleaded.

A sympathetic nurse stood in the doorway listening. "Miss, you need to leave now. You can come back first thing tomorrow."

"Please. I can't leave him now. This man saved my life once, and I can't abandon him at a time like this."

"I understand, but visiting hours ended some time ago. So you need to leave." She stated it more firmly this time.

"Look, this is my fiancé." She lied. "Please don't make me leave."

The nurse glanced at Scarlett's left hand. "Um-hum. No ring yet, huh." She eyed Scarlett. "Better be careful of this one girl." Then, pausing, she looked over her shoulder and down the hallway.

"Alright, but not a sound. There's no bed here, just this one chair." The nurse pointed. "Don't get me in trouble."

Scarlett knew precisely what she was going to do. When the nurse left, she climbed onto the bed beside Jack and took his hand.

"Don't leave me, Jack." She wept. "Don't you dare leave me. You've been so good to me, so respectful. Do you know how rare men like you are? I felt so used and unappreciated by my last boyfriend. You're an answer to so many prayers."

She checked the door to see if anyone had noticed and snuggled closer. "I know this is right. We have such a bright future together.

Remember who you are, Jack. A fighter who always takes care of himself. You told me that once, remember?"

She stopped to stifle her sobs before whispering again.

"You have always been there for me when I needed you, and Jack, I need you now. Do not leave me. You've stolen my heart. Bring it back to me." She allowed her head to rest gently on his shoulder, and the tears flowed.

Scarlett awoke at 3 AM when a different nurse came to check on Jack. She was black as midnight, and when the whites of her eyes flashed at finding Scarlett in Jack's bed, Scarlett found it frightening.

"Honey, you can't be in here. I don't know how you got in, but you can't stay."

Scarlett moved across the room to the single chair, sat down, and crossed her arms. "I'm not leaving my fiancé." It had worked once before, and the lie came naturally this time.

The nurse huffed and thrust both hands atop ample hips. "Then you stay out of the way and don't leave that chair. Understood?" Her eyes flashed, and Scarlett nodded. She watched the nurse complete her check of Jack, then quickly asked before she left the room. "How is he?"

"He's stable, and that's a good thing. Bruised lungs are nothing to sneeze at." Then she caught herself. "I'm sorry I didn't mean it to sound like that. Fortunately, his right lung functions normally, and his oxygenation level is improving. We are giving him antibiotics to prevent pneumonia. I expect to see a big improvement today."

"Praise God."

"Girl, he'll be alright, and I'm sure his healing will be sped up because he has you at his side, but you've got to give him some time."

Scarlett smiled meekly. "Thank you. I won't be any trouble, and I'll stay out of the way."

"It's a deal then." She flashed a tender smile. "You cooperate, and I'll look the other way. I can't speak for the doctor, but I'll give him a good report about you."

She started to leave and then turned back. "I know it's none of my business, but if that boy is your fiance, child, you should drop him like a hot potato. A real man would have a good-sized diamond on the hand of someone as pretty as the likes of you. You mark my words."

"He's promised me," Scarlett said softly. "Humph! Don't hold your breath, honey." The nurse huffed and spun on her heel. Scarlett listened to her shoes squeaking down the hall before returning to the side of Jack's bed. Taking hold of Jack's hand, the feel of calluses and the strength found in his fingers brought new tears. The same hands that were once frozen stiff, pulling her from the car, had also been so gentle with her. Now, they lay still and unmoving.

"I hope you didn't hear what I said to that nurse. But I do love you, Jack, in a way I didn't know I could love someone. She says you're getting better. That's encouraging." She squeezed his hand. "If I could just see your smile and those brilliant blue eyes again." She squeezed his hand again and felt a weak clench in return.

"Jack?" She held her breath.

Then, the faintest of smiles surfaced on his pale face. "So we're engaged now?"

She wanted to smack him but carefully threw her arms around him instead.

"Easy." He moaned. "These ribs are gonna take awhile."

"Oh, Jack, I'm sorry." Her hands flew to her mouth, and she recoiled at what she'd done.

His smile was more assertive this time, and a light emerged in his eyes to chase away the dullness she'd first seen there. "It's alright. We just have to be careful."

A couple of hours later, after the doctor completed his check-up, he told Jack it would be a couple more nights to ensure no complications developed. The doctor then turned to Scarlett and winked. "It's my understanding the two of you are recently engaged. Congratulations."

Jack began to protest, but Scarlett cut him off.

"Yes, quite recently, in fact."

"Well then. I will arrange for you to spend the night if you like, so you don't have to sneak in again like you did last night."

Scarlett blushed. "Would you really? Thank you so much."

The doctor left, and Jack cleared his throat. "A-hem, just how far are you going to take this fiancé thing? You haven't even proposed to me yet."

Scarlett's blush added a little more color to her cheeks. "As far as I have to take it to stay by your side. And Jack, I'd marry you in a moment, but I know it's not right yet. So relax. I haven't stolen your thunder."

"But Scarlett."

"Hush." She put a finger to his lips before kissing him. "There's only one thing that matters. You, getting healthy and back on your feet so you can romance me just like you were doing."

"You're a strong woman, Scarlett. I don't know if I can deal with that." he winked.

"Oh, you'll deal with it, alright. I'll make sure of it. But enough of this. We have a long way to go to get you back to health."

CHAPTER SEVEN

JACK WAS RELEASED FROM THE HOSPITAL FOUR DAYS LATER. The fall of 1974 was a tender season for Jack and Scarlett. Except for staying home at night, she cared for him nearly every moment of the day, and Jack responded with a quick recovery. The autumn reds, russets, yellows, easing temperatures, and brisk morning air also assisted with his recovery. Though summer was fading, their romance bloomed in full color, and Scarlett invited Jack to come to Seattle and meet her parents during Christmas break.

On the day Jack was to arrive in Seattle, a rare Christmas snow left nearly a foot of snow on the ground. When Scarlett saw Jack pull up in front of the house, she rushed out the door to greet him. Unprepared for her vigorous greeting, she slid into Jack and knocked him to the ground. After rubbing snow in his face, a good-natured wrestling match occurred.

Determined to get on top, Jack soon pinned Scarlett's arms to the ground. Scarlett flashed a feisty, ear-to-ear grin. "I told you I'd teach you to deal with a strong woman."

Her parents remained standing on the front porch, arms folded and waiting to be introduced. Jack bent down and kissed her full on the mouth. Then, after helping her to her feet, the snow-covered couple turned hand in hand to meet her parents. Facing them with tousled hair full of snow, Scarlett suddenly realized this may not have been the best way to introduce Jack to her parents.

"Mom, Dad, I'd like you to meet Jack."

Her Dad's eyes went wide over Jack's ponytail and overall rough look. But Scarlett's mother looked away so her husband wouldn't see her discreetly smile at Scarlett, acknowledging she understood what Scarlett saw in the man. Her secret wink to Scarlett didn't get past Jack, but "Dad" would be a tough sell.

Now I know where she gets that flirty wink. Jack thought.

Jack and Scarlett spent their days riding ferries and seeing the sites in and around Seattle. She took him north to Marysville and showed him the old house she grew up in near Deception Pass. They hung out together at Pike Place Market, where Jack especially liked the head shops with their black light posters and Jimi Hendrix music. Scarlett had to wrestle him away each time they passed one by. It was the only issue to arise between them during an otherwise magical visit.

Their time together in Seattle went much too fast, and soon, Jack was back in Pullman partying with his friends as usual. He was anxious for Scarlett to return to school, but the partying life he enjoyed filled much of the void.

A couple of months later, when both of them were back in school, Scarlett began to feel like Jack was partying too much and taking her for granted. He'd stood her up several times because he was too out of it to remember their date. It seemed like a habit the man couldn't break, even to the point of preferring it over her. After confronting him and threatening to break up if he didn't change his ways, he swore off partying and doubled down on his commitment to her.

On the day she showed up unannounced, pounding on the front door of the house he rented, Santana was pouring forth from every door, window, and crack. The music was so loud he couldn't hear her knocking.

Upon opening the door and stepping inside, she found Jack on the floor, slumped against the couch. At first, she thought something was wrong, but after shaking him and seeing the lazy smile, she knew he had fallen back into the same old habits he vowed to give up.

Scarlett stormed from the house, struggling between crying and screaming. This time, she would lay down the law. And she did. After ignoring his week-long phone calls, she called him and arranged a meeting.

After the warning, Jack fell in line. His attention shifted back to Scarlett, and the partying ended. For a few weeks, all was well, and once again, they began looking to the future together.

They shared secret dreams and made plans for the spring after they finished college. 1975 looked to be a promising year. But it all blew up when Jack made plans to go kayaking with his friends on their annual trip during spring break. A severe fight ensued. Scarlett's fury displayed the fiery crimson her name symbolized in full regalia, but all it did was cause Jack to get his back up. Who was this woman to tell him he couldn't pursue one of his favorite pastimes? Especially since he had been doing so well at keeping his promise not to do drugs and party.

It pissed him off, and he told her so! Jack had never experienced a fight like the one that followed. Her high, shrieking voice was unrelenting until he finally reached his limit and told her he'd had enough. They were through!

The week-long kayak trip with his buddies gave him ample time to digest and rehash the words they'd yelled at one another, hash being the key component of his event processing. The river trip and time apart allowed him to gain a little perspective. How had he gotten so tied down? The freedom he'd given up for Scarlett, regained while kayaking confirmed his thinking that he'd made the right decision to break up with her.

A week passed after returning from the river, and Jack was getting comfortable being single again. A second week passed, and he was fully embracing it. Scarlett had called twice in the last couple of days, but he had yet to return her calls. He couldn't see anything good coming from it and didn't want to get all tangled up in another fight full of angry emotions. He just hoped Scarlett was doing alright because his intent was not to hurt her.

Three weeks later, on a Friday night, Jack relaxed comfortably at home alone. The weather was unseasonably warm, and he'd removed his shirt and opened all the windows to the house before settling in for a good smoke. Cranking up some Alice Cooper and stretching out on the couch with a beer and his joint, Jack was at peace. His business was booming, he would soon graduate and finally be free of all the college bullshit. A new and promising future beckoned, and he looked forward to it!

CHAPTER EIGHT

THE POUNDING ON JACK'S DOOR SHATTERED HIS PEACEFUL mindset. "Alright, alright. I'll turn it down." The neighbors were always complaining about his music.

He'd barely sat down again before the banging resumed.

"Oh, alright!"

Upon answering the door, he was shocked to find Scarlett standing outside and immediately threw back his shoulders and struck a pose against the door frame. He had to admit she looked pretty darned good.

"Hello, Jack." She stood tall, faced him squarely, and spoke directly. "You haven't returned my calls."

"Uh, well. I told you. We aren't good for one another, and I think we should move on."

She seemed reticent and anxious at the same time. Scarlett swung her foot at a piece of gravel atop the concrete steps and looked down. "I was thinking maybe we should give it another try."

"Seriously? After the things you said about me."

"I was only making it clear I don't feel I'm number one in your life."

"But of course you are, uh, were." Jack corrected himself."

"You sure have a funny way of showing it." She looked up into his blue eyes, knowing full well the effect her beauty had on him. Though Jack tried not to notice, it had the desired result.

"The drugs, alcohol, girls, even the guys count for more than I do!"

"Aint never been any other girl, and you know that."

"I do? How would I know that, Jack?" She spoke softly to him, but her eyes conveyed a withering look that never strayed from his face.

The dead air between them carried notes of the snowstorm he'd rescued her from – cold and frosty - signaling the end of the conversation, but Scarlett persisted. "I think we should try again. What we had once is worth fighting for. I'm asking you to think about *us*! If you can put our relationship first, I'm willing to start over. It will be your last chance, our last chance. After you think it over, if you want to get together, call, and if you can convince me things will change, we'll try this one last time. I love you, Jack, but I think it's pretty much a one-way street right now."

"But Scarlett..."

She held up her hand. "Don't prove my daddy right about you."

"Scarlett, don't leave. Please come in."

"Not now, Jack. It's time for me to go." She reached up, took both his bare shoulders in her hands, and kissed him on the cheek.

A week passed, and Jack had to admit he was still smitten. She had that kind of hold on him, and it wasn't easy being without her. *What was the deal?* He wondered. *No woman ever affected me like this.*

When he called, she sounded busy, and an unexpected chill shot up his spine.

"Scarlett."

"Hello, Jack."

The cold response shook him. "I'd like to meet with you and put things back together. What's a good time?"

"I'm not sure it's a good idea." Having had time to think more about it, she was having second thoughts about getting back together.

"Please, Scarlett. I can change." He hated begging, but the image of the most beautiful woman he'd ever known walking away chilled him.

Reluctantly, she agreed. "We'll see Jack. I know the man inside. He's the one I want. But I'll remain skeptical until you can win the battle with your demons."

"You'll see. They don't control me."

"Alright. I'll see you one more time, but no promises."

The cold conversation ended abruptly after agreeing on the time and a place to meet.

The following day, standing on the lawn under a massive weeping willow covered in fresh green growth, Jack spied Scarlett.

More beautiful than ever, he knew he could be all she wanted.

After agreeing on a burger and shake at the old A&W. Scarlett drove them. She wasn't about to get on the back of his bike and sit so close to him. Besides small talk, little was said during their meal, and afterward, the two went for a short walk along the Palouse River. Scarlett even allowed him to take her hand.

When they returned to her car, and Jack leaned in for a kiss, she turned away. "It's not like nothing has happened between us, Jack. I don't think you understand that. You cannot wave your magic wand and expect things to return to how they were before. Can't you see how you've hurt me?"

"I'm sorry Scarlett. How many times do I have to say it?"

"Saying it's one thing. I need to see it. I gave you my heart, and it meant nothing to you."

"That's not true."

"Sorry, Jack, but you have much to prove." She turned away and got into her car. "I'll let you think about that on your walk back to get your bike. And if you still want to, I'll see you in a few days." Then, more to herself than Jack, "If you can stay sober that long."

"You're just gonna leave me here?"

"It's not much fun, is it?" she glared, backed out of the parking spot, and headed for Stadium Way.

Over the next few weeks, the two reconciled, made up, studied together and things seemed to be going well. The relationship they'd previously enjoyed appeared set to bloom once more. It lasted about a month.

When Scarlett took a three-day weekend to return to Seattle and visit her parents, Jack fell victim to some old habits. Freedom beckoned with powerful enticements, and it didn't take long for a full-on party weekend to begin. The day she returned, all hell broke loose.

Scarlett fixed her hair just how Jack liked it, left Seattle early and drove back to school faster than she would typically drive. Dressed in the cut-off jeans she knew he loved, she was anxious to see him.

After knocking on the door to his house, she impatiently waited. When there was no answer, she knocked again. It was quiet inside. No music was playing. Maybe he was out grocery shopping or something. After trying the door again, she reluctantly turned away and returned to the sorority.

Late that evening, she knew something was up when he didn't answer the phone and hadn't returned home. After calling some of Jack's friends, she sat down alone in her room. Dejected at not being able to see him as she'd planned, the old haunts of past betrayals troubled her.

Don't judge Scarlett. You don't know there's anything wrong. Sure, you're disappointed you didn't get to see him, but you don't know anything is wrong yet.

But he knew I was coming back today. He should have been there waiting for me.

After a glass of wine, she went to bed, wrestling with her thoughts and more than a little disappointment.

It was after two AM when the phone rang and woke her.

"Scarlett, sorry to wake you, but you'd better come get Jack." It was Jack's friend Buzz. "He's pretty out of it."

"No way! You can throw him out in the street for all I care!" Maybe it was because she was not fully awake yet, but her quick-to-rise anger surprised even Scarlett.

"Scarlett, come on. He's only this way because he misses you. The guy loves you more than he knows how to deal with."

"Sorry, Buzz. I'll come get him, but he gets no sympathy from me."

When Scarlett arrived, she found Jack on the floor, leaning against a couch, passed out. The remains of the joints he'd smoked were in a bowl next to him. His arm rested atop a girl's hip, asleep on the couch with her back to him.

Scarlett's face blazed red, lighting her hair like a burning sunset and setting ablaze the sprinkling of freckles across the bridge of her nose and under her eyes.

"You never should have called me Buzz. Hard telling what I might do to him."

"Come on, Scarlett, have a heart."

"I can't, Buzz!" She bellowed. "Because Jack has it." She looked across the room at a near-comatose Jack. "We are through!"

"Just get him home safe, and you guys can work it out later. He's a good man, so don't be so hard on him."

"Bastard!" She stomped.

Scarlett drove Jack home, helped him stagger inside, and laid him out across his bed. Consumed with rage, she vacillated between physically attacking him and breaking down in tears. Fists clenched at the sides of a body rigid with anger; her face blazed in resentment. Looking down upon his rugged face, she could no longer contain her tears or fury.

"You son-of-a-bitch!" She yelled. "I thought it was real. A love so deep we could overcome anything together. What we had was special, Jack!

Can't you see that? It was all I ever dreamed about, and *you* destroyed it! *You* ruined everything! I trusted you in every way, Jack. You took advantage of me, and I owe you nothing. *I HATE YOU!*"

Jack roused just enough to greet her with a drunken half-smile. "Sometimes you just gotta let the horses run." He slurred.

Scarlett sobbed, wiped the tears from her eyes, and stormed from the house.

CHAPTER NINE

THE WEIGHT OF ALL THAT WENT DOWN THE NIGHT BEFORE crushed Jack when his mind gained consciousness the following morning. His body railed against the way he'd treated it, and his soul convicted him at every level. Suddenly, he found himself unable to climb out of the dark hole his life had become without Scarlett.

When she refused his calls, it rocked his world. There was nowhere to turn. Acknowledging it was entirely his fault but with no idea how to fix things, it was one of those rare moments when Jack didn't feel in control. Used to having command of nearly every situation, Jack felt the stirring of old feelings deep inside.

The world will knock you down, kick you in the nuts, and no one will care. It's just how it is.

Faced with regaining control of his life, Jack swore *no one* would ever get close to his heart again. It was all about Jack now, and he would make sure it stayed that way. He'd gone back on the promise he once made to himself, never to give his heart away, and was burned again. He swore it would be the last time.

Jack quickly sold his paint company and prepared for an extended road trip. He used the money from the business to pay off his debts, buy some weed for the road, and some gear for his Harley.

On a Friday night the day after finals, Jack found himself back at the same bar in Idaho where he and Scarlett had once hit it off. Joined by Buzz and a few other friends, they celebrated the end of another year of college. Jack was swilling fifty-cent glasses of beer when he heard the unmistakably spontaneous and joyous laughter that belonged to just one woman.

Looking across the dance floor to the other side of the room, he spotted her. What was left of his heart fell. Scarlett had cozied up with one of the better-known drug dealers in the area. Though he knew what his reception would be like if he intervened, Jack felt obligated to warn her. If she thought she was hurting now, look out.

Jack threw his shoulders back, stood tall, and puffed out his chest before strolling across to their table. The band was on break, and the dance floor was unoccupied. He walked straight up to their table and asked for a moment with Scarlett. When she refused, the guy got to his feet. At once, Jack put a hand in the middle of the guy's chest and shoved him back down in his seat.

"We've known each other for years, Johnny, so you'll believe me when I tell you this ain't between us. Now, just back off a moment and let me speak to Scarlett. Then you can have you're wh..." Jack checked himself. It may have been how Johnny treated the cheap women he dated, but Scarlett didn't deserve to be called that.

"...Your woman back. Then she'll be ALL yours." Scarlett didn't miss the insinuation.

Johnny grunted. He was no match for Jack, even if the guy had been drinking.

"Scarlett. I need a moment with you." Jack directed her to an area a few steps away.

She leaned in toward Johnny, and he appeared to give her permission.

Stepping from behind the table and smoothing her black skirt, she approached. "Make it quick, Jack. What do you want?"

They moved a few more steps away before Jack spoke. "Scarlett, the guy is the biggest drug runner in all the Palouse. I'm trying to save you from a lot of trouble. Stay away from him."

"Save me from trouble! Yeah, that's what you do, isn't it? What a joke! You're an asshole, Jack, and you can go straight to hell!"

Something wasn't right. This wasn't Scarlett. No matter how mad she got, she rarely swore. Jack turned and pointed at Johnny. "Leave her alone, Johnny, or you'll answer to me. Plenty of other girls are out there for the likes of you." Jack walked to their table and smashed his fist down to make his point. "I'm telling you here and now. You let her be!" Jack slapped him to make his point, then turned and slowly strolled across the dance floor, daring the guy to challenge him. It never happened.

Slaps on the back greeted Jack when he returned to his table, and Buzz ordered another round of beers.

* * * * * * *

JACK MANAGED TO GRADUATE, BUT THE DIPLOMA, A PERFECT example of "higher" education, meant nothing to him. He'd done it for Scarlett, and now that she was gone, he was as detached from school as she was from him.

Preparing to hit the road, he stored his 65 Ford Falcon in the old three-bay shed on the farm where he'd worked harvest. Covering it, he said goodbye. "You're the only girl I have left to say goodbye to. But I'll be back. I promise. I just can't tell you when." He patted the car's hood, sighed, and momentarily stared across the green wheat fields before leaving.

These wheat fields are home to me. I've known such good people here and had such wonderful times. Frank has taught me so much. Danny has been a good friend. I'm going to miss working harvest this summer more than anything else.

The breeze rattled some of the aging wooden shingles and waved the giant spider webs stretched between the beams. It stirred the musty scent of moldering hay, oily rags, and a diesel-fueled 1935 Caterpillar tractor resting in the next bay over.

Jack took a moment for one last look around before walking back to the farmhouse for his ride back to town.

A few days and a couple of parties later, he was packing up and preparing his bike for the road. When the phone rang, it reminded him he needed to have it disconnected. At first, thinking to ignore it, he hesitated to answer, then figuring it could be important, Jack grabbed it on the seventh ring."

"Hello."

"Jack! I need your help!" It was Scarlett, and she was frantic. "You gotta come get me outta here."

"Slow down and tell me what's going on." She was nearly hysterical, and Jack was having trouble understanding her.

"It's Johnny. I'm locked inside his bedroom."

Bedroom. And you're calling me? Was Jack's first thought. It was all he could do to keep from hanging up.

"He's gone crazy, and I'm afraid of what he will do to me."

Yup. The guy got some bad stuff. I've seen it before. It was just a matter of time.

"Jack, are you there? Please don't leave me here, Jack. I need you."

There it is. She was tugging on his heartstrings again. *It was to be expected, I suppose.*

He sighed deeply. "Scarlett. What'd I tell you about that guy."

"Jack, please! This is no time for a lecture. Please hurry!" She was in tears now, and Jack found it impossible to ignore her pleading voice.

"Alright. I'm on my way. Whatever you do, don't let him in."

Jack hung up, shrugged, and sighed. "Shit. Nothing good gonna come from this." Speaking to himself made it more real. He didn't want to get involved but felt duty-bound to do what he could.

"Damn it, Scarlett!"

He threw on his riding leathers, stashed the last bit of clothing he was taking in one of the bike's saddlebags, and roared off to Johnny's. Ten minutes later, Scarlett heard the rumble of Jack's motorcycle outside. Johnny did, too.

"Bitch! You called your ex, didn't you? Damn you!"

He began kicking and beating on the door. Scarlett pushed back and screamed for him to stay out.

Hurry up, Jack.

Jack's voice boomed from the living room.

"That's enough, Johnny. I told you not to touch her. Now get the hell out of the way and let her go."

Johnny turned on him, flipped open a gleaming seven-inch blade, and began stalking towards Jack. "You don't come into my house uninvited and tell me what to do." He flipped the knife once and caught it by the handle. "Unless you want to be carved up and fed to the pigs, you'd better leave."

Jack took a step back. He hadn't asked for any of this, and for a fleeting moment, he thought of leaving, but he'd never forgive himself for abandoning Scarlett. Much of the blame for her being with the guy lay with him, and now he was stuck in a situation he'd never asked for.

Reaching behind his back for the pistol he always carried on the road, Jack retrieved the snub nose .38 from his waistband as Johnny lunged. Jack fired twice, striking Johnny in the chest.

The shit had just gotten deep. *A woman got you into this mess, Jack. Never forget that.*

At the sound of gunfire, Scarlett shrieked and raced from the bedroom. Johnny was lying at Jack's feet, the gleaming blade still in his hand and a dark pool of blood growing around his torso. Scarlett's suddenly saucer-sized eyes looked at Jack.

"You killed him!"

"Thanks to you." The realization of how dire things had just gotten washed over him. He needed to think fast.

"Now listen to me carefully, Scarlett." He took her by the shoulders and got in her face. "I came here to help you out. Now it's your turn to help me."

She nodded mechanically.

"After I leave, you're going to call the cops and tell them you were in the bedroom sleeping when a loud fight broke out. Then you heard gunshots and came out to find Johnny dead and the sound of squealing tires outside. You will describe it as a drug deal gone bad, and that's all you know. It should throw the cops off my trail, if not the dealers who are sure to follow."

"What are you going to do?"

"I'm leaving town. I was finishing packing when you called."

"Leaving? No Jack. Please don't." Her fists clenched at the front of his shirt. "What about us?"

"Us?" Jack threw his hands up. "There is no us!"

"I've missed you, Jack. I know we can work this out."

"Don't waste your time on me, Scarlett. I'm sorry, but I'm not good for anyone right now. It's better if I go."

"No, Jack. It's not. You're just running away."

He took her by the shoulders again and stared into her emerald eyes for the last time. "Sometimes there are things a man can't help. If I had known when I met you that I'd fall in love and that you'd be the reason my heart would be broken again, I still would have loved you. I still do, but my heart is never going to heal from this, and I need to go."

"Jack, please."

"I need time away from here. Time on the road, new places, new experiences, new people. Understand?"

"A new woman." Tears were forming in the corners of Scarlett's now red eyes.

"If that's what it takes!" He yelled.

Her eyes searched his face, looking for an answer. "We had a good thing, Jack—a rare thing. It's not something you will find somewhere else. It's here now, right in front of you. Don't turn your back on us. We can get through this."

Jack grunted and shook his head. "Been down that road. We had our chance, Scarlett. It's not in the cards: oil and water and all that. You're a big-city sorority girl; I'm a farm boy. We had no chance. You know that as well as I do." He took her hands from his shirt and placed them at her side.

She responded by embracing him, but Jack's arms remained limp at his sides.

"Please sit down, Scarlett. I need to go." Jack was unmoved and coldly sat her on the couch.

"Why? Where are you going? Who are you going with? When will you be back? What are you doing, Jack?"

It was typical Scarlett - always a million questions. Most of the time, it didn't bother him, but other times, it tended to push him over the edge.

"Searching for my soul." He mumbled, primarily to himself, before stalking down the hallway to search the bedrooms. Jack found nothing of interest in the room Scarlett had come from except her bathrobe hanging on the back of the door.

Disgusted, he slammed the door and marched to the other bedroom across the hallway. There, he found a massive bag of cash and a nice stash of weed hidden under a pile of dirty clothes at the back of the closet.

Returning to the living room with a bag in each hand, he stopped at the front door to say goodbye. "You understand your instructions?"

She nodded.

"Drug deal gone bad. Never saw the shooter. Are we clear?"

"Yes, Jack." She sniffed. "But please, my life is a wreck. You can't leave me now."

"Your life is a wreck? Give me a break!" He turned to go, then stopped. "Take care of yourself, Scarlett. You're a tough gal. You'll be fine."

"How will I get in touch with you?"

"You won't."

"Come on, Jack, you can't just walk out of my life."

"I can, and I am. Your Dad will be thrilled. Goodbye."

He turned for the door.

"Will I ever see you again?" Her strained voice beseeched him.

"No, it's over. Goodbye." Jack's words were hoarse and weak as he struggled to control his emotions.

Scarlett rushed to the door and grabbed his arm. "There has to be some way I can get in touch with you if I need to."

Jack was about to boil over, and he shook her off. "Scarlett! I'm not anybody's white knight riding to the rescue. Forget about us! I'm leaving now. I have no plans to come back. We're done!"

In the end, he shared the address of a friend in Texas.

"Not promising anything, but if that gets me out of here, then fine. Have a nice life, Scarlett."

"Jack. I love you."

He didn't bother looking back and stormed out. The sight of his ponytailed back, clad in black leather, and the sound of his Harley fading away in the distance would be Scarlett's last memory of him.

A war raged in Jack's heart - passionate love versus fiery anger. His heart told him yes, but his head said no.

Nothing some time on the road can't fix.

CHAPTER TEN

JACK WANTED NOTHING MORE THAN TO GET OUT OF TOWN, and his bike had never sounded better as he roared east. Hell-bent on doing things his way now and swearing no one would ever have control over him again, he flew down the road, racing to leave his old life behind. He didn't know where he was going and didn't care as long as he left the past and all its troubles behind in the dust. He'd build a new world with his own hands and prove everyone wrong! He just needed some time to put it together.

The wind in his face and blowing through his hair told him he was free now. Free of the shackles binding him to school, the town, the girl, the job, everything! And it felt marvelous. The feeling of leaving life's wreckage behind was exhilarating. Wherever his bike took him would be good enough. The thrill of it all electrified him.

Jack rode east to Moscow. The mysterious dark, leather-clad silhouette racing through town caught the eye of a group of college girls hanging out on a downtown street. Two bikers parked alongside Highway 8 at the eastern edge of town noted the same stealthy form.

"Gotta be him, Jake."

"Timing is right. It's gotta be him."

The two pulled out and followed at a distance.

Jack relished the ride through the rolling hills of pine trees and farmland. The cool air and feel of the bike beneath him felt like home. He soon came to the timber towns of Troy and Kendrick before descending the canyon to the Clearwater River. He passed cars recklessly, uncaring, and received numerous single-digit salutes in the process. He didn't even bother saluting back.

His mind raced with thoughts of Scarlett. It enraged him. Whenever he got close to someone, he hurt them, they hurt him, and things soon fell apart. Why? Jack was determined to find the answer somewhere. And he wouldn't think of returning until he had.

By the time he reached the little town of Juliaetta, Jack knew Lolo Pass and the wide-open country of Montana were where he needed to be. Following the Potlatch River down to the Clearwater, the memories of that fateful day when he'd nearly drowned consumed him. Scarlett's angry lecture about God saving him made no sense then and less sense now. What was he missing? He had no idea and didn't want to think about it.

Riding hard through the curves in the vast open country soothed his nerves and took his mind off things. He could feel himself unwind. The ride kept getting better the further he traveled along the Clearwater River. When Jack rolled into a gas station in Orofino, Idaho, many miles later, an old timer in a straw hat, overalls, and clenching a straw between his teeth ambled out to pump his gas.

"Tell you what…" He pointed with the piece of straw retrieved from his mouth. "That's one nice bike, Mister. Think I'll just be letting you pump your own gas." He stepped back, still admiring the machine. "Ain't seen nuttin' like that round here for ages."

Jack smiled and took hold of the pump handle. Moments later, he handed the attendant $5.00 for $1.16 in gas.

"Thank you, Mister. Safe travels now, ya hear."

Jack flashed him the peace sign before continuing upriver along Highway 12. The two riders following him since Moscow pulled out of an alleyway across the street and continued to track him. A short distance upriver, Jack found a site that would make a good place to camp. The open space and lack of developed campsites were perfect. He always looked for places on private land where no one else would be. If he were quiet and picked up after himself, no one would know he'd ever camped there.

The dulcet sounds of the river were comforting, and Jack quickly settled in. About the only traffic he heard that evening was two bikers passing by on the highway at dusk. Unaware they had missed him pulling off the road, they continued searching for him further upriver.

Jack picked through his travel bags and kicked himself for rushing out of town with only a single can of pork and beans. He pulled out the bottle of rye whiskey, figuring it would fill in the gaps after he finished his meal of beans.

Before kicking back for the night, he walked to the river's edge and sat down next to a cool, clear brook entering the river. The placid stream waters sang to him as the burdens of school, work, and obligations faded. Thoughts of Scarlett, not to mention the fact that he'd just killed someone, continued haunting him.

Somewhere along the line, I lost myself. Life got so fast and crazy. He puffed a small cigar to life. *This is what I've always connected with. This peace, this calm, this slower pace of life. Gotta learn how to hang on to it.*

Kneeling at the creek's edge, he looked down into a still pool of clear water, expecting to see his reflection looking back. Instead, Scarlett's tear-stained face peered up at him. The poignant green eyes, flaming red hair, and grief-filled look startled him. He fell backward, forced back by the image. Resting on the moist ground, the wrestling match with his thoughts continued.

Should I go back?

No. You blew it, Jack. You've searched all your life for a woman like her, and what do you do when you find her?

We are different people. It could never work.

Got that right.

The accusing voices were unrelenting. *Ok, OK, you made your point—stupid me. Go ahead and kick my ass. I'll do better next time. Now, just leave me be.*

Earlier, he'd rejected the idea of smoking any of the weed he'd stolen, but that was then, and this was now. Jack climbed the bank, strolled to his bike, pulled out enough grass to roll a joint, and kicked back with his bottle of whiskey.

His only concern for the night was the drug gang to which Johnny may have owed the money. If Johnny hadn't settled up with them before his death, Jack was likely being tailed. And it was always possible they had gotten ahold of Scarlett and forced her to talk. Would she talk, he wondered? He'd left her bitter and angry. Not a good combination. He couldn't know if she would rat on him, but he was getting obliterated anyway.

The following morning, Jack made the short ride back to Orofino. The bear grass was blooming and filled the open areas near the side of the road with its cream-colored flowers. The fresh air and beauty of the land freed Jack of any lasting concerns. He had a long, possibly never-ending road trip to look forward to.

Arriving in Orofino, he turned into the first Mom and Pop restaurant he came to: a mound of hash browns and gravy foremost in his mind with numerous cups of coffee.

The "Turn It or Burn It" eatery looked like the perfect place. Removing his helmet while standing astride his bike, Jack watched two bikers in black leather pull in and park next to him. One wore a black helmet, and the other wore red. He'd keep an eye on them. After parking their rides, they sauntered inside, seemingly unaware of him.

The cute young waitress who brought his coffee and took his order flirted. But Jack was in no frame of mind for it and made it clear he wasn't in the mood for conversation. Returning with his plate of hashbrowns and gravy, she made sure to lean over right in front of him.

Not today, honey. Find another sucker.

Later, his meal was over, the waitress returned and made one more attempt.

"Saw that bike you rode in on. Where are you headed?"

"Don't honestly know," he smiled.

"Honestly?"

"Honestly."

"I always dreamed of wandering the country on the back of a motorcycle." She thrust out a slender hip to rest one hand on.

Jack hung his head and smiled. She was young and cute and perfectly represented the shackles he'd just freed himself from. He looked up into willing eyes.

"See those two guys over there?" he pointed. You never know, but you might be able to hitch a ride with them. Two guys, one gal." Jack raised his eyebrows. It could be a lot of fun."

The insinuation had the desired effect. "She slapped his bill down on the table.

"I'm not that kind of girl."

"Just sayin." He chuckled to himself.

After paying his bill and walking out to his bike, he pulled on his helmet and took a moment to observe the two riders emerge from the restaurant. Jack watched the black-clad men briefly glance his way while lingering about their bikes.

Just keep an eye on them, and you'll be fine.

Jack checked for the .38 in the back of his waistband, fired up his bike, and rolled out of the parking lot in search of a grocery store. Moments later, he pulled into a Safeway parking lot and walked inside. Standing just inside the door, behind a shoulder-high display of dog food, Jack watched through the front window. Would they follow? He noted a lone police car at the far end of the lot, and a plan began to form.

Moments later, the two bikers followed. Jack decided to shadow them once they were inside the store to see what he could learn. It didn't take long. The two men weren't there to shop and were deep in conversation as they moved about the store.

Jack stood with his back to them in front of a cooler containing milk and half and half. They passed by and disappeared down a nearby aisle. Quickly ducking down an adjacent aisle, Jack picked up snippets of conversation.

"We can't do anything until he's out of town."

"Told you we should have done it last night."

"But we didn't know where he was camped, idiot."

"Uh, ya. Well, we got him now."

Later, a couple of aisles over, one of the bikers approached Jack as he selected some apples. "That your bike outside?"

Jack nodded.

"Nice ride. Which way are you headed?"

Jack turned and eyed the guy.

"Probably east."

"Yeah, us too. Nice country out here."

"Sure is. Now, if you'll excuse me, guys, I need to hit the head."

Jack briskly walked to the front of the store, set his groceries down, and exited before they could see where he'd gone. At his bike, he pulled some of the stolen weed from one of the travel bags. Glancing about, he noticed no one near the rider's two bikes and quickly stuffed the marijuana inside one of their saddle bags.

Then, walking over to the cop's car, he told the officer about the weed and suggested there was stolen money with it as well. The cop told him to stay clear, and Jack returned to the store. The two bikers were about to leave when he passed by and wished them both a good day.

"Have a safe ride."

Jack quickly grabbed a few more things off the shelves, checked out, and, upon leaving the store, noted how the cop already had the two riders in handcuffs and sitting on the ground while he went through their bags.

Passing by, Jack tilted his head and frowned as if in sympathy. "Tough break, guys."

That should slow them down for a while.

Jack felt the weight of the last thing shackling him to the past fall from his shoulders. Feeling victorious over the trick he'd pulled, he rolled on the power and roared away. Racing through corners, leaning one way and then the other, Jack celebrated outwitting the two riders and distancing himself from the past.

He motored east, along the Clearwater River, until it split into the Selway and Lochsa Rivers. Then, continuing into the mountains along the sparkling Lochsa on Highway 12, Jack settled in and began to feel more at home and relaxed. His old camping and kayaking stomping grounds brought back memories of the good times shared with friends.

What was his hurry? The river was beautiful, and if he spent some time reminiscing, so what? Unshackled from all demands, he found permission in his newfound freedom to do whatever he felt; maybe revisiting some of his best memories was a good way to begin the trip.

Climbing the winding highway into the mountains, he shunned the developed campsites at Powell campground, preferring the riverside places of his choosing, much like they did when kayaking. The mild weather in the spring of 1975 had already melted off the snow, providing Jack with a handful of dry campsites to choose from.

He spent the next few days camping and fishing along the Lochsa River, sometimes doing nothing but sipping a beer and smoking a cigar. Leaning against the trunk of an ancient ponderosa pine in a sunny spot on the river bank freed his mind to wander. The river sang nightingale songs, soothing his psyche, and a head filled with the yearning for the past good times shared on the river yet tortured by the recent events with Scarlett, not to mention the fact he'd just killed a man.

After just a few days, his inner drive to be on the move again conquered him. The next day, he would leave and continue over Lolo Pass to Missoula, Montana, before heading south towards Salt Lake City and some country he had never seen before.

It was mid-afternoon when Jack crested Lolo Pass and descended the east side of the mountains before stopping for a cold one at Jack Saloon. *How fitting.* He thought. Situated just off the road, Jack Saloon was built in 1974 by lumberjacks so they could have a place close to their work. Thus, the name "Jack" saloon.

The wooden floors, hand-hewn tables, bar, and chairs inside the log building comprised everything Jack loved about the mountain country. Only a half dozen souls populated the place, and he quickly found a comfortable table in the corner with a view of the front door. After perusing the menu for just a few minutes, a middle-aged waitress approached and asked for his order.

"How are you doing, stranger?" she asked, not waiting for an answer. "I Haven't seen you in these parts before. Now, what will you be having?"

Standing ready with a pencil and pad, she patiently waited.

"I'm doing quite well, thanks, and no, I haven't been here before."

She nodded, pencil hovering over her order pad.

"Think I'm going to go with the steak dinner and a Coors beer."

"Good choice. The beef is local, and you're going to love it! I'll be right back with your beer. You're just ahead of the evening crowd. Won't be long for your dinner.

"Thank you."

The waitress soon returned with his beer, and relaxing back in his chair, Jack followed a game of pool taking place near his table while sipping his beer and waiting for the meal he ordered. He always found it comical watching a smoker squint through the cigarette smoke, climbing his face while the player bent down to line up his shot.

When the game ended, Jack turned down a friendly invitation to play. Wanting nothing more than to enjoy the comfortable surroundings of rural life, Jack was content.

While eating his dinner, the place filled with people. Hard-working men laboring in one of the most dangerous jobs in America, these were people Jack held in the highest esteem. Though he was a stranger, there were no snide remarks about the hippie or long hair sitting in the corner. He did catch a few sideways glances and a couple of stares, but that was all. Thinking of the money in the saddle bag on his bike, Jack decided on something he'd always wanted to do.

Walking over to the bar, he introduced himself. "Hello, Sir. My name is Jack," he said, extending his hand to the barkeep.

The bartender smiled and, in a friendly way, kidded Jack about the name. "No foolin. Think I haven't heard that one before, stranger?" He smiled.

"No doubt you have." Jack acknowledged. "But how many of them have bought a round of beer?"

"I could count 'em on one hand."

"Well, you can add one more to your list. I want to buy a round or two."

"Two?"

"Sure. Let's make it two."

The barkeep stepped to the side and rang a triangle-shaped dinner bell hanging over the bar. The din filling the saloon subsided as each patron turned towards the bar.

"Just a minute of your time, folks. I want to introduce this fella here." He extended his hand and directed their attention to Jack. "His name is Jack."

The place erupted with laughter. Then, a loud voice from the back of the room said, "Ask him what he's been smoking." More laughter followed.

"Well," the bartender chuckled. "Whatever it is, it must be pretty good stuff because he's offering to buy a couple of rounds of beer."

The resulting whistles and cheers were deafening. Soon, the bar was rocking with merriment, and Jack was welcomed with firm handshakes and slaps on the back. When he left early that evening, he was feeling good about himself for the first time in many weeks.

About a quarter mile down the road, Jack found a private little spot in the pine trees to pull over for the night. He slept late the next morning. The last few days' stress had taken its toll, and with the bed of pine needles cushioning his sleep, it was time for some healing rest.

The long sleep was needed for Jack's body, but the demons tormenting his mind never rested, and he remained unsettled. A walk through the woods did little to ease his psyche, and he soon returned to the road headed north toward Missoula.

Jack rolled into Missoula late that afternoon with a deep hunger and a steep thirst. The hunger was for Scarlett, and the thirst was for the whiskey needed to drown the memory.

After pulling into the first watering hole he came to, Jack ambled up to the bar and took a seat. "Whiskey, barkeep. And keep 'em coming."

A few shots later, the guy sitting beside him, the one he'd barely noticed up until then, spoke up.

"Trying to drown out a memory, right?" His gravelly voice hooked Jack's attention.

Jack rolled his eyes and inclined his head toward the gent. "Ya, so what about it?"

"She ain't worth the whiskey, man."

"What?" Jack growled. "What are you talking about?"

"I've known a lot of women, and none of them been worth the whiskey I wasted trying to forget them."

"Ya, well, this one was."

The guy leaned back on his stool and belly laughed. "Knew you'd say that. Word for word."

"You don't know Jack." Jack smiled to himself over the subtle joke.

"Well, maybe not." He grinned. "Names David."

Jack took the hand, extended his way, and shook it.

"I'm Jack."

David laughed again. "Well, now I do know Jack. So listen here, *Jack*. I've got a few years on you, more likely a few decades." He saluted with his glass. "You forget about her. A guy like you, you'll meet plenty of women, and when you do, take hold of the one with integrity."

Jack grunted and motioned for another whiskey.

"You mark my words, son. The one who isn't looking in the mirror all the time and chasing money or the latest trends, that's the one."

"Ya think." Slumped over the bar, Jack didn't bother looking up and continued staring at the scars scratched atop the wooden surface.

"Forget the fluff. You want the woman on the inside, the one she only reveals to the guy she's serious about."

"That would be Scarlett, and I just blew her off."

"Sorry, man." The guy offered a toast and the two clinked glasses.

Jack turned to have a look about the place. "So, anything happen around here on a Friday?"

"Huh. This place? Same old thing, warm beer n' cold women."

When Jack stumbled out of the bar that evening, it was all he could do to walk. After struggling to roll his bike to a nearby grove of trees just beyond the parking lot, he stumbled and grasped the trunk of a thick oak to steady himself. Sliding down the rough bark, Jack passed out.

When he awoke the following morning, the world was not where he'd left it, and there was a steady pounding on the sole of his boot, or was it his head? He couldn't tell. Rising on one elbow and squinting through bleary eyes, Jack thought he saw a cop.

"Rise and shine sonny. You have a beautiful day ahead of you." The hearty laugh was irritating. "You can't stay here."

"Occifer," Jack slurred, "I told myself to quit drinking last night."

"So why didn't you."

"I don't listen to drunks." He tried to laugh, but doing so nearly split his already splitting head.

The cop pointed. "Six blocks down on your right is a cheap motel where you can work on recovering."

Jack groaned.

"Gonna make my rounds son and be back in an hour. You best be gone by then, or I'll have to haul you in. Keep in mind there are some guys down at the station who'd love to take a spin on that bike of yours. Capiche?"

It took Jack two days to recover from the hangover. Returning to the highway on the third day and feeling more like himself, Jack felt the excitement that was the freedom of the road stir within once more.

He was rolling on the power outside Missoula when he spotted a hitchhiker standing beside the powder blue Highway 90 sign. Jack often stopped to assist hitchhikers, and this was no different, though most weren't built like this one. Dressed in black leather, long and lean with all the curves in the right places, the blonde held her thumb high while her waist-long hair danced in the slight breeze. Jack slowed, turned around, and pulled to a stop next to her.

"Lookin' for a ride?"

She approached the bike, eyeing him closely, and a sly grin crossed her lips. "You could say that." She smiled invitingly and set both hands on her hips.

"So what's with the leather pants? Did you lose your ride somewhere?" he chided. The black pants were skin-tight and matched the leather vest she wore.

Her dark eyes flashed. "As a matter of fact, but something tells me I just found it." She cocked her head and raised a flaxen eyebrow.

"But first, I need to know your intentions." Her eyes gleamed and hinted at more than his trustworthiness.

"Just out here looking for signs that point to the truth."

"Bullshit. Heard that kind of crap before. You some pothead or something?"

"What?"

"Never mind. Where are you headed?"

"Well," Jack scratched his chin. "The devil always rides along, so who knows for sure." He shrugged. "Right now, we are headed east, just like the song says." Recalling the song, a smile crept over Jack's face at the thought of a pleasant memory.

"The devil rides along? I'm not so sure about that part."

"Look. I have a philosophy about life. It's a mixture of joy and pain. We spend our time trying to avoid the pain, but the pain is what makes the good times so much fun. I'm putting all the pain behind me, so it looks like nothing but fun up ahead. Interested?"

"Sounds good to me."

Jack removed his helmet and offered it to her. "Climb aboard." It was a phrase they would share many times in an entirely different context over the coming days.

Pulling back onto the freeway, the feel of a woman's arms around his waist evoked strong memories and reminded him how right it felt. She drew close and rested her head on his shoulder.

A few days later, the two bypassed Salt Lake City and were crossing through southern Wyoming on Highway 80 when Jack turned off the freeway toward Green River so they could get something to eat.

He pulled into the first diner they found - a tidy little café directly across the street from a truck stop. After parking the bike, Jack stretched his back and the long legs of his six-foot three-inch frame.

"Rock Springs is nothing but trouble, so we'll stop here to grab a bite and pass straight on through there." He said.

"Sounds like the voice of experience."

"You could say that."

"Just as well. You probably heard my stomach grumbling." She smiled after removing her helmet and shaking out her long, straight hair.

The two strolled casually through the parking lot to the cafe entrance, relishing the parched desert air and the chance to exercise their legs.

Entering the front door, a row of chrome-sided pedestal seats covered in red vinyl greeted them. They stood aligned the length of a blue vinyl countertop just ahead and to their right. Large picture windows lined the wall on their left, where three tables were available. The black and white tile floor looked to be straight out of a malt shop.

Jessica took Jack's hand as the two slowly walked the aisle between the tables and the counter. Jack wanted a window seat where he could keep an eye on his bike and chose a table with a perfect view of the parking lot.

Two men dressed in jeans and T-shirts that looked as if they had been worn for several days and whose trucks were likely parked across the street at the truck stop occupied the first few seats at the lunch counter. At the end of the aisle, a group of men in overalls and sweat-stained John

Deere ball caps sat in the far corner. Hunched over coffee and newspapers, they looked up as Jack and his girl found a table.

Jack already knew what he would order – a bacon burger with fries and a chocolate shake. He gazed out the window, and his mind wandered amongst the few puffy clouds gliding across the cobalt sky. So much had happened in just a few short days. *A man contemplates the past and the future, which seem so far apart, rarely realizing the overall timeline is infinitely short – a bug splat on the timeline of life.*

"Jack, Jack!" She snapped her fingers to get his attention.

His eyes shifted as he took in the soft features of her smile. "Sorry," he grinned in an aw-shucks manner.

"Where do you go? It worries me sometimes when you drift off like that."

"Ah, it's nothing."

"I just hope it doesn't happen when you're driving."

He shook his head.

Moments later, the waitress showed up and asked for their orders.

Jack answered, "Dying for a bacon burger with fries and a chocolate shake."

"Sounds good. Now, what would you be having, honey?"

"Names Jessica and I'll have the same as him."

The waitress paused a moment to look her up and down. "Alright, sweetie. Not sure how you keep a figure like that eating burgers and fries, but I'll be happy to bring it to you."

"Sheesh!" Jessica hissed after the waitress left with their order.

"Can't a girl have a burger and some fries without all that?"

"It's cool. She means well." Jack said.

Moments later, the caustic comments he'd heard far too many times before began to rain down—all the same old clichés.

"Can't tell which un's a girl and which un's a boy, Clyde."

"Maybe theys both girls, Buck."

Their raucous laughter irritated Jack, and he had to stifle an urge to flip them off. There were three too many, five in total.

Soon, the waitress returned with their orders. She was the kind, motherly type Jack knew worked hard and put in too many weeks of long hours—the kind of person he'd always respected.

Resting one hand on a heavy hip after setting their meals on the table, she nodded to her right. "Ignore the fellas in the corner. They're generally good guys and just having a little fun."

Heard that before, too. Jack thought.

The trouble began when some ugly cowboy type with a pinched head and a matching I.Q. approached and tried to stir things up, but the waitress sent him away with a slight push on his back.

"Go sit down, Buck."

After their meal, the waitress returned and asked where they were headed. That's when pinched-head Buck approached and pulled her aside. He was looking to create a scene, and Jack knew it. It was time to move on. After rising from his seat, Jack left a nice tip and the money for their meal atop the table. That's when he heard something in the vein of "stay away from the hippie boy and his whore."

"Buck, that's enough." The waitress scolded.

Life's recent events had honed a sharp edge to Jacks's attitude, and he was in no mood to take any crap from ol' Pinched Head.

What else have I got to lose?

Jack turned on the turd dressed in overalls, towering over him by nearly a foot.

"So you don't like long hair, huh? But you're not smart enough to come up with something more original than old clichés."

Jack stared down at the guy with his most formidable, blue steel gaze. "I suggest you head on back to the munchkin farm stubby before you lose a couple more inches. Got me?"

Two beats passed between the two while the guy made up his mind. Those few seconds allowed Jack to figure Stumpy was right-handed and that his fist would come from that direction. His buddies in the corner watched closely, waiting to see who would make the first move. That's when the waitress stepped between them and backed the guy off while he mumbled something about Mama taking care of the long hair.

Well, if that saves his pride, then whatever. Jack's glare remained steely for another instant before winking at the waitress and turning to go. She was a good woman.

Watching their backsides while crossing the parking lot, Jack saw two men step outside from the table of five. They yelled obscenities and challenged him to fight. Buck wasn't among them.

Jack turned and took one step toward them. "You want some? Come and get it," he shouted.

"Come on, Jack." Jessica took his hand and pulled him away. "You got nothing to prove."

Then she spun him around, grabbed his hand, and slammed it against her butt while kissing him deep.

"That was for them, not you. Now let's go."

The jeers about the girl being tougher than him cascade down around them as they mounted the bike. Jack revved the engine, the angry sound blocking out their voices. Shooting up the nearby on-ramp to the freeway, Jack wondered if life would always be filled with such a vast bowl of self-righteous nuts.

One season of life left behind and another one beginning.

Just a bug splat on the timeline of life.

CHAPTER ELEVEN

Days later, Jack and Jessica rolled into Amarillo.

"WHY AMARILLO JACK?"

"Looking to catch up with an old buddy. I'm sure he'll be happy to put us up for a while, plus I'd just like to see the guy. It's been too long."

They found 'Carson' working behind the bar at the Velvet Hammer. Carson was happy to offer them a place to stay, especially after Jack offered him some of the weed he'd stolen from Scarlett's boyfriend back in Washington.

They spent the days catching up, and Carson informed Jack he was now the new owner of the Velvet Hammer.

"Congratulations! You always said that's what you wanted."

While catching up, Jack explained about his painting business, which he'd just sold.

"Stop right there, Jack. You're on the road because of some woman ain'tcha."

"How'd you figure that?"

"You're an easy book to read, Jack. Always have been." Then, nodding his head toward Jessica, who was leaning over the jukebox, her hips swaying back and forth to the music while making selections. "Looks like you've found a shapely replacement."

"Let me say this before Jessica returns. No one can replace the woman I left. I blew it, Carson, and I'm finding it very hard to live with myself. Ok, end of discussion. Moving on."

"I'm sorry to hear that. You always did have a big heart, my friend. Maybe she's the one who sent this letter."

Carson retrieved a folded envelope from his back pocket and handed it to Jack, who, after glancing at the return address, quickly stuffed it into his back pocket." Thank you, Carson."

The place was filling with the Saturday night crowd, and Carson excused himself to tend to his patrons.

Jessica stayed close to Jack's side all evening. "You doing alright? You've kinda drifted into never never land again."

Jack shook himself. "Oh, I'm alright."

"You never said anything about this other woman nobody can replace."

"Other woman?"

"I overheard you and Carson talking. So what happened?"

Jack finished his beer and set the glass on their table before facing her. "Look. It's nothing I want to talk about."

"Ok, no need to be so touchy."

Later in the evening, when cheap beer fueled the crowd and the band was on break, the trouble that never seemed far from Jack walked in the door. Two guys approached Jessica as she returned from the restroom. After turning down their advances, she began walking away when one of the men slapped her butt. She spun on him, delivering a closed fist punch that bloodied his nose. Preparing to punch him again, the other guy grabbed her from behind.

"Let's take her outside and have some fun, Tom."

She struggled to break free and screamed for Jack, who immediately landed in the middle of them. The resulting brawl broke tables and chairs, brought the cops, and left Jessica alone after the cops hauled all three men off to jail.

The next day, someone put up bail for the two thugs, but Jack remained alone in his jail cell for another two days. During that time, he checked his back pocket to read the letter Carson had given him, but it was gone.

On the third day, Jessica came to visit. She was short and abrupt with him. Standing defiantly with both hands in her back pockets, she told Jack it was over. "Jack, I'm leaving. This is not what I bargained for."

"Told you right up front; the devil rides along."

"Well, I'm not, Jack."

"I don't understand. I didn't do anything but try to help out."

"Yes, and I appreciate it. But it's time for me to move on. I'm sure you understand."

"Well, not really, but get me out of here before you go. Did Carson happen to store my bike away after the cops hauled me off?"

"Yes, I believe so. Saw him walking it around to the back of the building."

"There's money in one of the locked saddle bags on my bike. The cops have my keys. If you can talk them into giving them to you, then take some of the money and pay my bail. Alright?"

Jessica smiled, reached into a pocket at the front of her jeans, and dangled Jack's keys in front of him. "No, they don't. After the police hauled you off, I grabbed the keys you'd left lying on the table."

"So yes, I can do that much for you, Jack. Back soon."

A couple hours later, she returned, and Jack was set free. In the Velvet Hammer parking lot, Jack shook hands with Carson and thanked him for taking care of his bike.

"And thanks for getting me out, Jessica. Will you be alright?"

"Carson says I can stay as long as I like."

Jack had already assumed the two were hooking up and smirked.

"You do look like his type."

She wasn't sure how to take the comment, and Jack chuckled to himself because it wasn't intended as a compliment. Thankful to escape the jail cell, he fired up his bike and roared away, ensuring he was across the state line into Oklahoma before dark.

A full moon greeted Jack as he walked his ride through the open gate of a barbed wire fence and into a grove of poplar trees. The lights of a farmhouse were visible on the other side of a hay field about a quarter mile away. Jack hoped he'd been discreet enough to avoid detection.

After locating a suitable campsite next to the tiny stream percolating through the trees, Jack lay his sleeping bag in a grassy area that allowed him to view the gate and nearby highway. Only after setting up his meager camp and settling in for the night did he discover that all the money in his travel bag was gone except for a single twenty-dollar bill.

What else, Lord? Jack threw up his hands and stared into a black, starlit sky. *Lord? Have I fallen so far that I can no longer rely on myself? Sometimes I feel so messed up.*

He tossed the idea aside and took another pull from his bottle of whiskey. Since when did he call on God for help? The thought stirred him. After finishing a cold can of pork and beans, he enjoyed a few more sips before slipping into a tortured sleep.

When morning arrived, Jack had one thing on his mind: Florida, sunny beaches, island music, bikini-clad girls, and drinks with umbrellas.

The ride there took him through places he'd never been. New Orleans was his first extended stop. Jack spent two weeks there. He never thought he'd say it, but the place was just a little too weird for him. Or maybe it was just his state of mind. New Orleans was probably a lot of fun, but his heart craved the peace of a quiet beach.

With his money gone, he needed to find a job. Two weeks later, a solid weekend of tips from the bartending job he landed gave him enough to hit the road again and get out of town. He knew it wouldn't last long, and a few days later, Jack found himself a job as a deckhand on a commercial fishing boat in Naples, Florida. He wanted nothing to do with the Miami to West Palm Beach area on the overdeveloped west side of the state.

The work was physical and required some quick learning of rigging, its maintenance, fishing gear, and the ability to assist in docking and undocking procedures. The owner said he'd give him a chance to prove himself and made it clear that getting along with the crew would go a long way toward staying on.

When his new boss learned of his plans to stick around and his need for somewhere to stay, he offered Jack a place in his office to shower and clean up after work. An old mechanics shop, it wasn't anything special, but it would work until Jack got his feet on the ground.

"Don't know if I can trust you, son, but it would be good to have someone around when we aren't here. Show me I can rely on you; you can call it home. Do otherwise, and you'll be out on your ass." The burley fisherman motioned with a thumb over his shoulder.

Jack reached behind his back, grabbed his ponytail, and grinned. "Ya, I wouldn't trust me either."

The guy waived him off. "Don't bother me none. Some of my best workers have had long hair. Everyone gets a fair shake. Work hard, show me some integrity, and we will get along just fine."

Jack shook his hand. "We should get along just fine then."

Turns out Jack was a natural for the job. The owner may have been gruff, but Jack always found a way to get along with people. He loved being on the open water in the salt sea air, handled the crew's rookie initiation harassment well enough, and soon fit in like a brother. The money was pretty good, too, and sleeping on the beach meant he spent little of it. The work kept him in shape, and the summer sun tanned his muscular body.

Late one Friday afternoon, the crew taunted him on the way in after a day of fishing. "We're going into town tonight for a couple of drinks, Jack."

Jack leaned in to hear over the wind and the roar of the engine as they made their way back to port.

"But you're not invited." The crew roared with laughter.

"Cause you don't associate with rookies?"

"Oh hell no, Jack. We always take rookies and make them pay. But looking the way you do, you think we could even get a glancing look from any of the ladies?"

Jack shrugged while they laughed at his expense.

"Let's get real, Jack. Tanned and sculpted as you are, not to mention young, you think any of us old boys can compete with those blue eyes and dark Italian looks."

"I'm not Italian, but hey, fine with me. I've had enough of women for a while."

The men turned to one another and spoke as if he couldn't hear but ensured he did. "Look at that long hair, Earl. Maybe he prefers the company of men."

And they all moved away, laughing and acting like he had the plague.

Jack grinned and waved them off. "You guys are too much."

Then his eyes lit up, and he took one step towards them. "But I do like working intimately with you guys, and what a close-knit crew we've become!" He emphasized close and winked for effect.

As one, the group pulled back further. "Whoa!" The laughter and back-slapping continued.

After stowing the ship's gear, Jack showered and walked the half mile into town for dinner. He decided on a shrimp shack he'd been to a few times before. Jack decided to order a crab and shrimp Po Boy with a side of hushpuppies. A tall Coke completed his order.

Stepping to the counter to place his order, a long-haired brunette greeted him.

"Hello. I think I've seen you here before."

"Uh ya, I work on a fishing boat down the beach away." Jack pointed in the general direction.

"You work a lot?"

"Yep. Long days mostly."

"Uh-huh. I never seem to get away from this place, either. I live just a few blocks away." Her warm smile was inviting.

Jack could see where this conversation was headed and quickly changed the subject before placing his order. A few minutes later, when he picked up his food, she tried again.

"I know some fun places to visit next time you have a few days off. I could show you around."

"Sounds good. Next time, I have some time off." Jack was being polite and realized he'd have to steer clear of the place in the future if he wanted to avoid getting drawn into something he wasn't ready for.

CHAPTER TWELVE

TWO WEEKS LATER, JACK MOORED THE BOAT AND BEGAN cleaning gear with the rest of the crew. After ten days without a break, the captain had given them three days off. The tired but excited crew worked quickly to wrap things up. Before leaving, they asked Jack for a moment of his time.

"We've taken a vote, Jack, and would like you to come with us into town tonight."

It was good news. Jack had earned his stripes and their respect.

"Sounds like fun, guys, but I smell like a week-old fish wrapped in newspaper. I won't be ready until after a shower."

"Uh-oh."

"What? What'd I…"

"Turn around, Jack."

Strutting down the dock in cut-offs and a white crop top with a tiny pink bow in front came the girl from the Shrimp Shack. Her straight brown hair swung loosely, and she approached Jack without hesitation.

"Hello, Jack. I haven't seen you around, so thought I'd see if you are free tonight?"

"Um well…" Jack turned to face his crew from the boat.

"It's alright." One of them said. "Why don't the two of you join us, and you can buy that drink you owe us all."

Jack turned back. "That sound alright?"

"Sounds good to me."

They agreed to meet for margaritas at a local bar in one hour.

Walking towards the maintenance building where Jack could shower, he asked. "So, how do you know my name?"

"I asked around. My father knows the captain you are working for."

Jack tilt his head to look at her. "Well then, I think it's only fair I know your name."

"Sheina."

"Alright, Sheina. Come back in half an hour after I get cleaned up, and we can take my bike downtown to meet the guys."

"Not a chance. You're not slipping away this time. I'll be happy to wait while you get out of that nasty fish wrapper you're wearing." Her smile was intoxicating, and Jack began to look forward to spending an evening with her.

After showering, Jack put on jeans and a Hawaiian shirt he'd purchased locally. He was brushing out his hair while walking through the vehicle maintenance bay of the metal building.

"Here, let me do that."

"Um, well..." Jack handed her the hair brush.

"Your hair is nearly as long as mine. It's easier if someone helps."

"Thank you. Ahem, you know the couch you were sitting on is what we call greasy Dave's. He was the previous owner. Turn around."

She turned slowly, showing off shapely legs.

"I don't see any stains on your shorts."

"See anything else?" She teased.

"Uh...I think it's time to go. You ready?"

"Almost. Ponytail or free and easy?"

"Ponytail."

They all gathered at the "White Rabbit" a while later, sipping their first margarita.

"Hey Tom, how many do you think he owes us?"

"Oh boy, I'd need to do some calculating. He was pretty rough on us those first couple of weeks."

Jack rolled his eyes.

"I'd have to say at least two rounds, but probably more like three."

Jack attempted damage control. "I'll be glad to buy two rounds, guys. After that, you're on your own.

"Kind of a tightwad, ain't he, Tom."

Tom looked across the table and winked at Sheina. "Well, considering the expensive company he keeps, we'd better go light on him this time."

Jack took the jabs in stride; knowing he was accepted as part of a rough crew that didn't easily allow strangers inside their tight circle of friends meant a lot.

Suddenly, from across the room, a booming voice demanded. "Whose bike is this?" The huge leather-booted biker with a red bandana around his head pointed outside through the door he'd just come through. "I want to know who parked in my spot!" His voice boomed throughout the bar.

Then he spied Jack's helmet on the tabletop and stormed over.

"That your bike out there?"

Jack nodded.

"Well, you're in my spot. I'm giving you three minutes to move it."

"Sorry. I didn't see a sign with your name on it."

"Smartass."

"Frank. Cool your jets." Sheina looked up from her drink. "He's with me."

"What? Are you hanging out with some bait jocky now? You can't be that desperate."

Jack stood and stepped between them. Frank bumped Jack with his barrel chest as they stood with faces inches apart.

"I think you'd better go easy, Frank. She didn't ask for any of this. If you want to step outside, I'd happily accommodate you. If you want to join me for a drink, I'll gladly buy you one."

"Seriously?"

"Your choice, but you look like a man who is all mouth and no trousers, so why not get off your feet and let me buy you a drink?"

Frank looked over his shoulder to see if anyone was looking. "Well, maybe just one, and we can talk about this. All mouth and no trousers, huh."

"Uh-huh, just means you look like you need a drink."

A few snickers from Jack's crew drew a baleful look that quickly silenced them.

Sheina helped to soothe the tension with Frank, and after a couple of drinks and in-depth talk about their bikes, a stranger would never have known the two were not best buddies.

"How'd you like to come out to a little party we've got going on." Frank offered.

"You sure, Frank?" Sheina asked. "You know strangers aren't very welcome out there."

"Well, ol' Jack here, he ain't no stranger anymore. Why don't the two of you come on out? We've got a keg of beer, a bonfire, and one of the guys is bringing his pickup, which is really just a jukebox on wheels. We'll have us a good time. I think the guys got some real fun planned for tonight."

Jack looked across the table to his crew. "Oh, go ahead, Jack. Have some fun. Just be sure to pick up the tab on your way out." A round of laughter escorted him across the room as he went to pay the bill.

With Sheina's arms wrapped tightly around him, Jack followed Frank and the rest of his biker gang into the countryside. The party was loud and raucous, and when it lasted deep into the night, Jack had more to drink than would allow him to ride home.

When a scuffle broke out, Jack pulled Sheina aside. "We don't want any part of that; let's have a seat over here. Things could get a little dodgy."

Jack sat down and leaned against the trunk of a pine tree to steady himself. Sheina sat next to him.

"Man, that last beer hit me like a sledgehammer."

Sheina could see his lights beginning to dim. "Why don't you lay back? You sure you're alright?"

Jack never had a chance to answer before gunfire erupted, and everyone scattered. Sheina searched Jack's pockets for the keys to his bike and quickly hid them just before Frank grabbed her around the waist and hoisted her over his shoulder.

"You can't just leave him here."

"And I wouldn't feel right leaving you here either. He'll be alright, now let's go. We gotta make tracks before the cops arrive."

Jack woke the next day, peering through the bars of another jail cell and wondering what had happened. *There had to have been something in that last drink. I've never blacked out like that before.*

He stood and walked over to rattle the jail cell door. "Officer, I need to talk with you. Why am I in here?"

A burly man with a strong Southern accent strolled up to the cell. "Wattchu want boy?"

"Why am I in here? You just let me sleep off my beer or what?"

"Son, you done killed Trapper Dan. I spect you gonna be spending a long time looking through bars like those."

"What?"

"You heard me. Now shut up."

"I'm at least allowed a phone call."

"Ha ha. Nice try. You tried calling some woman last night. She didn't want to have nothin to do with you. Now sit down and shut up."

Called last night? A woman? Sheina? Jack rubbed the back of his neck.

He reached into his back pocket and found the phone number on a scrap of paper. He didn't recall using the phone, but there was a lot he couldn't remember about the evening after leaving the White Rabbit.

No one came to see him that day, and without the ability to make a phone call Jack found himself out of options.

The following day, Jack was moved to another facility. Six weeks after that, he found himself serving a life sentence in Lake Correctional Institution located in Clermont, Florida.

CHAPTER THIRTEEN

WINTER OF 75/76 BROUGHT TEMPORARY RELIEF TO THE HOT prison grounds while Jack struggled to accept the stroke of bad luck that got him there. He'd never felt so abandoned, not even when his family left him on the farm as a little kid. But nothing compared to his feeling of rejection when no one came to help after his arrest.

No way. This couldn't be his fate, yet there was little to provide even a thread of hope about the state of things changing.

The words he'd left Scarlet with kept echoing through his head. *And if I don't come back, don't come looking for me.*

Sitting on his bunk, Jack ran both hands over his scalp. The fact they had shaved his head pissed him off nearly as much as being locked up. But the real burden was not having contact with anyone outside the prison.

Maybe I'll write Scarlett.

You really blew it there, didn't you, Jack? She wanted to work things out, but you had to run off and see the world. One of the dumbest things you ever did and...

Shut up. What's done is done; there's no reason to beat myself up. But what a beauty. Not likely she's still single, either. A looker like that rarely spends much time alone. And what would she want with someone locked away for life anyway?

The internal debate raged on just like it did most days. *It can't hurt to send a postcard. It's probably too much to hope she'd write back, but maybe it's worth a shot.*

"Jack! Wake up. What planet are you on anyway? Get that lily-white ass of yours out here. We only have an hour for recreation, And times a ticking."

Only time it ever does.

"Sure Rocky." Jack brightened. "Thanks for not leaving me here to sulk."

Rocky was the epitome of his name. A black-as-coal mountain of rock-hard muscle, he played bass in the prison band and had taken a liking to Jack. Rocky recruited him when their previous drummer was paroled and began giving Jack drum lessons.

Their group had gathered together, ready to practice, and were waiting for Jack to show up. Sometimes, the guards allowed them to play longer than their one-hour recreation time. The group was getting better and beginning to sound pretty good, but they had no singer, so they all sang.

Jack protested about the requirement to sing.

"You want to play with us, you sing with us." Rocky threatened, then flashed a smile of gleaming white teeth. "Besides, I've heard you sing. You're as good as any of us."

Jack knew that wasn't the case, but who was he to argue? The drums were a good distraction, and he enjoyed the guys he played with.

That evening, after suffering the slop in the mess hall, Jack penned a few well-chosen words for a postcard to Scarlett. Unbeknownst to him, it would be his last day of relative freedom in prison for a while.

The following afternoon, Jack lost it while having lunch in the mess hall. Ranting and raving, he was not supposed to be there, that it was all wrong, and he didn't deserve what had happened to him. Jack tore up the place. He was overturning tables, tossing food trays, smashing drink coolers, and filling the place with gut-wrenching screams about being railroaded before the guards could overpower him.

The outburst earned him seven days in solitary confinement. Christmas came and went, and no one wished him a Merry Christmas. The loneliness buried him in the deepest, blackest pit of despair he'd ever known. The walls he had so carefully constructed to hide behind were crumbling. At the end of himself, Jack fell to his knees on the concrete floor of his isolation cell and prayed to a God he didn't know. *Lord, if you are there, I need another chance. If you can somehow get me out of here, things will change. I just need one opportunity to prove I can get things right. Please.*

But all he heard in return was the utter silence of cold, hard concrete. Before his release two days later, Jack's depression deepened. Lost in the dark hole that had become Jack's world, he curled up in a corner and lay there. When they released him from solitary confinement, the guards led him to his cell in a semi-comatose condition.

The day after his release, Rocky came to visit him. Concerned about Jack's stupor and apparent disorientation, he asked the guards for medical attention. His request was denied, so Rocky plied Jack with water, forced some food down him, and began reading to Jack from the bible. Slowly, Jack returned to the land of the living.

"I don't want to come back to reality Rocky. I just want to go away."

Rocky continued to encourage him. "No you don't Jack. And don't you dare make me force-feed you again!"

"I don't know how you do it, Rocky. You're here for life, yet somehow you've found peace in this hell hole that I couldn't find when free on the outside."

Rocky encouraged Jack to accept Christ. "It's where I find my peace, and you will too."

Jack blew him off, but Rocky continued.

"I messed up, Jack. I deserve what I've gotten. Jesus has forgiven me, and my time here is not forever. Forever, or eternity as the bible calls it, happens when we die, and when that happens, we will either spend it with Christ or we will spend it in hell."

"You believe that stuff?"

"To the core. God is using me here. I have a very fulfilling purpose that I never had on the outside."

Jack shook his head. "I can't see it, Rocky. Everything I touch turns to crap. How am I to find peace in that?"

"You have to let go. Quit trying to have everything your way, or as the bible teaches, stop serving yourself and serve others instead. You are not in control."

"I grew up in a world where no one cared. Self-preservation couldn't be more deeply ingrained in me. It's how I survive."

"Control is resistance to trust."

Jack immediately thought of Scarlett.

"Let go of your grip on life. You're strangling yourself."

"I can't do that, Rocky."

"And how's that working out for you?" Rocky grinned.

"Shove it, Rocky. That's not fair."

"You need to let go and put your faith in Christ. That's enough for now. We'll talk again later, but let me leave you with this thought. God is pursuing you, and if you think you're in a dark place now…"

Rocky stood, placed a massive hand on Jack's right shoulder, and looked toward heaven. "The Lord had to take me to the deepest, darkest place I could ever imagine before I saw His light. He will do the same with you someday if you don't turn from your ways and accept Him as your Savior. His desire is for no one to perish."

The conversation left Jack with a lot to think about, but he struggled to wrap his head around the things Rocky told him. He swore there was no one else he could trust, and he could do it all himself. He just needed one more chance to prove he could turn things around. If he ever got out, he would prove it!

Jack got his chance two weeks later when two guards came to release him. At the gate, they wished him well. "Happy New Year, Jack! You lucked out big time. A few months versus life in prison – we hardly got to know you. Stay out of trouble, and don't be tearing up any more dining rooms." Their boisterous laughter faded as the two walked back inside.

Standing outside the gate, he was shocked to find Sheina waiting for him. She drove him back to her apartment in Naples, where they spent the next few days.

"So what you're saying is that it was a setup right from the start?" Jack questioned.

"Sure was. Frank doesn't like to be snubbed by anyone. When you stood up to him at the bar, the wheels immediately started turning, and it didn't take him long to devise a plan."

Jack shook his head. He wanted to get as far away from Florida as possible.

"The only reason you were released is someone ratted out, Frank. The factions in his gang are going after one another. It's all coming apart. Taking out the top dog was viewed as the way to take over."

Jack shook his head in disbelief. "Look, I can never make up for getting me out of that place, but I can't stay here."

"Why not? The guys said to tell you they'd welcome you back on the boat."

"The only place I'm gonna feel at home is back on the road."

"Yes, I get that, but why not stay for a while." Her eyes pleaded, but Jack was determined. Tempting as it was, Jack remained steadfast in his decision.

"I'm sorry. But I just need to get out of here."

"I have a feeling that's always been your out, Jack. But never mind." She turned her back and walked away.

"What do you mean? Always been my out?"

Spinning back around, Sheina yelled. "You were running when I met you, and you're still running. It's not the answer, Jack. Someday, you'll figure that out!"

Jack gazed out the window for a moment. It wasn't the first time someone had told him that. "Look, this isn't a good time for me to commit to anything. I'm sorry."

"Fine. I understand."

But Jack knew she didn't. Changing the subject, he asked, "So how is it you managed to get a hold of my motorcycle? Figured I'd never see it again."

"After the shooting, I took the keys from your pocket and dropped them into a knothole in the tree you were lying beside. Frank was in too big a hurry to get out of there and never saw me do it. I knew the cops would impound the bike, but without keys, they stored it away awaiting auction. After your release, I took the keys in and asked for the bike. They said no way, of course, and that's why I had to take you back to the police station to get it."

"Last place I wanted to be." Jack mused. "Wouldn't have gone back for anything else, but Black Betty is part of me, part of my soul."

Sheina continued. "Frank never got over your attitude at the bar. So he spiked your drink at the party with every intention of killing Trapper Dan and leaving you behind as the guilty party."

"Damn."

"When everyone was rushing to get away after the shooting, Frank grabbed me. It was part of the setup. I was one of the few who could testify where you'd been and what you'd been doing that evening. So Frank kidnapped me. I've been locked away just like you."

"So why am I struggling to believe you?"

"Look, Frank and I go way back. We had a thing once, and he's always wanted to get back together. He's even gone so far as to threaten me. Police record and all that, but I never thought he'd go this far." Sheina paused and shook her head.

"Long story short. He ripped off one of the bikers in his gang after a big money drug deal, and the guy went to the cops. The cops found me and freed me when they came to arrest Frank. My testimony was the final nail in the coffin that got you released, and now Frank is the one sitting in prison for the murder of Trapper Dan. Believe me. The authorities in Florida have little tolerance for this kind of thing."

It made a little more sense now, but it didn't change a thing. The following morning, Jack thanked Sheina for rescuing his bike and freeing him from prison.

"I'm sorry, but I can't stay." He took her by the shoulders and kissed her forehead. "I appreciate all you've done for me, but I've worn out my welcome around here, and it's time to hit the road."

Standing in the bedroom doorway wearing only a nightshirt, she leaned against the doorframe with one hand on her hip. "Well, you haven't worn out your welcome around here."

Jack smiled, acknowledging the seductive look, but remained resolute. "Could I borrow a few bucks for the road?" He pulled out the insides of his jeans pockets. "I seem to be a bit light and will need to pick up some cold-weather gear before going north this time of year. The cops seem to have emptied my wallet. Pay you back as soon as I find a job."

"Jack, you're one of the few real men of integrity I've ever known. Of course, I'll loan you whatever you need." Then, putting her arms around his neck, she hugged him. "Someday, you'll learn that running is not the answer, and when you do, man." She sighed, looked up into his face, and smiled. "The woman that finds you then won't believe her luck."

"Not sure I can buy all that B.S.."

Jack saw it as part of her last plea for him to stay and ignored the comment, fully believing he could never be that guy. He'd always found it easier to leave than face the consequences of whatever mess he found himself in and saw little reason to believe otherwise this time.

But back on the road, free once again, he thought of Rocky, still locked away in prison, and of the oath he'd sworn to himself while in prison. *Life's gonna be different from here on out. I've paid too high a price not to change.*

CHAPTER FOURTEEN

THE JANUARY WEATHER BROUGHT JACK TO THE FRONT DOOR of a motorcycle shop in North Carolina. After outfitting himself with the gear he needed, he continued north, still having no idea where he was going. He'd know when he got there.

His trip north ended in Vermont, where he found a job working for a family that harvested and sold maple syrup. The elderly couple told him he was an answer to their prayers. The sap wouldn't run for another month, but there were plenty of chores to do before the sap came on.

"Well, son, you know what they say."

"I'm new here. Enlighten me."

The old boy chuckled. "Around here, the measure of a man is determined by the size of his wood pile, and ours ain't nothing to brag about. So let's get you started with that."

There was also equipment to repair and animals to tend to. The elderly couple sincerely appreciated his help. God had provided, and though Jack wasn't so sure about it, they told him he was the answer to their prayers.

I think I've pissed God off enough by now, and I certainly ain't gonna be the answer to anyone's prayers.

Jack's doubts aside, he suddenly found himself at home in the country, working for this elderly couple. The bunkhouse that would become his home for the winter reminded him of the place he'd been forced to stay in when he was a kid on the farm. The time alone would do him good.

When the sap began to run in late February, the work began in earnest. Jack found the cool, frosty mornings invigorating and threw himself into the work. The old man drove the horses that pulled the sled upon which a large wooden tank was mounted, and Jack emptied the buckets they took from each tree into the tank.

The maple tree sap was drained from the massive tank on the sled at the sugar shack and heated over a fire in a separate boiler. Cooking off the water and concentrating the sap yielded the sweet concoction everyone loved.

The physical labor, coupled with the time alone, had Jack feeling more like himself than he'd felt in a long time, and he was sorry when it all ended. At the end of the last day of work, Jack was paid a handsome bonus on top of his wages.

Feeling a little like celebrating, and it being a Friday, he figured he might head into town for a beer or two and maybe a game of foosball. It had been too long since he played, and he looked forward to it. He'd not been to town in all his time at the farm, and now released from his responsibilities, he felt the pull of freedom. It's not that he was looking for a wild night out, just a change of scenery and maybe some good music.

Riding slowly through town, he passed a bar that advertised maple tree harvest specials. The special turned out to be cheap pitchers of beer and no cover charge to get inside, plus a buy one get one free pizza special.

Stepping through the doors of the tavern, Jack immediately felt at home. The faint smell of beer, the smokey haze, and the three regulars at the bar who were already deep into their cups and would likely still be there at closing time felt like home. The dance floor was empty as the band had yet to begin, but the jukebox belted out familiar country favorites.

Jack avoided the last empty booth at the far end of the tile dance floor opposite the band and chose a nearby table off to the right-hand side instead. Resting easy and sipping his beer, Jack felt good about things. He'd always been at home in places like this.

Before long, the band arrived to check the sound system and bounced a few chords from the guitars off the walls. Jack recognized it as the signal for management to shut down the jukebox. Soon, the jukebox music seized, and the boom, boom, boom of the bass kick drum told him the band was about to begin.

The place rapidly filled, and by the end of the band's first set, he was sharing his table with a couple of guys who had just finished their maple syrup harvest. The threesome shared stories and asked Jack where he was from and where he was going. He didn't mention his time in prison and simply told them about working on a fishing boat out of South Florida before coming north.

Jack was enjoying the company of the two local boys and shared in their laughter when they poked fun at him for turning down two different requests to dance.

"I've sworn them off, guys. They always seem to bring trouble. Life is pretty good right now, so I'm good just the way I am."

He even laughed along when they kidded him about being gay. That was the moment when Jack realized for the first time in as long as he could remember, he was comfortable with himself and who he was—the experience changed him. He had nothing more to prove, and suddenly, life took on an entirely different outlook.

By the time the band was into their third set of the night, Jack was feeling the effects of the beer. For no reason other than he wanted to dance and celebrate his newfound self, he walked over to one of the booths at the far end of the dance floor, where a single woman sat alone and asked her to dance. It felt good to approach a woman with no ulterior motive, and Jack had no plans of hitting on her.

After two dances, Jack walked her back to her table and thanked her for the dances. Turning around, he was met by her drunk friend, who threw a weak punch that connected squarely with Jack's jaw. Shaking it off, Jack squared up and delivered two knock-out punches to the drunk's face.

Thinking that was the end of it, Jack was surprised when he was grabbed from behind by two men who looked like they moved pianos for a living. The massive fireplugs severely beat Jack before bouncers could break it up. Accused of starting the fight, the bouncers threw a barely conscious Jack out into the parking lot.

He was leaning up against the building, trying to clear his head, when the two guys he'd been sitting with approached to see if he was alright.

"I'm ok." Jack shook his head while wiping at the blood around his nose and mouth with the wet towel they'd brought him. "Wh-what's up with those two guys anyway?"

"Sorry you had to run into them. That's Merl and Earl. They're locals here, twins from the Pearl family. No one messes with them."

"No foolin." Jack winced. "But why me?"

"Well, the guy you punched out is a good friend of theirs."

Jack grunted. "Guess that would explain it."

Thanking them for the towel, Jack shuffled to his bike a couple of parking spaces away. Struggling to get on the bike, he nearly knocked it over, before steadying himself.

"Doesn't look to me like you should be riding that thing, Jack."

"I'm alright," Jack growled and swiped the back of his hand at the blood still trickling from the corner of his mouth. "Just give me a minute."

Jack fired the bike and warmed to its sound. Then, turning to his newfound friends, "I've enjoyed meeting you. Like I told you, I'm headed out of town tomorrow. You guys take care."

His goodbyes said. Jack slowly motored away from the parking lot and headed home. His head throbbed, but it was the pain in his jaw that had his attention. Tomorrow was going to be a rough day.

The next day, the old man laughed when Jack pulled up a chair at the breakfast table.

"Gotta say, Jack, ain't never seen a pair of raccoon eyes quite like the pair you sportin' this morning."

"Oh honey, let me see." The old boy's wife turned Jack's head from side to side for a better look. "I'm getting you some ice for those."

"Please. I'll be alright."

"Don't argue, boy. Only make your headache worse."

She quickly returned with a towel filled with ice. "Don't pay any attention to the old goat. You wouldn't know it now, but he was a real brawler in his day. Stupid fool wouldn't give it up until I laid down the law."

Jack winced at her ice application, then looked up without so much as moving his head. "How's that?"

"Oh, don't bore him with that old story, Melissa."

"You hush. Now, where was I? Oh yes. We'd been dating for nearly a year and were getting pretty serious when I told him I'd leave him if he didn't stop fighting."

"If he was so bad, why didn't you leave him? I'm sure you could have had your choice of other guys." Jack's attempt to wink with his swollen left eye failed.

"Oh, stop it, Jack, before you make me blush."

She gently moved the bag of ice to the other side of his face and continued. I could see something deeper inside him. Something I'm not sure even he knew was there at the time." She paused, and Jack didn't interrupt, allowing her to think momentarily. One thing he'd learned over the course of his ventures was that these old-timers possessed real wisdom—something the world didn't have to offer.

"Jack." She patted his shoulder. "You need to learn to look a little deeper than the surface. So often, what a person holds tightly inside, at their core, is the nugget, the gem you're looking for. You just have to know how to unwrap it."

"And you saw something there worth fighting for?"

"Sure did. Why else would I spend time with a barroom drunk and brawler."

"Now, hold on, Melissa."

She held up one hand. "Quiet. I'm speaking here, and this young man needs to hear it."

Strong woman. Jack thought.

"You may have to dig and scrape to get through a tough external layer, but as long as you know what's in the heart, the fight is worth it. Look beyond the beauty that is so fleeting and find what's in the heart, Jack. Then you'll know if it's worth the trouble of getting past the outer layer that messes up so many couples. Fifty years later, I can tell you it's been well worth the fight to straighten out this old coot."

Jack looked at the old man, who shrugged, grinned slyly, and sipped his coffee.

"I think I've had to learn this lesson the hard way."

Her questioning look solicited more.

"I knew someone like that once, Melissa. But I was too focused on myself to see it."

"Well, get back in touch with her. If you're sure that's her heart, then fight the fight."

"It's been a couple of years, and I wouldn't have any idea how to get in touch." He shook his head. "We didn't part on the best of terms."

"I'm sorry, Jack. But the lesson learned is golden. It will pay you back someday with interest."

Jack smiled meekly. "I hope you're right."

"Like some more coffee."

"Sounds good." She set the ice on the table and went to get the coffee pot. Jack carefully tipped up his cup to empty it.

Melissa soon returned with a fresh pot of coffee and filled his cup, then grabbed the ice bag and gave it to Jack.

"Hold this right here. I brought some aspirin to help with that headache."

Jack moved it to his forehead, where a headache pounded. "Hope you folks don't mind if I stick around a couple more days while this swelling goes down."

"Jack, you're everything we could have asked for. Sorry, the accommodations couldn't have been better."

"They were perfect. Hard to complain about free room and board." He looked up at Melissa through slits of steel blue. "You have no idea what this time has meant to me. It's been a blessing, and I thank you for everything from the bottom of my heart."

Three days later, when he shook hands with the old man and hugged Melissa goodbye, he knew he was leaving behind a cherished time he would never forget. The freedom, isolation, physical labor, and company of a Bible-believing family would likely never happen again, and he recognized it as the special moment it was.

CHAPTER FIFTEEN

HE DIDN'T KNOW WHY, BUT THE PULL TO GO WEST GREW SO intense he couldn't deny it any longer. The further south he went, the stronger the feeling grew. But Jack wouldn't leave until fulfilling a lifetime dream to visit the Civil War battlefields.

After spending some time at the first two battlefields, Jack was surprised by how moved he was when visiting each battlefield and lingered. Brother fighting brother, father fighting son, slaughtering one another in the most gruesome ways. Evil versus good. It was one thing to look at it from a distance, another thing entirely to think of a father killing a son or a son killing a father. Jack found it hard to imagine, but there it was, right in front of him. Undeniable.

Standing in the middle of the various battlefields he visited, Jack couldn't help but feel a connection with the men on both sides of the line. It was as if the spirits of those killed at each battle site continued speaking to visitors willing to listen. He'd heard the same voices years before when visiting the battlefield that was Custer's Last Stand.

I'll bet the voices of the Jews gassed and cooked in those ovens speak just as loud to people visiting the old extermination camps. Jack thought.

Touched by his experience, he decided to spend more time visiting the battlefields and various monuments than planned. The nation's history captivated him, and denying the urge to go west, he turned eastward to the

Smithsonian and Thomas Jefferson's home in Monticello. The brilliant man who wrote the Declaration of Independence had always fascinated him.

On the road again, Jack left the last battlefield, wondering how man could be so cruel to man. Though he knew there would always be someone who coveted power over other men, he still couldn't grasp it. But history was full of the kind of oppression Jefferson and others had attempted to escape by leaving Europe for America. It was a sick feeling, and he couldn't understand why it had to be.

Weeks later, when he'd finished visiting one last monument and satisfied his curiosity, Jack decided it was too late in the season to travel west. He wanted good weather for crossing over the Rockies and the opportunity to find work once he arrived. Wondering if the old couple back at the syrup farm would take him back for another winter and one more harvest season, Jack returned to Vermont.

Knocking on their door, Melissa broke into tears and threw her arms around him in a big hug. "You are such a blessing, Jack. We would love to have you stay with us."

Even her crusty old husband briefly hugged Jack after shaking his hand. "Your presence here will help us remain on the place for one more season."

Storing his meager gear in familiar digs of his bunkhouse, Jack sat for a moment and marveled at how wonderful it felt to be wanted. Returning to the syrup farm was the right choice. The winter of 76/77 on the sap farm was brutally cold. An extended period of single-digit temperatures kept Jack busy splitting and hauling firewood, caring for the animals, and making grocery trips to town.

One cold night about 2 AM with temperatures hovering around 3 degrees, Melissa banged on Jack's door . The loud cry for help frightened Jack. Jumping from bed, he rushed to the door in only his underwear. When Jack opened it, he was greeted by a distraught Melissa and a fierce winter storm.

"Jack. Sorry to disturb you like this, but I need your help. Please hurry."

Her husband was having trouble breathing, and she wanted Jack to drive them into town to the emergency room. "I don't dare drive in this storm, Jack. Can you take us to the hospital?" Jack knew all about driving in the snow and quickly agreed.

A trip to the emergency room stabilized Melissa's husband, and after a three-day stay in the hospital, they released him to home care. It took the old boy most of January to recover from pneumonia, and though weakened, he wasn't about to miss another season of maple syrup harvest when February rolled around.

Each morning, Jack would assemble the two horses they kept, hook them up to the sled, and prepare to head into the maple trees for a day's work. Melissa's husband sometimes struggled to climb aboard the sled, but once he took hold of the reins, he was back home where he belonged. Jack hoped he had the same grit and endearing, faithful wife at his side when he reached that age.

Spring of 1977 was beautiful. The weather couldn't have been better as if nature was attempting to compensate for the cruel winter. Warm rain for the flowering plants and balmy temperatures tempted Jack to stay. But the call west had grown inside Jack all winter; this time, it would not be denied.

Jack found it difficult to leave the sweet old couple a second time and wondered how they would do without him. They might last another couple of years, but he knew their time remaining on the place was short. If they could find good help, they might make it a few more years.

Melissa gave him a tearful hug goodbye. "Don't know what we would have done without you this winter, Jack. Take care of yourself. And like we've talked about this winter, you'll figure out who the real Jack is, and when you do, you'll find that singular woman to build a life with."

Jack shook hands with her husband and turned to go.

"Oh, and Jack." Melissa giggled. "I'll never forget the image of you answering the door in your underwear that night." She smiled and winked. "Be safe."

A couple of hours down the road, the dark clouds of a massive thunderhead threatened, and for a moment, Jack considered taking shelter. But the pull west was undeniable. Jack didn't understand it but wouldn't stop for the threatening storm. Whatever was driving him west seemed determined to get him there soon.

The road was straight, with little water pooling on the surface, so he rode on. Suddenly, he felt alive again. Free on his Harley with the road stretching out in front of him always had that effect. When huge raindrops ricocheted like bullets off his helmet, Jack embraced the machine gun rhythm hammering at his head. He allowed the rain to wash away the remnants of his prison time and the rest of the mess that was Florida.

Miles later, after the rain eased, a drenched Jack embraced it all as part of the adventure of life on the road. It was part of the experience, an experience he loved more than anything else. Then, his thoughts drifted back to Melissa's parting comment. Could he figure out who he was? Ashamed of his past and the whole lot that led up to prison, he determined a new start would take priority over everything else. Washed clean by the rain, he swore he'd use the storm as a renaissance moment.

Outside Des Moines, he slowed for a hitchhiker, thumbing her way west.

Reel it in, Jack. You swore an oath to yourself. Don't take the bait. As the song says, 'Could have tripped out easy today, but I've changed my ways.'

Accelerating, he passed her by, and she flipped him off.

Ouch! That hurts.

Maybe so, but don't outsmart your common sense, Jack. You're on a new road now. Remember! Don't be looking back at the old temptations.

The wrestling match going on inside him grew with each passing mile. Could he do this? Did he want to do it? The old man within loved the old ways. Sex, drugs, and rock and roll, as they said. What was wrong with having a little fun? And indeed, all sorts of fun was promised, though the associated heartaches were never mentioned.

On no account had Jack learned how to say he was sorry, finding it easier to walk away instead. *That probably has to change as well.* He mused. And though he thought he was free, Jack was learning how the freedom he once cherished wasn't all it was cracked up to be. Well, it wasn't everything anyway.

What kind of life is this, Jack? Face it. The type of life you thought would be so great cost you the best woman you could ever hope to have. Not to mention a stay in prison.

Yeah, yeah. Don't remind me. That's part of the deal, remember. I let go of the past, and you quit reminding me about it.

The tug of war continued while the miles stretched out behind him and his past. Just west of Rapid City, he turned northwest on I-90 towards Sturgis, fully intending to leave the highway of regret behind. When two riders merged onto the freeway from his right, he motioned a greeting, and they soon fell in close behind.

Jack's thoughts continued to wander. Florida was the bottom of the barrel. It was the worst experience he could have imagined. But on the flip side, working for the elderly couple during the two maple harvest seasons was among the best times he'd ever known.

Opposite worlds, for sure.

His life in Florida was the world and all it represented. The elderly couple represented love and what he would have once referred to as bible thumpers. Except they weren't. They were the most pleasant, loving, compassionate people he'd ever known.

There seemed to be no end to his internal struggle. Could he honor the oath he swore to himself in prison, or would the old man's temptations win out? Suddenly, the two riders following behind raced up beside him, one on each side, and began speaking to him. He wasn't sure how he could hear them above the wind and road noise, but he heard them clearly.

The one on the left began taunting him with all the good times he could have had with the hitchhiker he refused to pick up. The one on the right was calmer, peaceful, and speaking reason.

"You know the trouble it brings. Not to mention the oath you swore in prison and recently recommitted to."

"Come on, man. Don't listen to that guy. He's never had any fun in his life!"

"It's not about fun; it's about eternity."

"Seriously, you gonna listen to that guy? Did God really say…"

"There we are." The rider on the right interrupted. "The original lie. It's been going on since Genesis."

"Oh, please. Don't feed him that old line. Come with me, Jack, and you can have the time of your life!"

"Don't do it, Jack."

And with that, both riders vanished into thin air right before his eyes.

Jack shook his head. *Did that just happen? I haven't done any drugs, but they seemed so real. What's it matter, Jack? Even if they were ghosts, it pretty much paints the picture, doesn't it?*

Following the internal call that pulled him west, Jack continued through Montana. The rolling wheat fields stirred a place in him he'd nearly forgotten about.

Days later, upon arriving in Washington, the waving fields of wheat greeted him like an old friend, and Jack knew he was home. He pulled into a Mom and Pop grocery in Davenport for some beer and basic supplies. The place was right out of the thirties and forties. The creaking, worn wooden floors, narrow aisles, and, strangely enough, an aged scent straight out of the past had him feeling right at home.

Near the cash register up front was a glass case displaying fresh-cut meat from the butcher shop in the back and a glass jar full of pickled eggs.

"There a place where a guy can get a meal around here?" Jack asked while his purchase was rung up.

"Bout five or six blocks down on your right, and the only motel in town is directly across the street from it if'n you're lookin for a place to stay."

Jack picked up the paper bag containing his purchase and thanked the man.

"If you don't mind my askin, you planning on stickin around for a while stranger?"

"That depends if I can find work or not."

"Well, you might check with the widow Rachel. Poor old gal lost her husband some time back and is still trying to make a go of it herself."

"Hmmm. What kind of work?"

"She runs a wheat ranch northwest of town and a few head of cattle."

"Old gal, working a wheat ranch alone? Seems a bit strange."

"Oh, she's not old. Maybe forty, and pretty easy on the eyes. Tough as nails, though, and she won't take any guff. She might be looking for help this time of year if you can handle it."

"So where do I find her?"

Reaching into a pocket in the front of his overalls, he pulled out a pen and wrote down a number.

"There ya go, Mister. She won't have you out to her place unless she feels comfortable about it. You understand, her being single and all, she's careful with strangers from out of town."

"I understand. Sounds like I need to nail the phone interview."

Jack smiled and stuffed the slip of paper in his jeans pocket. "Much obliged. We'll probably see each other again if I get on with her."

Jack stepped out the creaking front door and heard the bell over his head ring when he stopped on the wooden front porch to breathe in the country air—the hint of dust and the familiar smell of wheat fields took him back to his roots. Wheat fields rolling out in all directions as far as the eye could see surrounded him.

Few cars passed by while he stood outside the storefront, confirming to himself he was home. Something about small towns, the hard life, and free-thinking people drew him like a magnet.

Mounting his bike, he was reminded of the many days, months, and miles of the last couple of years. The long distance he'd traveled to reach this point and how all the days on the road were a journey through so much more than the places he'd visited. The time away and the lessons on the road gave him an understanding and perspective he hadn't known before. A hot bath would feel mighty good, too, but first, he needed a beer and a meal.

The classic greasy spoon restaurant was right where the store owner had said, and after a couple of beers, a bacon burger with fries, and some of Grandma's raspberry pie, Jack leaned back in his chair and reflected. It was a new beginning: the old self and much of the past lay in a roadside ditch somewhere. Washed away in the wind and the rain, sweated out on the deck of a fishing boat and in a maple tree forest under a blanket of frost, or beaten out of him behind prison walls, the person he'd once been was gone. It was a good feeling, and Jack reminded himself of his oath. He would not fall into the traps he'd once set for himself. It was the start of a new life, and Jack grew excited about it.

He checked into the motel directly across the street from his window seat at the restaurant and spent the afternoon soaking in a hot bath. He'd call the widow Rachel in the morning.

CHAPTER SIXTEEN

AFTER BLACK COFFEE, HASH BROWNS AND GRAVY, TWO EGGS over easy, and extra bacon, Jack tipped the motherly waitress, who didn't take long to figure he was new in town.

"Watcha up to today, cowboy?"

Jack chuckled. "Well, I ain't no cowboy, but I am looking for work."

"I know a few places that need help."

"Well, I've got a lead to check out today."

"Mind if I ask who that might be?"

"The widow Rachel. Know anything about her?"

"Ohh! Well." She rocked back on her heels with raised eyebrows as if the statement struck her hard. "Be on your toes."

"Alright. Shoot straight with me. What's the deal with her?"

"Straight up. She's tough to work for. Pretty rough on the help, too. They don't seem to last long."

"Thanks. I'll keep that in mind."

"Just be careful. She's hell-bent on proving she can run that place by herself."

That last comment left Jack more concerned than anything else she had said.

After returning to his room and calling Rachel, Jack wondered what all the fuss was about. The widow seemed pleasant enough, well, that is, once she knew he was calling about work. A meeting was arranged for late afternoon.

Jack arrived promptly, passing beneath a massive log entryway from which a hand-carved wooden sign hung. Blackhorse Ranch was burnished into the wood in black. There was no gate, just a cattle guard that he slowed for before crossing.

Idling slowly down a long dirt lane bordered by barbed wire fencing on each side, Jack took in the property. In every direction, gently rolling fields of golden grain waved in the breeze. After rounding a corner, he came face to face with a beautiful but aged two-story farm home.

He was idling down the lane, nearing the farmhouse, when a rider on a black horse shot out from behind a red barn and approached at full gallop. Jack pulled to a stopped and waited for the rider who soon reined her horse to a hard stop beside him.

"What the hell are you doing on my property?" The sharp, accusing voice could have come from a crusty old cowboy with a mouth full of chew. But she neither chewed nor was crusty. Jack was shocked more by the disconnect between the beautiful blond woman sitting atop the horse and the sound of the voice than by the gruff greeting.

Before Jack could form an answer, she added.

"I suggest you turn that thing around and head back the way you came."

The small dark eyes peering from beneath a black cowboy hat drilled holes in Jack. She was slim, probably about five foot ten, and her long blonde hair hung straight down her back in a braided ponytail. The blue snap-front western shirt she wore was partially open but not in a suggestive way. Her right hand on the side away from Jack concerned him. Though he couldn't see it, Jack had little doubt it rested atop the butt of a sidearm.

Having taken a moment to collect himself, Jack responded, "I'm supposed to meet with a woman named Rachel about a job."

Now, it was her turn to be flustered.

"You're the guy who called about work? You have to be kidding. I'm sorry, but we don't have much use for your type around here. Though I must admit, you look fit enough." Her eyes raked Jack, taking him in.

"Lordy, what have I gotten myself into." She sighed. "Follow me up to the house, and let's talk."

The woman was all business. Jack liked that much about her. The fact she was easy on the eyes didn't hurt either, but the comments he'd heard about her quickly came to mind.

At the farmhouse, the two took up seats in the kitchen on opposite ends of a bare wooden dining room table. Looking about, Jack could see the place had been top of the line at one point. Now, the out-of-date cabinetry, worn linoleum floors and carpet, and the apparent need for a paint job both inside and out tied the house to another time and another place.

The initial small talk included questions about Jack's background and what he was doing wandering about the country on a motorcycle. Jack purposely avoided mentioning his prison time.

"Just wanted to see the country. I've been on the road for a couple of years and now I'm kinda finding my way back home in the Pacific Northwest."

"Any farm work in your background?"

Jack shrugged. "Just bucking bales on occasion."

"Can you run equipment?"

"I've run tractors and pulled hay sleds if that's what you mean."

"I'm thinking more like combines."

"Can't be that tough, can it?" Thinking of his combine accident, it was more of a tease to take charge of the conversation.

Rachel smiled, and her face softened. "I like your confidence, and your blue eyes don't hurt either."

"Well, thanks." He shrugged. "I don't mean to be rude, but what's a woman doing trying to run a huge place like this all by herself?"

Rachel's face quickly hardened into the granite look she sported when first greeting him, and Jack immediately knew he'd stepped in it.

"Look, I'm sorry, that's not what I meant…"

"But it is what you said; A woman can't manage a place like this. Right!"

Jack wished the fire in her eyes was there for any other reason but for what he'd just said.

"My apologies. Look, maybe I should be going."

"Sit back down." The authority in her voice set Jack back in his seat. "I didn't say you could leave yet."

"So I'm hired?"

"Not so fast. To answer your rather rude question, you need to understand that I lost my husband three years ago when he was thrown from a horse. But I love this place and have no plans to leave."

Jack nodded. "Understandable, but it sure looks as if you could use some help around here."

"I can, and that's why you're here. But before I hire you, I have one more question."

"Shoot." When they first met, Jack recalled the hidden handgun and wished he hadn't said it quite like that.

Rachel's face softened again as a devilish grin began to form. "What's your claim to fame?"

"What?"

"Everyone has a past, and this question often tells me more about a person than all the other questions I could ask. What's your claim to fame?"

There was no way he was mentioning his time in prison, but Jack figured it was his opportunity to turn the tables just a bit.

"I played flag football in college on an intramural team known as the Closet Queens."

Her nervous, high-pitched laughter burst loose, filling the room before she quickly slapped a hand over her mouth.

"You?" She laughed out loud. "So I'm about to hire a real live closet queen." Her laughter bubbled up uncontained. "Man, will the harvest crew ever love you!"

"EX-closet queen," Jack emphasized.

"I'm almost afraid to ask how a football team would accept a name like that. But..." She gestured with her hand for him to continue.

"We were just a bunch of cazy guys having fun. The name comes from a James Gang song called The Bomber."

"Yes, I know it."

"Well, the guys and I figured it would be so insulting for a football team to lose to another squad named the Closet Queens; we couldn't pass it up."

"Were you any good?"

"Won all our games and went to the playoffs."

"And..." She waved her hand again, signaling for him to continue.

"First playoff game, we defeated a fraternity, Phi Kappa Crappa or something like that."

"Bet that went over big."

"My claim to fame came out in the college newspaper when the headline across the top of the sports section declared in big, bold print, 'Closet Queens defeat Phi Kappa Krappa.' That was a sweet moment."

Rachel's girlish laughter bubbled up again.

"The next playoff game, we played another frat. The frat boys from all across campus gathered on their sidelines to cheer for their brothers. Musta been a hundred of them." Jack laughed. "It was one hell of a battle. I threw a pass to our high school sprinter for our lone touchdown, but we failed to get the extra point and lost 7 to 6. Even though we lost, it was a physical game, and no one mocked the Closet Queens afterward."

Rachel leaned back in her chair, enjoying the moment. "Ok, Jack, that's just too funny. You take the prize for the best answer to my question. So anyway, it seems you're a man of many abilities, a renaissance kind of guy. I like that in a man."

Her charming smile suggested many temptations, and Jack reminded himself of his vow.

"So, back to business. I always ask that question of new employees because you never know what you will learn. And I have to say I've never heard anything quite like that. Now, time to get serious. One last question: Can I trust you to see harvest season through to the finish if I hire you?"

"I always keep my word."

"It's a long, some would say grueling season?"

"Look." Jack leaned forward, resting his elbows on the table and looking her straight in the eyes. "I may have screwed up a lot of things in my life, but I never go back on my word. I'll be here for you and see the harvest through to the end."

"Alright, Jack. You're hired."

She stood and extended a slender but hard-looking hand. Jack stood to his full height and reached across the length of the table, only to be surprised by the tender touch he found in the firm grip. "I won't let you down."

"Well, we'll see about that." She placed both hands on her hips. "For now, I'll have to take your word for it. Let me show you to the bunkhouse where you'll be staying."

The one-room bunkhouse was no more than a twelve by twelve shed with two single beds and one window. There was no door to the building besides the screen door meant to keep the bugs out. Jack had stayed in rougher places, and compared to his prison cell, it looked like heaven.

"You can move in tomorrow. I hope you're ready to work. There are fences to build and plenty more to do before we begin harvest. And you might think about cutting that hair."

Jack's quizzical look solicited another response. "I don't care myself; in fact, I kind of prefer it, but the harvest crew that's coming will give you all sorts of hell for that ponytail." She tilt her head sideways. "You'll see."

He waved her off. "I've heard it all before, Redneck humor and all that. I can hold my own."

"Having had a look at you, I've no doubt about that, but you're here to work, and I don't have time for trouble. Are we clear?"

"Perfectly."

Idling back out the gravel drive, Jack felt a sudden urge for the road, wind in his hair and the rumble of his bike between his knees. It had been a stressful day compared to freewheeling it on the open road, and he questioned whether he was ready for this kind of commitment.

She's a tough old gal.

You can't run forever, Jack. Deal with it.

Instead of heading back into town to his motel room, he turned west on Highway Two and rolled on the power. Damn, it felt good!

A couple of miles out of town, traveling at about seventy miles per hour, he roared past a tavern called *The Minstrel's Oasis* and made a mental note to stop and check the place out on his way back into town.

A few miles further west, he whistled past Creston, a spot in the road with a population of less than two hundred. A few more miles and Jack slowed to a stop in the town of Wilbur. *Who wouldn't stop in a town with a name like that?*

It reminded him of the talking horse show "Mr. Ed" that began airing in 1961. Allen "Rocky" Lane was the voice of Mr. Ed, and as a kid, Jack always laughed at the way the horse said Wilbur. Allen Young played Wilber Post, the owner of the horse and the only one Mr. Ed would speak to. Jack loved the show and couldn't help but think of it as he rode through town.

After slowly cruising the tiny town's streets for a look-see, Jack turned around and headed back towards Davenport. A few miles outside Davenport, he was approaching *The Minstrel's Oasis* and decided to make good on his promise to stop for a beer. He was surprised to hear a band playing on a Tuesday afternoon, when hardly anyone was in the place.

Jack ordered a Ranier to go with his bacon burger, chose a table near the dance floor, and sat down to listen, but mostly heard more discord than guitar chords.

"How are we supposed to practice without a drummer?"

It was the bass player doing most of the grumbling.

"Ricky said he'd be here."

"Yeah, well, he says a lot of things and never comes through. We need to find someone else."

"Just walk out into the middle of a wheat field and take our pick of all the drummers lining up to play for us, huh, Jake?" The singer mocked.

"Give me a break, Alan. This problem with Ricky is nothing new."

Jack enjoyed his burger, and the group attempted its next song. They weren't bad, but rock and roll, or even the country song they were working on now, wasn't the same without the solid backbeat of the drums.

After the band finished its song, the debate began again.

"What about Tommy?"

"Naw. He's back east for the summer."

The band was about to hang it up as Jack finished his meal. Having had time to think things over while enjoying his burger, Jack tipped back his beer for the last swig before leaving. He was halfway to the door when he turned around.

"You boys lookin' for a drummer?" Jack stuck both hands in his back pockets and waited for their reaction.

All three band members stared. The tall, dark-haired stranger in black leather with a motorcycle helmet under his left arm didn't look like the answer to their problems. Jack overheard one of them mumbling something about him not looking like much of a cowboy.

Then Alan, the singer, addressed him. "I suppose you overheard us."

"Was hard to miss," Jack replied.

"Sorry about that, but yeah, we could use some help. You telling us you're the guy?" He scrutinized Jack with a cynical look.

"Nothin' fancy, but I might be able to help with some basic beats. Its about the only good thing that came out of my time in prison."

"Prison! Shit man, you ain't from around here, are you Mister."

"You could say that."

Well, I don't know. We're just a bunch of locals, and we ain't lookin' for any trouble."

Jack looked down and chuckled. The prison moniker always drew the same reaction. "Like I said, I know some basics, but it looks to me even that much might help you guys out."

"Give us a minute so we can talk it over."

"I'll be over at the bar."

When the brief meeting ended, one band member stepped outside while the other two strolled to the bar and introduced themselves to Jack. After ordering beers for themselves and some small talk with Jack, the third one returned from outside.

"That you're Harley out front?"

Without looking, Jack replied, "Yep."

"You know we all work around here and can't afford to get into trouble. Are you with some sort of gang or something? I mean, with a prison record and all."

Jack scoffed. "That's funny. I'm either a felon on the run, or I'm part of a gang."

Jack relaxed against the bar and smiled before saluting them with his beer.

"Run into many felons looking to join a band around here, do you?"

"Well, you certainly don't look like the farm boy type." Alan was the largest of the three band members, and he took a step towards Jack. "Just trying to keep our noses clean, if you know what I mean. We have families to support. So, do you work around here, or are you just passing through? Not much point in you playing with us if you're not hanging around."

"I work for the widow Rachel."

The guy Jack recognized as the bass player spoke up. "Holy crap, man. You definitely aren't from around here. Aint, nobody local will work for that woman. Sounds like trouble partnering with trouble to me."

"Why do you say that?"

"She'll drive a man into the ground to keep that place running. She doesn't know when to quit."

"Hard to believe you're working for her," Alan said. "You don't look much like a farm hand to us."

"I'm a man of many talents," Jack smirked.

Alan continued. "Look, the woman is trying hard to prove she can make it without her old man. He died a few years back. And though I give her all the credit in the world for not packin' up and leaving, she doesn't know much about farmin'."

Jack took another pull from his can of Rainier. "Guess I failed the interview, guys. It's cool." He laid a tip down on the bar with the intention of leaving and turned for the door.

"Hold on there." Alan put up a hand to stop him. When Jack grabbed it, turning it into a handshake, he made sure the guy felt more than a friendly grip.

"If you're going to be sticking around, the boys and I thought we might give you a shot." Alan looked to the other two band members who nodded their agreement. "Why don't you come over, and we'll see if you're as good as you say you are."

"Never said I was good. But I might know just enough to help out."

"Alright. Let's give it a whirl."

Jack noted the band's name stamped across the bass drum before settling in behind the drum set.

PLOWBOYS AND COWBOYS

It took a few attempts at different songs before Jack began to get on board with the group's style. They would need some practice to bring it all together, but in the end, they agreed Jack could join them.

"You're now officially a Plowboys and Cowboys band member, Jack. Welcome aboard, Renaissance man." Taking a jab at Jack's comment, he was a man of many talents.

They agreed on a practice time, and Jack rode home in the dark to his motel room in Davenport.

CHAPTER SEVENTEEN

THE FOLLOWING WEEKS WERE FILLED WITH HARD WORK AND an occasional practice session with the band. Rachel seemed pleased with his efforts, and Jack grew comfortable with the routine, thankful the harvest crew wouldn't show up for another week or so. He enjoyed working alone with the ground squirrels and Redtail hawks as his only company. With no one else to be accountable to and working at his own pace each day, Jack found the freedom he loved.

One afternoon, Rachel rode out to where he was building fence. Jack couldn't help but notice the long flowing hair and how the sun brought a healthy glow to her face. Leaning on the saddle horn, she greeted him with a smile. "The fence is looking good, Jack. Nice and straight."

Jack set the post pounder down and wiped the sweat from his eyes. Shirtless and pounding fence posts in the blistering heat made his bronze body glisten with sweat. Had he caught her eyes lingering over him? No. He dismissed the idea.

"Thanks, Rachel. Is there something I can do for you?"

"You've done a right nice job around here these past couple weeks, and I appreciate all the hard work. Initially, I was skeptical, but things seem to be working out quite well. Why not knock off early today and have dinner with me tonight? Nothing fancy, but I'm told I cook pretty well."

I'll bet she does.......

Knock it off, Jack.

"Well, ok. If that's what you want. Sure enough."

"Relax. It's not an order. I thought you might like a little downtime for a change. You've done a nice job for me."

"Alright. I look forward to it."

She flashed a trim smile of pearly whites. "Dinners at six. Don't be late." Then, wheeling her horse around, she galloped away.

Jack couldn't help but wonder what was up. *Probably just lonely.* Jack pondered.

Later that evening, the crickets were just beginning to tune up when Jack made the short walk past the cottonwoods that showered the brown lawn with summer snow. Knocking on the door, he heard a light, lilting voice he wasn't sure he recognized inviting him in.

Thinking it might be some help she'd hired, he asked, "I'm here to see Rachel."

"Well then, come in." When she opened the door, Jack had to remind himself to pick his jaw up off the floor.

Wow!

She was wearing a stunning red dress Jack was sure hadn't been worn in quite a while. Sparkling eyes lit up her face, and merry laughter seasoned her voice. It was of a quality he'd never heard from her.

Putting a hand to his chin, he wished he'd shaved. "You certainly clean up nicely, Rachel."

The long blonde hair he'd only seen pulled up in a bun or ponytail, swept over her shoulders, and hung loosely down her back. There was a softness in her eyes he hadn't seen before, and her easy laugh led Jack to believe she'd already had a little something to drink.

"Dinner will be ready soon. I took the liberty of making you an Old Fashioned." She held the drink out for Jack. "But I can make you something else if you like." Her whimsical response implied more than the drink.

"This will be just fine, Rachel."

"Well then, sit down and tell me about yourself while I attend to dinner. A stranger riding into town on a Harley, professing to have all the talent I need for this job, must have some tales to tell."

Jack couldn't help but notice the deep slit up the side of her dress. That's when a familiar voice spoke up.

Jack, you know what's going on here. You can't deny the hunger in her eyes.

Jack waited to hear from the other voice that was always present to argue the other side, but all he heard was vile, cackling laughter.

The point had been made, and the battle was engaged.

"Come on, Jack. A man in biker leather always draws a woman's attention. Bet you're a magnet for married women everywhere you go." Her raised eyebrows indicated she knew the answer was yes.

He smiled. "Yeah, well, I've been around a bit, but it's not what you think."

Rachel gave him a doubtful look. "You know I'm not buying any of that."

Jack's brain overflowed with confusion. He faced a stiff challenge here and realized he had no defense.

Rachel brought two plates containing steak and potatoes and sat at the opposite end of the table from Jack. When Jack looked up after taking his first bite, he peered into the deep blue eyes staring back at him. Her chin rested in hands folded over the dinner plate, and blond hair framed her high cheekbones.

Jack was enchanted, and the glint in her eyes told him all he needed to know. The moonlight, the velvety touch of strong hands, and the hungry desires of a woman who'd been alone too long would combine to overwhelm him, and Jack soon surrendered. In an instant, the promises he'd made to God on the concrete floor of his solitary confinement cell were forgotten.

And like all sins, Jack would eventually regret its steep price, but he had no way of knowing that in the moment of temptation. Years later, golden wheat fields waving in the wind would always remind him of her, even when he held another in his arms.

That was the end of his nights spent alone in the bunkhouse, and when the harvest crew began showing up, it soon became apparent that outside of a little good-natured jesting, they weren't to mess with the boss's main man.

Just before harvest was to begin, Jack and the crew were forced to shut down their preparations when a rainstorm settled over the area. With some time off, Jack was asked to join the band for a few nights at the Minstrel's Oasis. The place would likely be jammed with out-of-work harvest crews enjoying a short break.

While he prepared to head into town, Rachel asked where he was going, and Jack invited her along. She may have been comfortable atop a horse but had never ridden on the back of a motorcycle. Clinging to Jack with arms tight around his waist, the two roared west on Highway 2 to the Minstrel's Oasis.

It was a Friday night, and the place was packed well before the band was scheduled to play. Rachel may have been approaching forty, but she drew looks from most of the men as she entered the bar with Jack. Her hip hugging jeans and white T-shirt drew much more than a casual glance.

Jack introduced her to the band, then led her to a table next to the dance floor reserved for the friends and wives of the band before taking his seat behind the drum set.

After warming up with a couple of tunes from the Eagles, Jack settled in for the evening. Most of those attending were recently freed from the demanding work of a dusty, blistering harvest and were clearly in the mood to party.

They were halfway through the second set, and Rachel had danced with several men bidding for her attention, but she could wait no longer. Approaching the low stage, she told the group's lead singer. "Tell the Renaissance man back there he needs to come out of his hidey hole and dance with me right now. And play a good country swing dance for us, would you."

The singer turned back to Jack. "Hey, renaissance man, your needed up front."

"What?"

"Some woman here wants to dance with you."

Jack looked up to see Rachel's shining eyes and grinned. "Her wish is my command."

As Jack stepped out from behind the drums, Rachel leaned in and asked the singer for a second song. "Be a nice tip for you if you play a long, slow one after this." She smiled and winked as Jack came around the corner of the stage and took her onto the dance floor.

Jack sometimes felt he was following instead of leading during the swing dance. This woman could dance, and every eye in the place was on her. She snuggled close during the slow dance, and when he returned to the drums after the song ended, one of the band members told him he'd never seen her smile like that before.

"This is not the woman people around here are used to seeing." Then, with a wry smile added, "You've been good for her, renaissance man. The woman's in love."

Jack shook his head. "Oh, come on. It's nothing like that."

"You don't see it? Shit man. Your blind. You're absolutely blind."

Jack harumped. "Come on, let's play."

"Alright. I got just the song." Turning to the rest of the band. "Still the One, guys."

Jack smiled and shook his head as they counted down: one – two; one, two, three, four.

It may have taken someone else to open his eyes, but over the next few days, Jack came to understand just how head over heels Rachel was for him. More than just a physical thing, she really was in love with him.

The realization was unsettling. Things were getting complicated, and he wondered why it always came to this. Did it have to? As much as he cared for the woman, what had once been so simple, straightforward, and uncomplicated now jumbled his thoughts.

Jack wondered where it was all headed. The woman was nearly fifteen years his senior. He had no answers, and though he was no stranger to walking away from a relationship, no matter how it might hurt someone, he just wasn't there yet. In some ways, he found himself feeling quite comfortable with it all. If only she hadn't gotten so serious.

Saturday morning, Rachel threw a smooth leg over Jack, snuggled close, and kissed him awake. "I have a favor to ask of you."

"Um, hm." He smiled, but his eyes remained closed.

"I've arranged with Tony down at the feed store to pick up some fencing materials first thing tomorrow morning. Can you be there just after sunrise?"

"Why so early?"

"It's the only time he's available."

"Ugh. Alright."

"He's got church after that and won't be able to open the store. I'd like you to work on that fence you were building while things dry out enough to begin harvest again." She rolled on top of him. "I'll make it worth your trouble."

Church. The thought had more of a bite to it than it should.

Guilty conscience, Jack?

Go away.

Unaware of the coming turn of events, Jack agreed.

PART TWO:
SCARLETT'S STORY

CHAPTER EIGHTEEN

HOW MANY TIMES HAVE I TOLD MYSELF I'D START JOURNALING? "Well, I'm sorry, it sure as heck isn't going to be today. Life is just too confusing, and there's no way I'll resolve it on some stupid piece of paper." Scarlett mumbled to herself as she prepared to lurch through another dull day.

The catastrophic end to her relationship with Jack left her feeling listless and unmotivated. The shooting and death of Johnny left her unsettled. Maybe she was still in shock because her mind could do nothing but float about unanchored. Mindlessly packing her bags for the short trip from Washington State University to Spokane, Washington, her mind ran hot with the recent events in her life, but her dead, cold heart remained empty and numb. She was coming apart inside, and there seemed to be no remedy.

Having taken a job in a department store in Spokane, she hoped the new job and new location would help to get her feet back on the ground and reset life's compass. The expectation of a new setting allowing her to shrug off college life and begin anew was all she had to cling to. The killing of her boyfriend by her ex-boyfriend boggled her mind, and she struggled to make sense of it. *How did I ever allow myself to get involved with Johnny? Rebound! Shut up. Don't remind me.* Yet the voice was always there, making sure she didn't forget.

But it wasn't just the shooting of her boyfriend by her ex-boyfriend that upset her. Her ex, the love of her life, had just blown town. The man she once believed she would marry had said goodbye without a trace of concern. *He said he didn't care anymore, and I'm finding that more challenging to deal with than I thought. This feeling of not being wanted is horrible. I have to find a way to put it all behind me and make a new start.*

Yet her heart told her Jack was the one, and she wondered how it could have gone so wrong.

You fool Scarlett. Go ahead, hang onto those memories with Jack, and make sure you never get over him. He blew you off just like he'd do with any other woman who meant nothing to him. If you had listened to your head instead of being so damn stubborn...

Scarlett grew angry with herself and slammed down the top of her suitcase. She and Jack had something special she doubted she'd ever find again. It left her so devoid of feelings, numb didn't begin to describe how she felt. *And the idiot threw it all away!* She flung a pair of shoes across the room in frustration.

Well, ok, I may have had a part in it, but aren't we supposed to be able to work it out if it's true love? And I swear. It is, or was, true love. Friends have told me better to find out now than later, and that's probably true, but there is a side to the man that is so very special. And that's the man I love. The other part of him is pretty messed up, and he allowed it to get the better of him, get the best of us!

Scarlett wondered what she was supposed to do with the business degree she'd just received. The spring of 75 was going to be a time of celebration with the completion of college and a step forward into a new life. A life with Jack. Instead, she was tempted to return to the Seattle area and the familiar comforts of the world where she grew up. But that would be too much like giving up and running home to Mom and Dad. They would welcome her, of course, and expect her to move back in with them, but the thought was disgusting. She was supposed to be building a life of her own now.

Her shoulders sagged, and she slumped down on the edge of her bed, fighting back the tears that came too frequent.

Seattle is such a beautiful city. I think of the times Jack and I used to catch a ferry at night and ride out across the sound. The brilliant lights were so joyful, and the atmosphere so peaceful. More romantic than I could have imagined; it gives me chills just thinking of it. Then stop thinking about it!

Her thoughts continued to race, leaping from the present to the stable life she'd known there as a child. Surrounded by good people in a stable world, she had thrived. People there trusted her and provided a safe environment for her to grow.

The Marysville community where she grew up was tight-knit. She'd always felt secure and happy there. Built around shared values, a strong work ethic, and a common foundation of self-reliance, she had fit in well. The people worked hard, be they fishermen, loggers, or farmers, and Scarlett identified with that.

At age twelve, she'd taken a summer job on Camano Island where they taught her how to milk cows by hand, not to mention mucking the manure out of stalls. It was hard work, especially for a girl of twelve, but she was proud of her accomplishments.

Though the milk shed had modern milking machines, the old boy she worked for told her she first had to learn how to milk by hand because there would be times when she would need to. Besides, who ever heard of a dairy worker who couldn't milk a cow? She learned the skill quickly and, over the years, would eventually work for two different dairies in the area.

She'd also taken summer work on nearby farms and ranches when they needed an extra hand. The memory of riding in from the field after a day's work on the lowered tailgate of a pickup, legs swinging in the breeze, warmed her heart. The farms comprised the backbone of the community, and she became a familiar and welcome face amongst the locals. The integrity embodied by the hard-working people there soon became a part of her.

Scarlett was particularly fond of one dear old man her mother used to send her over with food to deliver. He lived across the field from where they lived, and she developed quite a caring relationship with Mr. Baker.

His close-cropped hair was white as snow, as was the finely groomed mustache nestled below an average-sized but somewhat flattened nose. His dark brown eyes always sparkled with life. Something about the contrast between his dark skin and white hair made the man particularly handsome.

She felt much the same about his wife but in a different way. Her long grey hair shone nicely in contrast to the aged but smooth ebony skin, yet it was the light in her eyes she remembered most. They pierced Scarlett with an inner peace that caused her to wonder about the source of it. It was a peace she wished she could grasp hold of right now. Scarlett thought of her as quite the distinguished looking woman. Her quiet dignity was something she'd always hoped to personify.

The elderly couple lived in an old farmhouse sided with thick, heavily weathered wood a half mile down the road from Scarlett's childhood home. Sometimes,she rode a bike, and other times, she walked through the field to visit them. She always thought of them as poor, yet now, in hindsight, they seemed rich, and she longed for the peace the two of them possessed. It was as if the world outside couldn't touch them.

In her turmoil, the memory became a touchstone for the calm, stable life she once knew and now craved but feared she would never know again. Sadly, the two stalwarts Scarlett had long looked up to were gone. Just before Jack took off, her mother called to inform her they had both passed away. Mr. Baker died peacefully in his sleep. His wife passed a few weeks later, shortly after laying her husband to rest.

It was hard enough news to accept by itself, but with her breakup, Scarlett felt the foundations of life crumbling beneath her. Life was changing, and the feeling of being cast adrift was distressing.

Longing for the kind of peace and personal confidence these old friends possessed, Scarlett returned to packing. Promising herself that she would not let the recent events get her down, she prepared to venture into the next chapter of life in Spokane.

CHAPTER NINETEEN

December 1975

STARTING THIS JOURNAL MAY BE A BIT OF A PIPEDREAM, AS I expect to have little time for it. But it's always been something I wanted to do, so let's give it a shot and see where it goes. Now, where to start?

Let's begin with life after college or, should I say, lack of a life. I grew disillusioned with my job and everything else in Spokane and found little inspiration to do much of anything, including beginning this journal. More than likely, it was the fallout with Jack and his shooting of Johnny. Emotionally, I'm spent.

So here I am on Mercer Island, sitting alone in my parent's basement where Jack and I used to spend so much time together. The worn, beige tile is chilly and uninviting. The cold fireplace and aged sofa near the sliding door that once seemed like such a romantic hideaway is just an empty room now. There is no candle burning or soft music playing on the radio.

Probably a mistake, but I'm sitting in the same place on the sofa where I used to sit with Jack. My radio on the window sill remains in the same place as when Jack stayed and slept on this couch. The stupid picture of a dry flower arrangement hangs on the wall in the same spot opposite the sofa. We used to wonder how someone could be so taken with a picture like that; they just had to have it. The now dark and empty room leaves me wondering how our relationship came and went so fast. It wasn't supposed to be like this. Lord, what is your plan? I know you always have one. Care to share it with me?

Since I've little else to do, I've decided to spend this afternoon putting all these mangled thoughts together on paper, hoping to put them in some sort of order while simultaneously getting them out of my head.

I know I'll eventually move on. That's how life works, right? But for now, the world offers me little more than heartache. My heart is as frozen as the icicle hanging from the eve outside the door. I've grown so cynical these past few weeks. That's not like me, but there seems to be little to hope for. I hate the sound of that, but what's a journal for if not a place to dump all this junk?

In the middle of the darkest, lonely winter I have ever known, I chose to move back home. Spokane's leaden skies and long, gloomy nights were bitter, empty, and more than I could bear. My friends scattered like dust after college, and I felt so incredibly alone in that frozen industrial city where my soul could find no rest. But moving home may have been an even greater mistake. Memories of my time with Jack pop up everywhere I go, and it only serves to remind me of what a mess my life has become.

Of course, my parents are thrilled, not just that I'm home but that Jack is out of my life as well. After kicking him out during his last visit, I probably couldn't have ever brought him home again anyway.

So here I am, alone in my parent's basement where Jack and I used to sit on the couch together listening to the rock and roll station on my little transistor radio. We'd hold hands, making plans for things to do and places to go, and then make out after my parents went to bed.

This is hard. Writing down my feelings is much more difficult than I imagined, so this is enough for now. I need to get out of here and think I'll head down to Pike Place and the waterfront for a walk and a breath of air. I'll get back to this later.

In no rush, Scarlett meandered through traffic and parked a couple blocks away from Pike Place Market. She loved the rustic atmosphere of the aged wooden buildings and farmers market. Slipping into the bustle of holiday shoppers seemingly unnoticed, it felt good to disappear in the crowds and linger. It was the same as feeling alone in a room full of people, but she embraced the feeling this time. Dead inside and detached from the world around her, interacting with people was the last thing she wanted.

Pike Place was a familiar environment and strangely comforting. Scarlett drifted from the fish market, where she paused to watch and listen to the fishmongers toss fish, to the bookshops filled with incense and the head shops Jack loved to frequent. Wandering past several more small businesses, window shopping, and reminiscing, Scarlett fell into a trance. *I spent some of the best times of my life here.* Something about hanging about the place brought her a peace she hadn't found anywhere else.

A jewelry shop drew her attention, and she headed inside. Some kind of Indian mystic music was playing, and Scarlett found it strangely comforting. The lemon-scented incense was pleasantly surprising. After agonizing between a bracelet or a necklace on twisted gold chains, Scarlett chose the necklace. It would make a perfect Christmas gift for her mother.

After leaving the store, she floated aimlessly through a few more shops before descending a long flight of stairs that would take her past a couple of the head shops Jack used to enjoy visiting. She planned on visiting a fishing and hunting business near the bottom of the staircase, where she hoped to find a gift for her father.

Descending the stairs, she hadn't planned on stopping, but the familiar scent of patchouli incense drifting through the front door of the Pipe Palace, accented with a hint of marijuana, drew her in. She and Jack had visited here more than once, and the colorful memories both comforted and troubled her.

Walking past the "Let Your Freak Flag Fly" poster next to the front door, Scarlett turned to her right to browse a shelf of sweatshirts. Numerous tie-dye T-shirts hung on an adjacent rack. She was searching through the sweatshirts when a touch of lavender discovered her nose. Jack had purchased her favorite sweatshirt here, one she still often wore, and like a familiar song that takes you back to a specific moment in time, the scent of lavender did the very same.

"Can I help you with anything?"

The voice came from behind and startled Scarlett out of the daydream. She spun around.

"Oh, no thanks. Just looking."

"We keep the good stuff in the back, if you know what I mean." The guy caught himself and half chuckled. "What am I saying? College girl like you, I've no doubt you know what I mean."

"No thanks." *I'm not some 'college girl,' you idiot. And I'm already messed up enough without smoking a bowl of your weed.* "Just getting ideas for Christmas."

"Well, the Blackroom is open if you change your mind."

"Thank you."

The friendly hippie excused himself, and Scarlett continued browsing.

After perusing displays of beaded necklaces and counterculture items, Scarlett headed back outside. Wrapped in memories, she paused on the stairway landing for some fresh air before rushing down two more flights of stairs to escape the haunting thoughts.

Deciding to put off shopping for her father's Christmas gift, she dashed beneath the viaduct and across the street to sit at the water's edge near Ivar's fish and chips. Scarlett sucked in the sweet ocean air and fought back the tears. A nearby ferry was leaving its dock, and its deep, strident horn blast momentarily filled the air. The waterfront's familiar sights and sounds were both torturous and comforting, but they left her feeling empty and cold. Grabbing a cup of Ivar's chowder to warm herself, she sat in a covered area to watch the seagulls beg for scraps.

Wrapping her hands around the warm bowl, her thoughts overflowed with that blissful time when two people, so in love, were entirely oblivious to the world around them. Walking hand in hand, her mind drifted through their visits to Pier 101, the waterfront, and Pike Place Market, in and out of shops, absorbed in a wonderland of love.

She'd never been in a head shop before Jack tugged her into the Pipe Palace. It didn't take long for him to find his way to the blackroom where Hendrix, Joplin, and Dylan blacklight posters glowed on the walls, and the rhythmic music pulsed. He seemed familiar with the place and was soon furtively enjoying a bowl of smoke with a couple of other dudes and one girl. When he offered to share some with Scarlett, she declined.

"I'm driving, remember."

"Oh ya, man. That Volkswagen thingy." The smoke streamed from his nostrils, and he grinned sheepishly. The image was endearing.

It wasn't that she didn't smoke a little weed from time to time, but smoking it publicly went beyond her comfort level. As it turned out, it was a good thing she declined. Jack had gotten so wasted on the new supply of hashish the business owner had just received that he was in no condition to drive.

The two of them had stood together outside the shop on the stairwell landing, in the same place she'd just visited, and she recalled asking him how he was doing. His sleepy-eyed response now came to mind.

"Kinda hungry."

A seagull landed on the wooden railing in front of her, interrupting her revelry. It eyed her chowder and cried out Mine! The big bird's intrusion snapped her back to reality. Ok, enough of this. I'm ditching these memories right here, right now, on this bench where the Seagulls can crap all over them. I'm walking away. It's time to move forward, Scarlett.

The scolding seemed to work. Her mood brightened when a beam of sunlight broke through the gray winter clouds and landed in her lap. From behind, a mocking chuckle said *Good luck with that.*

Scarlett's head snapped around. She could have sworn it was a real human voice spoken by someone standing directly behind her, but she saw no one.

CHAPTER TWENTY

TWO DAYS BEFORE CHRISTMAS, SCARLETT STOOD IN HER PARent's kitchen sipping a hot cup of coffee and watching gigantic white flakes stack on top of the fresh foot of snow that had recently fallen. Colorful lights strung along the eves of the neighbor's houses remained on, completing the seasonal display.

Desiring a quiet morning away from her parents, she topped up her cup of coffee and turned from the window to head downstairs. After pulling on a down coat to ward off the chill, her slippers hissed a chilly greeting as she moved across the cold tile floor to the sliding door. Throwing it open wide, she stepped outside and leaned against the door frame to listen. The serene, tranquil fall of heavy snow was a symphony playing to the few who took the time to listen. Scarlett found it soothing, and her mind drifted back.

Jack's first visit here was on a snowy day, just like this, two days before Christmas, and nearly a foot of snow was on the ground! Lord, don't taunt me. I'm tired of being overwhelmed by memories like that.

But that singular moment in time was etched in her soul. After waiting most of the day and watching for Jack to arrive, Scarlett was filled with nervous anticipation, and her mother grew tired of her dancing about the windows at the front of the house, watching for him. After scolding her numerous times, she chased Scarlett downstairs.

Scarlett stood outside in the snow, picturing the moment when Jack arrived. She had raced out of the house to welcome him, and, not fully anticipating her exuberant embrace, he lost his footing in the snow.

Scarlett's shoulders shook with a gentle chuckle. *I tackled him straight to the ground. Dad hated him from that moment on.*

After rubbing snow in Jack's face, we wrestled in a flurry of snowflakes. There we were on the ground, grappling with one another like a couple of bear cubs right in front of my parents before I could even introduce him. Big mistake!

Even now, the thought of that moment warmed her inside. When she had looked up at her parents, standing stoically on the front porch with their arms crossed, she found her father's disdain more than palpable. But even now, the memory of her mother's reaction tickled her. Scarlett's mother had turned to the side to hide her face and secretly winked. Scarlett hugged herself.

If it weren't for Mom, Jack wouldn't have been allowed to stay. Dad hated him right from the start. Here was some ponytailed stranger entangled with his daughter on the ground right before him. It probably doomed any chance of ever having a relationship with Jack as much as his Harley and long hair did.

The memory filled Scarlett with longing, and she couldn't help but wonder what Jack was doing at that very moment. *Is there snow where you are at, Jack? Does he ever think of me when our song plays on the radio?*

Cynical Laughter.

We knew such magical times together on the Seattle waterfront, walking the piers hand in hand, and I...

Shake it off, Scarlett.

She continued with the memory.

We were so young and foolish. I never dreamed it could end this way. I'm still young, but it's not hard to see what a pipedream it all was. Strong and free with our futures ahead of us, we never imagined it could all come crashing down in such an ugly way! So much has changed since those days. I can scarcely wrap my mind around it.

Her father's voice startled her. "Scarlett. I'm about to whip up some pancakes. Care to join me?"

"I'll be right up, Dad." It was something of a family tradition. A day or two before Christmas, her father always made pancakes for the family. Though she didn't much feel like it, Scarlett didn't want to disappoint.

After breakfast and a little lounging about the house while sipping another cup of coffee, she showered and decided a walk in the fresh snow was what she needed most. Pulling on snow boots before grabbing a heavy coat and knit scarf, Scarlett ventured out in the new snow. Outside, she peered into a gray sky filled with one-inch flakes lazily drifting to earth. Breathing deep of the crisp, sparkling air, her button nose crinkled at the cold.

Stepping onto the sidewalk and testing for traction, she found it slick but manageable. Then, kicking up the snow like a young pup, Scarlett relished the rare heavy snowfall. The fresh air was invigorating. *I can do this. I can move on and leave all this college crap behind! It happened in another lifetime. One I have no use for now.*

Descending the hill that would take her to a viewpoint over Lake Washington, Scarlett half-skated down the sidewalk. She didn't care much for her parents' home on Mercer Island, but when dad hit it big financially, this was the place to be, and her parents never missed out on the latest trend.

Scarlett stretched out her long legs at the bottom of the hill. The three-quarter mile hike to the beach on Lake Washington, opposite Seward Park, was covered with untracked snow. Like kicking up leaves in the fall, Scarlett crunched through the snow with a cloud of exhaled air following close behind.

The snow-covered beach on Lake Washington was empty, and Scarlett eased into a leisurely stroll along the water's edge. Shallow waves lapped at the shoreline, touching the air with the only resonance in the snow-hushed environment. She loved these rare moments deep in the city. Surrounded by millions, there wasn't a single sound but the sounds of nature.

Strolling to the end of the beach, she stopped and stood in the same spot where Jack had held her in his arms before brushing snow from her wet hair and passionately kissing her. Then he'd jumped back and danced a sailor's jig before playing air guitar to some tune only he knew.

She'd laughed out loud when he told her that's what her kiss did to him. It was an enchanting moment, but from her present vantage point, a future without him looked like a disaster. *Maybe they were right about you, but Jack, I wish you were here to dance a jig for me now.*

The thought momentarily lifted her spirits. *That's life. It was a sweet and wonderful instance God blessed me with. There will be more. God has a plan for your life, Scarlett.*

Her stride took on an extra bounce all the way home. There really could be life after Jack. *The bastard.* She couldn't help herself.

Approaching her parent's house, she stopped for a moment to take it in. Surrounded by cedars and other evergreen trees, it was beautiful when snow-covered. The solitary string of lights her father always hung along the eaves burned brightly. Compelled by the neighbor's colorful holiday displays, she knew he would have never put them up without the peer pressure. Still, she enjoyed the look of the entire neighborhood.

Reluctant to go inside, she brushed back ringlets of red from her face and breathed deeply. Working to muster the strength required to deal with her parents on this night of entertaining, she sighed and braced for the challenge.

Entering the front door, she heard the familiar voice of Bing Crosby singing White Christmas. In the kitchen, her mother wore the red, green, and white apron she always wore at Christmas, and the smell of turkey cooking in the oven filled the home. As a family, they always had their Christmas dinner two days before Christmas since there were office parties to attend on Christmas Eve and sometimes on Christmas night.

"Where have you been? I've been so worried."

"Mom, I told you…"

"Don't track in that snow. I've spent my entire day cleaning. Don't you know the Martins are coming over for dinner? Now get those wet clothes off and come set the table."

Scarlett sighed. Her parents put her up and paid the bills, and for that, she was thankful, but living at home was suffocating. Her mood deflated.

Later that evening, Scarlett excused herself from dinner as soon as it was polite to do so. The Martins were decent enough company compared to most of the high-brow types Dad brought home, but Scarlett needed to breathe.

Escaping to her refuge in the basement, she retrieved her journal before deciding to step outside for a quick smoke. Telling herself she needed to relax, she removed a pipe from behind a loose brick in the fireplace and stepped outside into the quiet evening. Jack had given the pipe to her as a birthday gift. She fired up a small piece of hash she kept for emergencies like these and leaned back against the side of the house.

This isn't like you, Scarlett. You swore you were giving it up.

I will. It's just a little help until I get through this.

After a peaceful calm settled over her, she stepped back inside. It was easier to let go now. Returning the pipe to its hidey hole behind the brick, she turned on the radio and settled on the couch with her journal.

I had the most wonderful afternoon walk in the snow. My trip to the beach was amazingly peaceful, and I felt much better about things until I returned home. I have to get out of my parent's house. I love them, but their life is not mine, and it brings me down to stay here. I had to have a quick smoke to settle my nerves.

My thoughts drift back to when Jack and I were sitting outside Ivar's, eating clam chowder and fish and chips while laughing at the coded language the workers use to call the orders back to the cook. I can smell the unique salty scent of the waterfront environment, hear the ever-present call of the gulls feeding on anything the tourists toss into the air, and touch on that joyful feeling of love. I was crazy in love with a romantic man, which couldn't have been more exhilarating. But what an illusion! Stupid girl!

I knew it was expensive for him. Neither of us had much money, but he always delighted in treating me. I loved it, and it made me feel special. He was spending money on me he would have to work extra hours for. I knew I was special to him and was enchanted by the joy I saw it bring to his gorgeous blue eyes.

We certainly had our differences. Like all couples, we had our ups and downs and split up many times. During one of those break-up fights, he made me so angry I was slamming my fists into his chest as hard as I could with every ounce of strength I could muster. He just stood there taking it, waiting for my tantrum to run its course and for me to settle down. That is until the moment I slugged him in the face. A left and a right! That set him off, but he didn't hurt me.

He never said a word but instantly grabbed my arms instead, just below the shoulder, picked me up, and tossed me onto the couch. Though I knew him well, his raw strength still surprised me. He was never violent towards me, but he did put an end to my tantrum that once. The quiet, surreptitious power he possessed both surprised and silenced me.

Much of what I miss is his six-foot-three-inch height and ropey, muscular build. I go crazy thinking another woman is wrapped in those strong arms, sharing in it.

He is a simple man who was easy to read, and I often teased him about it. He'd shrug and say, "I'm an honest man, and I have nothing to hide."Pretense was not his thing; I adore that about him, even if I could use it against him occasionally. Despite it all, he possessed a bit of an attitude that would spark from time to time. And I loved even that about him, although it did piss me off many times.

That attitude put off some of the girls who clambered for his attention. But for me, I embraced it as a part of the rebel he is, and for some crazy reason, I was drawn to it. I can't explain it. I was – still am. Lesson learned, stupid girl!

But that same rebel aspect of him is responsible for all this trouble and splitting us up. The guy possesses a steel core and refuses to chase after the crowd or follow the latest trend, always choosing to go his own way instead. I love that about him, but the same attitude can also take him down the wrong road. Jack is his own man through and through. I find that measure of independence hard to resist and even a little sexy.

Jack's always worn his hair long, sometimes in a ponytail, but most often loose. He would occasionally take me flying down the highways on the back of his Harley. I loved the carefree, sometimes bordering on reckless, attitude he embodied. Looking back, maybe I should have seen it as a warning.

It made the other girls jealous when I hugged him tight, and we roared off to destinations unknown. (Daddy would die if he knew any of this.) Even though my friends would never have dared to find themselves on the back of that bike, they still envied it. That's no brag! Some of them were honest enough to tell me just that.

The guy feels he's bulletproof. It's an attitude I found hard to deal with, and it's been the cause of many of our troubles. A pitcher of beer and a shot of whiskey, and in his mind, he's bulletproof. But he's not bulletproof, and the demons that tirelessly haunt him are going to destroy him someday. He doesn't seem capable, or possibly even willing, to deal with the things that torment him. When confronted, he always runs. It's the only thing the guy runs from. He's more afraid of himself than anything else.

Though he maintains the appearance of a rebel, over time, I realized it's all just a front to protect an extraordinarily tender heart. The man would literally give the shirt off his back, and I've seen him share his last couple of dollars with someone who needed it. But it's a heart so closely guarded you must first dig through the cracks in his leather jacket to even get a hint of what is at his core. Attempting to explore beneath the barrier he presents to the world is a long and complicated task, and I got lost in it. A process that seems to have cost me my own heart.

But he possesses that rugged look I find so attractive, and unfortunately, I got caught up in it. Of course, it drew other girls' attention, which was the basis of many of our fights. For the most part, though, few take the time to know him. They don't see the man I found wrapped away and so closely guarded inside the leathery shell surrounding his heart. That man, the one hidden away deep inside, is the man who has stolen my heart. I pray someday he comes back to me. Ha! What a delusion, Scarlett. Give it up!

He always treated me with such respect. The gentle demeanor, caring soul, and manners sealed the deal for me. But my parents only see the Harley, the hair, and the rough exterior. When they threw him out of the house that summer – "what would the neighbors think?" - Dad said. I was so embarrassed, and when his Harley's loud, angry sound faded into the distance, I never expected to see him again. And maybe it would have been best if I had not, for this wound I live with is not one that wants to heal.

Lord, we've been through so much together. I can't understand why this happened. We were so good together. Yet, I trust you, Father, that you know best.

I didn't see him for quite some time after my parents threw him out, but we got together again in the last few weeks of college.

He'd moved on, of course, and I never once heard from him after the incident with my parents. Never one to settle in one place for long, I wasn't surprised when he disappeared into his own dark world. But like I said, I knew the man's heart. He would be searching, searching for something he *wouldn't find outside of me. Yes, I believe that. Am I kidding myself? I wonder. Yet I feel it in my heart. Why, then, are we apart? I can't begin to explain.*

At times, I would catch a glimpse of him walking across campus or hear the roar of his Harley in the distance. Most of the time, he had another girl with him. That part wasn't surprising. The girls flocked to him but couldn't have known how little they meant to the guy if they'd understood him. He was an outlaw in many ways and only used them for his needs.

Even though I knew all of this about the man, to my dismay, it would stir me up inside every time I saw him. I was the one who couldn't move on, and frankly, I couldn't help but wonder what it would be like to be held in his arms again. Foolish me! Writing this, I look back and wonder how I could have been so blind.

Occasionally, we crossed paths at one party or another, but each time, either he was with someone, or I was. Still, I'd attempt to catch his eye, only to get his dead man's stare in return. It was a look I'd always hated but knew to respect. And I'd be lying if I said that one look in those steal blue eyes didn't spark the ember that still burns inside me.

I think to Jack, I'm just part of his past. I have a hard time accepting that. It's clear he hadn't settled down in any way and, if possible, is an even greater rogue now than before. And it makes me furious how this draws even more women to his side. What right do they have to a man they know nothing about? I understand him, I know what he needs, and I know the inner man. They only know the ponytailed guy in a leather jacket with the cool Harley! They don't see the man who endured frostbite and risked his life to rescue me from a wrecked car ready to explode. They don't know the man who saved me from freezing to death. Damn!! I guess I never mentioned that's how we met. He risked his life for me at a time when we didn't even know one another.

Scarlett paused and gazed outside. Her parents were upstairs, showing off for her father's company. *Geez, look at me. I've written pages. Maybe that's what happens when you're stoned. Oh well...*

As college came to an end, I couldn't bear to think of allowing all of this to pass and letting him walk out of my life without ever seeing him again. Even though I had no hope of getting back together, I couldn't sit by and allow him to slip away without trying to mend things one last time.

So, one night, after sharing a bottle of wine with my roommate, who swore I would always regret not getting in touch with him again, I decided to go to his apartment. Results be damned! Well, she was wrong! I should have stayed home and drank more wine instead.

I don't know how long I stood outside his apartment door, working up the courage the wine couldn't provide. His music was loud. Nothing new about that. Made loud to be played loud, he always said. As I stood outside his door listening, Alice Cooper sang, "Is it my body that makes you want to love me?"

Yes! NO! It's more than that. The song ended, and before I could get the nerve to knock on his door, Rod Stewart began singing, "I'd rather go blind than see you walk away from me." I hoped that was precisely how he felt about me and boldly knocked on his door.

Stepping back, I was overcome with the thought he would answer the door with some blond bombshell on his arm. I wanted to run but stood my ground instead. My heart was hammering in my chest when suddenly he turned down the music, and I knew he was about to answer my knock. It was now or never.

I swear my heart stopped momentarily when I heard him walking toward the door. It was all I could do to keep from running away. Yet I stood fast as if my feet were in concrete.

When he opened the door, I saw the illegal smile and lazy look in his eyes. I was not surprised to find he'd been smoking something unlawful. That's who he was, and I paid little attention to it. Because, I mean, come on, girls, the guy was shirtless, and the rippling muscles in his chest and broad shoulders stole my breath away. What pissed me off was he knew it!

I'd heard he'd been working out with his brother, a competitive weight lifter, and how they'd been running and training together. But still...He leaned against the door frame in an obviously practiced pose that almost made me laugh and brazenly looked me up and down. Honest, though, it didn't faze me because I knew he liked everything he saw from our previous relationship.

Knowing him like I did, there was little doubt he was purposefully trying to rattle me. That was Jack to a "T." But I understood this man too well to allow him to unnerve me like that, and I wasn't going to let him get to me. Though my heart raced, I refused to show any sign of being flustered. Seeing he couldn't rattle me, he flashed his most charming smile and invited me in.

We talked all night and covered a lot of ground. We put some issues to bed that needed to be dealt with and agreed to give things a go one more time. Our on-again-off-again relationship was back on, and we were back together one more time for the last few weeks of college.

Well, this is far more than I planned on writing. My apologies for rambling. The weed seems to have that effect on me. I think I already mentioned that. I feel better already, getting this out of my head. I've poured everything out tonight, probably more than I should have. I'm ready to move on now that I've gotten it out of me and into this little book. It's time to step out of this hole I'm in.

CHAPTER TWENTY ONE

SCARLETT SOFTLY CLOSED THE DOOR AND HURRIED FROM the man's office. Having just completed the interview for a job advertised as bookkeeper/secretary, she couldn't wait to get away. The burly man with the bushy salt and pepper eyebrows, balding skull, and big cigar owned and operated one of the largest construction companies in the Puget Sound area. The pay he offered was excellent, but the longer the meeting lasted, the more apparent it became something more would be expected from his new employee.

His black eyes roamed her body continually throughout the interview, always returning to settle on her chest. Scarlett avoided wearing dresses or skirts to interviews because her eye-catching legs were often distracting. Scarlett knew she was attractive, but using it to get a job was inviting trouble. The longer the meeting went on, the creepier it got.

Rushing from the man's office and rounding the corner to catch the seventh-floor elevator, she collided with a striking young man carrying a cup of coffee. The spilled coffee soaked the front of her white blouse and splashed onto the stranger's finely polished shoes.

"Oh! Excuse me. I'm so sorry." Scarlett cried.

A warm smile creased the man's face as he searched Scarlett's eyes. "Well, I'm not."

Scarlett noted how calm and unshaken he remained.

"I never regret running into a beautiful woman."

Scarlett felt her cheeks warm and realized she was blushing. His eyes remained on her face instead of peering at her coffee-stained chest. The man's gentlemanly manner was a welcome contrast to the situation she'd just come from.

He stuck out his hand. "Hello. My name is Donovan, and it looks like I owe you a new blouse." He paused, "Or at least a ride home if you need one?"

"Uh no, no thanks." She sputtered. "I'll be fine. I just need to get downstairs to my car." Scarlett struggled to gather her wits about her.

"Are you sure? Please take my jacket to cover yourself before going downstairs to the lobby."

Donovan shrugged out of his jacket and held it out while Scarlett ran her arms into the sleeves.

The handsome young man was charming as well.

Finally gathering herself, "Thank you. My name is Scarlett. How will I return your jacket?"

He smiled again, and his blue eyes sparkled. "I have more jackets, but my card is in the front pocket. Now, if you will, please excuse me. I believe I'm about to be late for my meeting."

He stuck out his hand again. It was warm and soft but in a manly sort of way. "It was nice meeting you."

With that, he picked up his briefcase and disappeared around the corner.

Riding the elevator to the ground floor, Scarlett reviewed what had just happened. *Not creepy at all. Attractive, friendly. Quite the gentleman.*

She couldn't quit thinking about what happened during her drive home. The dark hair and square jaw line kept running through her mind.

She wrestled with her thoughts all the way home and soon forgot about his jacket after hanging it in her closet. A family birthday gathering and more interviews to attend quickly stole her attention. A few days later, in the still of a sleepless late night, Scarlett took to her journal again. Maybe getting some of the stuff swimming around in her head down on paper would help her get some sleep.

Those last few days together at school, we took his Harley on some long rides into the mountains in Idaho, and to be honest, we spent a few nights together. But it wasn't the same. Like they say, you can never go back. It's surprising just how much truth there is in that statement, and I soon began feeling like one of the other women I had seen him with.

Before school was out, we spent a few days together on the Oregon coast. It couldn't have been a more beautiful time. I have a photograph of him standing atop a sand dune there, and it still gives me chills. So wild, untamed, and handsome. Free of the shackles of school and liberated to do whatever we wanted, I couldn't help but think back to the times we first shared in Seattle.

During this last trip to the coast, I saw a side of him I'd never noticed before. It both hurt me and drew me closer to him. I knew better, but I was falling in love all over again. Stupid girl! I should have known better.

Like I said before, a part of him was so very restless. It both put me off and drew me to him. What kept the guy from settling down? He felt bound, was disillusioned with school (Oh, how I can relate to that!), and wondered if there wasn't something more. 'Is there life out there?' I remember him saying. he felt trapped in a world not of his making and was screaming for a way out.

I think the rebel side of him that I so love felt imprisoned. The rules, demands, orders, and everything else that stole his freedom fueled a need in him to be released and set free. I couldn't understand it then, though I certainly do now.

He made it clear during a walk on the beach that there would be no relationship. It crushed me. It was the second time he'd broken my heart, and I felt so stupid, so foolish. I should have known better.

We made love that night, and I knew then it would be the last time. He seemed detached, or maybe it was me, but I knew things would never be the same between us again. It all felt so empty.

Tonight, my heart aches miserably, like never before. No human is equipped to deal with the indescribable bleakness residing inside me. I know I got lost in the man, and God can't be too pleased with me. More than Jack, I've lost my way, and righting myself amidst this storm without the Lord is next to impossible. I should know better than to try to do this without Him.

After returning from our trip to the coast, we saw each other one last time before he left town. It was right after school got out. He asked me to pick up some of my things, so I went to his place before going out for a last dinner together. While gathering up my belongings, I came across an unopened letter resting atop his dresser, buried amongst some bills and other mail. I don't know what possessed me to take it, but I quickly hid it in the bottom of my bag and have it with me now. The writing was clearly a woman's, but the return address included no last name and simply said Susan. Why he hadn't opened it yet, I don't know. But I wanted to know if he had been seeing another woman at the same time we dated.

Anyway, we shared a couple of drinks over dinner while reflecting on the past and wishing one another well in the future. It was quite a pleasant evening together, and I remember it fondly.

At one point that evening, after the small talk, he reached across the table and gently took my hands in paws stained by grease and oil from working on his bike. I knew what was coming but sat quietly and let him have his say.

He had no plan for his life and explained how he would ride until he was tired of riding. Though I knew there was no future with him after our coast trip. I still couldn't hold back the tears.

He was kind and full of patience for me and attempted to make it all as easy as possible. That part made me mad. How could he be so gentle, so compassionate, and still walk away?

Our goodbye was about as dry, hollow, and cold as it could be. I'd allowed myself to be drawn in and hope for something that wasn't possible. Jack had no idea what the future would bring and said that was part of the adventure and the thrill of it all. And because of that, he couldn't be tied to anyone or anything.

He was both tender and honest with me but was clueless when it came to how much he'd hurt me. He said he might send a postcard sometime when I inquired about staying in touch. Really? After all, we had shared, was that all I was worth to him? A lousy postcard!

After saving me from my drug-dealing boyfriend (Oh, I guess I haven't mentioned that story, have I. It was the last time I saw him.) and kissing me goodbye, I stood there like a fool, fighting back the tears. I felt so alone and abandoned watching him leave and roar away without so much as a wave goodbye.

The cops did buy my story about a drug deal gone bad. It seems they won't be after him, but I can't say the same for Johnnie's friends, who showed up looking for the money he owed them.

Johnny was a guy I've known throughout college, and I took up with him after Jack and I split. We'd grown on each other over the years, and the growth of our relationship felt natural. In hindsight, I was stupid to take up with the guy and should have known better. It was just a weak moment in my life.

Moving forward, that's a part of me that will change. If there's one thing I learned from Jack, it's to be my own person and not be afraid to stand out from the crowd while standing on my own two feet. I had all sorts of examples growing up while working on the farms around here, and it's time I grow up!

This has been a painful time of writing, but strangely, I feel better now. At least I've gotten some of it out of my system, even if I've wasted much of the night pouring out my lament. Maybe I can move on now. I guess a diary might serve some purpose after all. Tomorrow is a new day. I'm turning my back on the past, including you, Jack! You SOB! It's time to get on with my life, and I'll be watching out for number one, just like you! Things can only get better from here. Right?

CHAPTER TWENTY TWO

SCARLETT QUICKLY GREW TIRED OF THE ENDLESS INTERviews for what, in most cases, were dead-end jobs. She had already begun preparing for her real estate license, which was suggested by her father, but had yet to take it seriously. Frustrated after her last interview, Scarlett decided real estate might be the way to go and began working hard toward obtaining her license. In the meantime, she considered which real estate company would be a good fit.

The evening after passing the exam, her father hosted a small neighborhood party to celebrate her accomplishment. She knew he was trying to build her confidence and help lift her spirits, and she appreciated all he did. But she also understood his ego was the likely motivation.

Eventually, she got on at one of Seattle's better real estate offices. She seemed to have a knack for the business and had soon made three sales. The people in her office were encouraging, telling her that even two sales are a lot for a beginner just starting out.

At work, a wonderful older gentleman befriended her and began teaching her the ins and outs of real estate. She welcomed his mentoring, embracing the experience he represented. It was primarily through him that she accomplished her sales. His name was Charlie, and he was preparing to retire in the next few months. His positive attitude and encouragement helped instill some of the confidence Scarlett lost at school and the disastrous way it ended.

Charlie told her she had what it takes. *Whatever that was.* She thought, but the support and kind words were welcome. Charlie said her easygoing manner and the fact that she wasn't pushy and seemed to care about the people as much as the sales made people comfortable and helped to develop trust. Before long, he began sending more and more of his clients her way, and she gained a lot of listings as a result.

Charlie reminded her of Charlie Chaplin. He wore tweed pants with black suspenders and a dress shirt every day. His white hair was thinning, but he was not yet bald. She found his little dark eyes nestled beneath bushy white eyebrows to be quite cute. Charlie was easy to be around, and Scarlett enjoyed spending time in his company.

Still living at home, she began forming a plan to buy a place of her own without her parent's help and bankrolled the money she made in hopes of moving out within the year. Through work, she met people her age and began going out on the town. Scarlett was beginning to feel alive again. It felt good, and she decided it was time to live a little. She'd been through enough, and it was time for some fun!

Outside of work, Scarlett let her hair down. *You only live once!* The side of her she kept bottled up at college in exchange for good grades demanded to be set free. *It's time I added a little excitement to my life! Sounds like Jack.* She told herself. *Don't remind me.*

Big city life was different, and she was soon fully immersed in it. The parties, the drugs, the guys! She found it to be a way of letting go, blotting out the past, and moving on to a new life of her own.

February 15, 1976

So what's wrong with having a little fun for a change? I worked hard and lived a straight life in college. I followed all those stupid rules, and what did it get me? A hole in my heart and a silly piece of paper they call a degree. Worthless! So I'm just going to hang loose and enjoy life for a while. What harm can it do, especially compared to "Miss Prim and Proper," I was a total loser! If living life right brings no rewards, then what the heck? I'm gonna have some fun living life my way. I think I deserve that much.

March 1, 1976

Recently, I've been spending time getting to know Donovan. Remember, he was the guy who spilled coffee down the front of me when I ran into him in the Smith Tower after rushing out of that terrible interview. I was surprised to find out he works in the same real estate office where I work. Our relationship, if you can call it that, has been quite casual and business-like. But this last week, we kind of hit it off.

His blue eyes and endearing smile make it easy to forget about Jack. Some of the older guys at work, including Charlie, don't care much for him. They say he's too slick and moves too fast. "Just another hot shot," Charlie scoffed and made a point of warning me, "He's not good for you, Scarlett." Charlie has taken me aside and cautioned me about getting involved with him. Maybe Charlie's age is catching up to him because I don't see it.

Donovan dresses in finely tailored suits and always looks impeccable. His dark hair is professionally cut, and his black mustache is perfectly trimmed. He's tall, trim, and fit. The fact a man like him has taken an interest in me is nice. I guess I needed a boost in confidence more than I thought.

He's talented, successful, and handsome as can be; he could have almost any woman he wants, and many of them at the party we attended last night made their play for him. The fact he drives a red convertible Corvette doesn't hurt either, and he promised to take me for a ride in it soon.

I find it easy to be comfortable around Donovan. It's nice to be appreciated and treated special again. Being the new girl in town, I can't help but think it's a passing fancy, but I hope not because, to be honest, I slept with him this weekend. Damn!

His family has a cabin in the foothills of the Cascades, and this last week, a bunch of his friends and a few people from our office spent five days there. I'm not sure I would have gone if I'd known what a wild scene it would be—not giving any details other than it was five days of drugs, alcohol, and sex. I've never seen anything like it and feel guilty for enjoying myself so much. But why? I lived a straight life, and it turned into shit. I won't feel guilty about living the way I think is best for me.

March 23, 1976

It's been a couple of weeks now since the bash at the cabin, and Donovan and I have begun seeing each other regularly. Last night, he took me to the top of the space needle for the most beautiful date ever! He'd made reservations, and after we were seated, the waiter brought out a dozen red roses Donovan had prepared just for me. We shared the most romantic evening, and I didn't get home until after three in the morning. I hope my parents didn't hear me stumble in—a definite downside to living at home.

CHAPTER TWENTY THREE

AS THE WEEKS PASSED, SCARLETT FOUND DONOVAN MORE and more to her liking. They shared expensive wine from his collection, nights together on the town, and Donovan's bed. Her parents grew suspicious and wanted to meet the man she spent so much time with.

"I hope to hell he's not another rabid long-hair like the last guy you brought home. Whatever got you wrapped up with…"

"Dad, enough." Scarlett held up a hand to silence him. "We've been over that one too many times." Then, smiling sweetly, she leaned in to kiss him on the cheek. "You're going to like Donovan. I promise."

"Donovan, huh? He'd better not be like that glassy-eyed, dope-smoking beatnik singer everybody's so crazy about."

"Daaaaad! You'll see. I'll bring him by soon."

A month later, in early June, Donovan's red Corvette rolled up in front of Scarlett's home. The top was down, and a laughing Scarlett leaned over to pound on the horn to get her parents to come out of the house. Soon, both of them appeared on the front porch, wondering what all the commotion was about.

Scarlett swept both hands through her wind-blown hair, attempting to bring some order to the red blend of locks, before stepping out of the car. Careful to hide the new diamond ring adorning her left hand, she hugged her mother and smooched her father on the cheek.

Donovan rounded the front of his car to stand next to Scarlett.

"Mom, Dad, this is Donovan."

After shaking hands, Scarlett's father began to go on about the car.

"This is yours?"

"Yes, Sir."

"Probably a big payment, huh?"

"Dad!"

"That's alright, Scarlett. He can ask anything he wants."

Then, turning back to her parents, "Actually, Sir, it's paid for in full."

"Well, you must be quite successful. Scarlett tells me you both work in the same real estate office."

"Yes, Sir, we do."

Scarlett's father continued walking around the car, appraising it, but Scarlett knew he was taking the time to appraise Donovan. She knew his polo shirt, boat shoes, and striking dark features would impress, and she breathed deep, preparing to share one more surprise.

"You don't own any motorcycles, do you?" Her father asked.

Scarlett grew impatient but needed 'Dad' to grow comfortable with this man.

Donovan smiled. "No, Sir. I've never even been on one."

Handled like the pro he is. She smiled.

Scarlett knew that was the final check, and soon, her father was inviting them inside.

They gathered in the living room around cups of coffee and polite conversation. Scarlett's father probed further, wondering how his daughter landed this gem. He was clean-cut, courteous, and well-established in the real estate world. The neighbors would be most impressed, and he had already grown anxious to hear their inquiries about the red Corvette parked in front of his house.

Donovan was patient, allowing her parents to ask questions and grow comfortable with him.

"Well, Donovan, it appears I've been doing all the talking, so is there anything you'd like to ask of us?"

"Yes, Sir, there is one question I have been wanting to ask you."

"Certainly. What would you like to know?"

"I'd like to ask for your daughter's hand in marriage."

Scarlett played the next card by holding out her hand and showing off the colossal diamond on her finger. Her father didn't even answer the question. Instead, he rose to his feet and announced,

"This calls for a celebration."

Drinks were poured, and food was ordered in. When the afternoon turned to evening, Scarlett's parents embraced their soon-to-be son-in-law as they prepared to leave.

Donovan said he would run out and put the top up before returning for Scarlett.

"Little different send-off than the last fella you brought home."

"Enough, Dad. That's old history, and I don't want to hear about it anymore."

"Agreed. Scarlett, you've done well for yourself, just like I always knew you would. Well worth the price of us running off the last ruffian you brought home."

She held a finger to her lips and shook her head. "That's the last I want to hear of Jack! Agreed?"

Grinning ear to ear. "Who?"

Donovan returned, took Scarlett's arm, and walked her to the car. After turning the car around, he honked goodbye to Scarlett's waving parents. They were standing in the yard near the same spot where she had once tackled Jack in the snow. *Why did that come to mind? She asked herself.*

To her father's delight, Donovan honked one last time. It would draw even more attention.

"Whew. What an evening. Can we just go to your place and crash? I'm drained."

Donovan smiled devilishly. "Of course, but I'm betting I can wake you up." His mischievous smile brought a slight blush to Scarlett's face.

"If my parents knew."

"I think they do. And your Dad is good with it."

She turned to face him with a puzzled look. "Seriously?"

Donovan shrugged. "And he even gives his approval."

CHAPTER TWENTY FOUR

SCARLETT AND DONOVAN BEGAN MAKING PLANS FOR A September wedding.

"Honey, don't you think this is a little fast? He's a nice man, but you've only known him a short time." Scarlett's mother expressed concern.

But Scarlett knew it had more to do with the money needed for their wedding plans than her marriage. Protests from Scarlett's parents about the cost of what they wanted to do and how soon they wanted to do it were put to rest when Donovan offered to pay for it all one evening.

After accepting the drinks her father offered, Scarlett and Donovan excused themselves, saying they had some things to discuss.

"Dinner will be ready in about twenty minutes." Scarlett's mother yelled from the kitchen.

"We'll just be downstairs, Mom."

Situated on the couch, Donovan leaned over.

"Daddy's money does come in handy occasionally,"

Scarlett had a glow about her Donovan believed was worth every penny.

"You've told me about your father's money and how you try not to abuse the privilege of its availability."

"I try to show restraint and, with it, respect. That way, he doesn't feel like I'm taking advantage, which I'm not, so when things like this come up, I feel comfortable asking him to help."

"Things like this?" Scarlett's eyebrows inquired.

"I'm sorry. It's something I don't like to talk about. I was briefly married once before. We both agreed it was a mistake and parted amicably after less than one year."

"When was this?"

"A couple years ago." The realization put a damper on Scarlett's enthusiasm.

"Relax, Scarlett. We were young and rushed into a blunder neither of us will make again."

He reached up and took hold of her chin, turning her face toward him so he could look into her emerald-green eyes. "I love you. I'll be with you always."

The months flew by as their plans came together, and the day of the September wedding was quickly upon them. Donovan's father used his money and influence to rent the Space Needle for one night. The entire rotating floor atop the Space Needle was prepared for the wedding celebration, except for a private room where the newlywed couple would spend their first night.

When Scarlett's parents arrived, they were shocked to find the Space Needle was reserved just for Scarlett and the wedding party.

"The neighbors will never believe this." Her father exclaimed.

The ceremony went off without a hitch, and when "You may kiss the bride" was announced, Donovan kissed her deep and whispered. "You're the most beautiful thing to ever happen to me. I love you, Scarlett."

The party might have lasted all night, but Donovan's friends were prepared to usher everyone out by midnight. When the last elevator descended with the final group of attendees, Donovan took Scarlett by the hand to a room specially prepared for their wedding night.

After entering the bedroom chambers, he asked Scarlett to close her eyes and remain standing. She could hear the clatter of something moving before all grew quiet.

Then she felt his arms come around her from behind and his champagne-tainted breath whisper. "Open your eyes."

Scarlett was stunned. Donovan had rolled back a partition, making up one entire wall at the end of their room. The view of Puget Sound and the city lights from their bedroom was breathtaking.

"I hope this sight from your bedroom on the first night of our marriage is something you will always remember."

"I'm sure I will." She turned to face him and felt his lips brush her own.

The following afternoon, the newlyweds boarded a plane for Paris. Their honeymoon on the French Riviera lasted nearly a month. Scarlett didn't want to leave, but they both had jobs and responsibilities to return to.

"I could live like this forever, Donovan. Free to wander Europe, sleep in each morning, make love to you, and enjoy this wonderful French coffee every single day!"

"But you would soon grow bored, my dear. Part of what makes it so special is knowing it must come to an end."

"One more trip to the Swiss Alps." Scarlett threw her leg over his and pulled herself close against his back. "One more time?"

He turned back to face her, working his eyebrows up and down. "One more time, she demands." His smile was devilish and taunting. "Of course, my dear. One more time." He sighed.

"As if it was some kind of chore." She giggled. "Then we go to the Swiss Alps.?"

The couple returned home to Seattle and Donovan's mansion four days later. Well, it was a mansion to Scarlett anyway. A well-appointed home, situated lakeside on ten timbered acres.

She had to pinch herself to believe it was real and wondered at her good fortune. Standing before a full-length mirror, toweling off after her shower, she took a moment to admire the gorgeous flaming red hair, highlighting brilliant green eyes and the scattering of freckles across her nose. She told herself she deserved all of this. The perfectly appointed kitchen, lake view, and peaceful quiet were all meant just for her. Jack was in the rearview mirror, barely an afterthought. *As if he could have given me this!* She deserved it all, she told herself again, and Donovan was the perfect treasure who brought it all to life.

CHAPTER TWENTY FIVE

EIGHT SHORT MONTHS AFTER THE WEDDING, EVERYTHING changed. The Seattle rains held off for a day, and the sunny May weather, highlighting yellow, red, and purple flowers, was striking. Scarlett scarcely noticed.

After taking time off for a funeral and family and friends, she found herself standing graveside. When the reverend concluded with his final words, "May she be welcomed into heaven with the rest of the saints and patiently wait for us to join her."

The comment stirred Scarlett, causing her to reflect on her life's direction. It provoked thoughts in a way she didn't care to consider. Once close to the Lord, speaking to and walking with him daily, Scarlett was forced to acknowledge how far away she had drifted. Donovan was not a believer, and the cold reality was that the luxuries he provided, usurped the relationship she once had with her Savior.

Shaken from her revelry by the touch of a warm hand, she looked into the eyes of the deceased's sister. "You know she loved you dearly. I can't recall how long she babysat you as a little child and later when you sometimes came home from grade school to an empty house, but I know you were special to her. Thank you so much for coming here today, Scarlett."

Scarlett's mother appeared beside her and took her arm. "She was a special person and a good influence on you."

"She was good to me, Mom. I always looked forward to spending time with her."

"I wish your father would have come, but he hates funerals."

"That's because he doesn't know the Lord, Mom."

"Well, I'm not so sure about that. He's a very busy man, you know."

Scarlett shook her head. "He hates funerals because he doesn't know the Lord and is afraid of dying."

"He believes in his own way."

Scarlett glared. It was a look her fiery red hair enhanced. "Sorry, Mom, but you have to quit making excuses for him. If he doesn't come to the Lord, he will find that 'his own way' doesn't do much for him in hell."

Scarlett's Mom gasped. When she started to say something in his defense, Scarlett interrupted.

"Save it, Mom. I've heard it all before. You know, I think I'll head home a day early. There are some things I need to think about, and a little downtime with Donovan will be good for me."

"Are you sure? Dad will miss having another day with you around."

"I'll tell him goodbye when I pick up my bags."

The funeral put a new perspective on things for Scarlett, who rummaged through the mountain of thoughts swirling in her head on the drive back from the funeral. Her partying lifestyle, the drugs, the men, and her prideful, self-serving desire for money suddenly came into sharp focus. *You live, you die, and what have you done with your life, Scarlett? Fifty years from now, no one will remember you. Billions have come before you, and no one remembers them.*

"*Let not the rich man glory in his riches.*" The scripture reverberated in her mind.

"What?" The voice was so clear and strong that she jumped, thinking someone was in the back seat.

Looking in the mirror, then turning around, she saw no one. Speaking out loud as if to reassure herself. "Where did that come from?"

All the expectations that came with chasing after the things of the world had taken her further away from the Lord than she had ever been. The funeral brought everything into focus.

How have I allowed this to happen, and what do I do now?

The freeway traffic stalled, and her thoughts piled up, but the accusing voices continued. Hanging her head in prayer, Scarlett suddenly saw the reality of what her life had become with great clarity.

Like the prodigal son, she'd wandered away, partaking of everything the world had to offer. And in the process, she'd deceived herself. *Lord, can you forgive me? I've strayed so far. Things are going to change when I get home. I promise. This is the beginning of a new day.*

Scarlett grew excited about spending some time with Donovan. They rarely made time away from all the distractions, spending less and less time with one another. The closer she got to home, the more eager she grew to see him. She would gently broach the subject of making some of the changes she knew needed to happen. He would be reluctant, but she had to start somewhere.

Arriving home, she eased down the long blacktop driveway surrounded by towering evergreen trees. Scarlett sighed, taking stock of the well-manicured landscape, the two-story four thousand-square foot home on ten acres of lakefront property north of Seattle.

I've been blessed and haven't even noticed. Lord, I promise not to take it for granted any longer.

It was so good to come home to a safe, comfortable place where someone loved and cherished her. The realization of how blessed she was brought tears, and her heart overflowed with thanksgiving.

Easing through the front door, Scarlett paused at the sound of soft music. The comfort of home and being welcomed by a loving husband nearly brought her to tears. Wrapped up in a sensation of love and filled with the anticipation of surprising Donovan with a big kiss, Scarlett stepped around the corner of the foyer and into the kitchen.

There, she came face to face with Donovan, standing in the kitchen, dressed only in boxer shorts. He was beside the stove frying bacon while a naked woman, attired only in black panties, hung on his shoulder, feeding him buttered toast. The two were so engaged with one another they didn't hear Scarlett's approach, but she overheard every word between the two of them.

The well-endowed stranger snuggled close and rubbed herself against Donovan's chest, cooing, "I'll fry your bacon if you'll butter my…"

"THAT'S ENOUGH!" Scarlett yelled through her tears. "Donovan, how could you!"

A startled Donavan dropped the pan, and the bacon grease caught fire on the stove. Briefly glancing over his shoulder before rushing for a wet towel to extinguish the fire, "Scarlett! You weren't supposed to be back until…"

"Sorry to disappoint you, but don't worry, I'm leaving! For Good! I sure hope getting your bacon fried by this bitch is worth all I'm going to take you for! And when your money is gone, and there's nothing left but the fat from the pig you are, she won't want you either!

"Scarlett, please." He hurried to extinguish the fire before following her to the bedroom, where she found the bed covers in disarray. "Let's talk about this."

"Get away from me!"

Scarlett slammed the door in his face and refused to speak with him. Throwing together a single bag, she flung the door back open and stormed past him.

"Don't try to get in touch with me. I'm never speaking to you again. My attorney will be the only one you'll be speaking with." Then, pointing towards the girl coming to Donovan's side, "And maybe bacon face over there if she's as dumb as she looks. Goodbye!"

Enraged, she stomped out the door. Scarlett's flaming red hair burned brighter than ever. Her green laser stare could have sliced through marble – or killed somebody.

Donovan backed away.

Squealing away in their newly restored red 65 Mustang, Scarlett wondered where to go and what to do now. A few miles down the two-lane county road, she pulled to the side and gave license to the tears bursting from her eyes.

"He betrayed me." She whimpered and sobbed before slamming both fists against the steering wheel.

Like you betrayed yourself and your faith. The accusing voice was back again.

Oh, shut up. I don't need that right now.

Scarlett slumped in her seat and spent the next twenty minutes parked under the heavy bows of a giant cedar tree, trying to collect herself. When her sobs subsided, her thoughts began to clear. There was no denying how far she had strayed.

"Lord, have mercy on me. I've fallen so far." She whispered. Before she could stop them, her thoughts drifted to Jack. She cursed him, beat on the steering wheel again, and screamed. Then she thought of Charlie.

"Oh, Charlie, you warned me. How could I have been so stupid? I was so deceived!"

More sobs shook her shoulders, and she fell back in the seat. Then, the thoughts of Charlie began to settle her nerves. She wiped her eyes and brushed away the fallen ruby colored curls hanging on her face.

Charlie will put me up for a night or two. I'm sure it will be alright. I just need a couple of days to pull myself together and make a plan.

When she arrived unannounced at Charlie's front door, he welcomed her with open arms. After inviting her in and patently listening while Scarlett shared with him what happened, Charlie and his wife offered comforting warmth, supportive counsel, and a shoulder to cry on. The smell of bread cooking in the oven didn't hurt either.

After dinner, some hot cocoa, and Charlie's encouraging words, Scarlett cried herself to sleep, snuggled beneath a thick comforter, and woke the next morning to the enticing smell of fresh coffee. Rubbing the sleep from her eyes and stumbling into the kitchen in flannel pajamas, she hugged Charlie and his wife. "I can't thank you enough. I panicked and needed a place to land to gather my thoughts. You've been so kind."

"Say nothing of it. I suggest you take the day off from work while I go in and see what things are like in the office."

"You'd do that for me? Oh, Charlie, you're so sweet. It's a great idea and will give me time to get the ball rolling with my attorney."

When Charlie returned from work that evening, he gave a quick report. "Was probably a good idea you stayed home. Donovan looked pretty rough like he hadn't slept much."

"Yeah, I can only imagine why."

"Scarlett, you need to let go of your anger. As tough as that might be, it won't help you move forward."

Scarlett nodded. "I know you're right. I'll do my best."

The next day, she found working in the same office as Donovan nearly impossible. After moving her desk to a corner of the office as far from him as possible, she refused to speak with him, though he attempted to do so numerous times. On the drive back to Charlie's that evening, she entertained thoughts of quitting.

A few days later, Scarlett thanked Charlie and his wife for letting her stay with them and moved into a one-bedroom apartment. Formulating a plan to escape her current situation brought with it a measure of peace. All that was left to do was to make it happen.

Then, one night after working late, Donovan was waiting for her in the parking garage. Cornering Scarlett between her car and the garage wall, he shook her by the shoulders and threatened consequences if she didn't back off.

"You get your attorney off my back, or something bad might happen to you."

"Let go of me, Donovan. I'll scream rape. It will only make my case against you stronger." The look in his eyes told her the man was prepared to kill. But the fire burning inside Scarlett disguised her fear in the blaze of green eyes. "Now let go."

The moment he released his grip, Scarlett kicked him in the groin with all her strength. How dare he threaten her!

He doubled over, trying to catch his breath.

"Go home to that slut who cooks your bacon because, by the time I'm done with you, it will be a long time before you eat bacon again unless it's your daddies. And what woman will want anything to do with you after the money's gone!"

"Scaaarlett!" He groaned.

"Get away from me!"

"We can work this out."

He called out again as she backed the car away.

A few days later, Scarlet turned in her resignation. She couldn't get Donovan off her mind and no longer felt safe around the man. There was no way sharing the same office with him could work.

Her attorney was confident of her case and told her it was just a matter of time. She informed him she was leaving town but would stay in touch. Scarlett didn't have much of a plan other than to get away, as far from Donovan as possible, and spend some time alone, putting her life back together. And it had to be somewhere he couldn't find her. He was not safe to be around, and there was just too much she had to work out for him to be near.

A few days later, after abandoning Donovan's Mustang at the side of the road, Scarlett walked across the street to a nearby used car lot. She knew exactly what she wanted. A Chevy van would fit her needs perfectly. There were two of them on the lot. One was three years old and the other two years old, but the two-year-old model had more miles on it.

She considered trading in the Mustang but quickly tossed the idea aside because the title was in Donovan's' name. After some haggling over the price, she used the money she'd once set aside to buy a house and purchased the three-year-old Chevy van. It was a plain tan color, equipped with a tiny kitchen, a bed, a fantastic sound system, no toilet, and some lovely hippie paintings on the sides.

Scarlett paid cash, cranked up the lone cassette tape left in the vehicle, and Cracklin Rose by Neil Diamond boomed from the speakers. *They must have left it behind because they no longer wanted it. I can't say I blame them.*

Leaving the parking lot, a sudden feeling of freedom overwhelmed her. The open road beckoned, much like it once had while riding with Jack on the back of his Harley. She would swing by her apartment, grab the few things she still owned, and head out. She didn't know where, but it didn't matter at the moment.

After returning to her apartment, she quickly picked up the place, but a thorough cleaning wasn't happening. She'd already agreed to let the landlord have her deposit and one month's rent so she could get out of the rental agreement.

While packing her things, she came across the letter lifted from atop Jack's dresser many months before. Having forgotten all about it, she couldn't help but wonder why it surfaced now and why she'd never opened it. Settling in with a second glass of red wine, she looked at the writing across the front of the envelope. Clearly, a woman's handwriting. A warm flush of blood-colored her face as she tore open the letter and immediately wished she hadn't.

Jack,

I've been trying to reach you, but you won't answer your phone, so I'm just going to say this straight out...I'm pregnant with your child. Don't you dare run off and leave me. I can't do this alone and need your support. You need to be here caring for me and your child. We can work things out. Please, Jack, don't run out on me now.

Scarlett's hands dropped into her lap. *Seriously. I have to read this about you now. You must have had quite the laugh at my expense. You played me for the perfect fool, just like Donovan, didn't you? Good Lord, are there any good men left in the world?*

She reached for her glass of wine and drained it, the red liquid brightening her neck and cheeks as her anger grew. *What next? Lord, I know what you're doing. You're telling me straight up to let go of my dreams of somehow getting back together with him. Message received, loud and clear! Thank you.*

Scarlett tossed the letter aside. She'd sworn off Jack once before and wouldn't be getting involved with this. Then, as if possessed of a mind of its own, her hand cautiously returned to the letter, picked up the envelope, and turned it over. After reading the return address, she knew instantly what she would do.

The following day, she loaded the van and pulled out her map to check the route north. She would head up I-5 towards Lynnwood and turn off on Highway 523 to Bothel before continuing northeast on 522 to a little town called Monroe. Vaguely recalling the area from her childhood, Monroe sat in the foothills of the North Cascades, where the wilderness and all its wild country were just steps away.

CHAPTER TWENTY SIX

SCARLETT WAS SURPRISED AT HOW GOOD IT FELT TO BE ON the road. There was little traffic, and the freedom of the highway soothed and summoned. After passing through Bothel, doubts about what she was about to do crept in, corrupting the good feelings that filled her earlier.

She wondered what she was doing as the dashed white lines slipped by. Visiting a woman she didn't know, about something that was none of her business was out of character. Yet somehow, the connection they shared with Jack was drawing them together. At times, it felt like the dumbest thing she had ever done, yet the closer she got, the stronger the bond grew, and she made up her mind to go through with it regardless of the outcome.

Easily locating the address in the small town of Monroe, Scarlett pulled up in front of a dilapidated old house with peeling paint and one shutter hanging from its hinge. The unmowed lawn, overgrown flower beds, and the door to the curbside mailbox standing open contributed to the ramshackle sense of the place. No car was in the driveway, and the windows were shuttered with poorly hung beige curtains. Scarlett wondered if anyone still lived there.

Stealing herself with courage while brushing out her hair, Scarlett's heart filled with compassion. If the poor woman did live here, she was not exaggerating her need for the help noted in the letter to Jack. Maybe she could encourage her in some way.

Stiffly walking the crumbling concrete sidewalk leading to the front entrance, Scarlett knocked on a weathered wooden door, pealing at the bottom, and stepped back. She was about to knock again when the door opened partway, and a disheveled, dark-haired woman peered out. The woman's brown eyes roamed over Scarlett, taking her in.

"You a bill collector?"

"No, miss."

The door opened further, and she confronted Scarlett. "Then what do you want?" Her abrupt reply threw Scarlett off balance. This might be tougher than she'd expected.

"My name is Scarlett, and I thought I might visit with you about Jack."

Smack! Scarlett's head snapped back. The attack was unexpected, and a startled Scarlett stepped away, shocked at the unexpected slap.

"I know all about you. You're the woman that son-of- a-bitch Jack ran off with! What are you doing here anyway?"

"I...I just wanted to speak with you." Scarlett's hand rubbed at the stinging side of her face, which was quickly turning red.

Susan remained silent for a moment, glaring and drilling holes in Scarlett's head with fierce coffee-colored eyes. "You want to what?"

"You may find we have more in common than you think. Would I be able to visit with you for just a moment?"

A puzzled Susan stepped back, still unbelieving. "I don't know. I hardly see a point in sitting down with one of Jack's lovers to have a friendly chat. Besides, the place is a mess, and I only have water to offer you. You should leave now."

The stern look and Scarlett's smarting cheek were nearly enough to convince her to turn around and leave. But looking over the woman's shoulder into a dimly lit and sparsely furnished living room, Scarlett got an idea.

"Look. Why don't I get us pizza and something to drink while you clean up? I'll be back in a jiffy."

Susan hesitated. Who the hell was this stranger, and what did she want anyway? Stepping behind the door as if to close it in Scarlett's face, Susan was intrigued and returned to the door, holding her son.

"I can't think of one good reason to do this, but the pizza sounds good."

"Alright." Scarlett flashed a smile. "I'll be right back."

"Um, Scarlett."

"Would you mind picking up a carton of milk for me?"

Scarlett was already headed to the car and looked back over her shoulder. "Of course. See you soon."

While she shopped at the grocery store, Scarlett knew the woman needed much more than a carton of milk and soon filled her cart with three bags of groceries. She purchased two giant pizzas on the way home, one for now and one for the woman to eat over the next few days.

Returning to Susan's, she grew apprehensive again. *Stuff it, Scarlett. Now you know why your calling to come here was so strong. She has his child, the woman needs help, and God has brought you here for that reason. Me? That's a laugh. I've been so far from you for so long, Lord; how can you even think of using me?*

The undeniable voice of the Lord replied – "I can work with that."

It might have startled her, but Scarlett knew the voice.

She smiled to herself. As lost as she was, God still believed He could use her. Maybe there was hope yet.

The afternoon slipped by, the pizza disappeared, and Susan even allowed herself one beer while the women conversed. The two strangers had only Jack in common, and cursing him together helped build a bond. They shared the same hurt with the same man. By the end of the afternoon, Scarlett had grown even more angry with Jack. Holding Susan's son, Jack's son, she was deeply moved by the woman's plight. Thinking of the money she expected to have soon after the divorce was finalized, she made a spontaneous decision.

Susan's refusal to accept the check Scarlett wrote was weak, and Scarlett had little trouble getting her to take it.

"My divorce will be final soon. The guy is as sleazy as Jack, but he's got a lot more money. Please take it. I'll never miss it."

Susan broke into tears when Scarlett handed her the five-thousand-dollar check and hugged her close until the shaking in her shoulders subsided. Scarlett helped her to the sofa and assisted with her son as she sat down. "We all go through hard times, Susan, but the Lord always sees us through. Pray, eat right, and pray some more; you will find yourself on the other side of this soon.

"We should stay in touch," Susan suggested.

"I'm sorry, Susan." She frowned. "Another time, maybe, but I'm shedding all connections with my past. The last contact with the outside world I plan on having is when my attorney tells me Donovan has agreed to the settlement and the money is in the bank. I'm not sure when that will be, but when it happens, the world isn't going to see me for quite sometime."

Susan smiled weakly. "I wish you the best, Scarlett. And thank you so much for everything."

"Don't get up. I can see myself to the door. Take care of yourself and that son of yours. You'll find your way through this, I promise."

Once outside, Scarlett breathed a sigh of relief and took a moment to collect herself. How was it she was always following in Jack's wake? Well, it was time to start making a wake of her own, however small and subtle it might be.

She shivered with delight after returning to the van and pulling back onto the highway. She hadn't felt this good about anything in a long time and soon realized one of the things missing in her life was the joy of following where the Lord led. Without His prompting, she never would have taken the letter in the first place and definitely wouldn't have shown up at a stranger's doorstep.

Scarlett pondered the string of events that brought her to this place. It felt so good to help someone in need, and she realized it was one of the things missing from her life the last few years.

It couldn't be more obvious. Follow your own path, chasing after the world's ways, and you will be lost. Walk the narrow path with the Lord and be filled with the simple but fulfilling rewards He has planned for you, Scarlett.

CHAPTER TWENTY SEVEN

A MOTEL SIX WOULD HAVE TO DO FOR THE FIRST NIGHT, AND after finding her room and freshening up, she headed out. Drinking her heartache away wasn't what she had in mind, but a brisk walk to burn off the tension and maybe a drink afterward to calm herself would be a perfect end to the day.

A few blocks from the motel, she walked through the parking lot and into the front door of an outdoor camping and recreation store. There wasn't much she needed, but wandering up and down the aisles couldn't hurt and would help get her mind off things and focus on the trip ahead.

By the time she left the store an hour later, she had a new stove, backpack, a new attitude, and a little more dehydrated food to add to her stash. Thinking of how she might put the new equipment to use on the trail invigorated her. After stashing her purse in the backpack along with the stove and dehydrated food, she continued her walk through town.

The new pack fit better than her old one, and for the miles she planned to hike, comfort would count for a lot. She was thrilled at the thought of returning to the mountains. It had been too long, far too long.

She pulled her jacket close against the cool breeze, and a quarter mile or so further, she stopped at a place called the Pencil Factory. The old brick building seemed safe enough from the outside, but she found it to be a bit sketchy once inside. A single beer and she would be gone.

Scarlett had nothing against the patrons frequenting a bar home to loggers, mill workers, and truck drivers. She'd grown up with those types and greatly respected them, but the ones she found in this bar seemed more likely to give her the kind of reception a single woman in a bar like this always feared, and it didn't take long.

"Hey babe, what's your sign."

His sunken front teeth made it possible to fill the space between cheek and gum with even more chew.

Scarlett sipped her beer and pretended to be preoccupied with her new backpack.

Undeterred, "You one of them hippie types from Seattle heading out to hug some trees and eat some mushrooms?" The guy leered, and Scarlett tugged her jacket tighter together.

"You probably would think that, wouldn't you?" She nodded, deciding to play his game. "As a matter of fact, I am planning to hug some trees tomorrow morning."

"Hot damn, I knew it the minute I laid eyes on you."

For the first time, he looked directly into her eyes. "Well honey, you know what, I'm a logger from right here in these parts, and we don't always take kindly to you tree huggers. But in your case," he paused to look her up and down again, "If you wanna step out back to my truck and rev up my chainsaw, I'd be more inclined to make an exception."

The guy's dirty old laugh had Scarlett gathering her things, preparing to leave, when a big, burly guy in a wife-beater t-shirt and a watermelon belly interrupted.

"Leave her alone, Billy."

"But Gus, we was just getting to know one another."

Gus never said a word. His look alone was enough to back the guy off.

"Sorry about that, miss." Gus tipped a greasy Carhartt ballcap. "He's drunk as a skunk, but I assure you he won't bother you no more."

The words had barely left his mouth when a chair broke over Gus's head. He sagged to his knees before righting himself, staggered sideways a few feet to his left, and leaned against a nearby table. Figuring to take advantage before the blow from the chair wore off, Billy jumped him.

Scarlett gathered her things as the fight rumbled through the bar and quickly slipped outside, untouched and unnoticed. The peaceful call of the woods grew even stronger now. One night in a cheap motel would be all she could bear before disappearing into the woods.

The following morning, Scarlett filled up on two eggs, hash browns and gravy, a side of bacon, and multiple cups of coffee. It hadn't always been her favorite way to start the day, but it was Jack's favorite, and she had come to love it.

After breakfast, she made the short drive into the mountains, parked at a nearby trailhead, and locked up the van. She adored the North Cascades, sometimes known as the North American Alps, and it had been far too long since her last visit.

Taking to the trail, the soft, needle-covered ground rose up to greet her. The scent of evergreens invited, and the peaceful quiet drew her deeper into the woods. Ferns and pinecones lined the trail, and squirrels chattered high in the trees above. The forest environment soothed and was just the medicine she craved.

With no plans and nothing to return to, she gave little thought to how long she might be gone. All she knew was that leaving the woods anytime soon was out of the question. She had enough food for at least a week and decided she'd figure things out as she went.

The serenity enveloping her after the first few miles on the dusty path rejuvenated her. Passing through the dense old-growth forests, Scarlett found each step brought more relief and more healing than the last.

Stopping for a break at an aged granite bridge arching across a talkative stream, Scarlett crossed halfway, shrugged off her pack, and leaned against the broad stone-sided wall. Allowing the sound of the creek to wash over her, she rested while listening to its calming, musical voice.

Sipping from her water bottle, she relaxed and took in more of her surroundings. Every little thing was perfect and in its place here. This was where she belonged. On the way to the ocean, the bubbling brook sang about the forest life cycle. The fish, wildlife, ever-changing seasons, and the perfect balance of God's creation were all woven together in the melody. The water would soon complete its journey to the sea and return to the forest, this or another one, in the form of rain and snow. A yearning for the same completeness exposed the enormous hole inside Scarlett.

Looking back, she contemplated her life, where it had been, and where it was going. God reassured her all would be well if she would turn away from the things the world offers and follow Him. But at the moment, she couldn't conceive how that was possible. She'd strayed, taken too many wrong turns, and wondered about ever finding her way back. Having experienced so much in so little time, she swore a pact to herself: *No more fast living. No more life in the fast lane.*

Breathing deep, the fragrant pine-scented air filled her with the forest's tranquility. It would take a while before the door to the person she'd locked away inside began to open, but this was the beginning. The forest surroundings and time alone would surely draw the old Scarlett out of her hiding place. Maybe not today, but the chains binding her to the world were loosening. She was already feeling it, and the person hidden away in her mind's dark, empty crawl space would someday be set free.

Breaking her train of thought, a black raven glided in and landed atop the stone wall she sat on. Boldly hopping near, it stopped and cocked its head to eye her. The giant bird's sizeable beak snapped open and closed twice as if begging for food. That's when she heard the voice.

You think you can lose me in these woods?

Devilish laughter followed.

You're in for a fight, little lady. If you think your life is bad now – more laughter – *just try putting me back in the bottle. I willingly granted every single one of your fleshly desires and worldly wishes. You embraced it all and reveled in the fun, and this is how you repay me? HA! I'm not some genie that goes back in the bottle when you're done with me. There will be a price to pay.*

Scarlett stepped forward to chase off the bird.

Do you think your charming Jack is safe? Its laugh was deep and threatening this time. *Back off, or you'll be sorrryyyy.*

The bird flew straight at her face when it took off, pulling up at the last moment. Scarlett felt the swoosh of its wings just above her head.

Momentarily stunned, Scarlett leaned back against the stone wall until the gentle voice of the creek below broke through her thoughts. Then, taking a seat again, she attempted to collect herself.

I know the bird didn't speak, but the voice was so authentic it frightened me.

Her alter ego was fighting back, promising it would not go away peacefully, even to the point of threatening her. It loved its freedom.

I've been down your road, and I know where it leads. I'm getting off that train here and now. Threaten me if you like, but I've learned my lesson.

Remorseful and filled with regret for the life she had lived, her Irish blood began to boil. Shaking off the threats and filling herself with an even greater determination, she threw on her pack and left the ancient bridge to rejoin the trail. The straight and narrow path, filled with the wholeness of God's creation, offered everything she needed.

Hours later, with the forest's harmony seeping deeper into her pores, cleansing, refreshing, and purging the world's waste, Scarlett slowed her pace. Every step into the wilderness took her further away from the city's temptations, and the hurried, rush-rush lifestyle faded behind in each tiny cloud of dust. Sad that she couldn't walk away from her memories in the same way, Scarlett embraced the cleansing the forest offered and invited it in.

Somewhere in these mountains, she would return to herself. She wasn't sure where and when that would be, but the search would continue until it happened. Six miles later, after cresting a steep ridge, Scarlett approached a massive tree trunk lying across the trail. The ancient body was bare of bark and had lain there long enough to exhibit extensive rot. Scarlett sat down and swung her jean-clad legs over to the other side. It was time for a break and a late lunch.

The view from the ridge top, slightly above the tree line, was bathed in brilliant sunlight and brisk mountain air. Scarlett sipped from her water bottle and relaxed. Then, setting it aside, she reached into her pack to retrieve her favorite lunchtime snack. Packed with the energy needed to sustain her throughout the arduous hike, she pulled the tab on top of a can of Deviled Ham. Using her utility knife, she smoothed the tasty spread across the top of a rice cake and savored the flavor of her first bite. There was nothing like it.

Soon, two Golden Mantled ground squirrels appeared to beg for scraps. Many called them chipmunks, and backpackers often called them camp robbers because they would steal food at the first chance. The two cuties approached within a couple of feet of Scarlett and stood tall on their hind legs. She tossed each a tiny piece of rice cake. Sharing her empty self with the two friendly critters energized her with a touch of life.

Packing up, Scarlett tossed two more pieces of rice cake to the squirrels. A giant raven swooped down and stole the treat at the same moment. Scarlett shooed it away and was threatened with more devilish laughter.

The squirrels didn't return, and after another drink of water, Scarlett headed further down the trail. A mile later, she left the path to pick her way through knee-high brush and stood at the edge of a thousand-foot cliff. Below, just a short hike down the mountain, a deep blue lake sparkled. A second lake lay further away down the mountain. It was quite large, and a handful of colored tents populated the lake's edges. She would not be headed there.

The closer lake was small but unoccupied and looked just like the place Scarlett wanted for her first night in the woods. An hour or so later, resting beside the smooth, crystal-clear lake she'd viewed from above, Scarlett called it a day.

Setting aside her pack, she took a few moments to skip stones across the water, breathe the air, and wonder how she had ever allowed this simple delight to escape her life. Wandering the shoreline, Scarlett congratulated herself, feeling strong and confident about completing the eleven-mile hike on the first day.

After moving back into the trees to set up her tent, she fired up her new pack stove, boiled some water, and made a cup of hot cocoa to sip while waiting for her freeze-dried meal to cook. There wasn't a single person around. The thought of being so completely alone was new, and she quickly embraced it. *It only feels foreign because the raucous noise of the city no longer fills my head.*

Her first night brought only snippets of sleep and a lot of wondering about the noises outside her tent. By morning, relaxing next to a small fire and sipping instant coffee, she admonished herself for being so skittish. Sure, there were bears in the area, but she'd hung her food high in a tree away from camp and cooked her dinner a distance from where she slept. She would be fine.

Each passing day took her further away from the ego-driven lifestyle that had brought her to such an abysmal place in life and drew her a step closer to the person she knew was inside. The person she'd always been proud to be. Each day's hike, each chilly dip in a snowmelt-filled lake, peeled away another layer, allowing a little more of the old Scarlett to come through. Her torn soul began the long process of healing.

By the fifth night, she eschewed the tent for sleeping under the stars. The brilliant spread of diamonds scattered across the dark void of a night sky enticed her. There was no view of creation like the one found high in the mountains. Laying on her back, gazing into the Milky Way, Scarlett wondered how anyone could deny the existence of God. It was right there before them if they were just willing to look. The forest itself was a remarkable living organism. With an ecosystem functioning so perfectly and in balance at all times, there was no way it came into being by accident. Just the cycle of water from the mountain top to the sea and back again was a marvel in itself.

Two days later, Scarlett finished the ascent of a steep, rocky mountain trail to emerge in a meadow well above the timberline. After leaving the woods and hiking another quarter mile across the verdant plateau, she stopped to set up camp near a diminutive green lake. With no one around, she stripped bare for a dip in the cool mountain water to wash off the dust and sweat after the day's strenuous climb.

Her calf muscles ached from days of hiking, but the cool water eased the soreness. Emerging from the lake, Scarlett dried herself, stood naked in the golden sun's delicious rays, and allowed its gentle fingers to caress her body. The tender warmth completed nature's spa treatment, and after retrieving clean clothes from her pack, she dressed.

The fading sun was low on the horizon and would soon disappear behind the mountaintops when Scarlett heated water for a hot cup of tea. Fifty yards away, a sheer cliff dropped over five hundred feet to a small lake below. Grabbing a bag of jerky to go with her mug of tea, Scarlett strolled to the cliff edge to watch the lake below for wildlife. After sitting on the ground, she sipped her tea and marveled at the healing force of being so isolated from humankind and closer to God.

A chill wind gliding down the snowcapped mountain dove between her neck and the collar of her down jacket. The resulting involuntary shiver brought to mind the image of being buried in a snow bank in an upside-down car flooded with gas fumes, and she shuddered.

Where are you, Jack, and what are you doing right now? I'm just wondering, not pining. She chuckled at her play on words. *There's no way you have the view I'm enjoying right now. Though I try not to, I can't help but wonder about you and how you are doing.*

In the next moment, a massive black bear walked out of the woods below and began making its way around the lake. Shuffling along, stopping to investigate before digging at things Scarlett couldn't see from her vantage point, the bear eventually made its way around the lake.

Entranced, she sipped her tea and watched. When the bear came to a massive log, only an animal its size could put its arms around, it began tossing the down tree from side to side, paw to paw, spilling out decayed wood, bugs, and worms. She watched in wonder at the animal's extraordinary strength.

The rotten parts of the log were flying off under the bears beating; then the animal would stop momentarily to lick up bugs, ants, and any larvae it found. When satisfied, it shuffled away and wandered up an adjacent drainage that would eventually connect with the lake Scarlett camped near. Though the bear could at any time emerge from the drainage on the south side of the lake opposite where she had camped, Scarlett slept deeply that night. She was growing accustomed to being alone in the woods.

A couple of days later, Scarlett stepped out of the woods after shedding her city skin in the forest, smelling as foul as an old sailor and welcoming the thought of a real bed.

She delighted in that special place where both worlds melded together, and the creature comforts of civilization mingled with the lingering peace of her time in the wilderness. She savored it. No more perfume, makeup, or phony persona. This was the honest, down-home, no-false-pretenses Scarlett, who'd grown up in the country with pigs, cows, and chickens. Sweat, stink, tangled hair and all. It felt good. And so did the thought of a shower and comfortable bed.

The first item on the list was to find a place to stay. After that, she would lay up for a few days before returning to the peaceful shelter of the woods. She could always sleep in the van, but wanting to get more settled than that, Scarlett returned to a spot in the road known as Index. There, she noticed a vacant house with a 'for rent' sign in the front window. After walking about the place and peering through the windows, she wrote the phone number on a small notepad taken from the glove box of her van. Locating a phone proved to be a bit more challenging. Eventually, she resorted to asking the owner of the only store in the five-building town if she could use his phone.

"You're not seriously considering renting Mrs. Kimball's place, are you?"

"Yes, I am Sir."

"Pardon my frankness, but what's a city slicker like you doing hanging out in a place like this? I'm afraid you're going to be sadly disappointed."

The comment was not intended to be disrespectful, but Scarlett still bristled.

"I would suggest you not judge this book by its cover, Mr.?"

"Sorry, I didn't mean to ruffle your feathers. It's just that I see so many from the city who are so totally clueless. Names Bob, Bobby Smith."

He extended his hand, and Scarlett shook it. It would be the beginning of a slowly evolving friendship.

"Well, Mr. Smith, I'm anything but clueless. I grew up milking cows and working on farms."

"Is that right?" He said with a nod, indicating he wasn't at all sure he believed her. "A pretty little lady like yourself milking cows." He laughed. "That I'd have to see."

Scarlett ignored him. "So, what can you tell me about Mrs. Kimball's place?"

"Mrs. Kimball will treat you right. Kitty's a widow now, and while she gets by, I know she will appreciate any income that old rental can provide. And don't get me wrong, she keeps it neat as a pin. Just that it's an old place set back in the trees, which makes it more'n a tad bit dank and dark."

"Well, I don't plan on spending much time there, so I'm sure I'll be fine."

"Keep your doors locked, missy. Not lookin' to scare you, but we get some pretty strange characters through here from time to time, being right off the highway and all."

"I appreciate the heads up, Mr. Smith. Now, if I could trouble you for the use of your phone."

Mr. Smith bent down to grab the device from under the counter and stretched out the cord so it reached across to Scarlett's side.

"Thank you."

"Don't mention it."

Thirty minutes later, Scarlett met with Mrs. Kimball to tour the house. It was precisely what she sought; no one would ever find her here. After agreeing on the rent, Mrs. Kimball handed Scarlett the key and told her someone would be out to hook up the phone in the next day or two.

After the front door creaked closed and the sound of crunching gravel from Mrs. Kimball's car faded, Scarlett slumped in an armchair from which Mrs. Kimball had just pulled the dust cover. Taking it all in, including the fact that she was actually doing this, Scarlett sighed, allowing the tension to drain from her limbs. The house was exactly what she'd pictured; a hideout in the woods, right on down to the musty smell and flowery décor. The place might have been old, but it was near to sparkling clean.

Sleep tugged at the edges of Scarlett's consciousness, and she allowed her mind to drift. Ideas about how she would spend the rest of the summer and what winter might be like flooded her thoughts. *But first things first.*

Before falling asleep, Scarlett forced herself from the chair and walked out to the van. After retrieving her gear and dropping it in the middle of the living room, Scarlett hurried to the shower, undressed, and slipped under the soothing stream of hot water. The shower was in an old iron, claw foot tub with a new plastic shower curtain wrapped around it. She was thankful Mrs. Kimball had stopped by and turned on the hot water tank before meeting with Scarlett at Mr. Smith's store.

Clean and refreshed, Scarlett wrapped a towel around her head and stepped before a full-length mirror. It had been quite some time since she'd paid any attention to the person peering back at her from the mirror. Green eyes sparkling above the fiery freckles dancing across the bridge of her nose, and the top of her cheeks looked back. The damp hair peaking from under the towel was dark but would regain its brilliant red as soon as it dried. Sometimes, she wished it wasn't so red.

Hands on hips, her jade-colored eyes – or were they jaded - drifted lower, taking in the rest of her body. Muscled, tan, and shapely, *Not bad.* She smiled to herself. *Girl, I wonder what puts the guys off once they get to know you. Both my ex's thought the grass was greener somewhere else. Well, it's their loss. This is my new life, and none of that matters now. Someone is going to love me just for who I am.*

Scarlett dressed, unpacked her things, and began making herself at home. Pulling out a transistor radio, she rolled the dial across the FM band to see what radio stations she might find. As expected, reception wasn't much near the base of the mountains. Fortunately, the signal that came in best was a rock and roll station with a fun-loving DJ playing almost anything he wanted.

After pulling out the antennae as far as it would go and walking about the living room's creaky wood floor, she searched for a place with the best reception. An end table hosting an old metal lamp with a stained beige lampshade next to the couch seemed to work best.

Scarlett sat and listened momentarily after dialing in the station as best she could. The DJ announced they were finishing up 60 minutes of Led Zeppelin music. Listening for a minute as 'Tangerine' began to play, the song took her back to times with Jack, and she remained transfixed in place on the couch.

When it ended and "Since I've been loving you" filled the room, she shook her head and tried to fight back the wave of emotion sweeping over her.

No one sings a song like that to me anymore.

Emotionally weak, she found there was little reserve left to contend with her negative thoughts.. It was one of their songs, but this one Jack used to sing to her in the most off-tune voice imaginable. But what always captured her was his face when he sang it and how much he meant the words contained in the song. What had happened to that?

And what are you doing dredging up all this stuff anyway?

I'm just tired.

You left it all behind, remember?

Then why does it still torment me? Does he ever think of me in the same way?

Ha! Get real, Scarlett. He was not who he said he was and left you for at least half a dozen other women.

Hey, half a dozen for one? Not bad, Scarlett.

Oh shut up. I need to get back to the woods.

Scolding herself, she got up from the couch to turn off the radio, then grabbed her keys and hurried out the door to Mr. Smith's grocery.

He greeted her with a warm smile the moment she opened the door. "Hello there, Scarlett, how are…" Stopping himself in mid-sentence, "It may not be any of my business, but are you alright."

"I'm…I'm fine."

"Well, missy, I know fine when I see it, and sorry to say, but you ain't it. Is there something I can help you with?"

"It's personal. I'll be alright."

"Alright. Whatever you say. But I'm here if you need help with anything."

Scarlett nodded thanks and began her search of the store. Of course, there were no groceries in her newly rented home, and basics like spaghetti, peanut butter, jelly, bread, milk, cereal, and fruit would fit the bill. *Oh, and chips. Can't forget the chips.*

Scarlett placed it all on the counter and reached for the cash in her jeans pocket to pay.

"Before ringing this up, I got to ask you again. I'm not trying to pry into things that aren't my business, but if there is ever anything I can do for you, please don't hesitate to ask."

"Thank you." She smiled. "You don't know how much I appreciate that. I've just got a few things to work through, and I'll be fine." She was grateful for the gesture and, thanking him again, gathered up her things.

After she turned away for the door, Mr. Smith smiled and nodded. *Heartache. I can see it a mile away.*

Making the short drive back to the house she'd just rented, the desire to pack for her next trip and escape into the woods was overpowering. The past still haunted, and the memories dogged her like a baying pack of wolves. It would soon be time to escape back into the woods.

CHAPTER TWENTY EIGHT

THE NEXT DAY, THE PHONE COMPANY SENT A MAN OUT TO connect the phone, and as soon as he left, Scarlett called her attorney. Things were still a bit up in the air, but he felt confident the case would be settled in her favor in another week or two. "Just a few details to clean up before closing the deal." He told her. "You're going to do well."

What a relief. Scarlett poured herself a single shot of celebratory whiskey and sat down to spend some time with her journal.

So here I am, divorced and alone. AND LOVING IT! So, a quick update.

I cannot describe the hurt of discovering my husband with that other woman. It was so much like what Jack did. But in this case, if I could have jumped on the back of Jack's bike and road off into the sunset, I probably would have. But there was no motorcycle to ride off on. That's perhaps a good thing.

To top it off, the whole real estate world rubs me wrong—greedy, self-serving people. I wasn't smart enough to figure that out at first. Their influence wasn't the only thing that fed my ambitious desire for money, but it certainly didn't help. Donovan was at the center of it, but I had no way of knowing that when I began working there.

So, not long after filing for divorce, I quit my job, bought a Chevy van, and left for the mountains. Yeah, me. Imagine. I had to get away. The little burgs they call towns scattered in and about the North Cascades will be my home for the foreseeable future. (Gold Bar, Startup, Index, Mazama, Haze, and Darrington to name a few) I plan on hiking throughout the area and intend on settling into a very peaceful and secluded lifestyle here. I don't miss people or the rat race of the city and feel most comfortable with myself alone in the woods. Hey, I'm great company!

The North Cascade Mountains feel like home to me. They weren't far from where I grew up, and I love them. My plan is to spend as much time on the trail as possible. Am I running from something? I don't know, but I can barely sit still right now.

I just got word my divorce will soon be settled, and I will be one rich girl! The money means little, other than taking that bastard for all I can, but what does mean something is the freedom it buys me. Free to escape a crazy world filled with crazy men.

I find such peace here in the mountains, out of reach of what most would call civilization. On each trip, I'll hike until I run out of supplies and then hike out, clean up, rest, and restock before leaving for the forest again. That's my only plan for now.

The next day, Scarlett loaded her pack and walked out to Highway 2, where she put her thumb out for a ride to the Pacific Crest trailhead near the top of Stevens Pass. From there, she would begin a seventy-five-mile hike south to Snoqualmie Pass through the Alpine Lakes wilderness. Beautiful and remote, it was just what she needed.

It never took long for the long-legged redhead to catch a ride, and by the end of the day, Scarlett was setting up camp beside a clear, sparkling alpine lake. The pine-scented air revived her, the forested landscape soothed, and the sounds of the birds in the trees calmed her. In a word, peace. This was where she belonged. Alone with her thoughts, free of demands, soaking up all of God's creation.

Except for a single tent on the opposite side of the lake where she chose to camp that first night, there was no one about it. With the sun slipping behind the mountains and the shadows growing long, Scarlett heated a small pan over her camp stove and fried some Spam. Jack loved Spam; he cooked it often, and she had learned to enjoy it.

Stop right there. Jack is off the menu. Have you got that? He's not a topic out here.

Enjoying a cup of tea and watching the lake for wildlife, Scarlett leaned back against a mossy log, absorbed in the setting. Leave this serenity and peace for the clamor of life below? No way. She could do this all summer and never go back.

At sunrise, Scarlett stepped from her tent and slipped into the brush for bathroom duties. The air was moist, and the slight chill raised goose bumps. She knew it wouldn't last and would soon be sweating under the load of her pack on a dusty trail. But the woodsy scent was always most pronounced in the morning, and she took time to enjoy it.

Sipping from a cup of instant coffee and chewing on a piece of jerky, Scarlett noticed the tent across the lake was gone. *It's nice to be completely alone again.* A ruffed grouse called, and she listened for an answer, but it was the splash in the lake that caught her attention. A black bear, checking out the campsite on the other side of the lake, had decided to go for a swim.

Scarlett kept an eye on the bear while she packed but didn't expect any problems. Eventually, the bear wandered away, and she shouldered her pack to head south down the trail toward Snoqualmie Pass.

The time passed quickly, and after a delightful day of hiking in and out of the timberline, she set up camp, gulped down a pint of water, and walked to a nearby stream to filter drinking water for her water bottles.

Upon returning to camp, a couple of sips from her flask of whiskey and a nice cigar completed the day. *Do you do that to catch the eye of the guys?* Jack had once teased. Of course, she'd responded no. It was just something she enjoyed. *Uh-huh.* Jack had smirked. *The guys will embrace you as just one of the guys and....you wanna be just one of the guys?*

She recalled the conversation, told him it was something she liked, and saw no harm in it. Simple as that. End of discussion, though she was never convinced he believed her.

Well, Jack, here I am, whiskey in one hand and a cigar in the other, and there's not a single guy around. Now, what do you think of that?

"Hello, Sir."

Lost in the past, the voice startled her so badly that she dropped the flask she was raising to her lips and scrambled to pick it up before it spilled too much. Looking to her right where the voice came from, she replied.

"Sir?"

"Oh my gosh. Pardon me. I smelled the cigar, saw the hat and plaid shirt, and assumed..."

"Assuming can get you in a lot of trouble."

"Agreed." His smile was easy and disarming.

A short conversation ensued, after which he wished her well and headed a bit further down the trail to camp. "I'll be nearby if you need anything."

He was polite, pleasant, and easy on the eyes. Scarlett scolded herself for feeling comfortable with the fact he would be close by. *You can take care of yourself, girl, and you know nothing about that guy.*

Three days later, she arrived at a portion of trail chiseled straight out of the side of the mountain. The trail builders carved back the granite just enough for someone to pass across the vertical face of the mountain. The path was approximately a quarter mile long and straight down for at least a thousand feet. A person could see the opposite end of the trail from either side, and a sign warning riders that there was only enough room for one horse to pass was posted at each end.

Scarlett had just begun crossing when she saw two people on horseback approach from the opposite side. She waved them on and returned to the shade of two alpine fir trees to wait for them to pass.

The riders were nearly across the passage when she heard a voice behind her.

"Waiting for me?"

It was the agreeable man from a few nights before.

"Just waiting for them to pass."

"Mind if I join you? We could hike together for the last bit of this trail if you like."

Scarlett agreed, and after the horses passed, they headed across. She found him to be knowledgeable and very pleasant. He also had a car at Snoqualmie Pass and was willing to give her a ride home so she didn't have to thumb her way back.

They spent the next two days hiking together and getting to know one another. During their car ride home, he suggested they plan another hike together.

"Would you consider the Wonderland Trail around Mt. Rainier?"

"Oh, I'd love to." Scarlett thrilled at the thought. "I've always wanted to hike that route."

"It's not easy. Three thousand foot climbs, up and down, day after day for ninety-three miles." His look said he doubted her

She looked him in the eye. "Try me."

"I'd like to." The glint in his eye said he was expecting more than hiking.

Scarlett cut him off at the knees. "Look. I will gladly hike with you, even share a tent, but I will not share my bed or sleeping bag. Are we clear?"

"Very. Still want to go?"

"Of course."

He would pick her up in four days, and they would drive to the trailhead at Paradise.

After dropping her off in Index, Scarlet quickly showered and sat down at the phone to call her attorney.

"Scarlett. I've been trying to contact you. Donovan has agreed to our terms, and the case is closed."

"And..."

"I think you will be quite pleased. The court awarded you some cash, of which you will even have some left after paying me." He chuckled. "But to top it off, you get the million-dollar house."

Scarlett gasped, sucking in her breath.

"Well, it's not quite a million, but I have a buyer if you're interested."

"Of course I am. I want nothing to do with that place."

"The buyers are offering eight hundred ninety-nine thousand for it. I suggest..."

"Done. Sell it."

"You sure? I think we could get more."

"I want to be done with it. Sell it for what you think is best, but just sell it."

"Alright, Scarlett. Will do. Just one last thing. There are some papers for you to sign. I will send them to the P.O. Box you gave me for Index. Sign and return them as soon as you can."

Scarlett thanked him and took a deep breath. That was that. Her past life was history; the shackles were cut free, and she could make a new beginning without all the baggage.

CHAPTER TWENTY NINE

THREE DAYS LATER, SCARLETT PICKED UP THE DIVORCE papers from Bob at the local market. He'd given her permission to use his post office box for any mail she might receive. They were the only two in the store when she opened the envelope and immediately spread them out on the counter to sign.

Looking up, she smiled at Bob. "Signing these papers is like putting the key into the chains locked about my ankles and setting myself free."

"I'm happy for you, Scarlett. You headed out again?"

"Tomorrow, I leave to hike the Wonderland Trail around Mt. Rainier. I'm so excited."

"I hope you find what you're looking for, Scarlett. When can I expect to see you back?"

"Probably in a couple of weeks."

"Be careful and stay safe."

Scarlett thanked him for the use of his post office box and walked outside to drop the envelope into the drop box. She paused there, absorbed in the moment. Dropping the papers into the mail was a landmark on the timeline of her life. She was free now, and her spirit soared high with the ravens flying overhead.

Ravens? There they were watching again.

Just then, Mr. Smith stepped out the door to his store and, observing her looking up into the sky, asked. "Do you know what a group of ravens are called Scarlett?"

She shook her head. "No idea."

"Well, they are most commonly referred to as an Unkindness."

"Seriously? An Unkindness. Well, I hope they stay away from me then."

The hike around Mt. Rainier went well. It was more strenuous than Scarlett had expected, so they slowed their tempo and took their time. After the first few days, Scarlett began to find her pace. They'd planned for a couple extra days in case of weather or if they needed more time and packed plenty of food for an extended trip.

Scarlett enjoyed hiking with this man. He was a knowledgeable, experienced outdoorsman who knew the names of many birds they saw and the best times and places to traverse some of the more dangerous stream crossings. And he behaved perfectly, though she was sure he expected a little more than she offered.

At the end of the trip, and thinking of the successful hike they'd just completed, Scarlett suggested one more hike during the drive home. He told her about the Glacier Peak wilderness in the North Cascades - a one-hundred-and-twenty-seven-mile journey through stunningly rugged terrain and finishing in Canada. Second only to the difficult John Muir trail, it would provide the challenge they both enjoyed. Scarlett agreed, and the two planned to begin the trip in two weeks.

Back home, Scarlett continued running to a nearby rise early most mornings, further conditioning herself with hill workouts. Though the two weeks passed quickly, she grew anxious to get going. Filled with anticipation, she studied the map, knew the route, and committed much of it to memory. The fact they would gain over 26,000 feet and lose over 25,000 feet was a little intimidating. But the rugged, wild, one-hundred-and-twenty-seven-mile hike across unforgiving terrain was just the kind of challenge she longed for.

On the day of the trip, Scarlett pulled on her backpack, locked up the house, and made the short walk to see Bob at the market. The two of them visited while she waited for her ride. He'd become something of a father figure. His concern for her was genuine, and having someone in her corner felt good. When her ride arrived, he reminded her again to call him if anything unexpected came up for which she needed help.

She thanked him and noted that his phone number was stashed inside her pack.

"You ready for this?" Scarlett smiled and adjusted her window to allow in some air during the drive.

"I've been busy at work and have so been looking forward to this. Beer in the cooler if you like."

"Hmm, a bit early, don't you think."

"Yes, but it's our last chance for a cold one before we hit the trail."

"I'm good for now."

"Well, if you don't mind." He reached into the cooler and pulled out a can of Rainier. Then, smiling, "Just didn't want to drink in front of you."

"Just one," Scarlett told him. "You're driving."

It wasn't a long drive to the trailhead, and the two were quick to get on the trail. After leaving Stevens Pass and beginning the hike north, Scarlett's enchantment with the area's rugged beauty surpassed all expectations. They saw few people and nearly as many bears. The rugged trail was challenging, but in top shape now, Scarlett embraced it with each new step deeper into the wilderness.

Days later and a little more than halfway through the trip, where the trail circled the west flank of Glacier Peak, a massive thunder and lightning storm forced them to shelter near the edge of the tree line. Exposed to the element's raw fury, the only shelter to be found were little groves of trees scattered about the meadows. Choosing a small grove of older trees because they had obviously been there quite some time, the two set up their tent and sheltered inside.

Nearby trees cracked with lightning strikes as thunder boomed and shook the ground beneath their tent. The raging wind uprooted tent stakes, forcing them outside in the driving rain to re-anchor their tent. Staying dry was impossible.

It was three days before the rain subsided, and in that time, stuck together inside their small tent, Scarlett learned all she needed to know about her traveling companion.

After the rain abated and resuming their hike north, she was relieved to be back on the trail. Some stream crossings became more challenging with the storm's runoff raising water levels, but generally, the trip continued smoothly. Scarlett marveled at the beauty of the area's natural wonders.

God's creation is so incredible. I wonder how people miss it?

But she was growing tired of her company as they approached the trail's northern end and began planning an early exit. The desire to be alone grew with every step. He'd made some subtle advances. Nothing more than any other guy might have done, but he was a carbon copy of Donovan in too many ways. His outdoor knowledge notwithstanding, he was all about returning to life in the city and making big money.

Their time together on the trail provided plenty of opportunities to share past history and what they each dreamed of in the future. The guy was always happy to talk about himself, so Scarlett frequently held back and let him go on.

A day later, they camped near an icy stream filled with glacial melt rushing off the mountain. The brook provided the perfect background music for a comfortable evening by the fire. After feasting on dehydrated dinners, the two kicked back with cups of instant coffee. With the end of the trip coming up in the next few days, the discussion turned more to their plans for the future, and the conversation continued long into the night.

"Like I told you. After breaking up with my college sweetheart, I went to work in a Seattle real estate office. I met a guy there who seemed like everything I wanted in a man, and it wasn't long after that we were married."

"Let me guess, he didn't treat you right."

"Well, yes, you could certainly say that. I'd describe it more as a flash-and-cash kind of romance. There was no depth to the guy whatsoever, but I couldn't see it. Less than a year after we were married, I caught him cheating on me. It's left me a little jaded, and I swore I'd be much wiser about any future relationship."

'So you blame him and your college sweetheart for everything." The naked statement struck home. Scarlett swallowed the coffee she sipped while his words disappeared into the forest.

"I certainly do, but looking back, I wasn't ready to be married. As hard as it has been, I know God is preparing me for something better. After college, I went my own way and missed out on His plans for me. Still, I see His hand at work in so many different ways. Molding me, keeping me from trouble, and preparing me for all the blessings He has intended for my life. Someday, that will include a husband of integrity."

"Seriously. You believe all that God stuff?"

"Look, I'll be the first to admit it's been rough these last few years, but God grows us by allowing challenges to come into our lives. He knows what's best, and when we get on the wrong road or involved in something that will harm us, He redirects our path."

Scarlett paused to think, and instead of interrupting, he waited patiently. "Look." Scarlett knelt by the fire ring, stirred the coals of their small fire, and added a few sticks of wood. "My past is a daily reminder that when I do things my way, I get into trouble. If I remain faithful and trust in the Lord, I have confidence all will turn out just fine because He has shown He is always watching out for me."

"Wow. You really do buy that religious stuff. That's wild. I'm sorry. I'm more of a self-made man. I'm building my own life, and I'm the one who knows what's best for me, not some mysterious outer space entity."

Thinking of Donovan, Scarlett chuckled softly. "I'm afraid you'll have some hard lessons to learn."

"Oh?"

"Look. After college, I moved on. I found a good job, a job I was good at. I partied, tried all the things I'd denied myself in college, and made good money, yet there was always this missing piece, a piece I could never find. It took a while before I came to understand that God himself was missing from my life. Not some guy who revved my heart to the red line, but a merciful God who grounds me, forgives me and prepares me for a blessed life. I had to learn that God comes first, and His blessing will follow when He does. And don't misunderstand. I'm not talking about wealth and riches."

"Unreal. Sorry to say it, but you've been brainwashed, kid."

"I've heard worse. An old friend of mine once told me, Gotta keep it real, man." She smiled at the thought before continuing. "I've tried the phony, lame life in the fast lane. It's empty of any substance. You'll regret it."

He scoffed and shook his head. "Don't think so, Scarlett. I know where I'm going. It's all coming together. Life is looking good."

"Life can be good without all the Stuff." Using her fingers to make quotations around stuff. "Your investment in this life will only last as long as you do. But the reality is, our life is a vapor, and before long, someone else will have everything you strived for. You should invest in eternity, not the here and now."

"Wow. What a trip." He shook his head. "You been smoking something I'm not aware of?" He chuckled and leaned back to take another pull from his whiskey flask. "Well, good luck with that, Scarlett." He wiped his mouth with the back of his hand. "You're a good kid, and I've enjoyed getting to know you, but I think we best stick to hiking for now. Agreed?"

"Agreed." She sighed. "Differences aside, I've enjoyed hiking with you as well. We are different people headed in different directions, but that hasn't interfered with enjoying this amazing backcountry."

Though she did enjoy their travels together, her new life was all about getting away from worldly, money-grubbing people looking out only for themselves. And spending more time with him wasn't helping. The guy was so corporate she was surprised he didn't backpack in a suit and tie. Always scheming ways to make the big money. It turned her off. They'd shared an adventurous summer together, but that was it. Scarlett was wise enough to know the road to riches was not the road she wanted to travel.

He chafes my soul!

Nearing the one-hundred-mile mark, Scarlett was ready to disengage.

"I think I'll branch off here and call it a trip. I can hike into Stehekin and take the ferry back to Chelan. My thumb will get me home from there."

"Are you sure?"

Scarlett stuck out her hand. "I'm sure. It's been a pleasure hiking with you."

The two shook hands and separated at the fork in the trail while he headed toward Canada and the trail's end. Scarlett completed her hike by walking to Stehekin. While there, she couldn't help but fall in love with the place. Isolated from civilization, Stehekin sat at the edge of Lake Chelan on the far west end. Realizing she could both lose and find herself in that place, Scarlett devised a plan. There was no denying this was where she wanted to be.

The only access to the tiny little town, nestled in the heart of the North Cascades, was by plane, ferry, or foot. It was precisely the place her heart yearned for, so she stayed a couple of days to look into rentals. After chasing down several dead ends, she eventually found what she was looking for – a private home just off the lake.

It was a summer home, and as luck would have it, the owners were in the middle of spending a couple of weeks there before closing it up for the season. Scarlett approached them about staying throughout the winter. After a short discussion and numerous warnings about being completely isolated for months and unable to go anywhere, they struck a deal. After showing her around the property and walking down to the boat dock, they even offered her the use of their boat. On the stern was the name "She Got The House."

Scarlett laughed to herself. *I can relate to that.*

When she asked about the name, Scarlett learned the boat's owner was on his second marriage, and the previous wife got the house. The home she would be renting belonged to his new wife.

I guess I'll fit right in. She thought.

With her winter home arranged, Scarlett needed to return to Index and take care of matters there. Stepping from the ferry at Chelan after making the trip down the lake, she stood on the dock momentarily, looking back along the length of the lake to the mountains in the background.

I'll be back when the peaks wear a white winter coat.

Scarlett's hair served nearly as well as a red flag when it came to hitchhiking, and she never had to stand at the side of the road for long. Soon, a wildly colored Volkswagen van pulled over in answer to her thumbs call. Painted with flowers and a big-footed long hair, striding across the side of the van with the single word *Truckin* painted underneath, Scarlett knew it would likely be an entertaining ride home.

Approaching the passenger side of the van, a lazy-eyed man with a sleepy grin leaned out the window to greet her. "Uhhhhh, where you headed, man?"

Scarlett told them Index.

The driver leaned over, "We're headed back to Seattle, and that's right on our way. Climb in." He motioned toward the back with a thumb over his shoulder.

"Oh, cool man, you're from Index?" The passenger in front chuckled. "Mind if I look you up sometime?"

The woman beside the sliding door slugged him as Scarlett climbed in. "Don't mind him, he's harmless." She grinned.

Scarlett took a seat, and they passed her a joint. She shrugged. *What the hell? One last fling, I guess.*

The ride home was slow, but the music was cranked and good. Scarlett toked on the doobie and kicked back, happy to let someone else drive. At Index, she thanked them for the ride and wished them safe travels before briskly walking home, anxious for a long hot shower.

After settling in again at her rented home in Index, she sent off a check to the owners of the Stehekin house for the full amount of her winter stay. Ten days later, she received the key to her winter home. The lakefront property was costly, but the owners were happy to have someone there for the entire winter to keep an eye on the place and made her a pretty sweet deal. Besides, it was really Donovan who was paying for it.

CHAPTER THIRTY

CUPPING HER SECOND CUP OF COFFEE IN BOTH HANDS, Scarlett left the kitchen and returned to the back porch, where the finches greeted her with an energetic serenade. Alone and undisturbed with nature as her backyard, she counted her blessings. Some would have said she was already living alone and isolated, but Scarlett longed for her winter escape in Stehekin.

Her long-forgotten journal sat on a weathered wooden table next to her, and she contemplated an entry. It had been a long time and she was reluctant to start. Still, its call, like the voice of an old friend, beckoned; she reached for the book, deciding to give it a try.

I'm sitting on the back porch of a rented house in Index Washington. Yeah, Index. It's truly a slice of heaven, and I love the solitude here. I've been hiking the mountain trails and camping for days at a time and just returned from an extended trip around Glacier Peak. As much as I love the backcountry, I think it might be time to kick back.

My divorce is final, and I need some time to clear my head and plan for the future. The settlement means money is not a problem, and I have all the time in the world. What better than a place in the woods with no one to distract me?

Life has taught me some hard lessons these last few years, a failed marriage not the least of them. It didn't take long for God to get me off that road! Even through the pain of betrayal, I thank Him every day. I've learned enough to know to trust in Him and not myself, or some guy for that matter! I seem so capable of screwing things up when it comes to relationships, and from now on will leave it up to God if and when another man comes along.

Yet, I must admit that an ember for Jack remains alive in my heart. Is that just insane, or what? But I can't seem to shake it. How bad do I have to hurt to extinguish it? I shake my head. Everything I had with my old flame, faded as it is, never leaves me. I can be so stupid sometimes.

What to do? I trust my feelings for Jack will fade over time, but I can't deny that, for now, they are still there. I kick myself for it. I mean, the guy is off-running about the country and probably never entertains a single thought of me. Does he think of us when our song comes on the radio? Maybe shedding a silent tear when he hears it. Who am I kidding? I should be committed for thinking he still cares.

So stuff it, Scarlett. You know better than to let your mind go there. Bury those thoughts with the rest of the past and move on! I mean, get real! You've been burned by the guy twice! He'll never change. Now quit entertaining thoughts of him and move on! It would probably help if you had a drink. Yes. Agreed! First smart thing you've had to say.

Over the next two weeks, Scarlett took some short overnight hikes, relaxed in the quiet peacefulness of her place, and got to know Mr. Smith at the grocery store. Soon, thoughts of spending the winter in Stehekin dominated her thinking, and she grew anxious to leave.

Mr. Smith warned her about being so isolated and alone in Stehekin for what would be a very long, cold winter. It all sounded delicious to Scarlett, who couldn't wait to move there. She promised to be careful after telling him her mind was made up. When the time came, he offered to store her van and give her a ride to Chelan to catch the ferry.

A few more nearby hikes and, a week later, found Scarlett loading up her backpack and a single duffel bag. The house she was renting at Stehekin was fully stocked, and she was welcome to all of it, so she only needed to take a few things. The single, miniature grocery store within walking distance of the house would allow her to purchase any necessary basics. The store was nothing fancy, a throwback to the 30s when it was built, but that was the point. It was only open a few days a week since few people spent the winter there.

Mrs. Smith invited Scarlett for dinner the night before leaving, treating her like family. Scarlett knew nothing about her past, but one look in the woman's eyes implied a deep understanding. It felt good to have some friends.

The ride with Mr. and Mrs. Smith was comfortable, with Mrs. Smith asking numerous questions about where she would be staying and what she expected it to be like. Before she knew it, Scarlett stood on the dock, preparing to board the ferry. The wind whipped her hair, and the icy mountain breeze cut through her clothes. Though Mr. Smith had never before touched her, the hug he gave her was welcome. He reminded her to call if she needed anything. Scarlett glimpsed a tear glistening in the corner of one eye before he turned away.

Then, sharing a hug with Mrs. Smith, she whispered, "If I were a young girl, I'd be tempted to go with you. Enjoy your time away from this world."

Scarlett stepped outside the cabin to wave after boarding the ferry that would take her to the other end of the lake, which was far away from civilization. It would be a long while before she spent time with anyone she knew.

The view of snow-capped peaks in the background spoke of times to come. Fall colors painted the lake's shoreline in yellow, orange, and red splashes of blush, welcoming Scarlett to her new world. The empty sensation of leaving her known world behind, mingling with the idea of traveling to a place where no one could reach her, brought both peace and excitement.

The long ride up the lake with a few stops along the way would take just over four hours. Halfway into the trip, Scarlet left the comfortable confines of the ship's cabin and stepped outside to stretch her legs and stand at the stern of the boat. The cool, brisk air was chilly but invigorating. A touch of winter was in the air, caressing her neck with cold fingers. Would she always think of the night of the car crash whenever she felt winter's touch?

For Scarlett, leaving the world behind was equivalent to leaving her past behind. Relieved of these burdens, new life, like an artesian spring, bubbled up and began to fill her. It was incredibly freeing to disappear into a place unknown and as far from the past as possible. The depth of these feelings took her by surprise before realizing all those days spent hiking the backcountry was a search for the place she was now about to enter. The clean, fresh air, freedom from entanglement with anyone or anything else, and sense of adventure made up the perfect elixir her heart had craved all along.

Docking at Stehekin mid-afternoon, Scarlet felt like she'd been transported to another world. The hike from the ferry landing to her new home was just a mile. In no rush, she took every moment to soak it all in. The chill in the air foreshadowed coming storms and made the hike easy and comfortable. The touch of fall was in everything.

Arriving at her new home on the lake, she found it just like she'd left it and quickly settled in. It took a few days to adjust to the new setting and occasional lonely night before Scarlett felt a part of the rhythm of her new world. The October nights were cold, but Scarlett stayed warm, snuggling deep beneath a heavy down comforter. There was electric heat, of course, but she preferred the wood stove and kept the temperature cool at night to sleep well.

A morning fire in the stove, a large mug of coffee, and time in prayer with her bible may not have seemed like much to most folk, but the simple life was precisely what she'd come for. It was impossible to find anything like it in the city, and she was determined to take the path the Lord promised to meet her on. Cozy mornings seated in the rocking chair next to the fire, wrapped in peace and quiet, made it easy to get out of bed each morning to meet with her Maker.

On afternoons, when the sun came out and the lake was calm, Scarlett would often walk the gravel path from the house to the lake. Passing through a handful of ancient evergreen trees to the gravel beach where the trees retreated and the water advanced, Scarlett would sit at the picnic table, listening to the LBJ's call and sing to one another. Little Brown Jobs. That's what Jack called them. She often left bird feed out for them in hopes of keeping them nearby.

It was so peaceful, and even the crunch of the gravel path sounded inviting. On this particular morning, after leaving the path and walking to the far end of the dock, Scarlett sat quietly on the wooden bench there. She found the sound of water lapping at the pier soothing, taking her back to her childhood in Marysville.

There was so much to unwind; her mind spun, attempting to disentangle the mess that filled it. She sometimes would pull the cover from the boat and idle out into the middle of the lake just to think. Her past was such a whirlwind, and it still held the potential to suck her back in. But there would be time to sort it all out, and that fact alone allowed her to chill out, let her hair down, and work things out one day at a time. Sometimes, she journaled, but most often, she gazed across the lake's surface while contemplating the current Gordian Knot she was struggling to unravel.

Gradually, she grew familiar with the lake's mood and temperament and was surprised at how often it reflected her own. From still and dead calm to stirred up and threatening to storm, the lake and Scarlett shared a growing bond.

Then, late one afternoon in early November, a shift in the wind brought an icy breath straight out of the mountains. It descended over the lake and dock where Scarlett sat, gripping the entire area in its frozen embrace. The breeze exhaled its last breath in a sudden puff that turned the page on the journal resting in Scarlett's lap, and a hush fell over the lake. The tranquil air carried every little sound, but there was none to hear. Not even the LBJs called to one another. Minutes later, the sound of snow sifting through the evergreen trees reached her ears just before the snow did.

Scarlett let the snow fall around her until it covered her boots and colored her hair white. She stuck out her tongue to catch a few snowflakes before heading back inside.

After building a fire and changing out of her damp clothes, she cooked up a batch of macaroni and cheese. Settling in next to the fire with the mac and cheese and a glass of wine, Scarlett watched the snowfall. Memories of time with Jack and his antics in the snow rushed in. And it took every ounce of restraint she could muster to control her frustration and keep from throwing her glass of wine against the wall. She hated the fact her memory of him continued to haunt her but had to admit the ache was still there, though nothing like before. It was the hole in her heart searching for something that would fill it. The peaceful serenity of the life she was now living helped it heal, but it couldn't fill an empty space so large.

Trust in the Lord, Scarlett, and you'll be fine. As the scriptures tell you, "In this world, you will have trouble." Well, danged if that ain't true!

She stopped pacing, returned to her seat by the fire, took a large swallow of wine, and looked through the snow-covered trees to the lake.

And Jeremiah also tells you, "For I know the plans I have for you, declares the Lord, plans to prosper you and not harm you, plans to give you hope and a future."

Father. Thank you.

Scarlett rose early the next morning, anticipating the new adventure she'd planned the previous evening. Glancing through the sliding doors before building her morning fire, she noticed well over a foot of fresh snow had accumulated on the deck where the wood was stored.

A solid breakfast of eggs and toast, followed by leftover Mac and Cheese, prepared her for the day. Another round of Mac and Cheese came after coffee with Jesus. Then, filling a water bottle and packing a lunch, she dressed for a hike and stoked the fire.

Stepping out on the back porch, Scarlett took down one of two pairs of snowshoes hanging there. It was just over a mile to the tiny village of Stehekin, closed for winter except for the few hardy souls who remained there for the peace winter offered.

Though the near foot and a half of snow would make the hike more strenuous, Scarlett was in good shape from a summer of hiking and enthusiastically took her first steps towards the little community. The hike to town couldn't have been more enjoyable and filled another desire in Scarlett to prove she could do it alone.

The fresh snow was untracked, and she took to the task of making her trail. In fact, she relished it. With the lake on her left and a snow-covered mountain rising straight up from the edge of the road on her right, it couldn't have been a more beautiful setting.

Arriving at the village's only business open in the winter, Scarlett sat on a bench at the front of the store. Four wooden posts set in the worn wooden deck at the front of the building to support the deck cover offered a bit of shelter from the snow. A vending machine with five-day-old newspapers and a phone booth greeted her.

After leaning her snowshoes against the storefront and walking inside, a middle-aged man standing behind a yellow vinyl-topped counter smiled and greeted her. The little shop with its creaking wooden floors, had tall shelves, narrow aisles, and the walls were painted white. She was there to get a half gallon of milk, fresh fruit if they had any, some popcorn, and a bottle of wine. The house she was renting came well-stocked, but she was surprised to find no popcorn and selected two bags from the shelf.

Setting her basket on the counter at the single checkout, the middle-aged cashier greeted her a second time.

"Good afternoon. Don't think I've seen you around these parts before, miss."

Scarlett smiled. He seemed friendly enough. "This is my first winter here."

"Maybe I know your husband or boyfriend."

"Probably not. I'm here alone."

His eyebrows shot up. "Well, I'll be damned. I think that's gotta be a first. In all my years, I can't ever recall a woman spending a winter here alone. Occasionally, a guy will, but it's almost always couples."

Scarlett smiled politely. "Yep, just me." She grabbed a half dozen Snickers bars from the nearby stand and added them to her purchase.

He looked her over while ringing up the merchandise and thought to himself. *She looks more like one of those city chicks I sometimes see who come out here and get in over their heads: high-end camp store clothing and all. Pretty girls don't come here to spend the winter alone. She's feeding you a line. Yup. This ain't no experienced backcountry girl embracing the harsh isolation of winter in Stehekin.*

"Need help packing all this home?"

It was well-intended help, and Scarlett appreciated the offer. "Well, I've a bit of a hike. You probably wouldn't want to go that far out of your way."

"How far is that?"

"The Jackson place a mile or so back down the dirt access road."

"You're right." He chuckled. "You must be on skis."

"Snowshoes."

"Nice. Not a bad trek, but you'll get your workout on the way back."

"I look forward to it."

Butch gained a new appreciation for her. "Please be careful going home, and if you ever need anything, you can always check in with ol' Butch. I'll be glad to help out the best I can. I'm always here, Thursday through Saturday."

"Thank you, Butch." She extended her hand. "I'm sure you'll see me again."

Scarlett stored the groceries in her backpack and stepped outside. After slipping on her snowshoes, she shouldered her pack and began the trip home. The clean, crisp air was bracing. Looking at the heavy, overcast sky, she hoped it wouldn't storm again before she got home.

Following the trail she'd left in the snow coming in, Scarlett found it untouched. No one else had been out to break down her path. For that, she was thankful. It meant she was unlikely to meet anyone on her way back.

Falling into a comfortable rhythm of breathing, stepping, breathing, stepping, she warmed to the task. It felt good to move at her own pace. Entirely alone, she took in the snow-covered landscape and mountains. Her breathing steamed the air, and the vapor cloud trailing behind frosted her hair. Scarlett embraced the silent world surrounding her, broken only by the swoosh of her snowshoes through the feather-light powder.

Nearing the halfway point, a light snow began to fall before turning into a near whiteout without the wind. Soon, Scarlett could barely see ten feet in front of her. She stopped to listen. The only sound was falling snow—a unique and extraordinary experience. As the storm closed in and snow covered her head and shoulders, she couldn't help but think of Jack pulling her from the upturned car.

Guess in some ways I owe you, Jack. I probably wouldn't be here enjoying this rare moment if not for you.

The whiteout left her thankful for the trail she had to follow. Nearing home, the wind gained strength, and though she appreciated the workout, the appeal of escaping the ever-building storm grew. Thoughts of a blazing fire with a hot toddy or a relaxing soak in the tub, soft music, and a glass of wine filled her mind. With the wind howling outside, it would be oh-so-cozy. She needed only to decide which treat to go with. It had been a delightful day.

CHAPTER THIRTY ONE

THE QUIET DAYS ALONE CENTERED SCARLETT, BRINGING peace and calm to her soul. The solitude restored her and helped to find the path leading back to God. Repenting of the past freed her to forgive even her ex-husband, and she began to look forward to the coming new year with a fresh perspective on life.

A favorite time was cozying up to the wood stove when the storms were howling outside. A glass of wine and one of the many books stocking the small library at the back of the living room restored her. Sunny days sometimes found her sitting on the dock in snow boots and a heavy coat she'd borrowed from the back room. There, she would read, pray, and reflect on her life while soaking in the sounds of the lake's tranquil environment.

There was little chance of her contemplations being interrupted, and she found the lack of demands healthy and freeing. The days flew by; loneliness was kept at bay by the peace she found and the lack of wanting anything beyond what she already had. Content for the first time in as long as she could remember, the anger that possessed her lost its hold, and her frozen heart thawed.

Comfortable as she was, Scarlett could not escape a few pangs of loneliness on Christmas morning. The times she spent with her family during the Christmas season while growing up played across her mind. Then there was that one Christmas Jack visited, followed by thoughts of their first kiss. Those still-strong memories filled her with melancholy.

Christmas afternoon, the air stood still while the sun played hide and seek with puffy white clouds scattered across the blue sky. Scarlett was sitting on the porch enjoying the sun when she thought she heard singing coming from the lake. The frozen air carried voices further than usual, and she grew curious about their source. Stepping back inside, she hurriedly gathering up her heavy coat and refilled her coffee mug. Then the search for the singing voice began.

Shuffling her way along the path in the snow she'd created during frequent trips to the dock, Scarlett was careful not to slip. From the dock, she saw seven boats drifting gently on the lake's calm waters.

Each boat displayed a festive collection of lights sporting every color of the rainbow. Candle-lit lanterns hung from various places on each vessel; one even had a Christmas tree mounted atop the mast. The seven boats must have been communicating via radio because they all appeared to sing the same songs together, though some were too far away to know for sure.

Scarlett sat on the wooden bench at the end of the dock, soaking in the sight of it. When one of the boats saw her there, it turned and slowly approached. Soon, a second boat joined the first, and the two of them drifted closer. Then, the people on both boats joined together, singing White Christmas. Their voices rang clear as crystal on the bright winter's day. Scarlett couldn't help but join in, at first singing softly to herself and then in full throat, sending her voice up and out over the water to join the voices rising from each craft.

The boat people shared three more songs before applauding and waving goodbye. Scarlett was deeply moved, and the moment nearly brought her to tears. She was not alone this Christmas day; it was a moment she would long cherish.

Walking the quiet and slippery path back to the house, she was overcome with the desire to call home and felt guilty for not making plans to call her mother on Christmas day. There was no phone in the home she was renting, but she could use the pay phone out front of the store in Stehekin.

Tomorrow I'll go to the store and call her. I could stand to pick up a few things anyway. Hopefully, the weather holds.

That evening, a content Scarlett settled in beside the fire, reading her book and recounting the joyful day. Turning the page of her paperback, she glanced outside through the porch's French doors into the fading light of Christmas Day. Lazy snowflakes floated past the door, unwilling to land. *A dusting of snow will make my trip into town tomorrow morning so much nicer.*

Scarlett stoked the fire before returning to her book and glass of wine. It was getting late when she decided to head off to bed and get some rest for tomorrow's hike. She was brushing her teeth when the first blast of wind and snow rattled the house. After finishing up and slipping into a warm flannel nightshirt, Scarlett strolled to the French doors and flipped on the porch light. A powerful wind bent the evergreen trees, and the snow flew by horizontally.

By morning, the snow had drifted three feet deep on the porch, and the wind still battered the west side of the house. Scarlett hunkered down to wait out the storm. Two days later, when the storm abated and the skies cleared, she prepared to leave. It would be a strenuous hike. Excited by the challenge, she added an extra water bottle, two PBJ sandwiches, and an apple to her pack.

Little remained of her old path from two previous trips to town, and Scarlett made slow progress through the deep and heavy new snow. Arriving at the storefront, she sat on the steps to rest and was removing her snowshoes when Butch stepped out the door.

"You alright, missy? Sure didn't expect to see the likes of you around here today. Not after that storm."

"I'm doing well, Butch. I need to call home and pick up a few things."

"Everything alright?"

"Oh yes. I wanted to call home the day after Christmas, but this storm…"

Butch chuckled. "Oh, that's just the beginning. January will bring us more storms and a lot more snow. Don't be alarmed if your power goes out for a while."

Scarlett smiled. "That I can deal with. There's plenty of firewood for the stove and a propane cook stove to heat my meals on if I need to." The thought occurred to her that she had little idea how much propane remained. "And I can always heat things atop the wood stove, too."

"You sound like someone who won't freak out if cut off and isolated for a bit."

"Freak out?"

"Oh, you'd never guess. These city folk that come out here and…" Butch stopped himself short. "Pardon me, but I've already mentioned them to you."

"No offense Butch. As I told you once, I'm an old-fashioned country girl, though I seem to have forgotten that."

"Oh?"

"It's why I'm out here, but…" Scarlett waved him off. "Anyway, I look forward to some storms like that."

Butch grinned and shook his head. "You're a unique one, alright. Please come in and warm up, and I'll get you some change for the telephone."

A short while later, Scarlett stepped back outside to use the pay phone after stocking up on some essentials and a few bottles of wine. Ensuring it was enough to see her through the coming winter storms brought her backpack to the point of overflowing.

After dropping in her quarters and asking the operator to connect her to her parents' number, she waited for the connection to go through.

"Mom, how are you?" It was good to hear her voice.

"No need to worry, Mom. I'm just fine and loving my time here."

Her mother continued with concerns over Scarlett's safety. It was to be expected, and Scarlett patiently waited for the flood of worry to run its course.

"I'm safe here, Mom, so please don't lose any sleep about it. And actually, I'm hoping we do get a major winter storm to lock us in for a while. It's exciting!"

The operator interrupted to say her time was running out unless she added more quarters. Scarlett reached for the stack of coins she'd set on the shelf by the phone and dropped them in.

"I should speak with Dad now before we run out of time. Love you, Mom."

After a short pause, her father came on the phone.

"Dad. So good to hear your voice."

The discussion regarding her safety was more or less repeated. This time, when the operator came on, Scarlett said goodbye.

"I love you, Dad. Give Mom a hug for me."

The conversation ended with a brief moment of longing for Scarlett, followed by a fulfilling touch of joy. They were fine, and she had dutifully checked in to let them know all was well with her. The mixed emotions were quickly forgotten as her thoughts returned to the trail and her trek home.

She leaned inside the door to say goodbye to Butch, who hustled over with a baggy full of cookies.

"Might be a few days past Christmas, but my wife has made so many of these I'd be happy to send some home with you. If they make it that far." He grinned.

She hugged and thanked him. "A belated Merry Christmas to you, Butch, and to your wife too."

Thankfully, the weather held off while she hiked home, but the return trip with an overflowing pack was more strenuous than she'd figured, and she was glad to get back to her hideaway in the snow. Grabbing a bag of chips to go with the coffee she'd made, Scarlett collapsed into her favorite chair next to the fire she'd just kindled. Relishing the moment, she thanked God for the opportunity to spend the winter alone in such a magical place and for her good health to be able to take on the challenges of winter alone.

Three days later, the storms Butch had warned about began pounding the entire mountain range. Cold fronts pouring down out of Canada brought below-zero temperatures. The snow piled high, and the wind hammered the walls of her secret bungalow, where Scarlett burrowed in, hidden away from the world. She was safe, content, and loving every minute. Jack had told her she was a strong woman, and now she believed it.

After each storm, there would be a break when the sky cleared, and the sun would shine. The clear skies brought plummeting temperatures before the next storm rolled in. Scarlett loved every minute of such a grand adventure.

One evening, in the middle of a thunderous storm, Scarlett sat reading next to the fire. The fierce winds hammering at the house that night were frightening even for Scarlett. She was sitting in the golden glow of the fire in the wood stove, attempting to concentrate on the book in her lap, when the lights went out.

She waited a few minutes, bathed in firelight and thinking the light may come back on. When they didn't, and having prepared for this very moment, she carefully made her way through the dark to a drawer in the kitchen, where she retrieved two candles and some matches. After setting them next to her chair, she lit them and continued reading.

For eight days, Scarlett hunkered down, cooking over the propane cook stove and maintaining the fire. With all the supplies she needed in place, Scarlett quickly established a comfortable and reassuring routine. More than anything else, the time spent sheltered inside four frozen walls and wholly isolated from the outside world was the window of time she had been hoping for that allowed her to draw nearer to God. This moment in time was the very reason she had come to winter in Stehekin.

It was an adventure like she'd never experienced and never once worried about when the power would be back. The winter storms continued raging outside while she cooked meals on the propane gas stove and heated water for tea and hot chocolate on the wood stove.

Though the blizzard's fury might be roaring outside, a peaceful calm filled Scarlett's hideaway. She thought she'd left the rushed, hasty lifestyle of the city after holing up in Index and spending most of her time hiking in the woods. But now she knew exactly what it was like to live without the tension and demands of the world or, for that matter, anyone else. She couldn't have been more content.

After eight days without power, Scarlett awoke to find the lights extinguished by the loss of power were now back on. Immediately, she missed the quiet life she'd lived the last few days and was admittedly surprised by the feeling. Civilization was intruding again.

After turning off some lights, she entered the bathroom for early morning duties. She brushed her teeth before brushing out her long, ginger hair. She hadn't bathed for eight days, and a shower was at the top of her list as soon as the water heated up.

It's intriguing to me how much I enjoyed the time without power.

Only because most everything has been provided for you to do so. You didn't cut and stack the firewood or fill propane bottles or the cupboards.

Enough! You made your point. Don't try to ruin my day.

You have to move past this, Scarlett. God has given you a wonderful break from life's disappointments. But He didn't create you to be a hermit, either. Enjoy the time He has appointed you for healing, but life will move on, and you are being prepared for it.

Ha! Maybe so, but I ain't trusting no one!

She finished brushing out her hair and left the bathroom and its obstinate conversation for the kitchen to prepare a hot cup of coffee. Minutes later, she sat beside the newly kindled fire, chewing on a pop-tart and sipping hot coffee. Then, thinking to herself:

I got your message, Lord, and I don't disagree—you are right, of course. I only need a little more time.

And the Lord granted Scarlett more time, two months more. Cocooned away from the world, buried under all that snow where the people of the world couldn't get to her, she soaked up the peace she'd lost to the outside world and healed.

CHAPTER THIRTY TWO

THE WEATHER BROKE IN MARCH, AND THOUGH IT REMAINED chilly, a touch of spring brought the first hints of color to the south-facing hillsides. Along with the tender shoots of new grass emerging under the encouragement of the warming sun, the change in seasons brought forth a growing desire in Scarlett to move on with her life. She just didn't know what that was to be or where she was to go, so the search would continue.

The first step was to move back to the Index. She made one last snowshoe trip to visit Butch at the local market and purchased a ticket on the Lady of the Lake for her trip back down the lake to Chelan.

"So, what do you think of your winter here?" Butch asked.

"Loved every minute of it! And I'd do it again in an instant."

Butch shook his head. "You're something else, little lady. Well then, maybe I'll see you again."

"It's been good to know you, Butch. I always looked forward to my snowshoe trips in to see you. Take care, and maybe someday I'll make it back."

Standing in the sun at the stern of the boat for the first part of her ride back, Scarlett recalled the conversation while watching her winter hideaway disappear in the distance. Then, it occurred to her that her old self remained behind and she slowly raised a hand to wave goodbye. The changes occurring throughout that stormy winter would not be evident right away.

It was a strange feeling not knowing exactly who she was, though she had a good idea. Time would tell. Leaving behind the one place where she was safe and venturing forth, not knowing where she was going or how this new person would fit in outside her private escape, left her unsettled. The world would test her, dispute her beliefs, and shape her with its challenges. But she knew the Lord would be there to hold her up and sustain her.

As the mountains and the far end of the lake faded away, they took much of her past with them, and she filled with melancholy. Then, hearing the voice of her conscience, she acknowledged the wisdom.

Like a dog to its vomit, don't return to the things of the past, Scarlett. There is nothing but pain there. Instead, look ahead for that which the Lord promises to share with you.

The frosty breeze gusted, and tucking back her hair, she returned to the comfort of the cabin. Nearing Chelan, Scarlett looked to the distant mountains behind where she had backpacked just months ago and still slept under a heavy blanket of snow.

Then, gazing forward, searching for the dock where she would meet up with Mr. Smith, Scarlett looked directly into the wicked gleam of a raven's black eye. The bird coast along beside the boat, appearing to sneer. Scarlett closed her eyes and, after shaking her head, looked again. The bird was gone, and she assumed it was her imagination.

Minutes later, after stepping from the gangplank onto the dock, Scarlett caught up with Mr. Smith. She'd called from the Stehekin market to make arrangements for the ride. True to his word, Bobby Smith was happy to come to Chelan and give her a ride home.

When he greeted her with a welcome back hug, Scarlett knew rejoining the world would be alright. During the drive home, she answered his many questions and shared her stories. His warm welcome made the transition from isolation into the real world more accessible.

Once home, it took a few days to settle in and adjust to her new life in Index, but she kept in touch with herself by taking short hikes. The heavy snow in the high mountains had yet to melt, preventing her from taking the long hikes she preferred, and it wasn't long before she grew restless.

Anxious about her van starting after a long, cold winter in storage, Scarlett soon decided to check on it. Living within walking distance of the little store where the van was stored made for a pleasant walk through the pines to where it was parked.

The driver's side door squealed a greeting when she climbed in to get behind the wheel and slide the key in the ignition. She hoped it wasn't a sign of trouble. Then, turning the key, the motor spun nicely but refused to fire. At least the battery was still good. She pumped the gas a few times and tried again. This time, the engine fired but didn't catch. A few more pumps and it roared to life.

Relieved the van wouldn't be a problem, Scarlett took to the road to charge the battery and ensure everything else worked as it should. Upon returning home, she spent the day packing, then drove back to the store to purchase some supplies for the road and say goodbye to Mr. Smith.

"I wanted to let you know I've decided to move on. I'll be leaving tomorrow morning. You've been a good friend. Someone I could trust at a time I needed to find just one trustworthy person in this world. I want you to know how much I have appreciated that."

After saying goodbye, Scarlett drove home, sad for what she was leaving behind yet filled with anticipation for the following morning and the new life that lay beyond the horizon.

A familiar gray sky and light rain greeted Scarlett the following morning. As comforting as it had once been, she decided she'd had enough of the wet stuff. After a bowl of granola and some hot coffee, Scarlett filled a thermos with the remainder of the black stuff and headed for the door. Before leaving, she stopped and turned around for one last look.

It had been her home for a singular time in her life, and she invited the living room and kitchen to imprint in her mind. The single rose and envelope she'd left on the dining room table were there as a surprise for the widow, Mrs. Kimball. The envelope contained a $100 bill and a check for an extra month's rent beyond what they had agreed to.

Mrs. Kimball had been so kind and flexible enough to allow her to keep the place through the winter so she had a place to return to. It just seemed appropriate, and she could afford it, so why not? The money was a nice perk for all the hell she'd been through, and she was happy someone else could benefit from it.

Outside in the drizzle, Scarlett hurried to her van and quickly slid inside. The door didn't squeal this time because Mr. Smith had oiled it. She let the engine warm momentarily while deciding on some music for her first day on the road.

She was headed east, so it seemed appropriate to fire up a Head East album. Knowing how much she enjoyed the song she had in mind and the likelihood it would be played more than once, Scarlett took a couple of minutes to spin the Flat as a Pancake cassette tape to the song "Never Been any Reason" and fired it up. She loved the song's energy. It fit her mental state perfectly. After cranking the volume, she said goodbye to her home in Index and headed east into the rising sun.

After a long winter of inactivity, the van seemed ready to go as much as Scarlett. Pulling out on the highway, she became filled with the freedom of the open road and no particular destination.

Outside of her bank account, everything she owned was right there inside the van. After isolating herself for such an extended time, she was surprised at how exhilarating it felt to be free-wheeling down the road with nothing to tie her down.

The roadside to the pass was bursting with brilliant yellow flowers and new green growth. Waterfalls filled her view with each passing mile as the snowmelt cascaded down the mountains. Sunlight sparkled in the crystalline patches of snow alongside the road, and the air filling the van was crisp and fresh.

Scarlett took her time, enjoying the bright, clean air and taking in the views. At the summit where Highway 2 crested above four thousand feet, she pulled into the ski resort, now closed, and stepped outside to stretch her legs. There was no one in the back of the parking lot, and after sliding open the side door, she cranked up the music of David Bowie. Rebel Rebel filled the air, and stepping from the van, Scarlett raised her hands over her head and danced.

Slipping back inside after the song ended, Scarlett prepared a sandwich sided with cottage cheese and apple slices. Then, sitting in the open doorway of the van, soaking in the sun and relishing the clean mountain air filled with earthy notes of the woods she'd called home for the past year, she wrestled with leaving the mountains. The beauty and peace they encompassed grounded her and made leaving difficult.

After eating and a short hike, she returned to the road and headed for Leavenworth. Recalling a long motorcycle ride she'd once taken there with Jack, her memories of him flooded back into focus. *Why now?* She wondered. *I haven't thought of him for some time.*

Leavenworth was a rustic, relaxed little town with a bakery that produced the best-tasting bread she had ever eaten. She looked forward to stopping there and picking up a loaf or two.

The van ran smoothly, and the easy drive down the east side of the mountains freed her mind. She gave it license to wander. To her dismay, it continued drifting back to Jack, and she kicked herself for it. She'd left all her exes behind in Stehekin, yet some scenes played repeatedly, refusing to leave her alone.

Rounding a corner, she saw a hitchhiker up ahead. *No one is as free as those riding their thumbs to wherever.* She'd first met Jack this way. He was standing at the side of the road, thumb in the air, a drizzling rain dripping off the bill of the ball cap he wore. When she stopped to offer him a ride, he explained he'd run out of gas for his bike. He was just outside Ellensburg, Washington, and it was a short trip into town, so after filling a gas can, she gave him a ride back to his motorcycle. That was it. "Biker Man" was intriguing and left a memorable impression, but she never expected to see him again.

She was shocked when, sometime later, he was the very guy rescuing her from a gas-fume-filled car buried upside down in a snow bank. Something about that night held a grip on her soul she could not renounce. With no concern for his own safety, the man had risked his life for her and her friends.

She shook her head to rid it of the memory and pulled to the side of the road. The hitchhiker approached briskly and greeted her through the passenger side window.

"What, no Ass, Grass or Gas bumper sticker." He smiled.

Smartass. But an enchanting smile!

"I'm headed to Leavenworth if that works for you."

"Perfect." He pulled open the door and slid into the passenger seat. On the outside, he looked rough, leather jacket and black boots, but his countenance said otherwise.

Scarlett chanced a question. "Where's your bike?"

"Damn fools stole it from me last night while I camped. Something about the knife at my throat convinced me to give them the keys."

"Damn! Well, I'm glad to give you a ride to Leavenworth."

"Much appreciated. I hate dealing with the cops, but I need to file a report when I get to town."

Scarlett leaned to look out the window, ensuring the road was clear before returning to the highway. "Cold one in the cooler." She motioned over her shoulder.

"Don't mind if I do. I am just a bit dry. Thanks!"

The trip down the east side of the mountains went smoothly. The guy was a complete gentleman, and she wished him luck after delivering him to a friend's place in Leavenworth.

After dropping him off and refusing his offer of gas money, she turned back to the west and took a left down Icicle Road to find the bakery Jack had once taken her to. She was lucky to catch them just before closing and purchased three loaves. One pumpkin, one rye, and a still-warm bakery-fresh loaf of "Grandma's Best." Grandma's Best was so good there was no way it would last until tomorrow.

After dark, she quietly rolled into the back of a motel parking lot and settled in for the night. Deciding she wasn't ready to leave the forest environment just yet, Scarlett chose to remain in the area to hike and explore the mountains around Leavenworth.

A month later, she drove north to spend time in and around Winthrop. Much to her delight, the quaint little towns of Twisp and Winthrop rumbled with log trucks. The reminder of her childhood days near Marysville was comforting, and Scarlett settled in, hiking and getting to know the lay of the land. The van made for the perfect home when she was not on the trail.

Weeks later, she was ready to return to the road for sightseeing and general wandering about. After Winthrop, she drove north into Canada to visit Banff National Park, the Bugaboos, Kootenay, and Jasper National Parks. Canada was lovely, but there was nothing like the States. So, after exploring as far west as Prince Rupert on the Pacific Ocean, she grew anxious to return to the familiar comforts of America.

After crossing the border, she drifted south to Omak before taking Highway 155 to visit Grand Coulee Dam. Built in the 1930s and 40s and with a recently completed third power plant, it was the largest power station in the nation.

By now, the weather was quite warm, and spending every day on a scorching hot road was getting old. Her van was everything she wanted in a vehicle, but it did not have air conditioning, and Scarlett entertained the idea of settling somewhere to wait out the seasonal summer heat.

While passing through towns with names like Almira, Wilbur, and Creston, she found the ocean of wheat waving in the breeze, both beautiful and inviting. It reminded her of the Palouse country where she had gone to college, then shocked her with the thought of how long ago those days seemed.

Tired of the heat and needing a break late in the day, she pulled up to a mom-and-pop grocery in downtown Davenport. Like all the rest, the town was just another little berg along the way, in the middle of farm country. Stepping inside, she was warmly greeted by a balding, white-haired gentleman wearing a dark, rubberized apron smeared with blood. It was stretched across his barrel chest while he worked on a crossword puzzle in the newspaper.

Smiling reminiscently, as if he already knew from his own experiences what Scarlett was all about, he asked if he could help with anything.

"Oh, just picking up a few things."

"Where you from, young lady? I know most the folk around here, and I'd have to say you're from out of town."

"You guessed right. I'm just passing through, seeing the countryside."

A distant look came to the man's grey eyes before he spoke. "Can be quite the adventure, can't it? Traveling alone?"

Scarlett nodded. "Um hmmm. You wouldn't know a safe place to park my van for the night, would you?"

The guy pulled a pencil out from behind his ear and pointed. "Right this way, bout half a mile or so down on this side of the road, is Jake's feed store. Jake and I did some travelin' together in our younger days. He's got both a heart for wayward travelers and a large lot in the back of his store where you would be welcome to set up for the night."

"Thank you. That sounds perfect." Scarlett gave him the sweetest smile she could muster. "I appreciate that."

"Just make sure you park in the very back, out of the way of any trucks coming in to load equipment or feed."

"Who you talkin to, Roger? Thought you were back butcherin' the beef that came in." The voice came from a sixty-ish woman who'd just walked in from the back room.

"I was. Just takin a little break and visiting with this young lady here."

"Well, for heaven's sake, why didn't you just say so."

Roger winked at Scarlett. "I think I just did."

"Never mind him. Is there anything we can help you with?" The apron-clad woman was sweet as pie and reminded Scarlett of Aunt Bee on the Andy Griffith show, only slim and trim.

"Thank you, but Rogers has been very helpful. I just needed to pick up a few things."

Scarlett headed towards the back of the store and soon returned with some fruit, bread, cheese, and some cold Rainier beer before setting them on the counter. After taking her money, Roger bagged them up and handed her change back. "You'll be fine down at Jake's. Be safe on the road now."

"I will. Thank you very much."

As the bell over the door jingled with Scarlett's exit, Roger's wife teased, "You seem to have an eye for redheads. I saw that look."

Roger slipped his arm around his wife's waist. "You mean like the look I gave you nearly fifty years ago?"

It was early evening when Scarlett rolled up to the long wooden building that was the feed store. A 'closed' sign hung in the front door window, and no vehicles were out front in the parking lot.

A bit relieved that no one was around, Scarlett drove up the left side of the property, past the red-sided building, and into a large graveled lot in back. A pair of metal fuel tanks elevated on an iron stand sat directly behind the store at the very back of the property. Near them but well to the left and out of the way was a vacant area ideally suited for parking the van.

Before settling in for the night, Scarlett wanted to get familiar with the property and left the van for a short walkabout. She always slept better knowing her surroundings. A relatively open field of sagebrush lay to the north, directly beyond the fuel tanks and the place where she'd parked.

She strolled east across the lot. The crunching gravel under her sandals seemed especially loud in the otherwise silent twilight. Approaching the east end of the lot bordered by a four-strand barbed wire fence, a single meadowlark sang out a welcoming melody from the top wire. Scarlett stopped to listen. The bird sang out again, flicked its wings once, looked Scarlett straight in the eye, and took flight.

Scarlett strode forward to stand at the fence where the bird had been and observed a farmhouse on the far side of the field the fence bordered. Yellow porch lights burned on the back deck, but she saw no one about the place. Turning to her right, Scarlett saw that the gravel lot turned into a narrower two-track road curving past the east end of the building and around to the front,

Turning back, she strolled along the side of the old, weathered wood building, reaching out to feel the rough surface slide beneath her fingertips. About halfway along, she stopped at the loading dock and the large sliding doors on the side of the building. She imagined all the traffic it must have seen over the years there. Men working to move bales of hay, sacks of feed, lumber, and metal farm and livestock equipment, all under the watchful eye of some blue-eyed Healer.

Moving beyond the loading dock, Scarlett took note of the coiled hose hanging on the side of the building and the water faucet below. *Perfect.* She would return and fill a couple of water containers for use inside the van.

It was getting dark when she returned to the van with the filled water containers. Scarlett quickly prepared a simple dinner of cheese and crackers with a sliced apple and kicked back with a cold Rainier. The place was tranquil, and she couldn't have felt more secure as darkness fell.

She awoke just before dawn the next morning and, feeling the need for a shower, cautiously found her way through the murky light to the back of the building where the water hose she'd seen the night before hung. She knew the water would be cold, but it's hard to put off washing up when you begin to smell yourself.

The morning light was barely enough to see when she searched for the faucet and turned it on. She wasn't about to go running around completely naked in such an unfamiliar place, but wanting to get out of day-old stinky clothes, she stripped down to her panties and turned on the hose.

The water was cold but not as bad as expected, and after getting used to it, she enjoyed the refreshing feeling of getting clean again. After lathering up, she scrubbed away at the oily grime accumulated over the last few days of travel and began feeling more comfortable in her skin again.

Finishing up after rinsing out her hair, she bent over to turn off the water when a male voice caused her to jump with a yelp.

"Well, well. Damned if that backside don't look familiar."

The calm, easy voice and chuckle that followed sounded too familiar to believe, and Scarlett nearly spun around to see if it was who she was thinking of before remembering she was half naked. Swiftly grabbing the towel she'd left hanging from a nail on the side of the building, she wrapped it around herself and slowly turned.

"No - way." The words escaped her lips before she could even think.

"Is it really you? I hope not, I mean, I hope, I mean…"

The young cowboy laughed so hard at her predicament that he could barely collect himself. Bent over at the waist, the hilarious situation overwhelmed him, and he staggered backward a few steps.

Attempting to gather his breath, he tried to speak.

"They told me someone…" Laughter interrupted again before he could continue. "They told me someone would be here to help me get what I need – what I need for my fencing project, but the last person I ever expected to see here is you. And in your birthday suit as well!"

Scarlett turned the color of her name as the man fell into another fit of laughter.

"Jack. Let me get dressed. I'll be right back."

"No hurry. I parked in front and need to go fetch my truck."

His easy chortle followed her across the gravel lot while she raced to the van. Her bare legs prickled with goose bumps in the cool morning air, but it was nothing compared to the warm blush on her face.

Quickly pulling on a pair of jeans, she caught herself. *The air isn't that cool, yet you have goose bumps. Maybe you're just embarrassed. Yes, that must be it. I couldn't have been more uncomfortable. But imagine, it could have been someone else showing up early to help Jack with his supplies. If not for Jack, it might have been some employee showing up to greet me with a good morning.*

She shuddered. *And then I most certainly would have died.*

While finishing getting dressed, a store employee raced in to help Jack load his truck with fencing materials.

After Jack's truck was loaded and he was ready to leave, Scarlett slipped out of the van and quietly walked across the lot to see him. It had been years, and though Jack seemed perfectly comfortable with the strange circumstances, Scarlett was apprehensive. It wasn't her best look, dressed in flip-flops, a faded Stones T-shirt, and her wet hair hanging limp.

After all these years, if someone had told me this was how I would eventually see him again, I most certainly would have made sure I was somewhere else this morning.

Years later and a lot of water under the bridge, his easy going manner hadn't changed. Coupled with his still delightfully good looks, Scarlett relaxed.

He was leaning against the side of his truck with one arm resting atop the truck's bed and the other stuffed in the front pocket of his jeans. He looked good in a cowboy hat and reminded her of the Marlboro Man.

Scarlett extended her hand, and his rough palm engulfed it.

"Jack, what in the world are you doing here?"

He tipped back his black hat and greeted her with a beaming smile. For a brief moment, he just stared.

"To greet you good morning, of course." He grinned. "You're a sight for sore eyes, Scarlett." He said while shaking his head. "Seems we are always destined to find each other, one way or the other."

"I had the same thought. But how crazy to run into you here, of all places."

"At least it didn't require a car wreck in a snow bank." He winked, though his eyes never left her, as if he wasn't sure who he was looking at."

"So, Jack, how in the world does a guy like you end up in a place like this?"

"Scarlett, this is all pretty wild, and I would like nothing more than to sit down and catch up with you, but as much as I'd like that, I need to go."

Feeling as if he was putting her off, Scarlett frowned.

Jack shrugged and quickly followed with "Boss Man. You know how that works, and she'll be pissed if I'm late."

Wondering just what he meant by "she'll be pissed," Scarlett glanced at his left hand and saw no ring there. But a lot of men working around equipment chose not to wear them.

An uncomfortable silence filled the space between them before Jack offered another way. "Look, if you like, I can give you directions to where I'm working, and we can visit while I build a fence."

Her smile may have said too much. She didn't want to seem too eager, but she quickly accepted his offer, still not believing it would happen.

Jack finished writing down the directions on the stained napkin he pulled from under the front seat of his pickup and turned to hand it to Scarlett.

"I'll be there all day. So head on out if you want. It's easy to find."

Scarlett reached to take the directions, and that's when Jack took her hand in his big, callused paws. To her surprise, they were warm and reassuring.

"Scarlett, it was good to see you." His big blue eyes bore straight into her own. The sincerity she saw there surprised her, and she stumbled for words.

"Um, yes. This was more of a surprise than I was ready for this morning. I guess I'll see you in a little while." Then Scarlett winked.

"Oh girl, that's just mean. You remember perfectly well what that does to me."

"Maybe, maybe not," she pretended. "Besides, you winked first."

Scarlett saw him suck in his gut and swallow the "ooh" that nearly escaped his lips. Recovering quickly, he reached up and touched his hat in an old Hollywood gesture.

"Good to see you, ma'am. I best be going now."

A mischievous smile peered out from under the brim of his hat and conveyed the subtle humor well.

Scarlett watched his long, muscular frame climb into the truck's cab.

"If you're not putting me on, I'll see you in a little while."

Jack turned the wheel of his truck and began to drive away while leaning into the open window. "Wouldn't do that to you, ma'am."

Even though she knew better, his delightful smile filled Scarlett with a hungry desire to see him.

PART THREE:
JACK AND SCARLETT

CHAPTER THIRTY THREE

AFTER A BREAKFAST OF TOAST, SCRAMBLED EGGS, AND COFfee, Scarlett changed clothes, brushed her hair, and checked the image in the van's rearview mirror. She told herself no makeup. She hadn't worn any in nearly a year and wasn't doing so now. Then, smiling to herself – *I haven't shaved my legs for a while either, but he won't be seeing them. And I'm not dressing to impress. A clean T-shirt and a snug pair of jeans are what I wear, and that's not changing.*

Then, stopping in mid thought, with one leg in her jeans and one leg out, Scarlett began to wonder if seeing him was such a good idea. She sat on the side of her bed at the back of the van for a moment before slipping on the other leg of her jeans. Head in her hands, she doubted herself.

She had freed herself of the past. Why go back? Driving right on out of town just like she'd planned seemed like the smart thing to do. Though her head said no, her heart said yes, and she realized the only way to know was to pray.

Fifteen minutes, then twenty, and there was still no answer. She asked for a solid check about seeing Jack and received none. After another five minutes with no answer and no solid check, Scarlett decided to go. Confident that her strong relationship with the Lord, which had grown and developed over the course of the winter, would have resulted in a strong check against going if she was not to go, Scarlett finished preparing to leave.

After setting the napkin with the directions to Jack's work site in the passenger seat and placing her purse on top of it to keep the wind coming through the open windows from blowing it away, Scarlett took a new road into the unknown.

It was early afternoon when she drove west out of town before turning north. According to the bank thermometer, the blistering sun already had temperatures well above ninety degrees.

She doubted anything would come of the meeting with Jack, but maybe it would answer some questions and put to bed once and for all the things about their past that still haunted her.

Traveling north on a county road surrounded by blonde fields of wheat waving in the gentle wind, she was to turn right after about three miles. She relaxed when an abandoned homestead loomed in the distance, precisely where Jack had drawn on his map. It was the landmark he said to look for before turning off the county road.

Scarlett left the wheat fields behind after turning right onto a gravel road at the corner with the old homestead buildings. Traveling less than a mile through rangeland filled with bunchgrass and sagebrush, she soon spotted Jack's pickup near the side of the road.

After pulling up next to his truck, Jack set the post-pounder aside and greeted her with a colossal smile. This time, the re-introduction went easier, and the uncomfortable tension they both felt initially eased as they visited. Mostly, Scarlett talked while Jack pounded posts and stretched wire. The conversation was light, and they shared laughs while marveling over the crazy way they had bumped into one another in such an out-of-the-way place.

Scarlett was wilting under the blazing sun but couldn't pull herself away from the sweaty, hard body flexing in the golden light right before her eyes. She'd been close to this man once and couldn't help but recall the hard muscles and feel of his arms around her. The shirtless, tanned, sculpted back, broad shoulders, and chest created an ache that couldn't be denied.

Having forgotten to bring water, she asked if Jack would share his as he lowered the jug from his mouth. Holding the container out with one hand and dragging the back of his other hand across his mouth, he grinned.

"Got my cooties on it."

"Never bothered me before." She chided, then immediately wished she hadn't said it. *Too much too soon, Scarlett. This isn't old times.*

She turned away to collect herself while drawing deep from the water jug. Turning back, she changed the subject. "Never thought I'd see you with a farmer's tan, Jack."

"Well, I'm working on that. No shirt, as you can see."

Yes, I can, and you're driving me nuts.

An awkward silence began to grow between them. Jack took back the water jug and, excusing himself, moved to his next post, where he started working the post-pounder again. The muscles in his back and shoulders tightened and flexed each time he drove the post into the ground.

"Um, Jack. I think it's time for me to go, but I have a question."

"Sure." He grunted as he thrust the post pounder down on the fence post.

"You just vanished, Jack. Do you know how hard it was not knowing? We may have split up, but I still cared about you."

Jack turned to face her. His face showed regret before he could hide it behind a disarming smile.

"Obviously, we have a lot to talk about. So how about you? What have you been up to all these years?"

The perfect dodge. Turn it back on me. She thought. *He was always so good at that.*

"That's a subject for another time."

Jack tossed the post-pounder back toward the fence and approached her. Wiping the sweat from his forehead, a streak of dirt smudged his brow. Scarlett caught herself liking the look.

"Alright. Understood." Looking down, he shuffled his feet in the dirt a moment, and Scarlett knew he was working up to something. "I've enjoyed visiting with you. This whole thing, running into you here and all, it's just so crazy, actually, but…"

Oh no, here it comes.

"Well, maybe," he stammered. It wasn't like him to be nervous, and Scarlett wondered why. "Maybe, if you like, we could meet in town tonight."

When she hesitated, he quickly replied, "Just to talk."

A shocked Scarlett agreed. Jack described a place immediately west of town called the Minstrel's Oasis.

"They have live music there, and it's a safe enough place you can feel comfortable walking in alone."

Nice. He cares about my safety. Have to admit it feels good. Been alone for such a long time, Scarlett, you've forgotten what that feels like.

"I'd like that. A lot of water under the bridge since… well, you know. Since then."

"Alright." He seemed relieved. "Sometime around eight?"

"Eight it is. I'll see you there."

Like a ghost, their past together rose up from the grave she'd tried to bury it in to haunt her on the drive home, and Scarlett spent much of the day wondering if this was such a good idea. Each time she'd begin to think positively about him – this is a different time and a different place – their dark past would push those thoughts aside. The cutting, belittling, demeaning remarks they had once used to attack one another lingered and would not easily be overcome.

Then she scolded herself. *What are you doing, Scarlett? Why concern yourself with all this? It's just a couple of old friends catching up. Well, ok, old friends with a lot of history.*

That evening, her internal debate continued during the entire drive out of town to the country bar Jack gave her directions to.

Turn around, Scarlett. Don't start this.

I'll be careful. I might be sorry, but it will answer so many questions and ease my mind just to visit with him for a bit.

Scarlett arrived at the Minstrel's Oasis a little after eight and could hear the music from out in the parking lot—good ol' rock and roll. But walking through the gravel lot, the sun sinking low on the western horizon, she grew nervous and turned around. Back at her van, she again questioned what she was doing.

But why the chance meeting? There must be a reason, and I need to find out what that is.

Curiosity killed the cat.

Not this one!

With renewed determination, she marched to the front door, paid the two-dollar cover charge, held her hand out to be stamped, and stepped into a typical, smokey, dimly lit country western bar. The wood floor contained a mixture of wood shavings and peanut shells, while the jukebox on her left greeted with colorful red and blue lights.

A long wooden bar was straight ahead and to her left. Tables, the dance floor, and the low stage with the band were to her right. The tavern was packed, and passing through the stable of cowboys and plowboys, she felt their probing eyes scrutinizing the tall, lean, redheaded stranger in their midst.

Jack, where are you?

The place wasn't that big, and business was booming. Her eyes roamed the room as she approached the row of chairs lining the bar. Not finding him, she stepped up and ordered a beer. Turning about, she spotted a small round table adjacent to the dance floor on its right-hand side. It was unoccupied, and other than a couple of stools at the bar, where she knew she'd immediately be hit on, it was the only vacant table in the building unless she wanted to sit in the very back, where Jack wasn't likely to spot her.

Maybe he got stuck working late at the ranch? Oh well, it's been a long time since I've heard live music, so I don't mind hanging out for a bit.

Twenty minutes later, dreadful memories were prowling her mind, reminding Scarlett of the numerous times he'd stood her up for another woman or almost any other reason for that matter.

See. That's all the proof you need to know you could never trust him. Don't allow it to happen again.

Jack had often stood her up in college, and she began to sense the old resentment rising. Scarlett resolved to ignore the thoughts by telling herself it was ridiculous to think that way and that she'd long ago buried those hurts deep in some unmarked grave on the other side of the moon. She wasn't going to freak out over this. One beer, and if he hadn't shown up by then, she'd know it was not meant to be and would be gone without a word. His loss! But the threads of anger were already spreading from her back and around to her stomach, where they did everything they could to open the old wounds of heartbreak.

Of course, a woman sitting alone in a bar like that was a magnet for every guy in the place, and like bees to honey, it didn't take long. After turning down a number of requests, she finally accepted an offer to dance, if only to get a break from the continual demands.

The music was decent enough for a backwoods kind of place. It was a mix of country and rock and roll, and Scarlett tried to relax while continuing to hope Jack would show up soon. After the first dance, she wasn't ready to sit down again and hung around on the dance floor while the guy chatted her up for a second dance. Big mistake.

Over the speakers came a loud, deep voice that filled the bar. THE NEXT SONG IS DEDICATED TO…a drum roll followed…SCARLETT!

The band began a decent rendition of the Beatles's "Something in the Way She Moves," and a puzzled Scarlett, knowing something was up, began looking everywhere about the place. Thankful no one in the bar knew her name, she remained anonymous. A slow dance was the last thing she wanted, but at least the guy was well-behaved and keeping his hands to himself. There was no sign of Jack, but it would be just like him to pull some trick, and she grew suspicious.

Minutes later, the guy's cloying aftershave became too much. Unaccustomed to crowds, a feeling of claustrophobia began creeping in. Suddenly, she needed to be elsewhere.

Jack, where are you? I'm starting to get pis…

Turning about as they danced, Scarlett looked in the band's direction and was shocked to see him on stage behind the drum set. Their eyes met, and an undeniable glow filled her chest. A white cowboy hat had hidden most of his face until now. Upon seeing her, his face lit up from within, and a gigantic smile sparked blue eyes as if experiencing the delight of finding a long-lost treasure. Jack was very much enjoying the moment and the fact he'd surprised her.

He'd been watching her since she first set foot in the bar. Ever the jokester, it was part of his charm, and once again, Scarlett was reminded of how good it felt to know there was someone who cared and would go to the trouble of surprising her. The ache that surfaced reminded her of just how long it had been.

When the song ended, Scarlett excused herself and stepped towards the stage. Jack stepped out from behind the drums, thrilled with the trick he'd just pulled. Stepping to the front of the stage, he motioned for Scarlett to come close.

"I'll be done shortly. Break in two more songs." He grinned.

Scarlett returned the smile and said she'd be waiting at her table.

Jack returned the crazy-eyed look she'd once known so well. The one acknowledging just how much she got to him.

Two songs later, before the singer could finish announcing the band's break, two cowgirls dressed in full regalia made their way to the stage. One stopped to visit with the singer, and the other went around to the side of the stage to catch Jack as he exited the drum set.

No woman alive could have missed what this gal was selling, and as Jack stepped from the stage, she put her arm around his waist and pulled him close. Trying not to be rude, Jack removed her arm and graciously extracted himself from the one-sided conversation. But the woman wasn't getting it, and Jack soon turned to face her and pointed toward Scarlett. When the woman's face fell, Jack raised both hands in the air as if to say sorry and walked across the dance floor to join Scarlett.

Wow. Since when does that happen? Scarlett wondered.

This was not the Jack she'd once known. In the past, every good-looking girl that caught his eye had his attention. Even though Scarlett wasn't selling what this girl was offering, Jack had eyes for just one person: her.

Electricity heated Scarlett's belly. Jack had never been this way with her, and the fact he only had one person on his mind thrilled her in a way she hadn't known since first meeting her ex-husband.

Suddenly, Jack became more interesting as Scarlett realized she didn't really know this version of Jack.

He took a seat opposite her and set his callused hands on the table. His sparkling blue eyes and monster smile were all intended for Scarlett.

"Scarlett, I've been looking forward to seeing you tonight." He flashed the smile that always charmed her and reached across the table to take her hand.

"I was worried you might drive right on by after seeing this place from the outside." He chuckled. "It does kinda have that down home dive bar look to it, doesn't it."

Scarlett squeezed his hand. "Yes, it does, but Jack, I wanted to see you again and wasn't going to let it put me off."

"Even after…"

Scarlett interrupted. "Yes, even after, and let's not go there again. That's all in the past, and I don't want to be dredging it up right now!"

Jack nodded. "Agreed."

"I know it's been years, but it wouldn't have been right not to show up after the crazy way we bumped into each other again."

Jack's eyebrows shot up and tugged at one corner of his mouth. "Um, hum. You can say that again."

A slow blush crept up the sides of Scarlett's neck, and her freckled face began to glow.

"It was quite the memorable moment, alright." He squeezed her hand again.

Before things could get too awkward, Scarlett changed the subject. "When did you pick up the drums?"

"Oh gosh, it hasn't been that long. And honestly, I'm not that good, but these guys were hard up. It's that simple. They're helping me get it down and cover for my mistakes."

Scarlett smiled and returned the squeeze of his hand. "I hadn't noticed."

Jack shook his head while looking down at the table. "Believe me, it's a work in progress."

Deep down, Scarlett was enthralled. There was an undeniable energy between them. It had always been there, and all their time apart had not diminished it. Yet, it was also what had taken them down such a long, insufferable road, leading to a brutal ending. He may have seemed like a different man, but she knew the old, complicated Jack was also in there. The one she'd long ago fallen in love with. She sensed it more than saw it. But this was also the man who shunned her and broke her heart in a way that had never healed. And for that, she hated him. Shocked at how strong the feeling remained, she pulled back her hand. It wasn't like he'd changed into some slick new sophisticated gentleman – God forbid – but the rough edges seemed gone. It was a strange brew.

Dangerous territory, Scarlett. Her conscience warned. *Tread lightly.*

The two were interrupted when someone in the band yelled, "Hey, Renaissance Man. Time to go."

"Be right there." Jack acknowledged.

"Renaissance Man? What's that all about?"

"They're just harassing me." He reached across the table and took back her hand. "I'll be back soon."

The band played until just after midnight. During breaks, Jack would join Scarlett at her table, and she even got in a couple of jukebox dances with him. It felt good to be held in his arms again. She'd forgotten how good!

In a shadowy corner away from the dance floor and unseen by Jack, a blond-haired beauty was keeping a close eye on Jack's every move.

When the band finished up for the night, Jack walked Scarlett outside to her van and opened the driver-side door to let her in. But Scarlett didn't move to get inside. Instead, she stared at him.

"Did I say something wrong?" Jack shrugged.

Scarlett remained silent for a beat, finding the moment a little too big. Then, shaking her head.

"Nothing like that, Jack. I'm hesitant because I don't know where to go from here."

"Well, are you planning on hanging around for a while?"

"Mmm, honestly, I was about to leave town." She drew near and patted his chest with a flat palm. "So many things from the past are coming to life."

Thunder cracked overhead, and a light rain began to fall.

"Can't be good, huh?" Jack grimaced.

Scarlett slipped her arms inside the leather jacket he always wore when riding his Harley. Then, looking up into his eyes. "You talking about the weather," she taunted, or us?"

"Oh! There's an us now already?" Jack play acted, thrusting a hand over his heart. Then, in a high-pitched voice, "Oh, you're moving too fast for me, Scarlett. My heart is all a flutter."

Scarlett laughed softly. "Nice try."

"I'd like it if you stuck around. Get to know each other again?"

Tilting her head, "Would you like me to stick around for a while, or is this the old Jack I know so well who has other things on his mind?" She toyed.

"The old Jack?" He played dumb, and Scarlett slugged his shoulder.

"You know exactly what I'm talking about!"

"Kinda makes my point. We both have these impressions of one another from years ago. I'd like it if we could take the time to get to know each other as we are now. No strings attached."

Scarlett struggled for a moment. This was not what she had expected. "Let me sleep on it, alright. I'll think it over."

Jack eyed the red shock of silky hair cascading across her shoulders. The rain was picking up, and he pulled her close, sheltering her in his arms. She leaned in to kiss him and had her answer to the question if she'd stay when his lips gently caressed her mouth. The electricity between them was instant, melting away the years as if they had never been apart. The slumbering embers Scarlett thought she'd buried long ago sprang to life. She would be staying long enough to know the Jack of today.

Jack drew her close with one arm around her waist and the other behind her head. The deeper their kiss, the harder the rain fell until Scarlett leaned back and peered into his eyes.

Both looked up when interrupted by a loud truck at the back of the parking lot, revving its engine and roaring off, throwing gravel and dust into the air. When they returned their gaze to one another, Jack leaned in for one more kiss.

"Alright, Jack. That's enough." She pushed him back. "This is all happening too fast."

The rain's intensity picked up, soaking her hair and T-shirt. She looked hard at Jack. "We're not going back down that road, Jack. If I stay, it's to answer questions I'm sure we each have and get to know one another again.

He tucked a strand of rain-darkened hair behind her ear. "Agreed. Now you'd better go. You're getting soaked."

"What about you?"

"I'll be fine. I've ridden in the rain before."

"Be careful." Reluctantly, she pushed away.

"And tomorrow?"

"Let me sleep on it Jack. I've got a lot to think about. It was a crazy day running into you the way we did. I enjoyed my time with you tonight, but our past, Jack. What do we do with that?"

"What past?"

"Yes, it would be easy to ignore, wouldn't it? But if I stay, we will need to deal with it at some point, and that's what holds me back."

The dark shadows cast across Jack's face by the moonlight smiled. "Agreed. I'm not sure I would be willing to kill someone for you now."

"See what I mean. Let's not ruin a perfectly good evening. I had a good time tonight, and I'll talk to you one way or the other tomorrow. Can I find you at the same place?"

Jack nodded. "I'll be there." He leaned in for another kiss, but she pushed back and shot him a warning look. "See you tomorrow, Jack."

Driving home through the rain, listening to the wiper's rhythm on the windshield, Scarlett chastised herself. *How many times before you learn Scarlett? He can't be trusted and will tear your heart wide open again. Are you prepared for that? You saw what he was after.*

But the sensations running through her limbs were more potent than any liquor she'd ever drank, and her throbbing heart demanded she see him again. One way or the other, it was too late to back out now.

Scarlett, don't be a fool. Drive away, leave town, and don't look back. He doesn't deserve you. Your heart is on the line here, and you know better.

There it was again. That nagging voice. Did it have her best interest in mind? Or was she just that blind?

The argument within continued, but she could still feel the beat of his heart against her chest while they stood together in the rain, and the feeling of being encircled by his arms was nearly as overpowering as the bad aftershave she'd experienced earlier that evening. It had been years since being that close to a man. Did he genuinely care about her, or was it the simple longing of having spent so much time alone that drove her? She knew better than to get involved with him again, but knew she would.

Oh, Scarlett, what have you done?

When morning arrived, the debate continued while she made toast and sipped her coffee. *The heart says yes, and the head says no—the age-old conundrum.*

She shrugged, surrendering to the impossibility of knowing the answer. *You can run away or acknowledge the risk and accept the consequences.*

Just what would she be getting herself into if she stayed? She had no idea. And yet, she sensed something different about Jack. She'd seen it in his eyes and felt it in his arms. He didn't hang with all the guys in the band, cutting up and carrying on. His attention remained focused strictly on her, even when the easy women approached him. He seemed less focused on himself and, for the most part, had been the perfect gentleman.

But it was more than that. The hard parts, the calloused outer shell, the rough edges, and the self-centered demeanor all seemed worn down like a rock weathered and beaten in the surf. Had Jack been beaten similarly? Had all the time on the road worn him down? Was it enough to risk her heart again? She would have to stay if she wanted to find out, and that left little choice but to see him again.

Scarlett stopped in the town bakery on her way to see Jack to grab a couple of breakfast treats for him. Entering the white building with the red-framed front door, she noticed the help wanted sign as the bell over the door rang notice of her entry. They were hiring, and she decided to inquire.

After selecting three different doughnuts, Scarlett approached the counter to pay. A roundish white-haired woman wearing a red and white apron greeted her.

"Hello honey, what can I do for you?"

Scarlett held out the bag of doughnuts. "I came for doughnuts and saw the sign on the door."

"You're new in town, aren't you, hun?"

"Yes, Mam."

"Well, if I were to bring you on, could I trust you?"

"You certainly can."

"We'll see about that, but I could certainly use the help. Can you be on time, even early?"

"Yes, Mam."

The elderly woman rolled her eyes. "Stop it with that! My name is Mable, and we'll get along just fine if you can be here on time and stop calling me Mam."

The twinkle in her eye told Scarlett everything she needed to know.

"I can do that Ma...um Mable."

"You've been taught manners, ain't cha, child."

"I grew up with a lot of what you might call a country-folk influence."

"And with more than a dash of common sense, I spect."

"Yes, Mmmmable."

Mable chuckled. "What do you know about canning?"

"My grandmother canned and filled her basement with all sorts of canned goods, including homegrown veggies and sometimes even whole chickens. I was little then, but sometimes I helped."

Mable nodded in acknowledgment. "She was a woman who knew hard times, no doubt. A time when no one was there to help out but herself." The warm smile creasing Mable's face took Scarlett back to when she spent summers working with her grandparents in the garden.

"Bet she was a good woman. Hard worker and one who could turn a basic meal into a banquet."

How did this stranger know these things?

"Don't look so surprised, child. Those roots run deep. My grandmother was the same."

"But she would have been older than my grandmother," Scarlett noted.

"Same difference. The twenties and thirties were tough years. And then there was the war. I think we'll get along just fine, but I have another question for you. I've hired people who were passing through before. How long do you plan on staying?"

"Honestly, I don't know, but hopefully through summer and into fall."

"I appreciate your honesty. I'll be thrilled if you can make it to fall. I can normally find some help after harvest season finishes."

"So when do I start?" Scarlett's broad smile lit up her green eyes and highlighted her freckles.

"Tomorrow morning at five AM sharp if that works for you."

"I'll be here." She reached into her purse to pay for the doughnuts, but Mable held up a hand to stop her.

"It's on the house. See you tomorrow."

CHAPTER THIRTY FOUR

JACK UNTANGLED HIMSELF FROM THE TWISTED SHEETS HE'D thrashed about in all night. The sweat-soaked linen stuck to him and grabbed at his foot as he exited the bed, face-planting him on the floor with a grunt. He lay there listening to his windup alarm clock ring out the last of its wake-up call.

His tortured, nightmarish sleep left him exhausted, and now he was about to face the object of his struggles. The last thing he wanted was to lie to Scarlett. But how could he tell her he was living and sleeping with Rachel? Impossible! And he couldn't just walk away from Rachel either. He'd given his word he'd be there for harvest, and besides, nothing had ever worked between him and Scarlett, so why risk a good situation with Rachel? The equation was driving him up the wall.

Leaving Rachel was not an option. And yet, he couldn't deny the fire that still burned for Scarlett. It made no sense. She'd broken his heart, and he was crazy even to consider what the possibilities were with her. Still, he couldn't deny the instant connection the night before. They shared this crazy attraction neither could deny, and it hadn't dimmed one lick over the years. And yet, was it worth turning his world upside down for someone who'd wronged him and broken his heart? Not a chance. The two of them were incompatible, yet something was different. Was it peace he'd felt? That didn't seem likely. The natural hunger he'd always felt for her body was there, but looking deeper, he was sure something was different; something had changed.

Jack had never felt so confused. His life was mostly black and white, right and wrong, and he moved on without looking back once he'd made a decision. He'd jump on his motorcycle and ride off when things got too messy. Well, that is what the old Jack would have done. Maybe it's why he felt so twisted up inside now, because today, he couldn't just ride away. Instead, he had to go downstairs and face Rachel.

Breakfast was hearty. Hashed browns and gravy, bacon, three eggs, toast, and all the coffee he could drink. Rachel never failed to make a man-sized breakfast before sending him off to a man-sized day of work.

Pushing away from the table and reaching for the sack lunch waiting for him on the kitchen counter, Jack turned to leave.

"Forgetting something, Jack?"

He turned in time to see a slender, shapely leg extending from between the folds of Rachel's bathrobe. He always kissed her goodbye in the morning but let it slip in his perplexed state of mind.

Slipping his arms around her waist, he kissed her goodbye and immediately felt guilty. *Why? What's that all about?*

"Something else on your mind?"

"Oh, no. Just thinking of work today."

"Wouldn't want you to forget about me." Her smile teased, distracting Jack from the mischief playing at the corners of her mouth.

"No chance of that. I'll see you tonight, Rachel."

After loading his truck, Jack drove out to the work site. Engulfed in the turmoil inside his head, he drove slower than usual this morning. He and Rachel got along so well. They fit the same comfortable groove in life - single, content, and uncommitted, *meaning unentangled.*

He was wanted, respected, and needed. Nothing was missing, and he hated how this perfect situation had been disrupted. He did not love

Rachel, that much he knew. But it was an excellent place to be. Life hadn't been this comfortable for a long time, and he wasn't ready to throw it away on some long shot with Scarlett.

At the work site, Jack loaded ten fence posts in his bulging arms and, beginning where he'd finished the day before, started walking the fence line, dropping off the fence posts as he measured the distance between each with his strides. The dust his feet kicked up went unseen because his mind was already back in the ring, continuing the wrestling match with Scarlett.

Scarlett. What a beautiful woman. A woman he had once loved, but that was years ago when they were too young and stupid to know young love never lasted.

I'm older now, more mature, and I know better.

When did that ever stop you, Jack?

Shut up. It never worked with her, and we hurt each other deeply.

Do you love her?

The question stopped Jack in his tracks. He dropped the three remaining fence posts and gazed out over the rangeland. Prickly sage sprinkled amongst the perennial green grasses reminded him of the landscape of his life. *All we need is a hot, stiff wind to scorch and crack the surface of the land, sucking every bit of life out of it, and it would be the perfect mirror of my life.*

But the rain always comes, refreshing, renewing, and bringing forth new life.

Who asked you? I hate when you interrupt.

Jack turned and marched back to the truck. Removing the post pounder from the truck bed with one hand, he walked to the first post, stood it upright, and began pounding. The shock of striking the post rippled through his forearms and chest muscles. After fiercely driving the post into the ground and marching to the next, he set it up and pounded. Then, moving to the next, he did the same until he came to the last post, looked up, and saw dust rising in the distance.

Here comes trouble.

Stop it! You can't think like that. She's done nothing.

Yeah, but she's about to.

He stood there transfixed until the van came into view.

What do I do now?

A minute later, Scarlett stepped from the van and approached him. The long, toned legs in cut-off jeans immediately caught his eye, and his day instantly brightened. Her natural beauty was striking, and he felt his resolve melt away. The sunlight in her flowing crimson hair, the freckles he'd always adored, the smile that never failed to lift his spirits, and the laughter in her brilliant green eyes enchanted him.

Yup. Here comes trouble.

"Good morning, Jack."

"Hello, Scarlett."

"I wanted to tell you what a good time I had last night. I wasn't prepared for your little surprise."

"Just having a little fun. You know how I am."

"Ha, that's kinda the question, isn't it? I mean, I do know you, but yet I don't know you." Scarlett frowned. "Sorry. I don't mean to be so upfront. I didn't come here to talk about that. I had fun with you, Jack. It's just, just that…"

"We've always had fun together, Scarlett." Jack smiled.

"Um, yes and no, but we need some time to visit, just not here, not now."

"Did you have something in mind?"

Scarlett avoided the question by extracting a maple bar from the paper bag she'd brought from the bakery before handing the sack to Jack.

"Brought you a couple of snacks, Jack."

Jack took hold of the paper sack, looked inside, and licked his lips. "Well, thank you. Must think I need fattened up a bit, huh?" Jack patted his perfectly rippled and flat stomach.

"Hardly." Reflecting on the previous day when Jack was shirtless, Scarlett felt a tingle in her stomach. "Look, Jack, be honest with me; we both felt the connection last night. It's something that's always been there."

"Um-hmm. Agreed." Jack nodded but remained silent with a mouthful of doughnut.

"It's something we had years ago and doesn't seem to have diminished with time."

"Um – hmm." He nodded. "These are good." He lifted the bag to offer her one.

"Come on Jack. Don't make me do all the work here." Scarlett stomped her foot, raising a miniature cloud of dust. "We both felt it."

"Yes, but our past ain't so pretty."

"Yes, yes, the past. It does get in the way, doesn't it. But we were both young and dumb."

"Speak for yourself."

"Don't give me that shit, Jack! I'm not a little girl anymore. You'll find you can no longer sell me that crap. I won't be buffaloed so easily."

Reminded of how he loved her fiery spirit, to a point anyway, it was apparent that much hadn't changed. Then, remembering how her freckles would light up when her temper flared like they were doing right now, it tickled a place near his heart. This was a part of Scarlett he'd always found so endearing.

"Look." She continued. "You were pretty messed up when we parted. The question is, are you still? I'm prepared to leave this moment if I don't get an honest answer." Scarlet's face flushed an angry cherry color, and Jack knew he'd crossed a line.

"Look. I'm sorry. You have my apologies. And yes. I'm willing to admit I was pretty messed up." He glanced up and smiled mischievously. "And a lot of it was your fault, too."

"Jack, stop. No more games!" Scarlett held up her hand.

"Ok, ok. There's little doubt we've changed. Maybe this natural attraction we still feel is all there is? We could be further apart than ever, and…"

"I agree. We could be very different people now. It's what I'm trying to get to the bottom of. Do you think it's worth exploring what we once had or not? The years have passed, we've grown, and no doubt changed, but somehow this mutual attraction remains. Here we are, single and brought together in this far-flung setting, and I can't help but wonder why." She shrugged and looked to Jack for help, but absorbed in consuming the donut, he remained quiet.

"Did you ever think there might be something more behind this? Like God, maybe…Sorry, I forgot you don't buy into the God thing. Still…"

Jack held up a hand to stop her rant. "Scarlett, there's always been a place in my heart for you, but our past isn't so great. The smart thing to do might be…"

"Aren't you the least bit intrigued?"

Jack nodded. "Yes. Of course I am. But at what price?" His questioning gesture lit up both blue eyes. "And I find it so damn strange we've ended up together in this little one-horse town. I can't wrap my head around it. Don't you think it's just a bit odd?"

"Certainly. But maybe there's more to it than just some random occurrence, and there's only one way to know. Would you agree to sit down, compare notes, share what's been happening in our lives, and see if there's still something worth pursuing?"

Jack's smile split his face. "Sounds kinda sterile to me, Scarlett. But that's the Scarlett I once knew to a "T." Perfectly logical. Lay it all out on paper. This goes in the plus column, and this is in the negative column. It's all perfectly rational. No games, no wasting each other's time. Just straight down the road," He pointed down the gravel road with one hand.

"Jack, that's not fair."

"It's all gotta add up. Perfectly clinical. I remember it so well. At times, you drove me up the wall with it. No spontaneity, just an unending list of questions leading to a logical conclusion."

Scarlett jammed both hands on her hips. "That's not true, Jack!"

"Forget it. I agree we need to see if there's something more to this than two old flames bumping into one another. Now, how's that for logical?"

Scarlett couldn't help but chuckle. "I always enjoyed your humor, Jack. But I'm serious. I won't allow you to mess up my life, but I would like to see if there's more to this than old emotions. We both know the risk, but given what we once had, I think it's worth discovering the answer to this equation now that we are older."

"Equation!" Jack stomped his foot and laughed. "You know I was never good with math, and now I'm part of an equation!"

Scarlett was surprised at how his mocking laughter warmed her heart. It was hearty and full of delight.

"Ok, ok. As crazy as it sounds, I agree. We should get together and see if this spark we feel has life or is a dying ember."

"Wow, that's pretty deep for you." It was Scarlett's turn to laugh.

Knowing he had it coming, Jack endured it, then asked, "The band is playing again tonight. Would you be interested? I know it can be kinda boring sitting around all night, but I'd like it if you were there."

"Could you come by for dinner first?" She asked.

Jack thought for a moment. He'd have to give Rachel some kind of excuse for missing dinner. *I already hate myself because this isn't the only lie I will have to tell if I do this.*

"Sounds good. Where will you be parked?"

"Yesterday, you asked if I planned on sticking around. This morning, I took a job at the bakery, and the same people who own the store rented me a small house in town. I'm no longer parked in the far end of some parking lot."

"Or taking showers in the buff." Jack cracked himself up. Then his eye caught the dust cloud raised by a pickup racing down the gravel road. It could only mean one thing. Rachel would be here soon.

Suddenly, Jack found himself looking for a way out. The unexpected rush of adrenaline preparing him for being caught between two strong women, both of whom he was lying to, unsettled him. Already, he was getting caught up in the first trap of something far more weighty than he wanted. The thought shot through him like a poisoned dart and exploded in his gut.

He would be forced to lie about his relationship with Rachel if he wanted to move forward with Scarlett. Not to mention lying to Rachel. Suddenly, he hated himself. The open road and the feel of his bike beneath him called.

Scarlett saw the look on his face that appeared when she told him she would be sticking around. "Oh my gosh, Jack, I'm so sorry. I didn't know. I've been far too presumptuous. I should be going."

Jack reached out and took her by the shoulders. "Scarlett, it's not that at all. My boss is about to show up. I'll introduce you. She can be a bit of a hard-ass sometimes, but she's alright."

He glanced up to see the pickup drawing near and knew he needed to hurry up and say what had been on his mind.

"Scarlett, I'm the one who should apologize. We keep tippy-toeing around the obvious. I wasn't good for you, so I want to say this right up front. As much as I would like to see what we might have together, I think you'd be better off without me."

"Don't say that, Jack. I'm a big girl. I know the risk. I had all night to think about this. But I didn't expect you to be the one who chickened out."

The challenge bit hard. Jack surrendered and held up a hand. "Stop right there. What time do you want me to come by?"

Too late. Rachel roared up, covering them in a slowly moving cloud of dust. Quickly stepping from the truck, she approached Jack.

"What's going on Jack? I'm paying you to work, not fraternize with the local hussies."

"I'm sorry, Rachel. I want to introduce you to Scarlett. We go way back."

When Rachel leaned in to shake Scarlett's hand, her barely buttoned western shirt revealed more than Scarlett cared to see, and she immediately began to wonder about Jack's relationship with her.

Rachel stepped back and put her arm around Jack's waist, pulling him close.

"Way back?" Her stern look made it clear Jack had better give the correct answer.

"College days."

"Um hmmm. Sex, drugs, and rock and roll. Not sure she's a good influence."

Leaning against Jack, her blond hair cascading over his shoulder, Rachel peered into his face. Scarlett hated how she clung to him.

"I want to see this fence done. I'm headed into town and wanted to make sure you had everything you need." She kissed him on the cheek. "If you know what I mean."

Then she turned and strutted back to the truck. "See you tonight, Jack."

Scarlett noted her swaying backside and how her jeans couldn't have fit any tighter if she had been poured into them.

After the door slammed and Rachel was headed back down the road, Scarlett turned to face Jack. "I think this has been a big mistake. You never said anything…"

"Stop right there." Jack grabbed her arm. "It's not what you think."

"Sure. Like I never heard that one before."

He took hold of her other arm and turned her so he could look straight into her eyes. "I'm not lying! This is all a part of what we need to talk about. Give me a chance. I would have already told you everything if we could have spoken before this happened."

His pleading eyes were the only thing that convinced her he might be telling the truth.

"If you can pull yourself away." Scarlett looked in the direction of the pickup fading in the distance. "I will give you one chance. Are we clear?"

Jack nodded in agreement.

"One chance, Jack! We're playing with fire here, and I won't let you burn me again."

Jack started to reply, then clamped his mouth shut. The fact she'd been burned wasn't all on him. But this was not the time.

"Remember. I had a life before you showed up on the scene, so give me a chance. Give us a chance. Let's go over what brought us both here to little ol' Davenport and go from there. I won't hurt you, Scarlett."

"Ya, well, we'll see about that. After meeting your "friend," She emphasized the word, "I have my doubts. Now, I need to go. My new employer was gracious enough to give me this time away on my first day of employment, and I don't want to take advantage. "

The "friend" comment struck Jack hard and made his heart ache. He did not want to hurt Scarlett, but what was the way out of this mess?

Scarlett gave him directions to the house she'd just rented, and after agreeing on a time, she spun sharply on her heels and hurried to her van.

The emptiness Jack felt at her leaving struck him in a way he hadn't expected. What was it about her scent, her smile, right on down to how she walked, and the ribbon in her hair that never failed to drive him nuts? And just what the hell was it that connected them and brought them back together time and again? He could make no sense of it.

Rachel had nearly ruined any chance he had of even being able to sit down and visit with Scarlett. Then, it dawned on him. She never dressed that way or hung on him in public like she'd done. Something was up, and Jack was left to wonder what she was up to. He reminded himself that when it comes to women, guys are always the last know.

On the drive back to work, Scarlett began to regret agreeing to dinner with Jack. She'd seen all she needed to see. There was no way the guy had changed. Just look at how Rachel hung all over him! Who was she kidding, and what was she doing entertaining any thought of something developing between them?

Don't you give yourself away, Scarlett. Not for his charm, blue eyes, or even his sex appeal. Walk away.

But her heart still said yes, you will do this.

CHAPTER THIRTY FIVE

DURING HIS DRIVE INTO TOWN THAT EVENING, JACK WREStled with meeting Scarlett. There was little reason to believe it wouldn't turn into another of their train wrecks. The couple's history made that clear. He could back out now and avoid all the trouble he was picturing. Not showing up would tell Scarlett all she needed to know.

Hesitant to get involved, Jack rode past Scarlett's house, thinking it best if he forgot the whole thing. It was good to see her, to know she was doing well, and that was that. Life would go on. Making his way out of town toward the Minstrel's Oasis, Jack began having second thoughts.

Every decision I ever made regarding Scarlett has been the wrong one. Am I doing it again? She seemed glad to see me. Why not go and see what happens? Don't commit to anything. Just sit back, let her carry the water, and see where things go.

Jack made a quick U-turn and headed back to town. Pulling into the driveway and stepping away from his bike, he saw Scarlett through the kitchen window, and any questions about not showing up immediately vanished. She was gorgeous. He was suddenly overcome by a nervous sensation he hadn't felt since high school, like a kid on his first date.

Don't listen to this crap running around in your head, Jack. It's not like you're proposing or something. Get a grip. Besides, there's got to be more to it than her good looks.

He hated the internal battle tearing up the landscape of his mind. It was distracting and tied him up in knots. His peaceful world had been turned upside down simply by bumping into this fiery red-haired beauty he never thought he'd see again.

Scarlett greeted him at the door with a smile and a glass of red wine. She couldn't help but recall the time back at college when she stood outside the door to his apartment, half drunk on wine. She was scared back then, but today, it didn't take long for her to see that Jack was the nervous one.

She'd fixed comfort food in the form of spaghetti and meatballs. French bread with garlic added for spice. After initial greetings and a dash of small talk, Scarlett invited him to the kitchen, where Jack took a seat opposite her at a small dining table.

Between bites, Scarlett dove right in. "I know you need to join your band soon, so if I could be so bold, we agreed to share where we've been and what we've been up to since the day you walked out on me."

"Whoa." Her direct attack was unexpected. "Maybe this was a mistake." He slid back his chair and stood.

"Jack, I'm sorry. I don't know what happened. The words just came out. Please sit down. I'm so sorry."

Jack hesitated. "Well, that certainly clears the air. Now that we know how you really feel, are you sure there's any reason for me to stay?"

"I said I'm sorry. Please sit." She gestured towards his chair. "Your spaghetti's getting cold."

Jack slowly eased back into his seat.

"There's just so many things I need to know about you."

Jack ate slowly, enjoying the delicious food, and, for the most part, remained quiet for the next twenty minutes. Listening to Scarlett tell of her divorce, he felt terrible for her. And spending the last couple of years alone in the woods brought forth a side of her Jack had never seen.

Near the end of her story, he asked, "The divorce I get—damn city slickers anyway. You can never trust em, but I'm sure you know that by now. It's the time alone in the woods that surprise me. Doesn't seem like the girl I once knew."

"I've changed Jack. I'm not the same GIRRLLL," she added emphasis and stretched out the pronunciation, "You once knew."

"Point taken," Jack noted.

"And I've had time to figure out what I want in life." *And I think I want you, Jack, but you stupid clod, you seem so oblivious!*

"Now it's your turn. Where did you learn to play the drums?"

Jack grimaced and swallowed hard. "Uh, well, prison."

Scarlett choked on a meatball and reached for her glass of water. "Prison?" She gasped. "I think I need to hear about that, Jack. Am I sitting here with some rapist or murderer? What were you in for?"

Jack couldn't resist. "Littering." He kept a straight face.

"Truthfully? I…" Scarlett caught herself. "OK, I'm not falling for it, Jack. What did happen?"

The huge smile on his face lit up his blue eyes, and they sparked with sincerity as he began to tell the story. He answered her questions, briefly discussed his time in Florida, and shared his enjoyable moments working on the maple syrup farm.

"What kind of music did your prison band play?"

"A lot of southern gospel, some rock n roll, and a little country."

Scarlett nodded. "Southern gospel. Were you guys good, and did you all sing?"

"Yes, we all sang, but two of them were black boys raised in southern churches, and my gosh, how they could bring that place down with their voices. They were amazing. It was easy for me to hide beneath their vocals."

"But still, you sang? Right?"

"If you want to call it that. It was just a way of joining in. You know what I sound like."

Scarlett rested her chin in her hands, observing his sky-blue eyes and facial expressions. It was clear his thoughts took him back to the moment.

Then she asked him about fishing and what it was like working on a boat. Listening intently, trying to absorb it all, Scarlett pictured him shirtless, out on the water. The guy had certainly been around and paid a high price for it, too. Suddenly, it dawned on her. He'd failed to mention anything about the women in his life. It was too obvious an omission, and clearly, he was avoiding the topic. He was hiding something, and she wondered if he was again running away from another relationship.

When he finished, Jack reached for his glass of wine. He hadn't talked about himself like that in a long time.

"What about the girls?"

The naked question caught him off guard, and he gulped his mouthful of wine. "What?"

"Come on, Jack. Other than the girl who dumped you down in Texas, you didn't say anything about the women in your life. What are you hiding? I know your reputation with the ladies."

"First off, I'm not hiding anything, and second, that's kind of personal, don't you think; and three, she didn't dump me."

Scarlett laughed. "Come on, Jack. It's only fair. I told you all about my life. The only female you told me about was the highway trash you picked up. I'm happy to know you cleaned up the roadside rubbish, but please, tell me there weren't anymore."

Her sarcasm bit hard, but the truth was, it was something he'd always liked about her, just not when she used it against him.

Jack considered the grain in the wooden table top while gathering his thoughts. "Should have figured you'd come around to asking that question."

"It's only fair. I told you about the losers in my life."

"Well, Scarlett." He looked up and stared straight into the green globes looking back at him. She watched his eyes search her face as if the answer to her question could be found there.

"There were no other women," He said flatly.

A few beats of silence slipped by before Scarlett could respond. "Remember, we're being honest here, Jack. I can deal with it; just don't lie to me."

"I am being honest."

Scarlett hesitated, then burst into light-hearted laughter. "You're serious. There were no other women?" Both hands flew to her pink cheeks in surprise.

Jack was dead serious, and she saw the hurt in his face at not being believed. "I'm not in the habit of lying." *Though that's about to change, I'm afraid.*

"I'm not the same man you once knew, and obviously, you're not the same woman. It's why we need to take some time to get to know each other again and not allow our past to shape things if anything is going to come of this."

Scarlett grinned and raised her glass of wine. "Agreed. Remember that night I came to your apartment a little drunk with wine?"

A comforting smile crossed Jack's face. "Do I?" He shook his head. "If you only knew. It helped me get through every day while I was in prison."

She liked that. But prison? Was she seriously considering taking up with a felon?

"You thought about me?"

"Every day."

"Hmmm." She needed a moment to deal with his thinking of her. "I'm just a little surprised. The way you left…"

"Stop right there. We are both familiar with that territory and agreed not to dig it back up."

"Agreed. So where do we go from here?" Jack detected a note of hope in the open-ended question. They were about to cross a bridge into much more dangerous territory, and it made him nervous.

He answered in his best Clark Gable impression, "Frankly, Scarlett, I don't give a damn."

Scarlett laughed aloud, breaking the growing tension and lightening the mood. "I appreciate the humor, Jack." She chuckled some more while drumming her fingers atop the wooden table. "Now, what about my question?"

Jack sighed. "Just trying to lighten things up.

"Come on, Jack. We agreed there would be no games. I know you have something to say, so out with it."

"Scarlett, this is hard for me to say because my heart wants something else, but you asked for honesty, and with that in mind, I have to tell you again I don't think I'm the guy for you." It hurt to say it, but he'd chosen to put her first.

"Jack." She cried.

"I learned so much about myself on the road and in prison. I've hurt a lot of people. I've been selfish and self-serving. I wouldn't be good for you."

Scarlett smirked.

"What's so funny?"

"I could have told you all of that."

"Guess I needed to learn it for myself."

"So go on. There was something else you said you wanted to tell me."

"Alright. I'll lay it all out on the table. I'll play my hand, and you can trump me if you want. I'll pay with my heart, but that's the gamble, right?"

Scarlett nodded. "We each have a lot on the line here, Jack."

"My trip was mostly about seeking what I thought was missing. I searched for what, I don't know, whatever seemed would fill the gaping hole in my soul. But the more I looked, the less I found, and women only complicated things. And not just women. I gave up my cigars, the weed, and hard drinking."

The quizzical look on Scarlett's face said she still didn't believe him. Old doubts from the past crept in from the dark places of her mind, and an icy silence took up residence in the space between them. Jack sensed he'd better get on with it and tell her the rest of what was on his heart, or he may never have another chance.

"Scarlett." He whispered and reached across the table to take her hand. Hesitantly, she gave it to him. Its tender warmth filled him.

"I gave up all those things and spent time atop the mountain, so to speak, searching for the answers to all my questions. I needed time alone to sort things out, much like you did. Prison was tough on me. It brought a lot of perspective to things."

He stared directly into her jade-colored eyes. "None of the things I found, experienced, used, or experimented with satisfied or brought me the peace I once knew with you. I mean that from the bottom of my heart. I've never been happier than when we were together."

Scarlett was taken aback. "Jack, you've never said anything like that to me before." Looking into his eyes, she saw the heart-felt truth registered there.

"I mean every word."

"Truthfully, you gave up women and weed?"

Jack nodded. "I did. But to be honest, there is a little more to the story. I am repeatedly tempted to return to those creature comforts because there has been no payoff for giving them up. Those are the battles I fight."

Scarlett let go of his hand and leaned back. The man had never been so open about things.

"Scarlett." He leaned into the table to draw near and share his next words. "This is hard for me to say. I don't know why. It just is."

A tear gleamed at the corner of one of Jack's eyes. "As exposed and vulnerable as it makes me feel, I tell you this with all honesty. I've never found a deeper connection with anyone like I once experienced with you. Nothing was more satisfying than the serenity I had when we were together. It took a lot of crap and some tough lessons, but I've learned that now. All my faults aside, I'd like it if you stuck around to see if we can pick up the pieces."

There, he'd said it. The stake was positioned over his heart. All Scarlett had to do was bring the hammer down and drive it in. It was all in her hands now.

"Wow!" Stunned, Scarlett leaned back in her chair. "You never opened up with me like that before."

He huffed. "It's not easy to put your heart on the line."

Here he was, sharing his deepest feelings. It was so unlike him. What more could she say?

"I think I'd like that too, Jack. But before I agree to continue seeing you and stick around long enough to see where this goes, you need to tell me about your relationship with Rachel. She was all over you, and it's not hard to figure something's going on between the two of you. Please understand! My heart is on the line as well as yours, so you need to level with me."

Jack explained the situation and was surprised at how calm Scarlett remained. He fully expected her to kick him out right on the spot.

"Yes, so you gave up women. At least that's what you say."

"Scarlett, she came on to me. I'm not that strong right now. Do you know what it's like not to know the touch of another human being for over a year?"

"I certainly do."

Jack nodded in understanding. "Yes, I'm sure you do. So please keep in mind that everything with Rachel happened before I ran into you."

Surprisingly, she remained perfectly composed. Jack wondered what was up. The answer soon followed.

"Not sure what's so hard about all this." Her face filled with a Cheshire Cat smile, daring him to say the wrong thing. "The solution seems quite simple. If you mean everything, you just said to me, leave Rachel's place and give up your relationship with her. I'll give you one week." She raised her eyebrows. "Show me, Jack. Words are nice. Now show me you mean what you say."

Face in his hands, Jack sighed, then responded. "I would gladly leave her. Hell, I'll pump gas or bag groceries if I have to, but I promised her I'd stay until harvest is finished, and like I've been trying to tell you, my word is the only thing I have to offer anyone. I don't lie or purposefully deceive anyone. I made that promise to myself some time ago."

Scarlett's eyes blazed emerald cold and hard. She pushed back from the table. "You take me for a fool! I've heard your excuses before. Leave her or leave me. It's your call."

"Alright. Done deal. Just one condition."

"No conditions, Jack. Leave her, or we're done talking."

"What if I move out of the house and into the bunkhouse? It's where I stayed when I first arrived."

"No Jack! I'm not stupid."

Jack scratched his head. What could he do?

"Ok. How's this? I'll talk to Randy tonight and see if I can stay at the bar. There's a cot in the back room where he occasionally puts people up who've had too much to drink."

Scarlett paced the kitchen floor, then tossed back the rest of her drink. "I know I shouldn't do this, but OK, I'll go along with it. But one hint of anything going on between you and Rachel, or anyone else for that matter, and I'm gone. Are we clear?"

"Perfectly. I won't disappoint you."

She spun around and pointed her finger at him. "Believe me, Jack." She snarled. "You're the one who will be disappointed if you blow this."

Standing in a golden beam of sunlight, the last rays of the day's light shining through the kitchen window, highlighting her red hair from behind, Scarlett came to a sudden realization. At that very moment, it all coalesced. She knew exactly who she was, what she was about, and what she had to offer. The strength to stand up to this man, this heartthrob, galvanized her in every way. The moment's pressure and the past years' experiences came together, yielding a priceless payoff. Jack either fit or he didn't, and life's hard lessons were not about to be wasted or forgotten.

Jack smiled nervously. "I told you I'm not going to hurt you."

"Of course, you did, Jack." The patronizing comment nailed Jack right between the eyes. "Now, all you have to do is prove it. Should be simple, huh."

There it was, laid out right before him. The challenge was straightforward. It was up to him now. What did he want? Continue his nomadic life, wondering where it might lead, always searching for that elusive something, or sacrifice the freedom he loved for the one thing that might fill the empty place he could never fulfill.

"And I will. You have my word. Now, I need to go. The guys will be wondering where I'm at."

"Stop."

Jack remained seated.

"One more question. Did you have a child with Susan?"

It took Jack a moment to respond. "You know her?"

"I met with her."

"How'd…"

"I found a letter in your room back at school."

"Sheesh!"

"Your answer, Jack."

"No. The rabbit done died. It's not mine." With that, he got up to leave.

"Hold on. Were you seeing her while we were together?"

"No, not while we were together."

"Thank you for being honest with me."

"Told you I would, and I will. Can I go now?"

The terse conversation ended, and Scarlett walked him to the door, where he turned around to face her.

She placed a hand on his chest and felt the rapid beat of his heart. Jack noted the fierceness in her eyes.

"I'm willing to do this as long as you keep your word. Let's take some time and get to know one another again while doing our best to forget the things we did in the past."

Scarlett stood on her tiptoes and kissed Jack on the cheek. "Agreed?"

"Agreed."

"Now stay away from those cowgirls tonight, Renaissance Man."

Jack smiled and turned to go. "I gave you my word. You can count on it."

Scarlet followed him out the door to see him off.

"Someday, you're gonna tell me all about that name."

Jack straddled his bike and pulled on his helmet. "It's nothing. Just the guys giving me a hard time about my past."

The roar of his bike firing up drowned out her response, and Jack waved goodbye.

That's better than the last time we said goodbye all those years ago. Scarlett thought. *Well, maybe. Time will tell.*

CHAPTER THIRTY SIX

SCARLETT CLOSED THE DOOR AND LEANED BACK. *I THINK IT frightens us both. Who knows where this goes or if he can be true to his word? I'll be careful this time; one misstep and I'm gone.*

The decision to stay settled, Scarlett took to her work at the bakery and caught up with Jack whenever she could, which turned out to be not that often. He worked late, was up early, and it seemed like his boss demanded more hours from him with each passing day.

A couple of weeks later, shortly after harvest began, Jack invited Scarlett out to ride in the cab of his combine. Rachel had left for Spokane to pick up some parts. He knew she was furious about his move into town but wasn't about to fire him in the middle of harvest and continued making every effort to entice him back to her bed. With Rachel gone for the day, he used the opportunity to spend time with Scarlett.

She was reminded of her visit to the farm in Pullman when she surprised Jack by showing up unannounced one morning. Scarlett enjoyed riding high above the ground and watching Jack operate the ungainly equipment over the rolling hills. Focused on every detail and listening to every stray noise and sound, he seemed a part of the device. It gave her a new appreciation for his capabilities.

More importantly, she'd seen no sign of Rachel over the past couple of weeks, and Jack seemed to have no problem answering her persistent questions. For the moment, at least, all seemed well.

Back home at the end of a long, dusty day, she had time to reflect on their time together. How did this man remain unattached? No matter how closely she guarded her heart, Scarlett found herself falling for the guy again. *Am I just plain stupid, or am I crazy? He's a felon, Scarlett!*

Jack's long hours and seven-days-a-week occupation left little opportunity to see him. Scarlett could briefly speak to him over the phone in the evenings, though it seemed as if he was holding back, almost whispering on the phone whenever they spoke. Scarlett wrote it off as him being tired.

She missed her time with Jack. A side of him was emerging that calmed, comforted, and reassured her. This was new, and she wondered if it was real or if he was just trying to impress. However, nothing physical was happening between them beyond a few good-night kisses. His presence, his crazy humor, her hand in his when they walked together, and a growing mystery that there was much more to this man than she knew intrigued her.

As the days passed, an emptiness grew inside her when he wasn't near. It scared her at first. Having spent the last few years alone, entirely free and independent of anyone and any commitment, she felt torn between giving up the safety of living in her own world versus being with Jack. And as well as things seemed to be going, she refused to give up her heart to him. She'd done just fine keeping it locked away in its iron cage, and that wasn't about to change. At least not yet, anyway.

As promised, Jack had moved into the backroom at the bar. However, that was no guarantee nothing was going on. *Could a man change that much?* For now, all seemed well, and she would have to trust her intuition.

The long summer days passed slowly, and she soon grew claustrophobic in a town where Scarlett knew next to no one. Two weeks after she had last seen Jack, Scarlett decided she needed to get out of the house and headed out to the Minstrels Oasis, if only for some measure of distraction.

It was nearing nine o'clock when she arrived. Jack had indicated he wouldn't be done with harvest for another day or two, though they were getting close to finishing up. A little break from the monotony was all she needed until then.

Before leaving, she'd tried calling Jack but was told he was working late on a broken-down piece of equipment. She couldn't help but wonder about the laughter she heard in the background but chose to ignore it. The bar was busy that evening, and the buzz about the crowd was all about having some downtime as harvest came to an end.

She ordered a glass of beer at the bar and turned around to look for a table. The jukebox cranked out a familiar song, and a few couples were out on the dance floor.

"Hey, lady." The bartender yelled above the din of conversation and music.

Scarlett turned around, paid for her drink, and leaned back against the bar. Despite the smoke and clamor of the country bar, it felt good to be out of the house, listening to music and relaxing with a beer. She'd been cooped up far too long. If only she could be here with Jack. But it wouldn't be long now—just another day or two.

Thinking of when she could see him again, she sipped her beer and began tapping her foot with the beat of the music. Suddenly, her foot stopped in mid-air.

Was that Jack? No, it couldn't be. Her desire to see him was playing games with her mind. She continued watching the couple two-step around the dance floor. The woman had just placed her hand behind the man's head and engaged him with a deep kiss. When they turned, Scarlett could see his face, a face garnished with a massive grin.

Scarlett burst into a rage of tears. It was Jack! He'd played her for the fool with his lies once again.

Consumed with rage, she marched across the dance floor and threw her beer in his face before slapping him with every ounce of strength she could muster. A startled Jack backed away.

"You two-timing son-of-a-bitch!" She shoved him with both hands. "Just the boss, huh! Liar! I never should have trusted you. I knew better!"

She swung her fist for the side of his face, but it was engulfed in Jack's hand short of striking him.

"Let go of me!" She jerked her arm free. "I'll never speak to you again!" Her yelling drew everyone's attention, but she didn't care. She shoved Rachel aside before bolting from the place.

"Scarlett! Please, you don't understand."

Rachel took his face in her hands and caressed the side that was turning red. "Can't imagine what you see in her. She's an emotional train wreck." Rachel's syrupy voice added hellfire to the crimson sting of Scarlett's slap. "

Jack pushed her aside and rushed out the door into the dim glow of twilight. The confrontation that ensued took them both back to their days at college.

"Scarlett, we need to talk." He yelled.

She ignored him and was opening the door to her van when Jack rushed up from behind and grabbed her arm before slamming the door shut. She swung around, attempting to strike him with her free arm, but Jack grabbed it and pinned her against the side of the van.

"This is not what it seems, Scarlett."

She spit in his face. "You told me you'd never lie to me. It was the one ground rule we both agreed to."

"Scarlett, please hear me out."

"So you can tell me another lie?" She screamed

"No! It's just, just that you need to hear the whole story. I've been wanting to tell you…"

A hand on Jack's shoulder stopped him in mid-sentence. He turned around in time to be greeted by Rachel's smirk. "Time to go Jack. The band is waiting for you. Let your little plaything go. There's plenty more inside. Long as you come home to me."

Jack turned on her. "We are through. You can find someone else to finish harvest for you."

"I think not. Far too sweet a deal for you to turn down, Jack."

Jack wanted her to spill it all in front of Scarlett.

"Now leave her alone and come back inside."

Scarlett finished the conversation. "You're the worst, Jack. Stay away from me. Stay far away!"

A crushed Jack heard the guitars begin to sing and knew he had to go.

"I'll call you Scarlett."

"Don't you dare!" Her curses followed him into the bar, each word a diamond edged knife slicing off another piece of his heart.

Things didn't get any better when he returned to the ranch to settle things with Rachel that evening. Rachel had been drinking and began ranting about his leaving and his promise to stay. Jack grabbed the last few items of clothing remaining in the bedroom they'd once shared. After weathering her second torrent of verbal abuse, Jack stepped out into the night.

Rachel followed, stumbling out onto the porch. "You can't leave! There are two more days of harvest until we finish, and you can forget about being paid if you leave me now."

The moonlight gleaming on the black metal of his bike couldn't have looked more beautiful. His trusty steed was always there waiting, inviting him to leave his troubles behind, ready to sweep him away to the next refuge, far from the troubles that always seemed to find him.

Jack was stuffing the clothing he'd grabbed into a saddle bag when Rachel hurled an empty whiskey bottle at him. It bounced once before striking the side of his ride.

"You bastard, Jack. Don't you dare walk out on me!"

Jack chuckled as he straddled the bike and felt the comfort of its heartwarming rumble.

Son of a bitch - bastard? You've rung up a pretty nice score tonight, old buddy. Now, let's get out of here.

As was his way, he never looked back and left Rachel standing on the front porch howling curses at the moon.

Easing his way down the long gravel drive, Jack considered his options. How could he explain it to Scarlett? There had to be a way. He decided it was best to sleep on it and headed back to the bar. He'd let the air clear and speak to Scarlett in the morning.

Randy, the barkeep, had just finished cleaning up and was locking the back door when Jack rolled into the parking lot. Jack caught him at the door, and after a short conversation, the two men stepped inside.

"You've had a rough night, Jack, and from the looks of it, I'm thinking I only know the half of it." Randy handed Jack a glass of whiskey and poured one for himself. "Reminds me of a fight I once had with my old lady."

"Really? How's that work? You've been married for quite some time."

"We were young once, too, you know." He winked and drained his glass.

"Well, it must have worked out somehow." Jack tossed back his drink and set the glass down on the bar.

"Obviously, it did. It was a long road back, but true love seems to find a way."

Jack chuckled softly and shook his head. "True love. Is there such a thing? Because I've never found that to be true."

Randy leaned across the bar and poured Jack another drink. "Have some patience, Jack. Let the dust settle first."

"Think I'd rather be on the road," Jack mumbled into his drink. "No job, no reason to stay here, and there's no way Scarlett will ever see me again." Jack tossed his whiskey back.

Randy chuckled. "Gotta say Jack. I have never seen flaming red hair the likes of that before. Whoa! That woman is a walking conflagration when she gets mad. Sure you want to be around that long term?"

"I am." Jack motioned for another shot.

"I admire your courage. Why not stick around for a while? I can still use your help, and the bands counting on you for at least a little while longer." Randy raised an eyebrow. "Seems like it might work for both of us."

"I'll think on it, Randy. My world's a bit upside down right now."

"The band will miss you."

"Ha." Jack's grim smile said it all. "I'm not so hard to replace."

"I know you're feeling down, Jack, but the band has never sounded better." Whether it did or not, Randy did his best to cheer up Jack. "Look, we get damn busy around here after harvest is over. You can hang around as long as you like, no obligation, and leave when you want, but I can use your help. Take time for the dust to settle, and let the air clear. If you are as set on that red-headed maniac as you say, taking a few days to see how things go is a small price to pay. Sound good?"

Jack finished his drink and motioned for another. "I'll think on it."

"Sounds good. Now, I'm cutting you off, or you'll hate me in the morning for not watching out for you tonight."

Jack's head slumped against his chest. "Alright. Thanks, Randy. Probably best to sleep on it, though I still feel like hitting the road and leaving all this behind."

He ran a hand through his long, tangled hair and mumbled. "What a mess I've gotten myself into this time."

CHAPTER THIRTY SEVEN

THE FOLLOWING DAY, JACK WOKE WITH A NASTY HEADACHE and a guilty conscience. But it was Scarlett's earsplitting voice smashing against the insides of his skull that hurt the most. *She once told you she loves you, Jack.*

Yeh. Eon's ago.

So you're just going to walk away without giving things a chance? Buck up, old man. Give it the old college try. Oh, well, in your case, maybe not. That didn't go so well. So, um, just step up to the plate and...

Oh shut up.

Jack walked outside and took to the road, the only thing that ever gave solace to his mind. Passing through Wilbur, Coolee City, and across the Columbia River at a leisurely pace, he took his hog up the steep west side of the canyon to Chelan. The wind in his face and tugging at his hair, and the feel of the bike beneath him felt more like home than ever. The temptation to keep riding was overpowering, and he likely would have kept on going if not for his promise to Randy. He couldn't just walk out on the band, either.

After a quick stop at a grocery store, he found a comfortable lakeside site to eat lunch. Sliced cheese, French bread, and an apple washed down with a bottle of Coke made for the perfect lunch. Brilliant fall colors lined the lakesides, but the easy breeze still contained the summer's balmy caress.

Skipping stones across the water, he freed his mind to wander wherever it wanted. How did he always find himself in these situations, especially concerning Scarlett? The one and only woman he ever cared about.

He threw the next rock with all his might and watched it skip far out into the lake—*Randy's right. I have to go back and try. But I'm so weary of this. And what are the chances? I always find a way to muck things up.*

Jack took his time riding back to the Minstrels Oasis, enjoying the comforting freedom of riding alone while vacillating between leaving and attempting to speak to Scarlett.

When Jack pulled into the bar's gravel parking lot, he noticed Rachel's black pickup and quickly decided to remain out of sight. Pulling around behind the building, he walked his ride through the back door and parked it in the spare room out of the way.

Turning around, he came face to face with Randy.

"Glad you're back, Jack. I can use the help."

"What's going on? It's only Tuesday."

"Like I told you, it gets pretty crazy after harvest is over. I could use some help behind the bar taking orders and pulling beers."

"Can't do it, Randy. Rachel's truck is outside. I'm sure she's here looking for me, and I'm not up to dealing with her."

"What if I sent her away?"

"How ya gonna do that?"

"I'll tell her you left town. As you know, she's not made many friends here. I'm willing to bet she leaves if she thinks you're gone."

Jack shrugged. "Worth a try, I guess. And hey, in the meantime, mind if I have a couple of shots from the whiskey bottle you had out last night?"

"Be my guest, but don't get carried away, alright. As your friend," he took Jack by the shoulders, "You're not of the kind of mind that goes well with whiskey."

"No problem." Jack smiled.

"I'm serious Jack. I don't want to see anything happen to you."

Randy left the backroom, and Jack observed his conversation with Rachel through a small crack in the kitchen door. Rachel grew hot and animated, arguing with Randy.

When she threw her hands in the air, Jack heard, "That asshole!" Before storming out the door.

Randy returned with a smirk on his face and shook his head. "Jack, you get mixed up with the damndest of women."

"Tell me about it."

"I went down that road once." Then, shaking his head, he changed gears. "For now, you're good to go. She's headed out, but you owe me for that one."

"What was she saying to you?"

"Said she's sure you're over at Scarlett's."

"Don't I wish." Then the light bulb came on. "Oh no. She's probably headed over there right now. What a mess!"

"Unless you told her, she doesn't know where Scarlett lives. Keep your shirt on, and for now, let's put you to work behind the bar."

The following day, Jack woke rested, clear-headed, and ready for the challenge of seeing Scarlett. He showered, ate breakfast, and dressed in his motorcycle leathers because he knew Scarlett loved the look.

It had been a contentious part of their relationship when her roving eyes would catch on leather-clad bikers, and she was drawn away to visit with them, even when they were out on a date. Jack would sit alone while she visited, knowing full well this was not a two-way street. She always laughed it off when he brought it up and told him he was making too much of it.

Casting the thoughts aside, Jack rolled his bike out the backdoor and headed into town.

Scarlett would be working at the little bakery, and that's where he headed. Thinking he'd test the waters to see if she had cooled down enough to allow him to visit her at home, he began feeling more confident.

The bell above the door announced his entry as he entered the bakery and approached the counter. The smell of freshly baked pastries made his mouth water. He expected to find Scarlett behind the counter, but Mable greeted him instead.

"Good morning, handsome. What can I do ya for?"

"Good morning." Jack stood to the left of the counter, gazing through the glass at maple bars and bear claws. Stalling for time, he pretended to be undecided. "Well, it's all looking so good; I'll need just a minute to decide."

"Take your time, hun. I've got to check on my next batch. I'll send someone out to wait on you." And with that, she disappeared through a swinging door into the kitchen.

Jack stepped back from the counter, ready to order two maple bars. A moment later, Scarlett walked through the door and approached the checkout.

"What are you doing here, Jack!" She hissed. "We have nothing to talk about!"

"Yes, we do, and I'm asking for just one single chance to talk with you."

"You've had your chance. Now get out!" Scarlett's face was already turning red.

Mable returned at that moment. "Have you decided what you want, Sir? My help seems to be a bit star-struck at the moment."

"Hardly," Scarlett growled.

Jack extended a dollar bill, then took Scarlett's hand when she reached for it. "Scarlett, please. I need to talk with you."

Scarlett burned holes in his face with a green laser stare.

"Give the man his change, honey."

She made the change and slapped it on the counter so he couldn't touch her again. Then, turning her back, she marched into the back room. Jack picked up the change and the remaining pieces of his dignity and exited with the bag of doughnuts.

Mable rushed back to the kitchen as soon as the door closed behind Jack. "Scarlett, what's wrong with you? The man's a dreamboat."

"That's Jack! The asshole I've told you about."

Mable was silent for a moment. "Honey, he just wants to speak to you."

"I've heard enough of his lies! He can't be trusted."

Mable took Scarlett's hand in her own thin-skinned, age-spotted hands. "Honey, I could see it in his eyes from a mile away. That man loves you."

"Funny way of showing it." Scarlett spat the words on the floor.

"You don't find love like that around every corner, hun. Sure, there are cheap imitations that never last, but he came in here knowing if you got half the chance, you were likely to take his head off. Yet he walked in here anyway. A man like that could find a woman around any corner, but he came here for you, Scarlett. Of all the women out there, he came here for you. Do you hear what I'm saying? True love isn't always the storybook tale you read about as a kid."

Scarlett remained silent.

"Can't hurt to hear him out, and I can tell you care. That's why it hurts so much, honey."

Silent tears formed at the corners of Scarlett's eyes before streaking down her cheeks. "Mable. I thought this time would be different. Running into each other after all these years, it kind of seemed meant to be. What am I supposed to do?"

"Honey, you'd better think hard and get this right. Set your dog-gone ego aside because they don't make many like that anymore."

"My ego?"

"Sweetheart, we've become pretty good friends in our short time together, so I think I can safely say this to you."

Scarlett nodded for her to go on.

"You've told me about what you've been through and the winter you spent alone. You're a tough little gal who built a steel wall of safety around herself, and I can't say I blame you. You're proud of the fact you've survived and are out here making it on your own. Am I about right so far?"

Scarlett nodded again. "Yes." She whispered.

"I could see the chip on your shoulder the first day you walked in here. Figured you'd be a good worker if I could put up with you. Well, that part worked out just fine. So let me tell you, lower your guard just enough to let him in. I think you might be surprised."

"Mable, *he's* full of surprises. That's the problem."

"Sorry. Poor choice of words. Just give the man a chance and hear him out. It will cost you very little."

Scarlett's hands were busy twisting the hem of her apron when she looked up at Mable. "I thought we were getting things worked out. As much as I care about him, he's the same guy I broke up with years ago. And I can't go there again. I'm sorry, but I need to get away from him."

"Alright. If that's how you feel, honey."

"Oh, Mable, I've been so stupid." She fell into Mable's arms, and the two remained together until her sobs subsided.

A short while later, at the Minstrel's Oasis, Randy gave Jack a manly version of the same lecture. "Take this shot of whiskey, get on that damned bike, and go get the girl Jack. It's time to man up!"

Jack threw back the shot. He didn't feel like much of a man at the moment, having left the bakery with his tail between his legs like a spanked pup. Instead of leaving, he walked over to the drum set and began pounding out a solo.

Randy shook his head and yelled. "Whatever turns you on, son. When you're done getting that out of your system, I'd better see you riding off to get the girl, or I'm going to make you do that drum solo live tonight."

"Ha. Good luck with that." Jack muttered.

"About five o'clock that afternoon, after one too many shots of whiskey, Jack stood outside the front door of Scarlett's rented home. He had no idea what to say to her but had to try. After knocking for the third time, a shrill voice ordered him to leave.

"I'm calling the cops, Jack, if you don't leave this minute."

"Scarlett, please." Jack rested his head against the forearm he'd stretched across the top of the door. The woman whose warm embrace held everything he needed was inches away on the other side of the door.

"Now, Jack!"

The finality of it struck him with the force of a bullet in the chest. Trudging back to his bike, his soul screamed no. After all his searching, the time on the road, and the time in prison, he'd finally found that elusive piece, and it wanted nothing to do with him. Drained of everything that mattered, he walked away.

After mounting his bike, he screamed out of town and headed east. The concrete abutment where the railroad tracks crossed over the highway a few miles out of town flashed in his mind.

Don't do it Jack.

Why not?

I saw you through your time in prison. I'm asking you to trust me now.

Ha! You do that to bring me here?

Jack, we haven't spoken in a while because you've been making choices that exclude me.

You think? Well, watch this one. Better find someone else to haunt.

CHAPTER THIRTY EIGHT

SCARLETT HEARD THE SIRENS THAT NIGHT BUT NEVER thought twice about it. She was happy Jack was gone from her front door and out of her life.

A couple of weeks passed without a word from Jack. No way he gave up this easily, would he really? She wondered about her counting on his returning after the rant and chasing him off. *Maybe he did leave you, Scarlett?*

Mable's words rang in her head. *That man could have any woman he wanted, and he came here for YOU!*

"Fine." She mumbled. "Let them have him."

Feeling cooped up in the tiny little town with nothing but her thoughts and aching heart, she headed down to the Minstrel's Oasis for whatever distraction it might provide. Since it was a Wednesday evening and the band only played on Friday and Saturday, there would be little chance of running into Jack if he was still in town, which she doubted. *He always runs from his problems.*

With few options, the bar outside town would have to do. Before heading out, Scarlett fixed an easy meal of one of her favorite comfort foods. Pulling the Appian Way box of pizza mix off the shelf, she mixed up the dough and pre-heated the oven. Opening the can of pizza sauce that came in the package, she began thinking of what she would use for topping. Canadian bacon and pineapple would be perfect, and there was just enough left over from the last pizza. The one she had intended to fix and eat with Jack.

After sliding the pizza into the oven to cook, Scarlett changed into form-fitting jeans and a plaid midriff top. It was a look she knew Jack loved. Standing in front of the mirror, she approved the look.

Like I said, your loss, Jack!

Lose the ego, Scarlett. Mable's voice reminded.

After touching up her hair and applying the tiniest bit of makeup, the timer on the oven rang out. Removing the pizza and setting it on the table, Scarlett sat down with a glass of wine and blew on her first bite to cool it.

Kind of takes you back to Index, doesn't it?

Don't interrupt me. I'm eating.

Some lonely times, as I recall.

Look, it's a small town, and I'm just getting out for a break from the boredom.

Um hmm. Makeup and a midriff top?

Scarlett slammed the half-eaten piece of pizza down on the plate in front of her. In a huff, she slid the entire baking sheet into a mostly empty refrigerator before storming out to her van.

Why am I acting like this? Take a deep breath, girl.

Frustrated that she couldn't shake the calamity experienced with Jack and move on with her life, Scarlett found herself tied up in irritable knots. Tonight, she was going to shake the anxiety, free herself of her past with Jack once and for all, and move on. She was drawing a line in the sand, and it was time for a bit of fun.

At the Minstrel's Oasis, Scarlett walked straight to the bar and ordered a cold glass of beer. It was just coming up on eight o'clock, and the place was nearly full.

"Hello, Randy. I'd like some quarters for the jukebox, too, please."

Moments later, Randy returned with her beer and a handful of quarters.

"Excuse me if I'm mistaken, but aren't you Scarlett?"

She eyed him suspiciously. "Yes. Why do you ask?"

"Just thought I recognized you from the, um, well, the other night."

"Don't worry. I'm done with that loser. I won't be going off and cause a riot or something." Scarlett shot him a sweet smile. "Um, now that you bring it up, Jack's not around, is he?"

"Oh, you didn't hear?"

"Hear what?" A blast of adrenaline shot through Scarlett's veins.

"Well, you remember all those sirens we heard east of town a couple of weeks ago?"

"No! No no no no! Randy." She interrupted. "You're not talking about the motorcycle crash! Please don't tell me that was Jack."

Everyone had heard about the horrendous crash east of town. The sound of Jack's bike roaring out of her driveway two weeks ago reverberated in her head.

"I'm sorry, Scarlett. But…"

She turned and ran from the place.

"Scarlett!" Randy called after her but was too busy behind the bar to chase her down.

Scarlett didn't hear his final words as she raced from the building. Her blurry eyes and spinning head caused her to stumble in a massive pothole in the parking lot, rushing to her van. Steadying herself against the side, she bent over and threw up. After recovering, except for the occasional dry heave, she crawled inside and threw herself on the bed at the back of the van, where her tears flooded the pillow.

You fool Scarlett! You damned fool! Look what you've done.

A half hour or so later, Scarlett felt as if she was suffocating and stepped out of the van for some fresh air. Weak and drained of emotion, she wandered the parking lot. Conflicted in every way, confusion reigned, blame abounded, and a sizzling flame of anger began to burn. The realization that the feeling she once coveted of being free on her own, on the road with no care in the world, was gone, left her vacant, stunned, and paralyzed.

Jack was gone, and she had refused to speak to him just before his death. It shouldn't have unsettled her like it did, but suddenly; she couldn't have felt more lost.

Finding her way back to the van, she leaned against the hood before sliding down to sit on the bumper. Splintering thoughts broke into a thousand pieces and shattered her mind. She was chasing ghosts from the past when the laughter from a nearby pickup broke through. Incredibly, it sounded like Jack's laugh. Taking a couple of cautious steps along the side of her van, she saw them.

"Go ahead, Hank, you're the helping kind."

Laughter.

"I think I should at least check on her."

The smell of marijuana assaulted Scarlett. *Just a couple of good ol boys*, she thought. *At least someone's enjoying the evening.*

Realizing it was not Jack and her thoughts were playing tricks on her, Scarlett returned to sit on the van's bumper and searched the stars for answers. Finding none, she was about to move back inside the van when a voice only a few feet away startled her.

"You doin' alright, miss? I mean, you look a little lonely out here."

"I'm fine." She snapped.

"You don't look so good. Um, sorry, I didn't mean it that way. I mean, in that way, you look pretty darned good. But what I meant is, are you ok?"

The man stepped closer, and the smell of weed and whiskey enveloped Scarlett. He was about six foot tall, and Scarlett figured one hundred eighty to one hundred ninety pounds.

"Look, I'm ok. Now please leave me alone."

But the guy persisted and, taking her by the shoulders, began to force himself on her. His kiss was hard and forceful, cutting her gums with his teeth. When he pulled back, her cheek felt as if his scruffy beard had shredded it.

When Scarlett began screaming for help, he put his hand over her mouth and started pawing at her.

"Roger, that's enough!" His buddy snapped. "Leave her alone."

Distracted for a moment, Scarlett used the opportunity to kick him in the groin. While bent over, hugging his family jewels, Scarlett gathered herself and unleashed the most violent punch she knew how to throw. Her father had taught her the nose was the knockout punch, and she nailed it with a vicious uppercut.

The guy dropped like a punch-drunk heavyweight.

"Lady, you didn't need to do…"

"Drag him outta the way, or I'm running him over."

His buddy never hesitated. Her fiery look and rage in her voice convinced him she really would do it.

Scarlett climbed inside and fired the van's engine. Revving it to encourage the guy to pull harder and get his friend out of the way, she raced off, spinning the tires and throwing gravel over them.

CHAPTER THIRTY NINE

THE CROSSROADS OF LIFE RARELY OFFER EASY CHOICES. THE sharp corners are often difficult, crossroads painful, and both fraught with uncertainty. Except for work, Scarlett hid away at home and spent the next two weeks withdrawn, soul searching, and reconstructing the wall she'd once hidden behind. Even the motherly Mable had trouble reaching her.

After two weeks of wrestling with her thoughts, Scarlett gave Mable notice. The restlessness inside her was overwhelming, and she decided time alone, somewhere in the mountains, was what she needed. Maybe she'd return to Stehekin. It had been such a wonderful time of healing.

She said a sad goodbye to Mable and thanked her for everything. Feeling bad and a little embarrassed about running out on Randy the last time she'd seen him, she planned to stop and say goodbye to him as well.

Scarlett wore a faded but comfortable Led Zeppelin T-shirt over her most comfy jeans with the frayed cuffs. The only thing she did to get ready to go out was to brush her long hair, and had to talk herself into doing even that much.

The summer's events were never far from her mind and taking her time driving to the Oasis, she allowed the memories of Jack to wash over her. From guilt to some of her most precious memories of him back in school, she could never get past the question of why they had found each other again. *If I could have at least said goodbye or kicked his ass. Mmmm, and maybe one last kiss.*

Pulling into the Oasis parking lot, Scarlet was nearly in tears and cursing herself for losing grip on her emotions. She needed a drink and a chance to visit with Randy.

After circling the parking lot, which seemed much too full for a Tuesday night, and wondering what was up, she found her way to a parking spot in the back. Exiting the van, she was enveloped in a wave of marijuana smoke. Two men on the other side of some parked cars spoke softly at the back of the tavern, passing a joint back and forth.

"Glad you're on the mend, Jack. It's good to have you back." The guy drew deeply from the marijuana cigarette and passed it back.

Jack? No way, Scarlett. You didn't hear him right; he doesn't smoke that stuff anyway.

The gravelly voice that answered certainly wasn't Jack's, and dismissing the thought, she quickly strode toward the entrance at the front of the building. Once inside, she marched to the bar and asked the barkeep for Randy.

"Poor guys at the hospital with his sick wife. Now, what can I do for ya?"

Scarlett ordered her beer but was already feeling let down. She'd been looking forward to talking with him.

The band filed in while Scarlett stood with her back to the room, waiting for her order. When the woman behind the bar returned with her beer, Scarlett asked, "What's happening? You're full up on a Tuesday?"

"Small town. A good friend was just recently released from the hospital. We're here for him." She managed before rushing off to fill customer's orders.

Scarlett turned in her seat at the bar and began taking in the crowd. The packed place was loud, raucous, and filled with anticipation. The low lights highlighted a blue haze of cigarette smoke, and Scarlett took note it didn't entirely hide the smell of marijuana. The memory of her first night here after running into Jack flooded her mind and threatened to bring tears.

What was the point of that chance encounter if it was to end like this?

Put it behind you, Scarlett. Nothing you can do now. It's just another chapter in your story.

The band started the night with an old Hank Williams song, "Your Cheatin Heart."

Geez. Not what I needed.

The country boys quickly filled the dance floor with their gals in tow.

Then, as was their style, the band followed with a rock and roll song by Head East, "Never Been Any Reason." Reluctantly, Scarlett's mood began to lift, and she was soon bouncing a knee in time with the music.

When they sang the lines "Save my life, I'm going down for the last time," Scarlett felt the band could have been singing the song just for her.

The crowd cheered at the song's end, clearly excited to celebrate. Scarlett needed the diversion and allowed herself to be caught up in it.

When the crowd yelled for more, the band followed with another massively popular song that year, "Moving On" by the band Missouri. It spoke of a biker on the road riding on and on into the sunset.

You guys are speaking straight to my heart!

It wasn't long before Scarlett accepted a request to dance and jumped down from her stool to follow the guy onto the dance floor. The band continued playing rock music, and little by little, Scarlett temporarily crept out of her shell.

The fella was friendly; kept his hands to himself even during a slow country song the group mixed in, and was easy on the eyes to boot! When the group launched into their version of Hey Joe, her partner took her hands and led them in a slow dance around the dance floor.

Scarlett allowed the joyous atmosphere of the place to seep in. It didn't fill the emptiness inside, but she was enjoying herself for the first time in quite a while. When the song ended, the band paused, and she visited with her partner while standing amidst the crowd on the dance floor.

Moments later, the band's leader took to the microphone. "In just a moment, folks, I'd like to introduce a good friend of ours that many of you know saved the life of our bass player, Bobby Jones."

The place filled with cheers and applause at the mention of the musician's name. When it died down, an angry voice arose from the dance floor.

"Hey bitch! I know you!"

The voice came from her right. Unsure the insult was intended for her, Scarlett turned in time to see the man who had accosted her in the parking lot weeks before, and he was headed her way.

Grabbing her arm, he jerked her around and threatened to haul her out to his truck and have his way with her. "There's a price to pay for what you did to me." That's when a drumstick struck the guy in the side of his face. "Wouldn't touch her if I was you."

Scarlett looked to the stage, where the drummer stood tall and straight in a white t-shirt, sporting a cast on his left forearm.

"You don't scare me cripple."

"Probably not, but I've got a lot of friends here." He growled.

A group of men formed around Scarlett, and the guy quickly backed off.

Scarlett did a double take. Then, realizing it was Jack, she screamed and rushed to the stage. "You son of a bitch!" With fists flying, she attacked Jack, who held up his good arm to block her punches and backed away.

She may have been livid with him, but the anger quickly subsided, and she fell into his arms. The tears and questions flowed.

"Jack, how could you? What happened? I'm so glad you're ok. You said you'd never hurt me. I hate you! Don't you ever…"

When the verbal river of insults diminished to quiet tears, Jack leaned back to look at her.

"Do I know you?" It was the perfect comeback after the abuse she'd just inflicted, but his sly smile warmed her heart.

"I'm so glad you're happy to see me. Can't imagine the greeting I'd receive if you were angry."

Scarlett leaned back and smacked his chest. "I missed you," she whispered, "Can we talk?"

"Been trying to have that conversation with you for weeks now." Jack winked.

"Don't push your luck. Now play me a song."

"Alright. I know just the one."

She stepped back, preparing to leave the stage, then stood there instead, looking at him through her tears.

"What?" Jack said.

"You're alive." She winked and stepped down from the stage. Jack felt the years-old connection shiver up his spine and land hard in his heart.

Then, the band leader took charge. "Well folks, I can tell you that wasn't at all how we planned it, but I'd like to ask for a round of applause for our drummer, Jack. The way I understand it, Bobby owes his life to this man who paid quite a price himself assisting Bobby after his accident. Bobby's still recovering and can't be here tonight, but they tell me he's going to be alright. Please say a prayer for him."

Jack shook his head at the applause and held up his hands. Scarlett witnessed a shy, almost bashful man take center stage. *Well, that's something new.*

When the crowd demanded a "speech," he was given the microphone. Jack held up his cast-covered arm for quiet, then said, "It's nothing any of you folks wouldn't have done for him. I was fortunate enough to be able to help. Thankfully Bobby's going to be alright."

Inwardly, Scarlett wondered. *A humble Jack?* The moment took her back to the night he'd rescued her from a frozen car buried in a snow bank. That was her Jack through and through. *Your – Jack - Scarlett? What are you saying? You're the one who turned him away.*

Suddenly, she wished the night was over so she could speak with him alone. Jack turned to speak with the band, and moments later, he announced to the crowd.

"Men, grab your women. The little red-haired lady here," Jack pointed to Scarlett, standing near the front of the stage, "has requested a song."

She hadn't and wondered what Jack was up to.

"Free Bird!" Someone yelled.

Jack laughed. "Sorry. Not this time."

Jack returned the mic to the stand, stepped down from the stage, and took Scarlett's hand.

Then the band leader announced, "Folks, we're going to reach back to the sixties for a song you all know well." He softly counted, one, two, three, four, and the band took up an old sixties country song entitled "Stand By Me."

Jack did his best with the cast and took Scarlett in his arms for the slow dance. Finding it hard to believe it was Jack holding her, she gazed longingly into his deep-set eyes.

"You didn't forget."

"How could I forget? It's long been our song."

Scarlett rested her head on his shoulder, and like a timeout or the proverbial calm before the storm, little more was said during their dance as both enjoyed the close comfort of one another. When the song ended, Scarlett hugged Jack and reluctantly stepped away.

"See you in a while Jack?"

"You can count on it."

At the end of the evening, Scarlett wasted no time greeting Jack while the rest of the band stepped up to the bar for drinks.

Stepping down from the low stage, Jack asked, "You speaking to me now?"

"I could slap you for that!" Her rage bubbled up, threatening to return. "No bullshit Jack. We will set things straight and settle this once and for all. I'm happy you're alive, but it changes nothing!"

"Just trying to lighten the mood."

She took his hand and led him out of the bar. The cat calls poured down before they could reach the front door, but Jack ignored them.

Sliding open the side door to her van, Scarlett turned on Jack. "Don't get any ideas! We're here to talk, and you'd better shoot straight. Got me?"

Jack nodded. "Wouldn't have it any other way."

For a bit of light, Scarlett lit three candles, set them about the van, and opened a vent in the ceiling before taking her place in the passenger seat. She spun the captain's chair around to face Jack, who was sitting on the edge of the bed at the back of the van.

"Spill it, Jack. This is your last chance, and it damn well better be good. I might have missed you, in fact, I missed you dearly, but I'll be driving away, right out of your life tonight if you screw this up."

Jack sat up straight. Still sore and beaten up from the crash, she couldn't help but notice how his chest stretched the t-shirt he wore. *Meant to draw the women's attention tonight, no doubt.*

"Scarlett, I never lied to you. It's the honest to God's truth."

"Sorry, Jack. You've already lied to me. Strike one!" It hurt to say it. She was hoping for something different.

"Wow. Tough crowd. Got any whiskey?"

"Get on with it, Jack, or you're out the door!"

She peppered him with rapid-fire questions. Jack spent the next few minutes answering each and every one of her questions. And then, out of the blue. "You never wrote to me Jack. Just a postcard from your stinking jail cell in Amarillo complaining about the tiny size of the place where they locked you up."

"I was protecting someone from a couple of thugs."

"Uh-huh."

"I wrote one other time."

"Oh, that's right. The one that was supposed to make me feel so good by telling me how beautiful the Florida Keys are. Gee, how thoughtful. So I'm worth a total of two postcards to you."

"I'm sorry Scarlett, but I'd forgotten what it was like to feel the sun on my face, the wind in my hair, and all my troubles miles behind. All that mattered to me was chasing after the next horizon and feeling good about myself. Is that such a crime?"

"And the arms of a girl around your waist. You forgot to mention that part."

"Scarlett, come on."

"How often I pictured you relaxing on your bike with a Swisher Sweet outside some margarita bar. And then riding away, your long hair flowing out from beneath your helmet with some chick behind you, her arms wrapped around your waist while you rode over the bridges through the Keys."

When Jack smiled, Scarlett felt her temperature rise. "So it did happen just like that, didn't it."

Jack leaned forward to look into her face. "That's pretty much how I pictured it, too, but it never happened because there was no girl."

"You're lying again. Jack, you'll never know how often I had to chase that image out of my mind. And now you say it never happened. I can't believe it. Especially since you lied to me and pulled the same thing the very next time I saw you!"

They were going down the very road Jack feared the conversation might take. He rose to take her hand, but she ordered him back.

"Sit down." She commanded. "Look me in the eye and tell me the truth."

Jack took a moment to gather himself, then in the most solemn tone he could muster, looked straight into her glaring eyes. "Regarding my time on the road, it never happened because you weren't there."

"Don't toy with me Jack. You're saying that because you know it's what I want to hear."

"Need I remind you of your drug-dealing boyfriend."

"That was different, and I admit I screwed up. Johnny and I had known each other for a long time, and our relationship seemed natural." She straightened up in her seat. "I was stupid and weak, Jack! Is that what you want to hear?"

"Of course not."

"I felt like such a fool after you risked your life for me even though I had no right to expect your help. And by the way, the cops bought the story about a bad drug deal. More than anything, they were just glad to see the guy off the streets."

"Kinda figured. There were plenty of times the cops could have had me. I was stopped several times for speeding and figured I'd be cuffed as soon as they called in my information."

"Johnny's friends did show up looking for the money and the drugs."

"I had little doubt about that when two bikers came looking for me." He told Scarlett the story and how he'd set them up."

Scarlett got up and, after sliding back the door to the side of the van, stepped outside. "I need some air."

Jack followed her, and they took a moment to take in the star-studded sky while collecting their thoughts.

When she turned to face Jack, he was lighting up a small cigar.

"Strike two. You told me you'd given those up."

He puffed one more time before responding. "Took them back up after you stopped speaking to me."

When she took in his cast-bound bound forearm, the scabs on his chin, and the fading bruises on his face, her heart softened. She moved a step closer.

"It hurt so bad when you walked away. I felt abandoned and so alone when you roared off without so much as a wave goodbye."

"That was years ago in college."

She ignored him.

"It still hurt Jack."

"And then you jumped right into the arms of another winner." Jack chuckled and rolled his eyes.

"I've already told you all about that. Don't be turning this conversation around. This is about you."

"Good enough." His smile was disarming, but she'd been entrapped by it before and steeled herself for more questioning.

"Did you ever think of me?" She watched his jaw clench.

"Loaded question, and besides, that's all water under the bridge. What's it matter now?"

"It matters to me!"

"Alright, alright. Take it easy."

"Don't tell me to take it easy! Now answer the damned question."

"Of course I did, Scarlett."

"Come on, Jack. I'm looking for something a little more from the heart. Maybe your feelings for me aren't that strong. That's what I'm trying to figure out. I'm not ashamed to tell you I often thought of you and us over all these years. Do you know how many times I wondered if you were even alive? Not all of us can walk away without looking back like you did."

"Didn't know you cared."

"Smartass. Don't give me that bullshit. I won't ignore the fact you played our song tonight."

"Alright." An exasperated Jack held up his hands in surrender. "Yes, I've thought of you often and wondered how your life went, how you were doing, and yes, it hurt to think I would never see you again. We have a lot to talk about if…" He hesitated as if the following words would commit him to some unknown future. "If we agree to see each other again."

Scarlett blew out a slow breath. "Tell me about the motorcycle crash."

Jack told her about the night after he'd tried visiting her.

"Riding east out of town, another motorcycle traveling far too fast passed me, and I recognized it as Bobby's bike. He was carrying a passenger, and thinking it might have been stolen, I gave chase. One way or the other, I knew something was wrong.

I was just catching up when Bobby must have hit something in the road and went down. I only had a few moments to slow down before hitting his bike. I went down hard, the hardest I've ever experienced. The crash split my helmet and knocked me unconscious. When I came to, I was lying in the middle of the road, hurting like hell and trying to catch my breath. I knew I was beaten up, but it didn't feel like anything was broken until I tried to use my left arm.

Once I could clear out the LBJs flying around in my head, I stumbled back to Bobby's friend. He wasn't breathing, and there was no pulse. Later on, they determined he'd broken his neck. Then I rushed to check on Bobby and found he was bleeding freely from his leg. I was dizzy and shaking so badly I could barely function, but I still managed to figure out what was wrong. He was lying in a pool of blood from the cut in his leg." Jack shrugged. "I did everything I could just to keep him from bleeding out."

"How fast were you guys going?"

"I honestly don't know. Bobby flew by me when I was doing sixty, maybe. Thankfully, I was able to dump some speed just before crashing, but if I hadn't had my leathers on..." He stopped and shot a look at Scarlett

She shook her head, and half whispered. "You could have been killed."

"Dropping even the little speed I was able to lose before striking his bike saved me from a lot worse. Still, the full extent of my injuries didn't become apparent until after the medics arrived and examined me. I have bruises everywhere, and I'm still sore."

The conversation stalled. Scarlett was moved but forced herself to stay on target.

"I'm sorry about the crash, Jack." It seemed like a cold response, but she needed to maintain a keen edge.

"So we've covered your road trip and what happened the night of the accident. I want to believe you, but I guess none of that matters if I can't get on board with your answers to my final questions."

Understanding he hadn't blown it just yet, Jack took a breath and braced for her next barrage.

"You told me you'd given up marijuana, amongst other things. Were you out back tonight, sitting on someone's bike, sharing a joint with a guy?"

Jack frowned and tilted his head in a, dang, I've been caught kind of motion. "You saw that?"

She nodded.

Yes, that was me. I was with another band member."

Scarlett raised a burnished eyebrow. "Strike number three! You're out of here!"

"Scarlett, wait!" She was pushing too hard, and Jack was losing his patience. "The feeling of losing you again crushed me. Do you get that? Do you! Don't you see what you mean to me?"

Finally, she was getting past the outer shell he hid behind.

"Didn't know you cared. Funny way of showing it." She fired back the very same words he'd said to her.

What a hard ass. Sure you want this woman, Jack?

"Ok, I admit to having fallen back on some old vices."

Scarlett grimaced. "Does that include womanizing?"

"No!" Things were reaching the point of exasperation.

"I'm sorry, but I need to know these things before I can even consider investing more time in you. So the million dollar question 'Redneck Romancer.' Tell me about the night I saw you dancing with Rachel. You said you can explain. Here's your chance. Your one and only last chance!"

"Yes, I can explain. But the band is back from break, and I need to go."

"Walk away now, Jack, and you'll never see me again. Answer the question!"

Jack hated to stand them up, but the band would have to wait.

"We had just finished harvest. It was getting late, and I wanted to clean up before calling you. I had just stepped out of the back room and was talking with Randy when she wandered in. I could tell she was already half-plastered. She walked right up, grabbed my arm, and pulled me onto the dance floor. I'm thinking you arrived about this time."

"I have such wonderful timing."

"She promised to pay me for harvest, but I needed to come with her back to the ranch to get it. I knew that was trouble and told her I would come out during the daytime when she was sober. The point is that she was coming on to me, and I said no."

"I could tell by the way you kissed her."

"She did that after I told her I would not come to the ranch with her."

Scarlett ignored him. "Did you enjoy her kiss? Or maybe that was just the start of a long night together, all part of getting paid? Or should I say getting…"

"Stop right there." Jack was reaching his limit and jabbed at the air with his finger. "I've told you the truth. You can doubt me if you like, but that's all there is to it. Hell, go check with Randy if you need to, but I've answered your questions and tolerated enough abuse. I think it's time for me to go."

"Hold on. It all sounds good, but I haven't heard what I need to hear, Jack."

"Sheesh!" He sighed, thrust his hands into the front pockets of his jeans, and momentarily leaned back against the van. He was at a loss for words and beginning to feel as if all this was proving there was no way it could ever work between them. Searching for the right words, he tossed his cigar on the ground, and after rubbing it out with his boot, turned sharply and began again.

"Then let me be clear." His eyes blazed.

Scarlett noticed how the shadows silhouetting his face highlighted his features. The man was so stinking handsome. The dimpled chin, the sharp nose, and the deep-set eyes captivated her. She half enjoyed watching him struggle before telling herself to cut it out.

"At the risk of having my heart skewered one more time, I'll give you the bottom line." Though he found it difficult, it was time to put all his cards on the table.

Jack was always good at giving "the bottom line," and Scarlett was not comforted.

"Bumping into you and, ahem, your backside that morning." Jack smiled as the image came to mind, then chuckled softly. "Made me realize a lot of things about our past. Things I've done my best to bury but can't ever escape."

"And what is that?"

"All the things I've done wrong. I don't particularly like thinking about it because of how it haunts me and makes me feel."

"Now we might be getting somewhere. Care to share some of those things?"

"No."

Scarlett raised an eyebrow, and Jack looked down to study his boots. Then, collecting himself, he looked directly into her dark green eyes.

"Listen close. I can probably only manage this once. You weren't like all the rest, and…"

"And we know what a long list that is, don't we? It's not much of a compliment, Jack!" Hands on hips, she fumed.

"Scarlett, please."

"Go on." She dared him.

Jack sighed and looked away as if considering leaving. Then, gathering himself one last time, he began again.

"I didn't love you like I should have. I didn't treat you the way I should have, either." He paused, and she saw the pain behind his eyes. "I thought about you often, Scarlett, and sadly, only in hindsight could I see what I once had in you."

Jack fell silent. He had never spoken to her like this before.

Scarlett took a step closer and reached out for his good arm. "Jack. Running into you stirred up old feelings in me as well, but you were shacking up with your boss and didn't bother to share that with me."

"I never got the right moment."

"Jack." She shook her head. "See what I mean. What else aren't you telling me? If we were to move forward from here – and don't hold your breath - how could I ever trust you? You know as well as I do; this very thing sums up our history in a nutshell! And look how we've started out once again."

Jack couldn't resist the opportunity. "Oh, so we have made a new start."

"Shut up, Jack." But in the shadows of the moonlight, he detected a smile tugging at one corner of her mouth.

Scarlett continued. "How are we supposed to do this?"

"There's just one way. Build on what we have now – today. Let go of the past with all its hurts. That was a different time, different place, and all that. We don't have much of a chance if we don't. If we continue to use those old hurts against one another, we might as well hang it up now. I've told you how my situation with Rachel came about. I'd lost my way and was just drifting."

His eyes searched her face while considering what to say next. "Scarlett, I would never admit this to anyone else, but I'd reached the point of believing I was entirely unlovable because I always screw it up."

His look was more sincere than she had ever seen. When she started to respond, he held up a hand to stop her. "Hold on. You have to believe that you are everything to me." Jack raised his hands in a what else can I say gesture. "I've been honest with you in every way."

"Jack, I don't have to believe anything. I want to believe you, but I know your past. I know the real Jack."

"No, you don't!" Jack spit.

"Look. For all I know, this is just more bullshit, and nothing more than your latest attempt to get into someone's pants, my pants! One night stand at a time. That's the Jack I know."

"Ooooh, K." Jack spun on his heel and, feeling its call, gazed down the highway. Then, turning back, "So we're going down that road again, huh?" Jack kicked at the cigar butt he'd crushed in the gravel before continuing.

"Well, if that's where you're at, then there's no reason for me to be here. I've tried in every way I know to explain that's not me anymore." He tugged on the handle and slid open the side door to the van before turning to look back at her.

"I need to get my jacket."

Stepping back outside, he continued. "We've reached this well-known impasse a million times before. Our relationship always crashes right here in this very same place, and I see no way past it. Sorry to disappoint you, but I'm not here to argue with you. I wanted nothing more than to find a way for this to work. Now that we've answered that question, I think it's time for me to leave."

Scarlett grabbed his shoulders.

"Jack, don't leave." The words were out before she could think, and he watched as her hard exterior softened in the tender moonlight. "I've been hard on you for a reason. I had to be. I needed to remove every doubt I could. Now I'm asking you to stay."

"Is this where you hit me again?"

"I might if you don't shut up."

Resting his hands on her hips, he gently held her. "Scarlett, I never meant to hurt you. I needed to find a way out of my situation with Rachel and intended to do it without hurting you. It's the only reason I didn't tell you."

She put a finger to his lips. "Enough. I want to believe you, and I'm willing to give things a try. But Jack, if you ever." She paused to stare daggers before jabbing him in the chest with her finger. "I mean it. Lie to me. Cheat on me, and I'll kill you!"

Jack rubbed his chest and grinned. "Nursing is not a career choice for you." Then, breathing easier, he shrugged. "I'm good with that, but I have no job. Like I told you, I turned Rachel down and walked away, and she fired me on the spot. I'm still waiting for my harvest paycheck, and I'm not sure I will ever see it. The only thing I have to offer you is my word. That is the one thing of value I have for you."

She rubbed his chest with the palm of her hand where she'd jabbed him. "That's all I need from you. The rest will work itself out." She allowed a smile to grace her face for the first time. "I quit my job today, too. We'll have a lot of fun being unemployed together."

Then, running a finger along the side of his cheek. "I planned on leaving tomorrow morning but wanted to see Randy one last time. I'm glad I came here tonight, or I wouldn't have known anything about your accident and would have left town thinking you were dead."

"Honestly, Scarlett, it felt like that's what you wanted. I'm so happy you didn't leave."

"I never felt that way, but you made me so angry. I could have spit nails!"

"It was a misunderstanding. I think you know that now."

Scarlett beamed, and Jack saw the familiar smile he so loved brighten her face. "One more try?" He asked with hopeful eyebrows raised.

Scarlet sighed before answering with a hint of melancholy. "Yes. One more time. Now get out of here. I'll see you tomorrow."

CHAPTER FORTY

THE NEXT MORNING, SCARLETT ROSE EARLY, COMBED OUT her hair, and rushed in to see Mable at the bakery.

When the bell over the front door rang, Mable looked up from the cash register. "Couldn't stay away, could you." Her smile was comforting in a coming home sort of way.

"Oh, Mable, I need to talk with you."

"Well, why not do it while we make up this next batch of doughnuts? You know the routine."

Scarlett jumped right in, and as they mixed up the dough, Mable asked what was going on.

After explaining what had happened with Jack the night before, Mable offered some help.

"Well, of course, you can stay in the rental as long as you like. I haven't even had the cleaning people over yet so it will be like you never left." Then she raised an eyebrow. "Where'd you spend last night?"

"I slept in my van after talking with Jack."

"And Jack. Where'd he sleep?"

Anyone else and Scarlett would have been offended, but she knew Mable had her best interest in mind and wasn't just prying.

"He's been staying in a backroom at the Minstrels Oasis."

"He left the farm?"

"Um hmm." She nodded.

"So you two are back on for real?"

"I don't know. We agreed to try." Scarlett set down the bowl of dough she was working on and turned to face Mable. "Am I being foolish? I've told you about our history."

"Honey, I'm not about to tell you there's no risk in it. But girl, if my intuition is any good, plus the fact I've known a few guys in my lifetime." She winked and swayed her hips. "He's one of the good ones. You don't just walk away from them because they are rare finds. It's just that for some stupid reason, they all seem to have a bit of a crazy side that puts most of us gals off." Then, her face lit up in a sweet smile. "He's a lot like my husband."

Scarlett's eyebrows shot up in surprise. "How so?"

"Oh, you'd never know it now that we've gotten old, but that man had the toughest hide on him you ever did see. A gal could no more get close to his heart than a searing hot flame. A lot of girls gave up on him because of it." Whimsically, she giggled to herself. "Their loss."

"Why didn't you?"

"I grew up with three brothers, one of which was the kindest, gentlest thing you ever saw," she paused, "The other two had a lot of that on the inside, but their outside was so thick and tough you'd have never known. I had the strongest feeling my husband was a lot like those two brothers. I knew he'd be just as tough as nails when dealing with the world and providing for me. He'd take all the abuse the world could dish out while sheltering me in a safe place where I could thrive."

She stopped to wave her hand, indicating her business. "This is my business, and I've been free to build it as I wanted. I could do that because he deals with all the crap the world throws at us. He was a crusty, hard-boiled, and all-about-himself kind of man, which makes him the perfect shield against the world. But honey, his insides are a gooey mess. From what you tell me, your man is much the same. If you can get beneath that outer shell and put up with the hurts that come with it, because these kinds of guys honestly don't know when they're hurting you, you will likely find their hearts are just like that butter you're holding in your hands."

"You think so?"

"Honey, I don't know your fella. But I have to believe he is much like my guy. In my opinion, those are the best men. Besides, a solid-built clock stopper like your man is worth the risk."

"That's the part I struggle with."

"Sorry to do this, but must I remind you of your failed marriage? Some guys are perfectly smooth on the outside with no thorns at all. But as you found out. The slick ones that show no blemishes are often the most dangerous."

Scarlett found the twinkle in her eyes endearing. She must have been quite the catch in her time, and Scarlett began to understand that it was Mable who was the real catch.

She turned to gaze out the window, and Mable let her be alone with her thoughts.

When Scarlett finally spoke, she did so without turning around. Still gazing out the window at the little garden Mable kept out back, she said, "I hope you're right. I'll feel like such a fool if I'm wrong."

Mable took her by the shoulders and turned her around before stepping back. Then, placing flour-covered hands on her hips and pursing her lips, she whistled.

"Sweetheart, if I can be so frank, your trim figure, built the way you are with that flaming red hair and those delightful green eyes, you can have any man you want! Add in your charming personality."...the two of them shared a good laugh over that one, "and I have little doubt you already own his heart."

"Thank you. I hope you are right, Mable. After my divorce and my experiences with Jack, I've lost confidence in my ability to pick the right man."

"Scarlett. A lot of women are asking where all the good men are. They can't find them because they're looking for the perfect man without blemish. Those guys don't exist." She smiled. "If you are asking my advice, give the man a chance. Sometimes, you have to fight for these things."

"Thank you. You don't know what it means to have someone like you to talk with."

"You stay as long as you like. The key to the house is hanging on the wall behind you. And if you want to join me in the mornings like you've been doing, I'll have hot coffee ready, and we'll figure out something that works for pay and rent. Sound like a deal?"

"Deal."

After their discussion in the parking lot, Jack kept his room with the cot in the back of the bar, and Mable allowed Scarlett to stay in the rental as long as needed.

Returning to the bar one afternoon after running some errands for Randy, Jack found a check waiting for him in the office.

"Guess who stopped by today?" Randy smirked

"Gee. Lemme guess. Glad I missed her."

"I think that feeling was mutual, my friend."

"Not surprised. Still, just as well I wasn't here."

"Scarlett be here tonight?"

"She wouldn't miss it. Going to be a great party."

"Yes, as I've told you, it's our biggest and busiest time of the year when harvest is over. We'll be busy tonight, so before I forget, I want to tell you how much we will all miss you. It's been fun having you around here this summer, and you've been a lot of help."

"Thanks, Randy." Jack stuck out his hand, and the two shook. "You've done a lot for me this summer, and I'll never forget it." He paused for a moment to look about the bar. "I'll miss this place."

"You're funny, Jack. Not much here to miss. It's just an old bar."

"That may be, but I think I found much of what I've been searching for right here in this little back country town. We'll come back someday."

Randy grinned. "Got big plans?"

Jack shook his head and offered a grim smile. "Who knows, Randy. I don't deserve her. I want to say yes to future plans, and we've been seeing each other, but there's a lot to overcome. You and I have talked about these things before, and you know the inner battles I fight. We'll just have to see."

"Jack, we all have a past. It's a matter of what we do with the future."

Jack's sly smile said it all. "That bartender wisdom you're feeding me?"

Randy nodded. "Maybe, but consider this. If you want to write a memoir, that's one thing. Go write it and spend a couple of years living in the past. But if you want to move on, then move on and forget the past."

Jack toasted him and threw back the rest of his beer. "Can't argue with that!"

CHAPTER FORTY ONE

AFTER GETTING HIS BIKE BACK FROM THE REPAIR SHOP AND thanking Randy and the band for taking up a collection to pay for the repairs, Jack made a couple of test runs. Pleased with its performance, he packed his Harley, and Scarlett loaded her van.

When Randy noticed he was preparing to leave, he stopped him. "Jack. I'm glad I caught you. We had such a good time last night we are serving up one more round. So you can't leave yet."

"Seriously?"

"We've added the band for another night. You can't leave now."

"But Scarlett and I…"

"I know, I know, but it's just one night. You guys have been packing this place, and I signed the band this morning for one last blast."

"Well, I'll have to talk to Scarlett, but you've done so much for me, Randy. I owe you. If I can convince Scarlett, I'll do it."

"Would sure appreciate it. The wife's hospital bills and all that. Another big night would be helpful."

"You got it. And I'm so glad to hear your wife is back home and doing much better. Let me talk to Scarlett, and I'll get back to you, but I'm sure we're good."

Though disappointed she would have to put off their trip for a day, Scarlett readily agreed. "Should be fun, Jack. Just keep your eyes in your head and your hands to yourself."

"That's not fair."

Scarlett's raised eyebrows said it all. "Given your past..."

"You're relentless."

"Get used to it."

"Hey, I was perfectly behaved these last few nights with the band. We played well, things got a little rowdy, and I was a perfect gentleman."

"I know you were. I watched you turn down the groupies hitting on you. But was that just because I was here watching?"

"Scarlett, please. Can we forget about all that for a while and just have some fun tonight? It'll be a great sendoff to the future and our trip to the coast."

"I'm sorry, Jack. I'm scared about us. Please have patience with me."

He took her in his arms and tenderly kissed her. She snuggled close.

"I have all the patience in the world for you."

When they arrived that evening, Jack and Scarlett heard the cranked-up jukebox from clear out in the parking lot. The packed bar was rockin' long before the band arrived.

Jack led Scarlett to a table up front, next to the dance floor. For the band's last night, Randy reserved a table for the group's wives and girlfriends, and Jack introduced Scarlett to the other ladies.

Looking them over, she couldn't help thinking what a tough bunch of cowgirls.

"Yes, Scarlett, we've already met Jack." Ruby raised her eyebrows. "I must say, Scarlett, if I wasn't married... well, let's just say you'd have some competition."

"Well, I'm not married." A dark-haired beauty from across the table extended her hand. "I'm Diane. Welcome to the Minstrel's private fan club." She chuckled and looked to the other women at the table, who all returned her smile.

Scarlett looked across the table to the remaining woman.

"I'm Bobby Jo, Alan's wife. He's the singer. Quite the find you have there, girl. I'd keep a close eye on him tonight if you know what I mean."

"Thank you. I appreciate the heads up." *And yes, I will certainly be keeping an eye on him, and you for that matter.*

The band was in fine form. The music soared, the beer flowed, and Randy shot Jack a thumbs-up between songs. Jack was glad he stayed to help him out for another night. Every so often, the band would play a slow song minus one of their members so that each eventually had a chance to dance with their wives or girlfriends.

When Jack's turn came, he introduced Billy to the crowd. "I know I'm just a stand-in, and you all know Billy is the drummer who usually plays with this crazy bunch of guys. Please give him a hand. He's back in town, and I'm sure you'll be happy to have him back in the band. Thank you for putting up with me while he's been away."

Jack stepped away from the mic and applauded. Then, returning to the mic, he said, "He'll take my place for the next song. One I have specifically requested for my girl Scarlett!"

Your girl? Sorry Jack. You don't know that for sure.

Stepping from the stage, Jack strolled to Scarlett's table.

"Excuse me, ladies." He charmed them with his warmest smile. "Scarlett, would you have this dance with me?"

Before she could respond, Diane did. "And if she won't, I will Jack." Her tilted head and inviting smile said it all.

But Scarlett already had Jack by the arm. "Nice try, Diane." She looked at Jack and smiled. "But he's all mine."

Jack led her to the dance floor and put his arms around her waist as the singer announced, "It ain't country, folks, but I think you're gonna like this one. Grab your girls, fellas, and get out on that dance floor."

The band began a slow blues song called "I Want to Do Everything" by the group Nazareth."

Moving together, hip to hip, body to body, Jack led Scarlett around the dance floor. At one point, she leaned back to look him in the eye. "You requested this?"

He smiled confidently. "Sure did."

Scarlett didn't say much more, choosing to enjoy the moment instead.

The song ended, and Jack kissed her on the forehead. "Gotta go."

Scarlett held on and didn't let go. "Sing me a song Jack."

"What?" He grimaced. "No way, You know I don't sing."

Her smile imploded, and she put her hands on her hips. "If ever there was a time." She frowned. "Besides, you sang in prison."

"That was different."

"Jack, please." She pouted

"Alright, alright. If you promise not to laugh, I'll talk to the band."

Jack was headed over to join the band when someone called out to Scarlett as she returned to her table.

"Scarlett?"

At the sound of her name, she turned around in time to catch the full brunt of a closed fist. Cold-cocked, she staggered as her knees buckled but was able to catch herself when a man standing nearby kept her from falling. With a hand over her left eye, she struggled back to her feet and looked up just in time to see Rachel winding up to deliver the next blow. Scarlett ducked and followed the miss with a fist to the woman's stomach. But her attack was weak, and Rachel quickly retaliated with a shot to Scarlett's jaw. This time, Scarlett went down.

Rachel approached, ready to continue the assault, when three women grabbed her and roughly threw her to the floor, pinning her there. The wives and girlfriends of the band members held her down until the bouncers could take her away. All the while, Rachel spat, swore, and stormed at Scarlett.

"You bitch! You ruined it all. I hope you rot in hell. You had no business…"

Jack rushed from the stage and helped Scarlett to her table. Removing her hand from her eye, Jack saw it was already swelling.

"Let me see that. Oh ya. Going to have a nice one there. Be real pretty in a day or two."

Scarlett looked up at Jack and growled. "You'd better be worth it."

The rest of the women returned to the table and Diane brought a bag of ice for Scarlett's eye.

"Thank you ladies." Jack acknowledged.

Diane looked at Scarlett's eye again and responded with a quip to lighten the mood. "Sorry, Scarlett, that's not going to go well with your red hair. Now relax. Randy's watching the door. Rachel's been tossed and won't be allowed back in. So, how are you doing?"

"Ok, I guess. But I never even got a shot in."

"Uh-huh. Kinda tough to do when someone cold cocks you." Jack sympathized. "I can just imagine what people will think when seeing you with me."

Scarlett smirked. "Well, it is kinda your fault."

"I seem to recall telling you I wouldn't be good for you."

Ruby interrupted. "The song Jack. I heard her ask you for a song."

Jack looked back to Scarlett. "Damn, woman. You're going to feel a whole lot worse if I do."

"Jaaaack. You're hopeless if you can't do something just for me right now!"

"Alright. Alright." He raised his hands in surrender. "Message received." Jack headed back to join the band, and after speaking with the group's singer and then the rest of the band, the singer spoke to the crowd. "Folks, this is a little unusual. Most of you know we don't take requests, but this one is kinda special. And on top of that, my wife is giving me the 'you'll be sleeping on the couch' look if I don't do this."

The crowd roared with laughter.

"Please bear with us."

"Oh, and by the way, this impromptu moment is brought to you by our drummer, Jack. It's entirely spur of the moment, but we promise to do our best. Billy will be filling in on the drums for this one as well. The crowd cheered for Billy again, welcoming his return.

Then, the singer called Jack over to give him the microphone before speaking to the crowd. "The band and I have chosen a song we enjoy doing occasionally, one that we think is perfect for Jack. It's all yours now, buddy."

An embarrassed Jack addressed the crowd. "Well, folks, I'm no Rod Stewart." The place thundered with applause, laughter, and a few screams from the ladies.

"I'm doing this for one special woman out there, and that's the only reason I'm doing this. My place is hiding back there behind those drums." He pointed over his shoulder with a thumb.

He was interrupted when Alan approached from the side. Jack's comment was overheard on the mic. "No, not that song. That's not what we agreed to."

"You know the words, don't you."

"Well ya, but…"

"Then let's go." Taking back the mic from Jack for just a second, he addressed the crowd. "Gonna slow it down a bit, folks. Here's a hit from a couple of years back. "Feel free to sing along and help Jack out."

He returned the mic to Jack and whispered, "Have fun." His mischievous grin told Jack he should have expected something like this.

Then, breathing deeply and attempting to embrace the role thrust upon him, he pointed towards Scarlett, "For the red-haired damsel in distress right over there."

Jack looked directly at Scarlett and launched into a song by Elvin Bishop. His voice was low and smooth, a voice that would have sounded good if it were on key. It was not.

When Jack sang, "I must have been through about a million girls, I'd love 'em, and I'd leave 'em alone," Scarlett slammed the ice bag on the table, reached for her purse, and prepared to leave.

"You have to be kidding me!" She stormed. "The man has no heart. What an ass!"

Diane grabbed her arm and got in her face. "You sit your butt right back down there and enjoy the song!" Her unyielding look nailed Scarlett to the seat of her chair.

"The band's pulled a fast one on him and is having a little fun at his expense. Now, sit down and enjoy what he's doing. The guy is up there sweating bullets for you! So cool, your jets girl!"

Alan stepped in to help ease Jack's nerves and smooth out the vocals. Jack appeared to relax a bit, and his singing, such as it was, improved.

"That's my guy." Bobby Jo cooed. "He sings because he likes to sing." Then, turning towards Scarlett, she scolded. "Your guy is up there doing it just for you. I hope you appreciate that because you have no idea what it takes to sing in front of a live crowd." Her eyes bore into Scarlett with laser precision. "You hear what I'm saying?"

Scarlett received the cowgirls' message loud and clear, wondering why she had to be told to appreciate what was happening. Mable had warned her about holding on to her grudges.

Give the man a chance, Scarlett.

So she sat calmly and listened. When hearing the song's last few words, "I can't stop loving you." She became a bit more grateful for the band's choice.

At the end of the evening, Jack walked Scarlett out to her van. Standing there saying good night, he reached up with one hand to slip a loose strand of hair aside and tuck it behind her ear. "You be alright tonight?"

"I'm a big girl. I'll be fine."

Jack looked away and sighed. Then, turning back, "OK. Guess I'll see you in the morning." He turned to go, but Scarlett grabbed him.

"Jack. I'm sorry for being such a bitch. There's just so much I'm trying to figure out. It has me on edge. I need to be able to count on you, and I'm so afraid what we are doing could all go wrong."

"I won't hurt you, Scarlett."

"That song. Did you mean those things? The good parts, I mean."

Taking her gently by the shoulders and gazing upon her velvety, soft, freckled face, he saw a frown and a hopeful squiggly smile fighting for control. "Seems to me most everything in that song is true, much of which I'm not proud of. But the part I know you're asking about…yes, I most certainly did."

Scarlett pulled him close and laid a heavy kiss on his lips. "Thank you. I needed to hear that. I know you hated singing in front of all those people, but the fact you would do it just for me means a lot."

She placed a hand on her chest, and her eyes lit up. "A little balm for my heart. I'll see you in the morning."

"Just remember one thing."

"What's that?"

"This is the only time you will ever hear me sing in public." He leaned in and kissed her. "I'll see you in the morning."

Laying in bed that night with an ice pack over her eye, Scarlett replayed the events of the evening, making sure she would remember and never forget, then prayed what he'd said was true. *No man is an island,* she thought, *but how this one tries to be. Good Lord, can this work?*

CHAPTER FORTY TWO

BEFORE LEAVING TOWN THE FOLLOWING DAY AND HEADING for the Oregon coast, Jack and Scarlett stopped in the bakery to say goodbye and grab a few doughnuts for the road. For Scarlett, it was a tearful farewell.

Hugging Mable, "You've been good for me in more ways than you know, Mable."

"You've always had what it takes, dear. Now it's time to trust yourself." She replied. Then, stepping up to Jack and shooting him a stern look straight in the eye, she laid down the law. She may have been nearly a foot shorter, but Mable didn't hesitate.

"Now you listen to me, young man. You take care of this wonderful woman, or you'll have me to answer to."

"No worries there. I promise."

Pointing her finger, Mable wasn't done yet and the scolding continued. "Jack. I mean it. She's more special than you know. Forget about the past and take time to get to know her."

Jack attempted to charm her with his blue eyes and magnetic smile. "Got it, Mable." He winked, and Mable nearly blushed.

Back outside, Jack climbed on his motorcycle and waited for Scarlett to lead the way with her van. He would follow. Mable stood in the doorway to her little shop, wiping away the tears. Her husband came up from behind and put his arms around her waist. "What's wrong, sweetie?"

She turned and looked up to him. "We've had a blessed life, dear, but watching that young couple head out to discover their future together, sometimes, not often, but sometimes I wish we were young again."

There was a touch of a déjà vu each time Scarlett looked in the rearview mirror to check on Jack. Though not quite as long as it once was, his dark hair, blown back by the wind, took Scarlett back to their early days together.

An image of sunny skies, white lines flashing by beside them, blacktop rolling beneath, and her arms encircling his waist filled her mind. The scent of his leather jacket in her nostrils made it all too real.

The rebel that initially drew him to her was still alive and well. What was she doing trying to ring it out of him? Hell, even after the crash, he chose not to wear his helmet today. Then she wondered why he'd decided to wear it the night of the crash. The equation perplexed her. For now, she was content, but the future still worried her. Then Mable's words came to mind. *It's worth the fight. Guys like him are rare, even though it will sometimes hurt while they figure themselves out.*

Before heading out that morning, Scarlett had seen a different look in Jack's eyes. No longer were they filled with that distant, hungry, always looking-for-the-next-thing gaze she'd known in the past. In its place, she saw confusion amidst a comfortable peace that seemed to reside there now, and it gave her hope.

We'll see about that, though the guy does seem more at ease with himself. And the attitude I've always associated with the him is more under control. It's still there, but it takes much more for it to surface.

After a long day on the road, their first meal on the coast had to be comfort food, which meant a stop at Mo's. The clam chowder, fish and chips, and waterfront seating all combined for the perfect end to their first day together.

Jack was busy soaking up the last of his chowder with a piece of garlic bread when Scarlett chose that moment to bring up one more time her deeply held beliefs. There never seemed to be a "right" time, and when she'd attempted to do so in the past, Jack wouldn't listen. She wasn't going down this road with him any further without addressing the topic one last time.

Jack's hand froze in place, halfway to his open mouth, which hung open as time came to a standstill.

"You mean you got religion?" Jack said after gathering his wits.

His voice, filled with skepticism and mocking, momentarily froze the air between them. Then she laughed.

"Religion? Heavens no. Nothing could be worse."

"Then what in tarnation are you talking about?"

He didn't get it, and Scarlett knew she'd need to tread carefully here. Gazing out the window at his bike in the parking lot, she reminded herself that he hadn't left her at the table and taken off. Something he'd threatened to do before.

Scarlett looked across the table to Jack, smiled, and told him they could discuss it after their meal. After paying for their dinner, she took him to the beach and took up the topic again, but this time, she laid it out straight up, just like he asked her to do.

"I'll hear you out as long as you don't sound like another one of those crazy preachers on the radio. Send me your money, and all your prayers will come true. I don't know how people fall for that crap." He said.

Scarlett eyed him. "You've known about my faith for some time, but we've never really talked about it."

When Scarlett told him she'd accepted Jesus as her Lord and Savior, Jack about fell into the surf before growing very still. She tread carefully, feeling like she might lose him right then and there. But this was the way it had to be. If she lost him, she lost him because she was not about to give up her relationship with the Lord for Jack. Her future was in God's hands now because her Savior came first and Jack second.

Jack took off down the beach, head down, walking swiftly. Scarlett rushed to keep up. To her right, the incoming surf roared, breathing in and breathing out. Overhead, the gulls called and soared freely. The scent of seaweed filled the breeze, locking the moment in her mind. Above it all, she could almost hear the gears turning in his head and knew it was best to remain quiet, though the silence growing between them was killing her. That's when the raven flew low over Jack's head, and she rushed to shoo it away.

Suddenly, the dam burst. Jack spun around, and she struggled to keep up with all his questions. It wasn't the part about God creating everything. He could almost deal with that. But God loving him so deeply he would come to earth and willingly die at the hands of his creation to save him; that part made no sense.

"I've done so many things I'm not proud of Scarlett. I can't picture God wanting to spend much time with someone like me, let alone spend eternity hanging out together. And then you tell me I'm the one who decides if I'll spend eternity in heaven or hell."

The concept of heaven and hell wasn't anything new to Jack, but the idea of him being able to choose heaven by accepting Christ was beyond him. Scarlett answered his questions as best she could, knowing this was a spiritual battle and it wasn't up to her to convince him of anything. To his credit, Jack became more and more contemplative as twilight came and went.

Still deep in conversation about God and their possible future together, the two took their time strolling hand in hand along the surf's edge in the dark. The white-capped waves, highlighted by the moonlight and the sound of the breakers, accompanied them.

When Jack grew silent, deep in thought, Scarlett began to fear she was losing him. Returning to their hotel rooms hand in hand, Scarlet sensed how unsettled he was.

Stopping outside the door to her room, Jack drew Scarlett close and kissed her good night.

"I need to tell you something. In the morning, when you get up, I'll be gone."

"What? What's wrong, Jack? Did I say something – did I do something?"

"No." He smiled. "You're as beautiful as ever, but there are some things I need to work out."

"Damn you! Running out on me already!" She raised her hand to slap him, but he grabbed it instead. "I should have known better."

"Scarlett, stop it! Listen to me."

Instead, she cussed him and struggled to pull her hand free. "It's just as well I know now instead of dragging this out! It's the religious thing, isn't it?"

Jack took hold of her shoulders. "Listen to me. I'm not running out on you. I'll be back soon. Just give me a little time."

Scarlett stepped inside the door to her room. With hands on hips, she glared and gave him an ultimatum. "This is all way too familiar, Jack. You haven't changed one bit!"

"Hold on." Jack took hold of her arms. "I'm telling you I'll be back."

Scarlett shrugged off his hands and stepped behind the door. "I've been down this road with you before. I'm a fool to do this, but you have three days. If you're not back by then, I'll be gone. Do you hear me, Jack? Gone forever!"

"Four days."

"Three days Jack.

"Alright." He smiled and leaned in to kiss her on the forehead. "I'll be back. Wait for me."

"Three days Jack."

Scarlett slammed the door and sat down on the side of her bed, fighting back the tears. Tears that said she meant it. Tears that told her it was over and she would be leaving without him.

Her thoughts were racing through the events of the last few months when the words Mable had spoken to her returned. *"Men like him are worth the fight, Scarlett. Sometimes, they will hurt you while they figure themselves out."*

Then, the song Jack had sung to her came to mind. *He loves you, Scarlett. Well, if he did, he wouldn't be running off.* She fumed and began pacing the room.

You're acting just like you did when he began the song he sang to you. You overreacted then and would have stormed out of the place if those women hadn't stopped you. Its three days. Just three days. Don't overreact now.

The next morning, Scarlett discovered Jack truly was gone. She spent the day sipping coffee, dining on pastry, and eating the best seafood she could find. She prayed and watched the pelicans diving in the surf for fish during a long afternoon walk on the beach. Was she doing the right thing by staying? She kept telling herself no but couldn't force herself to walk away. *Three days, I can do three days.*

A darkening sky brought heavy winds and a fierce storm on the second day. A storm so gloomy and filled with rain that the menacing sky and tempestuous sea appeared joined together as one. Scarlett could see no break between the raging waters and torrid gray sky as if the ocean ran straight into the heavens.

Scarlett brooded at a dusty window-side table in her motel room and watched the near-hurricane storm pelt the coast with a fierce downpour.

Stunned at the turn of events, she spent much of the day observing the waves of rain march across the gravel parking lot.

She couldn't know it, but at that very moment, Jack was riding straight into the heart of the storm as he tried to make his trip in three days. He'd never attempted riding in a wind so dangerous but was determined to get back to Scarlett before she left him forever. The rain hammered, and as the storm intensified, he felt the temperature drop. When his hands grew numb, he was forced to pull over and wait out the storm.

Later in the day, Scarlett grew bored with sitting at the window, and when an elderly man from a few doors down ventured out into the rain to walk two little dogs, Scarlett knew it was time to escape her room.

She soon discovered how completely freeing it was to stroll on the beach at the mercy of the storm. The wind tugged at her, the rain searched every seam in her raincoat for an opening, and the howling gale secluded her in a world of her own. Extraordinarily renewing, she found her spirit soaring along with the dozen vultures wheeling in and out on the wind during breaks in the rain.

Was this how Jack felt when he hit the road? Little did she know that at the moment, he would have told her it felt like anything but that.

The storm began breaking up late in the day, and the vultures venturing out during rain breaks remained in the air. They seemed happy to follow as she strode along the beach. Was it an omen? Black birds flying overhead, ugly animals that feed on the dead, following her along the storm-ravaged beach. She refused to believe it, choosing instead to enjoy their company and ignore the warning they symbolized. Besides, they were the only other living thing on the beach. Maybe they were keeping the ravens away?

There was no sign of Jack upon her return to the motel. Soaking wet and frustrated with her decision to wait, Scarlett chose the comfort of a long, hot shower. After warming up and enjoying the luxuriant stream of hot water, she came to the realization she was kidding herself. There was no way the guy was coming back. *Why in the world would you believe otherwise?*

Scarlett went to bed that evening, accepting it was over with Jack. But she had promised three days and would stay for one more day. *And what a fool you've been! I mean, come on! Who am I kidding? And to think I was the one who was going to anchor this man, this wild stray of a human, to a different kind of life.*

The next day passed by slowly. Scarlett told herself there was little reason to expect him back, and she was right. After treating herself to a lobster dinner and more wine than was good for her, she returned to her empty room and slid under the covers of a cold bed, cussing his name until she fell asleep.

She'd made up her mind she would be leaving without Jack first thing in the morning. It hurt. There hadn't even been a proper goodbye. Well, what was new about that? Disappointing as it was, she eventually found a measure of peace with it all.

On the morning of day four, after coffee and a gorgeous but lonely walk on the sundrenched beach, Scarlett returned to her room. Jack had yet to return, and she felt the old familiar arms of betrayal begin to embrace her. She scolded herself.

Knock it off. You made this decision last night. And for crying out loud, what's the big surprise anyway? It's not like this is anything new; you knew you could never trust the man. So, what are you doing hanging around?

And yet, he'd seemed so sincere. Scarlett continued arguing with herself. She acknowledged deeply loving the man and was heartsick about leaving. Muddled thoughts competed with rational judgment to create thick-headed confusion. If she left now, it would be forever. Deciding it was too great of a decision to make while confusion reigned, she chose to go for a short drive and take in a little more sea air before hitting the road.

The passing storm left the air fresh, clean, and pure. Every whiff of pungent beach, salty sea, and rain-freshened earth was as authentic as she would ever know. Scarlett pulled off the road after locating a high point overlooking the storm-churned ocean. Alone at the unoccupied viewpoint,

Scarlett had time to think. Exiting the van, she found a smooth, flat boulder to sit on while looking out across the ocean and pondering what to do.

Like the waves on the beach below, a surf tide of thoughts crashed across her mind and surged amidst raging emotions. The seagulls soaring free overhead, liberated from the bonds of gravity, taunted her to fly away and be free as well. The rocky point she had found to sit on beckoned the opposite with its firm foundation.

'I've got some things to work out.'

What the heck was that supposed to mean? Was it his way of saying goodbye? No, he said he'd return. Then why wasn't he back?

It was mid-afternoon when the storm in Scarlett's mind blew itself out. Like the calm experienced when a ship slips out of the storm waves and into a sheltered harbor, Scarlett docked her thoughts. Having made her decision, she would wait no longer.

But the resolution brought with it the one question she could not answer. Why would the Lord bring this man back into her life? Was it a test or some strange blessing? She told herself God didn't test people in that way and decided the answer was to treat herself to a First-class seafood dinner and leave early the next morning.

Back in town, Scarlett drove straight to the restaurant she had in mind and found a table where she could sit alone on the deck overlooking the bay. Bundled in a warm jacket, she sipped a glass of red wine and turned her face into the rays of a stunning crimson and ginger-colored sun as the sea extinguished the last of the day's light.

Its burnished glow, painted across the waves of the incoming tide, seemed to confirm her chosen direction. There, she finally found a measure of peace. Things were going to be okay. The words of Mable came to mind once again. "You can have any man you want, Scarlett."

Except this one.

But her plan was set. She would pack up in the morning and head off to a new life. *I will walk away and leave this mess for you, Jack! Just like you've always done. It serves you right!* It may have been spiteful, but at this point, she didn't care. Life might be a bit empty at first, but that was alright. She'd just spent almost two years living alone; by comparison, this would be a piece of cake.

It's time to shed the old skin and the last of your tears, Scarlett, and grow into the new you that God is revealing.

CHAPTER FORTY THREE

THE FOLLOWING DAY, SCARLETT WOKE WELL-RESTED AND anxious for the next season of her life to begin. She just hadn't pictured it starting the way it did.

Loading the last of her things into the van, she was startled when a green Mustang roared in beside her. She paid no attention at first and slammed shut the sliding door on the van before turning to walk around to the driver's side.

"Scarlett?"

That voice. DAMN him! The man is always sneaking up behind me!

Scarlett froze in her tracks before slamming her fist against the van's hood. Slowly turning in his direction, she saw Jack standing on the driver's side of the car, leaning over the top of the open door.

And dang, if he didn't look good, though it did little to lessen the fury building inside her. She was tired of being jerked around.

"Scarlett. You're here!" He exclaimed. "I was so afraid you'd be gone."

"I am. You never saw me!" Her stiletto eyes carved him into pieces, and she turned to go.

"Scarlett, come back. Please don't be mad." He sputtered, searching for the right words, then spoke quickly before she could say anything more.

"Can we just go for a walk or something? I've got so much to tell you." He closed the car door and stepped towards her. "I don't know what I would have done if you were gone."

Probably just find another girl. But she kept the thought to herself. "I'm leaving, Jack."

"No no. You can't," he stammered. "I'm sorry. Please hear me out."

Scarlett frowned and chewed on her lower lip. "Alright. Let's go for a walk, and you can try to explain why I should even think about spending another minute with you!" She wanted to stomp her foot like a little child. He wasn't getting off easy just because his puppy dog eyes were pleading with her.

Her words struck him like a dagger through the heart, and she was a little surprised by its effect on him. The indomitable, full-of-himself man who could climb any mountain suddenly looked defeated. Scarlett began to regret the way she'd attacked him. Maybe she was the one who needed to change, even more so than him. Still, she stood her ground.

Jack faltered for words. He'd done all he could to return on time. The storm had cost him a full day's ride, and he'd risked speeds he'd never driven to return as soon as possible.

For an instant, he just stood there, toeing the gravel with his boot while struggling with what to say next. Scarlett changed the subject to give him a moment's break.

"So what's with the car, and where's your bike?"

"The cars for you. I know you've always wanted a 65 Mustang, and anyway, I've got my Falcon."

"Trying to bribe me?"

The question gave him the door he was looking for. Without a word, Jack stepped forward and cautiously reached for her hand.

"Please give me your hand."

Slowly, she extended her right hand. The feel of her hand in his rough paw took the edge off her nerves – just a bit.

Jack led her to the beach, a beach she'd already walked numerous times, sad and alone. Her anger surged again, and she nearly stormed off to the van, leaving him alone on the beach. He asked her what was wrong.

She ignored him. Was the guy so clueless?

They walked silently for the next few minutes while Jack searched for the right words. Then, after a stumbling start, he stopped, turned to face her, and tried again to explain how he had to go on one last ride and how a massive storm had forced him to take shelter off the road.

A last ride. How sweet. Scarlett thought. Her acerbic thoughts could have ripped him to shreds if she'd allowed them out.

Mable's voice rang in her head. *Reel it in Scarlett! The man's trying to tell you something.*

Following a long day with the wind whipping through his hair and the exhilarating freedom of being alone on the road, he'd found a private little beach on the California coast to spend the night. After hiding his bike from view in a stand of Scotch broom, he found a place to settle in for the night.

The surf roared like thunder that evening, and lying there looking up at the stars, he told Scarlett he found the answer to the thing he'd been struggling with and knew what to do.

Scarlett shot him a look of disbelief. *Right Jack.* It was all adding up to nonsense, and she began sensing another story full of BS. Except for the fact he seemed so serious.

"The next day, I tried to ride through the worst storm I've ever seen." He took her arm and turned her towards him. "I rode in conditions no fool would ride in, trying my best to finish my trip and get back to you by the end of three days."

The next day, I rode my bike all the way to L.A. because I knew the market was good there. I met with a friend who gave me top dollar for my bike. That's when I bought the Mustang."

Well, so what? Have you even noticed I'm holding my breath to keep from blowing up at you? Of course not!

None of it made any sense, and Scarlett's patience, spent long before they'd begun their walk, was wearing threadbare thin.

When they reached the end of the beach, where a rocky bluff jutted into the sea and numerous seagulls soared and called, Jack asked her to sit down.

Scarlett stood and stared at him with the eyes and hair of the goddess Medusa. Her angry eyes threatened, and her damp, windblown hair, with its livid copper color, expressed her pent-up fury.

"You want me to sit there?" She pointed. "It's wet!" She was being obstinate just for the sake of it. Then, suddenly struck by the thought: *what if he just walked away and left me standing here?* Scarlett relented.

As politely as possible, Jack asked her again to sit down, this time pointing out a large, flat, dry rock, and Scarlett plopped down. *Is this where he tells me why it would never work, why...*

Scarlett jumped to her feet and stormed off, not even completing the thought. *I've been a part of this scene one too many times, and I don't need to see it again.*

"Scarlett, stop! What's wrong?" Jack didn't understand but had had enough and rushed after her. The nice guy approach was getting him nowhere. It was time to take things into his own hands, and he firmly grabbed her by the arm and turned her around.

Scarlett fought him and nearly wrestled loose, but he refused to let go and pulled her back to face him. She screamed at him to release her.

"Jack! We've been through this so many times. I can't do it again."

She struggled some more and attempted to slap him.

"Scarlett, stop it! Stop it!" The robust, commanding voice froze her in place. She frowned and stood like a statue, awaiting his latest excuse.

"I don't know what you're talking about. Now, will you just shut up and hear me out for a minute."

More exasperated with Scarlett than he'd ever been, Jack gathered himself, said nothing for a moment, and stood silently with the sun backlighting his black hair tousled in the breeze.

Gathering himself and all the determination he could muster, he carefully let go of her arms. She didn't run. Then, tenderly taking her chin in one hand, he turned her head so she would look up into his eyes.

"Look at me, Scarlett."

The sneer on her face was enough to turn most men away, but Jack was not most men.

Though fearful of the words she was about to hear, Scarlett defiantly locked eyes with him, eyes that burrowed straight into his soul, eyes dark as a raven's because her heart felt just as sinister.

The contrast between her soul and the calm blue-green sea rolling in behind Jack's back was palpable. The sound of the surf mixed with the call of the seagulls soaring above them was a sound that would forever accompany the moment.

Barely in control of her anger, Jack chose that moment to kneel with one knee in the sand. With his left hand, he reached into the pocket of his leather jacket – the bike might be gone, but there was no way he was parting with the jacket – and suddenly Scarlett knew what was happening.

"Scarlett, I don't know why you're acting like this."

Her eyes flooded with tears, and she yanked back her arm. It was a purely visceral reaction that happened before he could say another word.

Patiently, Jack tried again. "Scarlett, if you will give me your hand, I'll try this again." His calm voice was reassuring, and suddenly Scarlett was overcome with confusion.

Slowly, she extended her arm. Jack opened a small jewelry box and removed a giant diamond ring.

Then, looking up into the green pools of her eyes, he continued. "Scarlett, I love you. You are a woman stronger than anyone I've ever known, and you are everything to me. I can't imagine life without you. Will you marry me?"

They were simple words from a simple man, and Scarlett knew the straightforward approach was coming directly from his heart.

Stunned for a moment, she faltered for words. Her world flipped upside down, and she hesitated, not knowing how to react.

Jack stepped back, thinking he had gone too far and that her answer was no.

Scarlett grabbed his worn leather jacket and pulled him close. "I'd say, Yes, yes, yes, but you told me to shut up." She began laughing nervously.

Jack's grin filled his face, and he whispered back. "Then speak, woman."

"Yes. I will marry you, Jack. Of all our times together over the years, I never pictured it like this. And I've never seen such an enormous smile on your face."

Jack's smile widened even more, if possible, then dissolved at her following words.

"Just one condition."

"Oh, brother. Knowing you, I should have expected this." Reaching out, he took back her hand. "And what is your request, my queen?" His smile reappeared, and he knelt on one knee before her again.

Jack always joked when nervous, but Scarlett didn't back off.

"I've told you before. I can't marry you unless you accept Jesus as your Lord and Savior. We would be unequally yoked, and the bible warns against doing that."

Jack burst into laughter, let go of her hand, and fell back in the sand. It was now Scarlett's turn for a moment of doubt, and she immediately took his laughter to mean it would never happen.

For Jack, it was a moment of great joy and incredible relief. The race to sell his bike, the storm, and the overwhelming fear she would be gone by the time he returned had tied him in knots. The chance to laugh and the relief it brought was overwhelming. He kicked his feet in the air like a turtle upside down on its shell.

After collecting himself, he stood and wrapped Scarlett in his arms.

"Scarlett, I'm way ahead of you."

A still peeved Scarlett replied, "Not likely."

"I've learned so many lessons on the road these last few years, and maybe that's the payoff. One of the things I've learned is that I want you in my life. Remember the night I told you I spent sleeping on the beach on the way to sell my Harley?"

Scarlett nodded.

"I lay there alone that night with just the sound of the ocean surf and stars of the Milky Way to keep me company. There I was, alone again like so many other nights on the road, gazing at the heavens when things suddenly became clear. There has to be a God. Not just a god, but a Supreme Being, an Almighty God who could not only create these kinds of things but hold them all together in such perfect order. The planets orbits, the earth's distance from the sun for the perfect warmth to sustain life and not freeze or cook us. There is just no way they could happen by accident. Of all the nights I've spent alone under the stars, I'll never know why it never dawned on me like it did that night."

Scarlett couldn't resist. "Hmmm, drugs, maybe."

Jack frowned and kicked at the sand, then quickly recovered. Scarlett had never seen him so serious or sincere and wanted to hug him, but she didn't dare interrupt.

"When the storm forced me off the road I took shelter at a rest area and was visiting with another biker taking refuge there. Turns out the guy is a pastor. Who would have guessed? He was wearing motorcycle leathers and rode a Harley just like mine. He looked no more like a pastor than I do!"

Scarlett chuckled at the picture he painted, relaxed, and let go of some of the angst she harbored. Jack was as cute and animated as could be.

"Anyway, the storm went on forever, and I told him about you and how we couldn't get married unless I was saved. He explained how simple it is and that all I had to do was admit I'm a sinner." Jack laughed. "Not like that was hard to do. And that I had to believe in Jesus and confess Him as my Lord and Savior."

"And how'd you do with that?"

"Well, honestly, I struggled. I told him I'd have to get back to him."

"And did you?"

"I knew if we were to be together, we would have to be on the same page about this. You've made that quite clear. Don't misunderstand. I'm not saying this so that you will marry me."

Better not be. But she'd never seen the man so earnest.

"You may not believe this, but Scarlett, you'd better. After that night on the beach, I realized that when I give it all up, give up living for myself, I get it all back. Everything I'd strived for on my own and never found would be given back when I turned away from serving myself. I knew then that could only be a God thing, something He revealed to me, and suddenly, the God you told me about, the God Rocky told me about in prison, became real."

"So good so far." She motioned with her hand to continue.

"I didn't think that rain storm would ever end, and I paced and walked around the place the entire time, wanting to get back on the road and fearing you wouldn't wait for me."

"I almost didn't."

Jack's face fell before finishing his story. "You know what a hard time I have allowing someone else to have authority over me. Like I just told you, I can accept the fact that everything works out when I give up living for myself. Still, the wrestling match I had with Jesus being my boss, my master, nearly tore me in two. It was like there were two forces or two people or something...I don't know what, grappling inside me."

Scarlett interrupted. "Two spirits?"

"Yes!" Jack's eyes lit up with the thought. "That's gotta be it. Later on, that pastor approached me and asked how I was doing. I told him about my past and how it was so hard for me to let go of being in control. It all crystallized when he asked me one simple question."

"And what was that?"

"Sounds stupid when I think about it, but it sure brought things together when he said, 'And how's that working out for you?'"

Scarlett laughed. "Prison couldn't do what that simple little question accomplished."

"It is kind of silly when I think back on it, but it had never been so clear to me."

"That was God, Jack. He opened your mind so you could see it."

"And then the guy asked me what I was more concerned with, eternity or chasing after my interests here on earth for the few years I have to live. When I hesitated, he said look at me. I'm seventy years old. One day, I'm twenty; the next, I'm seventy. It goes by that fast.

His challenge brought it all into focus, and I accepted Christ right there on the spot with the wind shrieking and the rain pouring down around us! He led me in a prayer he referred to as Romans 10:9, or something like that."

Scarlett's eyes went wide with shock and joy. She extended her left hand.

"But hold on!" Jack's excitement grew even more. "There was another thing that happened. The moment I accepted the Lord, the rain stopped, and that storm began to move out. It was like God was keeping me there until I made a decision for Him!"

The moment was precious, and she would long cherish it. Scarlett caressed his rugged face with both hands before stepping back and extending her left hand a second time.

"Yes, Jack. I will marry you. After everything I've been through with you and all we've been through together, if that's what it took, it was worth it. Now will you quit stalling and put that beautiful ring on my finger."

Afterward, the two casually strolled the beach, hand in hand, enveloped in the warmth of the moment. Scarlett struggled to wrap her mind around what had just happened. The suspicious side of her kept searching for what was wrong with this picture.

They returned to the motel, each to their rooms, to get ready for dinner out on the town. Later that evening, after strolling the waterfront in downtown Newport, Scarlett thrilled at sitting across the table from her fiancé. What a crazy road they'd each had to travel to reach this point and be joined back together again.

Scarlett gazed into his dark eyes. "Jack, you know I've sat across the table from my fiancé like this once before on the night of my engagement. And you know how it turned out. Does that kinda…kind of taint things for you?"

He reached across the table to take her hand, the one with the ring. "Don't be silly. It's not like I'm some angel. You know my past and what I've been about. I'm the one who should be asking you that question."

Their pasts may have been rough, but they acknowledged God's blessing of safely conveying them through it all and bringing them back together. It had been a wild and crazy trip that ended in the middle of nowhere.

Their meal of fish and chips and clam chowder took them back to their time together years before in Seattle. During the course of their meal, they became caught up in a conversation with a local fisherman who had taken a seat at the table next to them.

The man lived in Newport all his life, and in the course of the conversation, Scarlett leaned over and asked him if he knew of a local pastor who would be willing to marry them on such short notice.

The fishmonger flashed a toothy grin nestled atop a chin bristling with grey and black stubble. "Most certainly do." He nodded.

With the phone number the man gave them, Jack called the pastor first thing the following morning, and he graciously agreed to meet them at his church there in Newport.

When they met there a couple of hours later, he began by asking about how they met. They shared a brief version of their past to satisfy his curiosity. Then he started asking Jack all sorts of new believer questions. It wasn't long before Scarlett found herself at a baptismal where the pastor dunked Jack or, more like, drowned him.

Coming out of the water, he sputtered, filled his lungs with a couple of huge gasps, and shared his first words; "Praise the Lord." The pastor thought it had everything to do with being saved when it was all about being able to breathe again.

Scarlett laughed when he recounted the story over a late lunch the pastor's wife provided. "He held you under a bit long, Jack?"

"Oomph. He's a big man!" Jack's eyes grew big and round. "I was either gonna be saved or meet Jesus in the very next moment!"

Scarlett's light-hearted laughter filled the room, but Jack's bouncing knee spoke nervousness.

"You doing alright? You don't look well."

Jack looked away for a moment. When he looked back, Scarlett saw a single tear glistening in the corner of one eye. Jack never cried, and suddenly, she grew worried.

"Jack, what's wrong?"

Shaking his head and rubbing at both eyes before replying, Jack sniffed.

"I can't believe you are going to marry me. That you would have me for your guy." He rubbed at one eye again. "You are so beautiful. You have a fire in you that matches my own, and you could have anyone you wanted. I can't help but wonder why me."

"And you'd better not forget it!" Scarlett giggled, then grew serious. "There's no one else I want, Jack. You may think I could have anyone I wanted, but somehow, it seemed I would never be able to have you. There was never anyone else."

Jack joined her with nervous laughter. "Look at me. Its women who are supposed to get teary-eyed at their wedding. I'm a blubbering mess."

He was hardly that, but Scarlett was struck by how this mountain of a man who never showed his emotions had now been overcome by them.

After lunch, they went to separate rooms in the church basement and quickly changed into wedding clothes borrowed from a collection of donated dresses and tuxedos the church kept for moments like these.

Pastor John came for Jack and brought him to the sanctuary. "Just stand here, repeat the lines I give you, and don't pass out. Can you do that for this woman?"

Jack nodded.

"It's for her, Jack. Not you. This is her moment. Remember that." Then, a sly smile broke free from the corner of his mouth. "Your reward comes later."

A few minutes later, Jack was wiping the sweat from his forehead when the pastor's wife began the wedding march on the church organ.

Scarlet stood at the end of the aisle and began her walk at the pastor's beckoning. She'd chosen a beautiful white wedding dress with a short train from a closet full of dresses. It fit her perfectly, and she couldn't have been more striking.

Her radiance overcame Jack, and he suddenly understood why the pastor had warned him not to pass out. Then he heard the pastor hiss, "Unlock your knees, Jack."

Scarlett took her place across from Jack. Her long red hair shimmered, and her freckles glistened with color even through the veil. Pastor John quickly proceeded with the service, and after asking Jack if he took this woman, "till death do you part," Jack answered, "Are you kidding?" bringing an immediate frown from the pastor but a quiet giggle from Scarlett. "Of course I do!"

The pastor turned to Scarlett and proceeded with the same vow. Jack could no longer contain himself and began making faces at Scarlett, causing her to stumble over her words after a stifled chuckle escaped her control. Then, after shooting a fake glare at Jack and collecting herself, she finished her vows, and before Jack knew it, he heard the words, "You may now kiss the bride."

Jack reached across to her and lifted the veil. Scarlett's smile was striking, and her green eyes captivated him, causing him to hesitate momentarily to take it all in. Then the kiss, and though he'd kissed her before, somehow this one was different.

The ceremony took only a few minutes, and the two were soon on their way. Jack paid the pastor handsomely and couldn't have been more thankful.

The newlywed couple left town immediately, Scarlett in her Chevy van and Jack in their new Mustang. She had to admit she missed looking back and seeing the free-spirited Jack flying along on his Harley.

You're crazy, Scarlett! You know what that version of him cost you.

The two drove north to a little berg called Neskowin and spent their first night together as a married couple."

Sitting on the couch before a cozy fire that evening, Scarlett raised a toast with her glass of wine. "Looking back - crazy as it seems, God had a plan for each of us. A road for you and a path for me."

Jack appreciated the metaphor. "But man, we went through hell before finding our way back to one another and what we already had in the first place."

Scarlett leaned on his shoulder. "Agreed. Sometimes, it was unbearable. There were moments I could have killed you!" She grinned mischievously before leaning in to kiss him. "But we've both seen enough and been through enough to know His way is always the best."

"But dang, Scarlett. God sure can be tough on a guy sometimes."

"We both know you needed it." Her green eyes flared in the firelight, and she laughed.

"If only He'd shared with me that you were waiting at the end of that long, empty road. Sure would have made the trip easier to bear, and there's no doubt I would have shortened the journey."

"That would be cheating, and for you, Jack, that hard road is exactly what it took."

Gazing into the fire, he nodded. "Maybe so."

"It was God's plan, and we need to have the faith to walk the road he puts before us, no matter how dark it sometimes seems. If life has taught us anything, it's that very lesson."

"Agreed. Trust in the Lord with all your heart and lean not on your own understanding."

"Jack!" Scarlett exclaimed.

"Don't get excited. It's the only scripture I know."

"Good one to know. What about the rest?"

"In all your ways acknowledge Him." He frowned. "That's the hard part. And He will make straight your paths. Do not be wise in your own eyes, but fear the Lord and flee from evil. It will bring health to your body and strength to your bones."

Scarlett was pleased. "It's one of the promises He makes to us if we follow Him."

Jack slid an arm around her shoulders and kissed her. "There were times I felt so defeated, sitting in prison with no hope of getting out. Yet, He provided a friend to help me through that time and still led me back to you."

"Led us both back to one another." She corrected. "Though I would have chosen a more discreet way to be reintroduced to you."

Jack chuckled. "I happen to find that moment quite memorable."

"You would!"

A contented silence filled the room while the two gazed into the flames of the fire. Jack got up to add more wood. Then, turning back to face Scarlett,

"You may not have known it, heck, even I didn't know it for a while, but you were always the special one that made my life worth living."

From the couch, Scarlett launched a pillow. "Why didn't you ever just come out and say it?"

"I wish I had." He glanced back into the fire before continuing. "Guess I had some lessons to learn first, including some growing up to do as well."

Then, changing the subject. "So, where are we going to spend our honeymoon? We didn't have time to plan anything."

Scarlett beamed with a light bulb moment. "I know just the place at the far end of Lake Chelan. A little town called Stehekin."

"The far end of Lake Chelan! That's way out in the boonies! We'd be snowed in for months come winter."

A hungry smile lit up Scarlett's face, highlighting her freckles. "Yes, we would, Jack. And I'd have you all to myself there. It's exactly how I'd like to spend our first winter together."

She winked, and Jack's brain began to smoke. "You know this place?"

"You could say that. I'll call the people tomorrow if you think you are up for it."

"Is that a challenge?"

"Only if you're afraid to spend an entire winter deep in the woods alone with your newly married red-headed wife." She fluffed her hair and tilted her head.

"Afraid?" He laughed. "And Davenport is not that far from there. Maybe we could stop in at the Minstrel's Oasis and say hello before disappearing for the winter?"

"And say hello to someone named Rachel?"

"That's not fair. And besides, I would never choose to miss out on kissing those ruby-red lips of yours all winter long. Not a chance."

"Long as you're sure." She kidded.

"Hey, maybe we could even return to that feed store and re-enact the morning we met. You know, get reacquainted all over again."

Scarlett threw another pillow. "You're a sick man, Jack. Not a chance. Not a chance!"

Then she stood and walked over to the fireplace to hug him. Looking into his blue eyes and grinning coyly, she said, "Besides, we don't need to travel back to Davenport to re-live that moment."

She winked, and Jack's meltdown began.